# THE GOSSAMER MAGE

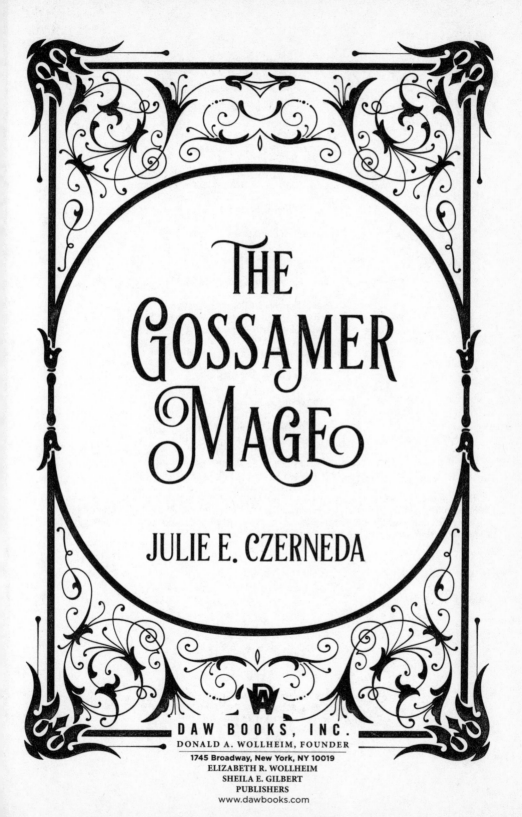

# THE GOSSAMER MAGE

### JULIE E. CZERNEDA

**DAW BOOKS, INC.**
DONALD A. WOLLHEIM, FOUNDER
**1745 Broadway, New York, NY 10019**
ELIZABETH R. WOLLHEIM
SHEILA E. GILBERT
PUBLISHERS
www.dawbooks.com

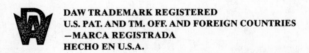

## DEDICATED TO

*Scott Aleksander Czerneda*

*Who walks in the woods*

*To hear the world.*

# WITHIN

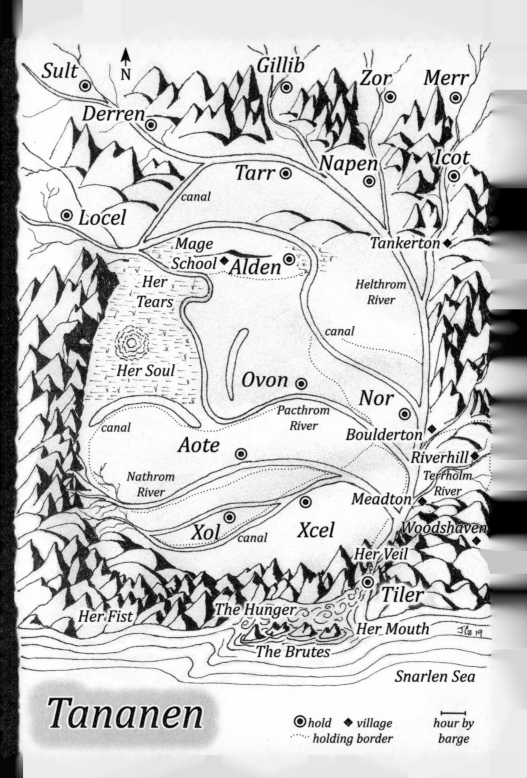

Tananen

# Fundamental Lexicon

*The world was not always thus.*

Keepers of histories agree on this, if little else. Those from the southern continents insist the world began as a frozen hen's egg, its yolk the ground beneath, its pristine white the ice, and its shell a sky of endless darkness and stars. When the shell cracked, in poured sunlight and warmth, melting the ice. Finally, the world was ready for people to live upon it, and so they did.

Historians and lore masters of the northern continent, experienced with ice, teach the world started in fire and it was only as it cooled that life of any sort could exist, be it hen or person.

Theologians both north and south avoid the topic, the present and future wellbeing of the souls in their care having the greater weight, the past being unalterable.

And perilous.

*We were not the first here.*

This is the truth no one—no person—dares imagine. That there were voices before ours. Hands. Hearts and love. Rage and a hunger so terrible it consumed the surface of the world, heaving mountains skyward, tossing continents, boiling oceans. Until nowhere was left unscarred.

Save one place.

This is a truth impossible to rediscover. Only in the names of places, only in that one place on all the world, could you glimpse it. For ages flew by and everywhere, even there, came new voices, new hearts and hands, to claim the land and write their truths upon it.

*Magic, once, was everywhere.*

Now magic is not, being confined to that one untouched place. Those of north and south might be curious. Might long for magic of their own. Might wish, in the fragile moment between twilight and the rise of the moon, to see a gossamer come to life before their eyes and transform the ordinary into wonder.

But there is only one place left in the world where you could. Where the words of those who came before linger. Where mage scribes write them down, to summon magic from the land itself.

Tananen.

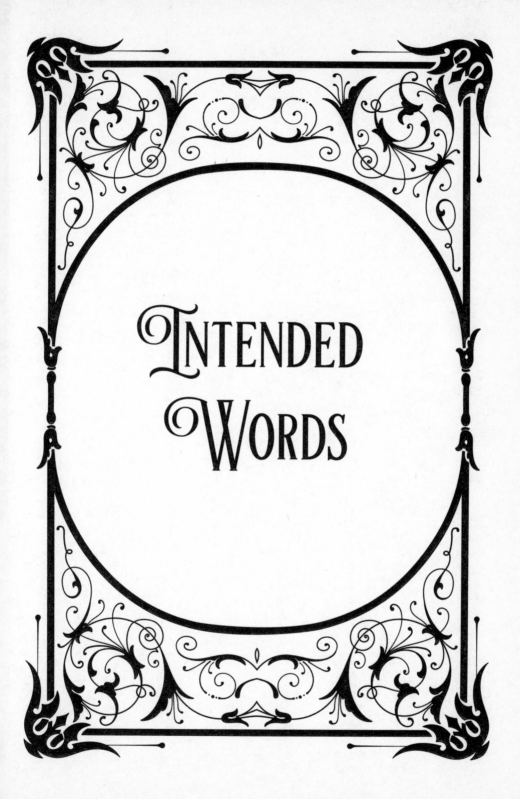

# Intended Words

# Intended Words

The body was beechwood, smooth and bronzed with age, of perfect balance. Silver girdled it, worn plain and tarnished, quickly warm to Maleonarial's fingertips. The pen had been an extravagant gift, from a father with neither coin to spare nor generous nature until a son proved of marketable talent. He remembered how the silver had glittered in his hand, that long-ago day, like some cheap gaud on a whore. He'd done his utmost not to use the thing in front of classmates or masters. Such a garish object demeaned the lofty position of mage scribe-to-be.

Had he ever been so young?

The new nib was old. Bone, weathered wood-bronze, carved silver-smooth. Simple, like the now-plain band, but with remembered complexity and purpose. He'd found the piece on his wanderings, tucked among reeds by a busy, impervious stream. A deer once.

Or a man.

A good choice. Now for the next.

Three small inkpots remained. Each was stoppered with thick yellow wax, a tiny russet curl imbedded as surety. Baby curls. Inkmaster Jowen Hammerson had courage to mock his aging guest. And a remarkable abundance of russet-haired great-grandchildren.

The contents of one inkpot, sold at Alden Hold where mage scribes clung like leeches to their famous school, would feed those children for a year. Maleonarial had left Tankerton with five wrapped in linen and bound against his waist, bought with the only coin he possessed: words.

Not any words. Names. He'd written the names of the Hammerson family in his clearest script; no more official rendering could have been asked by any hold lord or The Deathless Goddess Herself. It had taken the best of a night, but he begrudged not a moment. As each callused hand received its precious strip of parchment, as eyes wondered at the letters that bloomed in ebon permanence under the warmth of living breath, toil-bent backs had straightened. The raucous babble of dogs, children, and clanging spoons had fallen to a solemn hush. The parchments would be treasured and kept close; more importantly, the letters' shape would be practiced with care. None of them would again use a rude thumbprint to sign a document of importance, or be forced to wait on the uncertain—and expensive—arrival of a scribe. To write their own names was to gain respect and fair treatment from merchants and lawgivers alike.

The inkmaster counted himself well-paid. His kin whispered of marvels. But it hadn't been magic, other than that of skill.

Magic must be intended.

The night's breeze snapped and billowed the canvas overhead, a token against the pending rain. He slept in the open by preference. The fresh air and privacy of wilder places were a boon to his spirit; a shame they couldn't feed or clothe him. Not that he needed more than a stew or porridge under his ribs. Maleonarial plucked his threadbare, much-mended cloak. It would do another season.

His fellow mage scribes, having discovered his lifestyle—an unfortunate coincidence of storm and crowded inn, followed by a collision in a narrow hallway with a round bulk of rich velvet and gilt that had exploded in ire until he'd lifted his face to the torchlight and the other had stammered something aghast and apologetic—had sent along a beautifully penned and rolled parchment, levying a fine for inappropriate attire, unbecoming his high station.

Kind of them to overlook the dirty hair and sweat as well, not to mention bad breath.

Folded, the parchment made a fine lining for his right boot. They'd be aghast if they knew. Not that he'd apologize. As if he'd scrape it clean to reuse even if those were only words, however mean-spirited.

Magic required purity.

Though soaked, then left in heated sand to harden, the bone nib remained brittle and unforgiving. His gentlest touch would coax a smattering of words at best from it. Words and how many months from his life?

Maleonarial shrugged, shaking the tiny bells knotted in his hair. Mage scribes marked their lives by them, the quiet tinkling a constant reminder of magic's toll, collected by The Deathless Goddess. A bell for each intention. The first twenty or so accumulated quickly; schooling spent half—or more, for those prone to mistakes. The next thirty or so were reasoned, deliberate, considered. These earned what a mage judged of greater worth than time. Wealth. Security. The touch of a woman.

The moment came for every mage when that balance shifted, when the bells whispered: *"Life's short enough, fool."* A hundred-bell mage could write anything and make it live—for a fee to make even a heartland hold lord reconsider.

Having tied his three hundredth bell this season, Maleonarial counted himself fortunate to still have teeth.

He ran his tongue along their tips.

Most of them.

Enough for chewing.

To write with intent was, for those with Her Gift, an expenditure of life. A mage scribe used ink and pen, needed a surface on which to write, would study years to master stroke and technique, would above all else learn as many words of The Goddess' unspoken language as possible since those words were the means by which magic could be summoned.

To bring life.

At life's cost.

What matter the price? said those new to Her Gift. To the young, life was the deepest well, always full. When students gathered in hallways to gossip, it was of how their masters were timid, grown inept with age . . . that this was why mage scribes worked so little magic after the first wrinkle and ache . . . it couldn't be because those masters had been young once too and squandered the time they'd had . . . that they'd strutted from holding to holding to work magic, sustained by their confidence that the bells sang praise, not warning. Until too late.

The young believed their elders were indeed old.

They learned better. Come twenty years, each would find himself like a man of thirty. At thirty, more like forty-five. They would finally understand that no mage scribe escaped magic's toll. That they too aged not as nature but as each set of words intended, paying Her price for power. Until they too became masters, to hoard days, begrudge minutes, and scorn the young.

Until they refused to write magic again.

Rain on canvas echoed Maleonarial's bells as he bent to his task. Young once. Master once.

Fool, he hoped, no longer.

Cil was his name.

"Silly-Cil." Thick lips, bent teeth, twisted the whisper. They thought he didn't understand, thought him slow and stupid, but he knew what they meant. "Silly-Cil. Think me dumb. Think me meat."

With practiced ease, he stabbed the hollow tube into the calf's pulse, sucking warm rich life into his mouth as the creature bawled its torment. He was supposed to knock it dead with the hammer before bleeding it. The knacker would cuff his malformed ears, make his head ring. But the knacker was glad enough to have an apprentice, let alone one eager for the work.

Work no one else wanted to see.

Replete, he took another mouthful. Held it. Turned, his knee on the calf's neck, holding it down.

Spat at the plastered wall.

The blood flew through the air, a spume of death and anger.

Cil considered the result on the wall. The calf struggled, a distraction. He silenced it with a hammer blow. Wiped his lips on his sleeve. Admired the artwork of red on the wall's lime-plaster and rough-hewn wood.

It was *something*. But what?

There . . . an *eye*.

Lower down, where blood rilled along a crack . . . a *foot*.

The closer Cil looked, the clearer the image became. The eye *blinked*. The foot's clawed toes *flexed*. A sowbug popped free of the wood, bounced as it hit the floor, curled into a tight ball that rolled. Afraid.

He gave his laugh—the heavy snort and wheeze made others look as if they wanted him gone—and squashed the tiny thing flat with his bare foot.

Lantern light caught on a razor-edge. A *tooth*. There were more. Cil couldn't count, but he knew *more*.

He laughed again and moved aside to give *it* room. "Silly-Cil think them meat now."

Domozuk fussed with an uncooperative belt tassel, muttering under his breath. Saeleonarial stood still on the pedestal and waited, though he curled his toes within their ornate slippers. No hurrying his servant of these many years. His mouth quirked. A tassel askew or absent made no difference to him. It made every difference to the company surrounding this hold lord. He might as well wade with an open wound and expect leeches to ignore his blood, as that lot miss sloppy dress.

"I should write them something with spines. Something to climb inside their smalls," he murmured, fingers hovering over the generous beard Domozuk despaired of keeping silken smooth. Saeleonarial couldn't help him with that—he'd been born Sael Fisherson and men of that name sprouted wiry growths of red from chin and cheek to rival seamoss for twist and toughness.

And went bald.

The wig was bulky, overscented, and essential. How else to carry a mage scribe's weight of bells? Saeleonarial was in no hurry to don the hot, itchy thing. Domozuk humored him, letting it drape from its stand like a hide on display till the last possible moment.

"You won't," the servant said primly. He bent to snip an errant thread from a slipper.

"What—use magic on them?" Saeleonarial didn't risk the delicate pleats at each shoulder with a shrug, not before his audience. Instead he scowled fiercely. "Think I wouldn't dare?"

"I think I've enough gray to dye in your beard," Domozuk, ever-practical, replied as he straightened. His eyes sparkled with mischief. "Unless you'll let me commission something more modern." "Modern" being the contraptions younger nobles had begun attaching to their beardless chins: ridiculous conflagrations of precious metal, exotic feathers, and whatever else was too costly for commons; some hung to the knees and required bracing at the table. Equally witless mage scribes spent months of their magic penning tiny birds and gem-eyed lizards to live within the curls of wire. Saeleonarial pitied the servants assigned to clean that mess.

He crooked his finger for the damnable wig, quaint and sedate by comparison. "Point taken."

Scribemaster Saeleonarial knew his own worth. His rise through the ranks of his peers had more to do with honesty, a good head for names, and modest ambition than brilliance. Oh, he'd written one intention of memorable originality. The result still swam in the temple fountain of Xcel, all grave eyes and mischievous whiskers, trilling its song by moonlight to bewitch even dry old men with lust. Gossamer.

Not an accomplishment to share. He'd hastily destroyed that pen and done his utmost to forget those words and its shape. Though he dreamed it. When the world grew drab by day, predictability more deadly than age, he'd wake in the dark, blood pounding. At such a moment, Saeleonarial would swear he'd heard a faint splash, smelled musk on a warm summer's night. Been young and unafraid of the future again.

The Deathless Goddess wasn't above irony.

Just as well such moments didn't last. Someone had to keep his head. Magic wasn't to be squandered on useless marvels. The world might be drab for their lack, but it was calmer, more reliable. Like him. Another reason he'd been voted scribemaster.

No more need to write magic. He had wealth. Prestige. Some hair left behind his ears and still-reasonable bowels. What more could he want?

Surely by now he was safe.

Saeleonarial fidgeted.

Surely safe from that maddening, bone-deep, skin-crawling itch to create only magic's use could salve.

Surely now, he need no longer test his mastery of word and intention, waiting for the remembered and longed for and never-ever-enough climax of having those words take form and breathe.

He'd no need for magic. Knowing hands and a winsome smile would do him. The dimpled barmaid at . . . "Have done. It's fine," the scribemaster muttered peevishly as Domozuk fluffed the damned wig yet again. He was weary of standing. Weary of his own thoughts.

"It's not. It's flat on the side. You're the one who let the stable cat sleep—"

A head thrust between the draperies around the dressing stage; by the abundance of tousled brown ringlets, it belonged to Harn Guardson. If the sincere young student could learn to hold at least two words in his mind, he'd write his first intention and be renamed Harneonarial, "Harn, Debtor to the Lady," so all would know his life was now forfeit to Her and his masters could take a breath between lessons. If. To give everyone a welcome respite, the boy had come on this visit to Tiler's Hold to carry loads for Domozuk. Not to intrude in the dressing room. "My L-lord S-scribemaster—"

"Be off!" Bustling forward like an offended goose—an image his girth and abused nose made regrettably apt—Domozuk waved his free hand in fury. "Be off, boy! You know bet—"

Face red, Harn stood his ground, his hands clutching the curtains for anchor, doubtless leaving ink and sweat prints. He threw Saeleonarial a desperate look. "The Hold L-lord's entered the hall, Master. He's called your n-name. He's angry. He wants answers about the hermit mage. About Maleon—"

Domozuk's fierce "Hush!" overlapped Saeleonarial's no less forceful warning, "Have a care!"

Red cheeks paled before the tousled head dropped down. "M-my l-lord . . ."

Master's and servant's eyes met. Though blood fled his cheeks, Domozuk gave the slightest nod. He knew what to do. This wouldn't be the first hold a mage scribe had to vacate at speed, though Saeleonarial would regret becoming the first head of that venerable order to run for his life.

Hopefully he wouldn't have to. "Well done," he told the boy. "Stay with Domozuk. Help him. But in future, Harn, by The Goddess, keep your tongue."

Stepping down, Saeleonarial grabbed the wig from his servant and stuffed it on his head. At Domozuk's mute protest, he tugged it straight. Straighter. But didn't pause. No time to waste. The others got out of his way. They'd be on their own.

"Hermit mage," was it? Maleonarial had a new, unfortunate nickname. Old mage scribes tended to harmless eccentricity. They also stayed within the safety of the school, where no one else could notice and be alarmed.

Maleonarial might never be harmless, but he'd managed to fade from view well enough. What had he done to attract attention? Who had carried the tale? A spy in their midst? Or had one of the aging masters discovered secrets had a value loyalty did not?

Forget who.

Saeleonarial puffed as he hurried down the wide, too-empty hall. No one came late without consequence to an audience with a hold lord, not even the head of Tananen's only magic casters. There was malice in the delayed summons. Well done, Harn.

In this part of the new wing, the floor was polished marble, so smooth he had to be wary of a slip. The walls were of the same material, midnight-dark and shot through with copper gleams, arched in ever-lit openings that awaited treasure. Tiler's Holding bred wily, watchful lords, a consequence of owning Tananen's only deepwater port. The Lady's Mouth, they called it, through which poured what couldn't be grown, made, or mined within the lands under Her influence. Ships plied between Her Mouth and the strange countries across the Snarlen Sea, ships owned by those without magic.

The merchants and seamen who came on the ships were polite but curious, their heads stuffed with rumor and wild tales. It made matters worse that such had to linger here, waiting as much on the feet of made-oxen as the mercy of tides. All freight had to move by wagon past the rapids and falls of Her Veil, to where the mighty Helthrom widened and calmed, welcoming the barges that serviced the heartland. For this reason, Tiler's Hold boasted streets of brick warehouses, always full, and always expensive. Warehouses and inns.

For freight was welcome up the Helthrom, but not foreigners. The Deathless Goddess admitted no strangers past Her Veil. Only the cobbles of Tiler's Hold rang to their deep voices and booted feet. Only here did Tananen touch the wider world.

Tiler's Hold Lords kept it that way.

The latest, Insom the Second, was more than watchful. Unable to abide empty space on his charts, he insisted newcomers provide him with detailed journals. His ever-bright halls had nothing to do with vanity; he distrusted shadows and abhorred the dark. Little wonder word of a mage scribe outside the normal scheme of things would disturb him.

He would indeed demand answers.

Saeleonarial's hasty steps and puffing filled the space. His long sleeves lifted like wings, but his feet might have been stuck in mud for all the speed he could manage. Belt tassels and a wig doubtless askew were nothing compared to affronting a hold lord.

He was too old for this.

The bells around his ears laughed at him.

※

Words, once written, are free. They fly from their creator, bound only by limits set in syllable and phrase. A mage scribe can no more write magic for himself than magic write itself. The very act of writing sets him apart from his words' intent.

As well try, Maleonarial thought, to be both sun and shade.

Too much time to think, this morning. But he couldn't pass the abundance of galls in this meadow, full and ripe, their insects still inside. Crushed fresh, cooked in rainwater, filtered and let rest. A few of the beautiful green crystals from his dwindling supply to that infusion, plus a careful shave from his final small lump of desert tree gum, and he'd have a fine black ink.

Though the morning was chill and the meadow dew-drenched, he'd stripped to his clout. Easier to dry skin than clothing. His body reminded him how little time he had left. A dozen years ago—a hundred and thirty bells less—there'd been taut smooth skin over bands of strong muscle. Now, each shivering rib had its pale loose flap, and what muscle laced his limbs was more wire than flesh. His knees and elbows were the only parts left of generous proportion, and they were knobbed and indignant, inclined to complain of the damp.

Time. He shouldn't need much more. What he'd glimpsed as the merest possibility so long ago could become real with his next stroke of pen on parchment. He was that close.

Or that far. No telling what weakness corrupted him from within.

He would make his ink and find out.

If his ink-and age-stained hands trembled as they harvested the small, nut-hard galls, only The Deathless Goddess could judge it fear or cold.

Audience halls informed; a mage scribe learned to a nicety what a hold lord would want and what he could pay for that service with the first step inside. Those at the fringe of commerce were no-nonsense affairs, as often used to keep grain dry before shipment as to host grand suppers. Demands in such halls were usually practical as well. Livestock with special attributes: an ox that wouldn't tire; a messenger's horse able to see in the dark. Trees to replenish a damaged orchard. Grain sprouts to counter a too-late planting season. Hold lords knew well enough what a mage scribe could—and more importantly, could not—conjure with his words. Healing the sick wasn't possible. A living plant from which a worthwhile potion could be made was. Payment in such a hall would be gold or silver stripes, hammered flat and thin to fit a money belt.

That plus supper and a tumble with the hold daughter's selection, presumably willing, doubtless fertile. There was no proof Her Gift could be thrown like the color of a beard and fertility was very much a presumption in a mage of accomplishment, however willing. But men freely gambled on worse odds.

Including those mage scribes who clung to a belief that their hastened deaths were a sign of affection by The Goddess, that Her true intention was to summon those most worthy to Her assuredly ample and luxurious Bosom, there to dwell in whatever version of paradise suited the mage in every particular.

Saeleonarial snorted to himself as he paused in the doorway to Tiler's audience hall. The notion didn't help him sleep nights. Believers were wont to spent their lives with reckless haste, an abundance of magic that inspired dangerous expectations in hold lords.

The Deathless Goddess, being oblivious to belief or expectation, did nothing to make his life easier.

The holdings nestled in Her rich heartland offered more in payment—but expected more in exchange. Their halls were constructed of magic and architecture, with an emphasis on magic. How many years of life were paid to The Deathless Goddess to reproduce the glowing snakes illuminating Aote's hall of welcome—how many more to create the silent guardians that protected its treasury? Glorious Xcel itself required the constant attention of a dozen mage scribes to fill its hold lord's penchant for fresh flowers and frog-filled fountains regardless of season. Mage scribes there grew wealthy almost as fast as they grew old.

The audience hall of Tiler's Hold spoke of wealth accumulated, rather than spent. Little magic, other than what populated the beards of its court. Insom the Second preferred to display trade goods, the more precious and rare the better; his hall often hosted galas for foreigners. Birth wasted him on a throne. The man would have made an excellent merchant. There were, of course, a few graceful made-servants, waiting with their mute patience. Waiting with full trays.

Suspended service wasn't a good sign, not good at all, Saeleonarial fussed to himself.

His delay in the wide doorway drew the scrutiny of the made-guards to either side. Mauls, they were called. Each student was required to write a set before graduating as a scribe. Dogs, really, written taller than a man, of greater bulk. Written to stand like a man, too, but most remained bent, as if unsure written arms and hands shouldn't be legs and paws. Written to learn and obey one command: protect their hold lord.

Those hold lords who could afford to buy and replace their mauls, that is. The things did wear out. Another of their magical intentions, if unadvertised. A straightforward project that promoted peace in audience halls and reliable funding for the school, if not reliable results. Hard to convince students novelty of itself rarely meant improvement. Saeleonarial cast a critical eye over Insom's current pair. Dappled and drooling, with as much ability to intimidate as a leaky window.

Though there'd be teeth behind those loose jowls. Large, sharp teeth. Students always liked writing those.

Before his inspection seemed other than ordinary to those waiting, Saeleonarial entered the hall. The deep heavy carpet—a new acquisition from over the sea, woven as a desert-scape of yellow and bronze—resisted his slippers and made it necessary to step with the exaggerated care of being in his cups or risk lurching from side-to-side.

The nobles and their attendants parted at once, a bowing wave of sequins, feathers, and smirks that granted the scribemaster an aisle straight to the hold lord's impatient boots and themselves a good view. Another lesson to be read in an audience hall, he thought as he walked that gauntlet at a considered pace, trading dignified if meaningless nods. These placed more worth in bloodline than accomplishment.

No holding could support a crop of fools for long. Tiler's might be due for the attention of The Deathless Goddess.

Saeleonarial devoutly hoped to be anywhere else if so. The Goddess wasn't known for discrimination when She chose to clean house.

Almost there. The bows were stiffer, waists constrained by thicker tabards and girdles, though, small mercies, fewer of the dratted face confections Domozuk tormented him about. These were the cream of any hold lord's court: sycophants of use, rivals too powerful to ignore, heirs in waiting.

No smiles here, only frowns and pursed lips, as if he'd interrupted an argument. His stomach, contrary organ, clamored for sweets. Saeleonarial ignored it and came to stand before Tiler's Hold Lord.

In the fashion of more southerly holdings, Insom the Second sat on a plain chair, raised a single step above the floor. Behind him rose the latticework of the Daughter's Portion, in Tiler's carved from honey-colored wood. Mirrors filled a third of its square openings, their surfaces reflecting the bright-garbed nobles, like so many caged exotic birds.

Hands folded over his heart, the scribemaster bowed low, not to the hold lord, but the latticework. "Hold Daughter."

No matter how poor the holdings, the latticework granting privacy to the Daughter's Portion was a thing of beauty—be it a treasure of lacework created over generations or weavings of the freshest flowering vines. For any act of a hold lord to be legal and binding, she must be present to bear witness and record it. As the living voice of The Deathless Goddess and, not coincidentally, the sole person allowed title to a holding's land and life, she could also put an end to any hold lord's act or existence with a word.

Silks moved behind the latticework; shadow court or the true one? For mage scribes, the distinction was insignificant. In addition to the script of the land, every hold daughter could read and write the sacred words of The Goddess, a teaching passed from generation to generation. No mortal woman could write with magical intent or result, but these kept the key to that power. History was replete with proof that the school of mage scribes was above all a target. It didn't matter if this or that assembly of disgruntled hold lords attacked it in some vain effort to control what was never theirs to own, or a student rediscovered how to write living fire. It didn't matter if destruction came at the whim of The Deathless Goddess—who, truth be told, liked living fire but not disgruntled lords. The school burned to its foundation stones with deplorable frequency.

Five times, by common count, though some scholars claimed twice that. Saeleonarial doubted even The Goddess bothered to remember.

The magic remained, safe in the minds and hands of hold daughters, charged by their Lady to return it to those with Her Gift. A decimated school would be rebuilt on its scorched foundation by the obliging residents of Alden Holding, bright-eyed students would arrive, and any master wary enough to be out of the way at the right time but not enough to run beyond reach would be summoned back and put in charge of the new crop of mage scribes.

Not in his lifetime, Saeleonarial hoped uneasily. The holdings were at peace. Students well supervised. The Deathless Goddess?

Mages gave their futures for Her Gift, hoping She'd leave what remained of their lives alone.

Unfortunately, disgruntled was a mild word to use for the turmoil knotting the rank tattoos across the brow of Tiler's Hold Lord. Insom the Second was young for the post, Insom the First having the poor judgment to dismiss his horsemaster's concerns about a certain stallion and the cobbled streets of Tiler's Hold. The new lord was young, but not too young. The thick brown hair might be free of gray, but years at the helm of a barge had drawn reasonably distinguished lines on his broad face. Real muscle, not padding, stretched the velvet at shoulder, chest, and thigh. No hint of weakness or dissipation appeared in the keen pale eyes that now pinned the scribemaster. Temper, yes. And a worrisome glint of fear.

"Scribemaster!" Though toned to a civil note, a voice used to bellowing across a loaded deck easily filled a hall. "What do you know of this?" A gloved hand beckoned.

"This" stepped from behind the nobles. A tanned young man, sturdily built, with an upstanding shock of thick black hair. Country-bred, Saeleonarial judged with sympathy, clearly uncomfortable in his new, rich clothing. Those balloon sleeves suited a servant to one of the useless courtiers, not someone used to plowing a field or butchering pigs. Exhausted, from what Saeleonarial could see of his face past the homespun bandages encasing the left side. Exhausted and in pain.

"Saeleonarial," he offered with a slight bow. The unbandaged eye widened and the lad did his best to bow in turn.

"Nim Millerson . . ." The hesitation and worried glance at the impatient hold lord were clear. Young Millerson had no idea which honorific applied—to either of them.

"I'm a teacher and scribe, Nim," Saeleonarial said kindly. "'Sir' will do me—as you'd give any grizzled old man of your village."

"Yes . . . sir." Doubt remained in the tone. Not surprising. The niceties of court in the eastern holdings. Lost, poor lad, in a detestable maze of manners and mockery.

The glove made a hurry-up gesture.

"Tell me what the hold lord wishes me to know."

"I'm from Riverhill, sir. O'er by Tankerton. My uncles sent me past the Veil, here, to the Hold. For help." From the look on his face, Nim didn't think much of that help so far. "The rest—they stayed, sir. To guard what's stock left us. In case o' attack again."

"Attack?" Saeleonarial frowned. "By what?"

"A great beast, sir. Yesterday morn. Came a' nowhere. Tor—tor five of us t'shreds before run'n off." Nim's eye pleaded. "We can't lose more o'own. Not 'n 'arvest."

"A bear?" The guess drew impatient murmurs from the nobles behind him and Saeleonarial frowned. They must already know what he was learning from these painful gasps. He'd ask for a private audience, but delay now would only add to the distress of the honest young farmer.

"No, sir. I saw it. I swear it warn no natural beast, sir. The hermit must a'made it. The wild mage o' the hills. 'E set it o' us—t'push us from r'lands." Words tumbled like rocks downhill, faster and faster. "'E'll write anothern and anothern. You must help us, sir."

"Magic used for harm!" the hold lord thundered. "What do you know of this, Master of all Mages? Which of your kind has gone mad?"

In the profound hush, the whisper and soft click of mirrors being turned caught everyone's attention. Insom stiffened, but didn't look around. When the mirrors stopped, Saeleonarial could see himself and the injured country boy reflected over and over.

Unanimity of purpose. A terror shared. He could see it writ on his own face, and schooled his expression. Mouth dry, he bowed low, very low, toward the latticework and those behind it. There were no rules or customs forbidding magic as a weapon. There didn't need to be. Informed by a daughter of such transgression, The Deathless Goddess simply claimed all life left to that mage. At once.

"I accuse no one without proof," Saeleonarial told the hold lord as he straightened.

The bandage-free portion of Nim's face flushed. "Sir! I'm na liar!" Out of turn, impassioned . . . such was the fear in the hall, no one appeared to notice.

"I believe what you say," the scribemaster assured him gravely. "But did you see the mage write this ill creation? Were there witnesses to its first breath?"

"The dead." Flat and sure, shoulders squared. "Sir."

No wonder a distraught village trusted this wounded boy to plead their case. Saeleonarial was blunt in return. "Since they cannot testify— no, lad," this to forestall what was surely a protest. "Despite the tales, magic has no power after death. I must go myself. At once."

The hold lord pursed his lips, then nodded as if the scribemaster had asked his permission. "You'll take suitable company—"

"Here he is." Saeleonarial nodded at the farm lad. "If magic's been ill-used, best if only those already touched by it or those with Her Gift approach. My thanks, Hold Lord," this with a half bow, "but we go alone."

Insom scowled, but didn't press. "I expect a full reporting, Scribemaster, on your return."

Return? He hadn't left yet. At the mere thought of the journey, Sae-leonarial felt every ache in his once-young bones. Riverhill was not in the lovely heartlands, where civilized canals linked city to village and inns could be relied upon to have soft clean sheets. Once past Her Veil, it would be rutted mountain roads, and lucky to find a bed even if there was time for one.

But the hold lord was partly right.

Saeleonarial met a multiplicity of his own troubled gaze in the hold daughter's mirrors.

There would be a report, but not to Insom the Second. Not to anyone so predictable and powerless. The Deathless Goddess had daintier ears at her disposal.

Maleonarial, he fussed to himself. Old fool. What have you done?

Magic begins with intention. Intention is expressed as words in Her sacred language. Unspoken words. Words of only this purpose. The symbols of Her lettering are written in precise order, not from top to bottom, but over one another so ink blends all into the rest. What is written thus can never be read, as everyday writing could be, nor checked for error. Only in the mind and hand of the mage scribe will the intention of his words remain. There, and in the living result.

Ink and pen and parchment are the physical means. Students who struggle to master lettering soon learn they'll set fewer regrettable mistakes loose on the world if they use whole parchment, lump-free ink, and sharpen their quills. Masters, busy struggling to preserve what remains of their own lives, can afford no mistakes at all. They hoard fine parchment and carry their favorite pens on their persons. They buy only the best and rarest inks.

For materials have their own impact on intention and magic. Some dampen it, stealing more life than needful from the mage. Some enhance it, allowing a certain extravagance. Those inks and pens and parchments most worth using are those made by the scribe himself, an effort ultimately beyond aging bones.

The Deathless Goddess having a sense of humor.

Drizzle slanted beneath the canvas, found mends and gaps in his clothes, fingered the bones of his neck. Maleonarial shrugged his cloak tighter. His huddled body protected the tiny flame and the battered pot of ink bubbling merrily atop. Almost ready. His fingers twitched, practicing the words they would write this time.

Fewer than yesterday. Almost random. Almost. The words rattled around in his head while he did other tasks. They'd find their order when he wrote and not before. Though soundless, Her Words were as if spoken. Once said, once heard, forever gone.

Once he would have been flustered, unwilling to part with an instant of future without certainty. In the first years, at the beginning of all this, he prepared meticulous, thoughtful accounts of every potentiality, worked months on exact lists, planned for a flawless result. And failed, spending life for nothing.

He'd refused to let it be for nothing. The time since had taught him an important lesson. The language of The Deathless Goddess was itself perfect; he had only to trust and let Her Words flow as they would from his intent. Remarkably liberating, though he sometimes dreamed of being left with one word and no strength to write it.

Tucking his hands beneath his arms, Maleonarial stared into the pot. Fresh-made ink. Effort. The nib of bone. Chance. The tiny almost clear parchment he'd scraped and stretched from the delicate hide of a thrush. Skill. Would these be enough, this time?

Canvas snapped overhead, strained at the lashings. "Temper, temper," he murmured.

He dared not have expectation. Expectation was for those with a future.

Hope. That he permitted himself.

"Drive through the night?" If Harn's eyes went wider, Saeleonarial decided, they'd pop from his head.

Domozuk growled something rude from behind the wagon, busy repacking what he and Harn had hastily removed from their master's quarters. Most would stay behind—including court dress and the damnable wig, the scribemaster thought with some relief—to make room for the gear needed for the trip cross-country. Extra wheels and grain, tents . . . with luck, they'd use none of it. Nim, despite his injuries, was quick to help. The anxious student, however, stood beside the wagon, wringing his hands.

No question he had to come, however unused to rough living. Left alone, the curious hold lord would have him for questions Saeleonarial did not want answered. "The horses," he commented dryly, "do the work, Harn. You can nod in the back."

"Yes, Scribemaster." As if he'd sentenced the lad to lashes.

"Quick now. Make yourself useful." Trusting Domozuk to keep the glum student occupied, Saeleonarial walked alongside his team of six matched whites. He patted a pretty curved neck, admired the gilt-crusted harness and the red plumes crowning each head, and wished there was time to trade the lot of them for sturdy draft mules. As well wish for his youth back. A dozen bells ago and he'd have eschewed the big comfortable wagon to ride like a border raider. Now he'd count himself fortunate to hold his bladder more than an hour, let alone endure bouncing the long hours. The young didn't appreciate what they had.

Rid Smithyson, driver, groom, and pamperer of the expensive beauties, stood at their head, letting the lead right, a favorite, lip his fingers. He greeted the scribemaster with a scowl that joined his bushy gray eyebrows. "Ey'll na manage a rough road, boy. Na with yorn bloody 'ouse on wheels."

The "boy" from a man twice his years, if not age, made Saeleonarial snort. "This wagon's what we have. The team will get us to the foothills at Meadton and we'll buy whatever tougher stock we can there. The hold lord sent a courier ahead on our behalf."

A long, thoughtful chew, then spit to the side. "Nowrn ey'll be wait'n for a dandy'n 'is purse. Stick us wit 'ard-mout glueys a' best. Like to spook at yorn dingdangles n'run us inna ditch, if'n 'ey sound t'all."

Saeleonarial worked through that. Rid's hinterland tongue thickened when he wasn't happy with those in authority. It was almost incomprehensible now. "Dingdangles" were the tiny, almost mute bells stitched in rows around his travel cap. Better than the heavy and intolerably hot wig, however more impressive the latter. The tally was what mattered; Domozuk attached a new bell to both cap and wig with each intention Saeleonarial wrote. The Deathless Goddess hadn't protested. At least, he hadn't aged twice as fast. Not that he'd mentioned that particular nightmare to his faithful servant.

The rest? Not hard to guess. "Pick the best you can and keep us on the road."

"Aie." A gnarled hand rubbed the hollow behind an ear. Saeleonarial could swear the made-horse leaned into the caress. "Be rare trouble, 'is'un."

"It may not be a scribe matter," he countered, pitching his voice not to carry back to the wagon.

"An' I kin pull yorn bloody 'ouse misself." Another spit, accompanied by a too-wise look. "No one else fi'ta go?"

Trust the stables to have as much news as the full court, though the emptiness of the cobbled yard and curtain-drawn windows above were telling of themselves, it being a fair afternoon when the area should have bustled with those on their own business, let alone those curious about his. "No one else I'd trust," the scribemaster admitted. "The sooner we get to Riverhill, the better."

"'Ey'll be fast'rn wind o' flats—" Rid promised, only to toss his head abruptly like one of his charges. "Whossat, now?"

Saeleonarial turned and felt his blood congeal in his veins. "Stay with the horses," he thought he said. Hoped he'd said.

Slippers coated in pearls seemed not to care if they were stepped on cobble or into fresh droppings. Silks weighing less than air ignored the autumn crisp, though rouged cheeks took a brighter hue. An attacking army would appear—would be—less formidable than the five women who walked from the shadowed wall toward them. Saeleonarial bowed low and stayed that way, despite his back's protest.

"Rise, Scribemaster."

He knew the voice, very well, if not the face. "Hold Daughter." She was stout, round of face, hair peppered gray. Her lips were pale and thin beneath a regrettable nose; paler eyes gazed from the faint blue tattoos of her office. Without the voice, he'd have guessed someone's mother or aunt in the wrong clothes. The silks and jewel-laden ropes lay easier over the long, lithe bodies of her attendants. Their eyes, within curled black tattoos, stared at him with an unnerving intensity. The hold daughter was not at risk, in any sense, while these were with her, even though three were burdened with dark, polished boxes.

Saeleonarial gave a second, deeper obeisance. As he straightened, "What is asked of me?"

"Her Gift, Mage." The hold daughter reached within one sleeve to produce a pen.

His blood began to flow again. A request from the shadow court wasn't unheard of, merely rare and more discreet. Perhaps the speed with which he'd prepared to leave the hold had caught her by surprise. The boxes? If payment, all he wanted at the moment was a more travel-worthy wagon. "It is always at your service, Hold Daughter."

"Good. Leorealyon?"

The leftmost of the women flanking the hold daughter, the one without a case, stepped forward and bowed her head to the scribemaster. "I'm ready."

"Scribemaster. You will write eyes for this, Her Designate. She will accompany you to Riverhill and see this mad mage."

The Deathless Goddess was sending Her Witness with him? Saeleonarial was horrified. No, appalled. That was closer to the mark. The Goddess' personal attention was nothing a sane mage sought. Damn Maleonarial.

Which might be true by the end of this.

The pen tilted toward him, slightly. "Scribemaster?"

What could he do but take the thing? Too fine for his big, fisher-bred hands. Perfect balance. Gold, the body; for the nib, a gem had been cut and set into the end. A topaz. "Here?" His voice cracked on the word. "Now?"

"There's no time to waste. We're alone, save for those who should be with us."

No wonder the yard had a hollow feel. It hadn't been emptied by rumor.

He traded glances with Domozuk, who'd slipped out at the unfamiliar voices to stand by the wagon. The servant tipped his head at the rear
gate. He'd keep Harn and their farm lad safely out of sight. One worry
of thousands dealt with.

Another bell.

So soon.

Dread faded as his bones felt that itch. His heart pounded with excitement.

Not so safe. Not safe at all.

Saeleonarial braced himself. As if it were possible to prepare for the
body's abrupt decay . . . as if he had a choice. "This isn't a magic I've done
before," he cautioned.

Leorealyon's eyes lifted to his. They were the honey-flecked green of
warm summer afternoons. A man could find his youth in those eyes,
remember the sweetness of berry wine on his tongue. The suffix to her
name meant "Promised to the Lady."

The pen dragged at his hand.

"Need you be reminded of the words?"

Not an insult—fear. It laced the air, threw a chill the now-restive
horses seemed to sense. Magic as a weapon. Was he not being asked to
use it thus, in Her name? "I know what to write, Hold Daughter," he told
her, his voice flat.

She gave a regal nod. At that signal, two of her attendants stepped
forward, opening their cases. Within the first, lined with purple velvet,
nestled ranks of tiny crystal vials, the dark liquid of any one worth his
weight in gold. Within the second lay parchments of varied lengths,
each immaculate roll secured with a jeweled clasp. The true wealth of
Tiler's Hold, on display in its empty, breeze-swept horseyard.

Any of such quality would do. "You choose," Saeleonarial told

Leorealyon. Maybe having a hand in her own fate would ease what was to come.

Wordlessly, she plucked the closest vial and handed it to him. When it came to the parchments, her long fingers hovered over the selection and she gave him a questioning look.

Saeleonarial held up the pen. "That length."

She gave him one of the smallest rolls.

The lids closed and the bearers took a step back. The third came forward, offering the flat of her case as a table.

Saeleonarial tested it with one hand. Leaned. Steady as stone. He slipped the parchment from the clasp. It lay flat, uninterested in the breeze. A twist broke the seal on the vial of ink. A moment to clear his mind, to concentrate on the intention. Nothing but that. No words but what made it clear. The itch built inside him; his blood took fire.

Everything faded but the pen. He lowered it till the topaz nib penetrated the black surface. Ink climbed and held, dulling the gem. He lifted the pen and wrote what he must.

With the lift of the pen after the final stroke, a faint gasp broke from his lips. Even expected, remembered, and longed for, nothing muted the shocking exaltation that raced through his body as his words blurred into a thick line, then two, then four, then eight—lines that grew out from the parchment, that enlarged and swayed like rooted, hungry worms. Each had a head, of sorts. A closed eye. A closed mouth.

He'd done it.

Saeleonarial put aside the pen and curled the parchment in a loose roll. As he gathered it in his hands, felt the new life within squirm, his heart stuttered in his chest. He didn't dare move—couldn't move. Cold sweat dripped into his eyes. His legs threatened to fold under him. Not yet, he begged inwardly. Surely that wasn't the last of my life . . .

"Scribemaster?"

He didn't spare the breath to explain, merely . . . waited. His heart hammered once. Again. Then resumed an almost normal beat.

So. The Deathless Goddess wasn't done with him.

"Kneel, Leorealyon," Saeleonarial gasped. The girl obeyed, every motion of grace. When none of her companions came forward to brace her head, the scribemaster took hold of her jaw with his free hand and readied the thin, squirming curl of parchment in the other. "You must not move."

"I will not," she promised. Brave words. This would be the hold daughter's favorite, the best of those who attended her and so The Deathless Goddess, the one who couldn't be spared but must be spent.

He bent close. Silk from her sleeves whispered across his wrist, caught his doubtless grayer beard.

Saeleonarial wasn't sure if he pitied her or himself more as he tipped the roll into the first lovely eye and the worms opened their mouths.

Cil rubbed the rain from his face, blending it with tears. Cold and hot. Fresh and salt. Waste and frustration. "Dumb meat," he said through his bent teeth.

He wriggled farther into his hideyhole, his place, but squatted where he could watch the goings-on. Shapeless forms in the dusk gathered, guttering lanterns in hand. They carried weapons for a war against dirt, against weeds: staves and pitchforks, axes and picks.

They prepared for battle, but not against him. Silly-Cil was unimportant. Silly-Cil was useless. Silly-Cil was to squat in his hole, out of the way of his betters. "Mine. Mine!" he wailed. But none of them believed him capable of anything, not the creation of something magnificent, not even of being able to fight for himself.

They would wage war against a stranger, before noticing him.

It had been for nothing.

Cil hunched over the ache in his heart. "Not. Not. Not." His hand flashed down—they didn't think him quick, but he was, very quick, quickest—and scooped a bug fleeing the damp. He crunched it in his bent teeth, then spat his frustration and fury into the storm.

He didn't need to see the wings or razor teeth. Methodically, his hands worked the cold mud, finding anything alive to bring to his mouth.

Anything he could chew and spit and turn to spite.

Six holdings divided Tananen's lush heartland with its bustling canals and fertile soil. Their ancient holds were surrounded by sprawling cities of brick and cobblestone, though no other building could be taller and all roads, and newcomers, must go straight to the hold. Nine holdings carved an existence from the startling valleys and iron-rich hills of the north. Though together their sparse populations would be lost within a single heartland city, the nine sent a disproportionate number of students to the mage school in Alden. Regardless of wealth, numbers, or gifts, rule of each holding passed smoothly from hold daughter to her successor-designate; less smoothly, and at times with bloody argument, from hold lord to his heir.

Elsewhere? To Tananen's west spread the inhospitable fen called The Lady's Tears; beyond and in every direction, the jagged soaring rock of Her Fist.

To the south, beyond Her Veil, the Snarlen Sea.

Yet Tananen was bounded by nothing so common as sea, fen, or rock. Magic edged it, held it, defined it. Tananen was where The Death-less Goddess's gift answered a mage scribe's intended words, and only there could life born of that magic survive. Traders from across the Snarlen Sea, astonished by living wonders, would scoff at warnings and steal or barter for such treasure, only to watch it turn to ash and blow from their decks the instant their ships crossed that unseen line.

Those of Tananen stayed there. For who would leave a land of magic?

And who could be sure they themselves were not creations of The Goddess, to turn to ash beyond Her reach?

Maleonarial had stood at the sea's edge once, his worn boots lapped by bitter water, his heart worn and bitter too, wondering if it were true, wondering if he'd turn to ash if he swam too far toward the rising sun. Would She notice?

Or was every mage the same in Her eyes, and death Her intention?

He stirred the pot. Wisps of acrid steam danced over the surface of the cooling ink, teased at patterns, pretended secrets. Would it could be that easy . . . that his answer could be found by looking instead of dying a little more.

Maleonarial snorted to himself. The Deathless Goddess made the rules. As mage scribe, he made the choice. He closed his eyes to half slits and shivered inside his cloak. This old man would see another dawn. By that light, he'd write again.

If one more dawn was all She'd give him, maybe that was all he'd need.

Hooves splashed through puddles; wheels flung dollops of mud. Any section of wagon or clothing not sodden or muddied was soaked by wind-driven rain. With luck, he'd die soon.

The Deathless Goddess was being difficult. Saeleonarial's beard was now fully gray and the last of his hair had been left in the stableyard, but his heart, that contrary organ, cheerfully pumped icy blood from his hands and feet through the rest of his body. Merchants and traders claimed those over the sea prayed to their gods, sought their attention and favor. In Tananen, no one in their right mind tried for Hers.

Cushions made no appreciable difference to the hard seat; sitting shoulder to shoulder only made the bouncing worse. The Designate of The Deathless Goddess, it turned out, would see where they were going. Accommodating that requirement brought Saeleonarial out on the wagon box, since he wouldn't abandon poor Rid to such company alone.

For at the sight of Leorealyon's ruined face, Nim had shuddered and closed his good eye. Domozuk had cursed in his own tongue. Harn, after flinging himself to the back of the wagon to spew into the rush of dark road, had clung to the gate and refused to turn around.

Rid had given that visage a thoughtful look, then spat to one side. His hands on the reins eventually stopped shaking, but he never glanced around, even when their shoulders touched.

Saeleonarial shivered inside his heaviest cloak, this time not from the chill. It wasn't the empty, dark sockets or living horrors that could peer from them that filled him with dread. He knew who'd be looking back. Her. As well take pilgrimage to Her Soul and abase himself before the great, watchful tower.

Should have worn the wig, he fussed to himself.

The broad road that drank goods from the Mouth took the shortest path inland. Straight and paved with massive stone, it occasionally lured foreigners and local fools. They, and their unfortunate horses, were soon gasping as the road heaved itself up the steep slope without regard for such frail beings. If they persisted, they'd be drenched and blinded by spray as the road passed through Her Veil, deafened by the hammering of the great waterfall itself as it drained most of Tananen to the sea. If they passed that challenge?

The Deathless Goddess knew who belonged. Those who didn't, never left Her Veil.

Rid Smithyson had guided his matched whites through the gate of Tiler's Hold onto the second road that left it. This, though paved and wide, twisted its way up the sloping pass like a demented snake, sometimes almost touching itself again. A longer route, but safer. There were places to pull to the side and wait, for downward traffic had right of passage even over couriers. The team knew the road well, and had made good speed between the tight turns. They'd passed Her Veil at some distance, hardly noticing the lick of spray.

Sunset had caught them on a civilized road, with civilized traffic, lit by lantern, moving by rules. Heading to yet more civilization and comfort. Even the horses had hesitated when Rid asked them to turn off onto the narrow dirt excuse that led to Meadton. But the land was level here and the rains, however uncomfortable for passengers, hardly slowed them.

They'd be there by dawn . . .

The lead horse cried out and stumbled. The wagon jolted and Saeleonarial grasped in vain for a handhold, fingers slipping on the wet wood. Aged bones and the hard road beneath would be a disaster. But the Designate had him, hands like metal hooks. The driver hauled on the reins and worked the brake, alternately cursing and pleading until his team staggered to a safe halt.

The rain and wind chose this moment to ease as well. Rid snugged the reins and hopped down, splashing forward to find the trouble. Pointless to join him, the scribemaster knew, fretting. If the lead was lame, they couldn't slow to its pace. Favorite or not, the animal would have to be abandoned.

"A canal dancer blocks the road." Though flat and lacking intonation, the soft voice was Leorealyon's.

Saeleonarial blinked. He hadn't expected conversation from the Designate. Though this made no sense. "Impossible."

Canal dancers cleared the waterways that connected the three mightiest rivers of Tananen: the Helthrom, Pactrom, and red-tinged Nathrom. More traffic moved through the heartlands by barge than by any road. The immense dancers—a ridiculous name, since the beasts were long, flat, and shelled—crept along a canal's bottom and ate whatever silt and mud or worse had accumulated, deepening and widening the channel as they went. Their wastes appeared on shore each morning: tidy, serpentine mounds, odorless when dry. Superb fertilizer. Though, like most non-farmers, Saeleonarial did his utmost not to make any connection between his supper and the filthy beasts.

"Dancers stay in water," he pointed out.

"She takes the road tonight."

Of course. In nights of heavy rain, he remembered with dismay, the dancers availed themselves of darkness and mud-slick to slither overland from one canal to the next.

No one knew how long ago they'd been written. Magical creatures could not reproduce and most—mages being both practical and leery of expending more of their own lives than necessary—were written with a finite lifespan. Canal dancers were a different matter. Although the mage scribes claimed credit for the useful beasts, there was no proof they were the work of men. Like air, water, and magic itself, they could well be creations of The Goddess.

And tonight a damned nuisance.

By the paired lanterns on the wagon's roof, he just could make out the round rumps of the last of the team, some lines of harness. The lead horses could, of course, see in the dark. They were written that way.

Not a comfort to discover the Designate could too.

"Can't we go around it?"

"Na." The unhappy denial was from Rid as he came to stand by Saeleonarial's boot. The driver swept off his wide brimmed hat and clutched it to his chest. In the lantern light, his stubbled face was grim. "M'beauty slip do'in 'is best ta stop n'time. Leg's 'ole, but e'll be sore come morn. 'At beastie, it's filled the road. And na inna hurry te move."

"What could—" Nothing could budge a dancer. Ships rammed them all the time. Heedless barges went aground on them. Nothing harmed or perturbed the creatures.

Nothing natural.

He turned to the Designate. "Can you move it?" His mouth was dry despite the rain.

Topaz glittered. "Can you sing?"

"Sing." The worms must have ruined the mind as well as the eyes.

"She is a dancer."

A dancer. The name had real meaning?

Stay stuck on the road, or try the improbable. Saeleonarial sighed heavily, then rapped his knuckles on the peephole behind him. It slid open, Domozuk's face filling the gap. "Trouble?"

Anxious, the three in the back. No time for reassurance, had he any to offer. "We need Harn up here." The student was a decent tenor, if prone to singing too early in the morning, a habit his other masters lamented.

A lurch of the wagon, a thud and feet hurrying forward. Not only Harn; all of them. With confidence he most assuredly didn't feel, Saeleonarial explained the situation, ending: "Sing to it. Hurry."

"Sing to it? M-my lord?"

"You heard him." Domozuk gave the frightened young man a push. "Go on."

Harn balked. "Sing what?"

"She is a dancer."

The student stared at the Designate, then hastily averted his eyes. "A dancer." Shaking his head, he walked into the darkness, a hand on the loose rein for guidance.

An interminable wait. What was he doing? Had he run off? The scribemaster controlled the urge to call out to the boy.

Then, song filled the night, unsteady at first, growing more sure. A ditty from Tiler's wharves, rude and lively. Saeleonarial's lips twitched. What better for a creature of the canals?

Well done, boy.

At the second line of the song came a rhythmic grind and *whoof*, grind and *whoof*. Like no dance he could imagine, but the creature was moving! The horses startled but stayed still. Harn raised his voice and kept singing.

"She dances. There is room to pass."

"Rid."

"Aie." The driver shoved his hat back on and returned to the head of the team. His voice could be heard, coaxing them forward, comforting them as they pulled the wagon past the canal dancer. Grind and *whoof!* Saeleonarial covered his nose, grateful he could only smell it, not see. After a pause to let everyone climb aboard, Harn still singing at the top of his lungs, Rid clucked the horses up to a slow trot.

Harn stopped singing. The scribemaster sighed. They were clear.

"Faster." The Designate's eyes retreated into their socket caves. "There is no time to waste."

Saeleonarial nodded and huddled in his cloak. Rid clucked again and the horses resumed their fluid pace. The wagon lurched from side to side, bounced through ruts and potholes.

No time to waste and too much time to think.

The canal dancer was a creation of use, if not beauty. What had attacked the farmers, if not a bear . . . was a creation of harm.

Maleonarial . . . he wouldn't have done such a thing. Couldn't have.

Be truthful, old man. If only in your heart.

Of them all, only Maleonarial could.

Against his will, Saeleonarial considered the other side of his old friend, the mage scribe of astonishing, even terrifying, skill and imagination. The greatest hold lords for clients. Loremaster. Scribemaster. There'd been nothing he couldn't bring to life, it seemed. Yet twelve years ago, at the peak of power and wealth, Maleonarial had walked away from Alden Hold with only the clothes on his back.

The other masters were convinced he'd walked away from magic too. Wasn't Maleonarial past his two hundredth bell?

The scribemaster shook his head gently, so the bells of his hat merely whispered. We were all too small for him, he thought. Too bound by self-preservation. Too selfish. Maleonarial had never feared the price. He'd write magic until The Lady stripped the last life from his fingers.

But what magic?

And why?

Fingering his gray beard, Saeleonarial earnestly hoped it was nothing capable of disemboweling farmers.

Cil crept along the road that was his village. Buildings of wood and stone lined either side, connected by raised walkways to keep pants and pretty hems from the mud. He wasn't welcome inside. He wasn't welcome on top. There was room beneath either building or walkway to hide and crawl. They didn't like him there, but they liked him less in sight.

Not tonight.

Tonight he went down the center of the road, in plain view. Bold-Cil. Brave-Cil. His village, not theirs.

They—those not gone hunting—those not lying dead in the road—cowered inside. Trembled. Hid in the dark. No lanterns. Oh no. They'd learned. The spites liked lights.

Almost as much as flesh.

Cil twisted to his full height. Threw out his misshapen arms. Gave his snort and wheeze of a laugh. "My village!" he shouted.

"My village . . . my village . . . my-yy . . . vill . . . age . . ." The echoes mocked him.

They had to see him, had to know.

He'd make them.

The dead couldn't help. He'd tried the meat, to spit nothing but bile.

The village held more life. Life dozing in boxes and stalls. Life fenced and caged and waiting. Life he wasn't supposed to touch. Not his. Stay away.

"My village," he crooned to himself. "Mine."

They'd see him soon. They'd know he was important. They'd know what he could do.

Before they were meat too.

If the horse traders of Meadton had thought to cheat them, one look at the Designate by torchlight turned them into honest men. Or wiser ones, Saeleonarial mused. The weary, muddy whites had been led off to a livery Rid reluctantly pronounced acceptable, and the wagon harnessed to a pair of made-oxen. Unlike their humble namesakes, these were monsters of their kind, one stride the equal of three for any horse. They would not need rest, or food, or water on the journey. The weight of the wagon, driver, five passengers, and supplies would be as nothing.

Of course, the made-oxen would turn to ash in a few hours, being that close to the end of their intended lifetimes. The mage scribe who'd written this set hadn't returned to write replacements for the traders. From the pinched look of Meadton itself, and the alacrity with which Insom's haughty courier left for home once the made-oxen were hitched, the scribe wouldn't be back at all.

"Aie. Tol ye, din I," Rid commented, having made a thorough, silent inspection. "Hard-mout. Like'n pull off m'arms."

"They'll go in the right direction." Obedience was always written into something powerful. Mage scribes were nothing if not careful of their own skins.

The driver chuckled. "S'long as I na 'ave t'argue w'em." He sobered and glanced around. Domozuk had taken the lads to find food. The Designate sat on the wagon box; still for the moment, eyes empty of all but shadow. "I'd argue w'ye, boy. Stay 'ere. You're too frail for't. Send 'unters. 'Ere's som inna town."

So was he a boy or a frail old man? Saeleonarial kept his smile within his beard. "No need for hunters. If there was a monster made, it's ash by now. As for the mage . . . after that much magic, we'll be lucky to find him hale enough to explain himself."

Rid tipped his head toward the wagon. "She'd argue w'ye on t'at."

Warned, the Scribemaster knew what to expect when he looked up at the Designate.

Burst from their socket lairs, the worm eyes of The Deathless

Goddess shattered the torchlight, for beneath each lid was a topaz, faceted and clear. All of them stared down at Saeleonarial, as if to see every hair on his face, every sin in his past, every imagined trespass in his doubtless short future.

Under that inspection, the scribemaster stiffened. "There could be an explanation," he insisted. "Mistakes happen. Even to experienced masters. It's my duty to determine if this terrible business at Riverhill is a matter for fines and compensation, for discipline—"

"For death," countered the Designate in her toneless voice. "Her Gift must not be used for harm."

Harm. The word from this ruin of a vital, young woman, doomed to die herself when the worms finished their task, shuddered through his heart. His writing. His creation. Tears filled his eyes and the shards of light that were hers became all he could see, became all there was. Hands clawing at his chest, Saeleonarial began to fall.

Arms caught him. "'E'll na last the trip!"

The scribemaster could hardly believe his ears. Rid? Dared confront the Designate of The Deathless Goddess?

"He must." Utterly cold. Utterly confident. "Therefore he will."

Guided by a mage scribe's intention, magic could change what lived. Or it could produce something that had never lived, modeled on what did. And, every so often, guided by imagination and will, an exceptional intention could create something never before seen. Most such were dead before their misshaped hearts could beat. The school counted that a very good thing, given the inordinate amount of imagination and will exceptional students possessed.

Most such were dead.

But not all.

Gossamers, the survivors were called. They sprang from intentions that were more than the words of their making, that drew from something deep and unvoiced within the mage scribe. A need, perhaps. An unguarded whim.

For unlike all other creations, a gossamer was willful. Unpredictable. With a magic all its own.

Phantasms. Wonders. Large or small. Grotesque or glorious. Flesh or . . . not. Some lasted the moment it took to snare a heart, vanishing in a swirl of glittering bronze ash. Others could be immortal, for all the masters knew, since few lingered near buildings, preferring freer places. Those that stayed were harmless mischief-makers, perhaps amused by their effect on unmagical beings. Goddess Blessed, such gossamers were called, and no one would harm them.

Avoid them, yes. Every holding had its discreet signposts or hastily built walls to keep the unwary from a disconcerting encounter.

Maleonarial whistled tunelessly through his teeth as he worked. His own preference for wilder places had a practical side. Though a gossamer was not what he intended, he'd made more than his share over the years. So far, only the bells knotted in his hair haunted him. That, and an opinionated breeze.

Though in weaker moments, he feared the wind nipping at his ears had more to do with the opinion of The Goddess.

The parchment, stiff and almost clear, barely covered his palm. He held it in place with his thumb and smallest finger. The other hand held the pen, its bone nib ready with fresh-made ink.

His heart beat like a drum. Sweat chilled on his forehead; his hands were dry and steady. Welcome signs. Potent. He was here, in this moment, sure and set. His intention filled his mind, words arising and flowing together . . .

Not gossamer, with mind and desire of its own. Something controlled. Needful.

The nib touched parchment.

Magic itself . . . at man's bidding.

He always saw their faces at this moment. See every one of the latest crop of students waiting for his welcome as scribemaster, Saeleonarial's young brother among them. Look to his friend with a smile, a master himself and proud, and suddenly, like a bolt of summer lightning, see the toll of stolen time on that face. They weren't old men, but they were. And so, too soon, would be all those he welcomed, doomed the moment they became mage scribes.

Twelve years ago. He'd left the school that same day. There had to be an answer, a way to avoid Her toll. It couldn't continue like this. Not like this.

His intention was clear. The words were ready.

With every fiber of his being focused on his task, Maleonarial couldn't hear the pound of boots on rock, so like the pounding of his heart. The first inkling he wasn't alone came as rough hands grabbed his shoulders and flung him backward to the ground. A bag—from the taste and dust, a flour sack—was pulled over his head. Harsh cries rang out from all sides, more like seabirds than men. "Quick!" "Stop him!" "Fools! Grab the pen!" Hands wrested that and his parchment away. Something smashed. Something cracked. Something ripped.

He lay still as they destroyed his scant belongings, trying not to cough. Pots could be replaced; a canvas mended. Old fool, not to have heard them coming; careless, not to have kept proper watch. Brigands were a known hazard. They'd discover he had nothing of worth and leave. Hopefully with him still breathing.

Maleonarial freed his mind of the intended words, cast them away without trying to remember. Regret was pointless. There was no way to know if these would have been the ones, if this would have been his moment.

The pen . . . that he'd regret, if this time it was broken beyond repair. But he could make another.

Would.

He didn't resist as they searched his person none too gently, though he felt another regret as they discovered the remaining vials of Tankerton ink. But instead of the triumph he expected, there was another round of smashing, this time of porcelain against rock.

Thieves would know the value of those little pots.

"Who are you?" he croaked, for the first time afraid. "Why are you doing this?"

In answer, they seized him by ankles and wrists, carrying him away.

***

"Come out." Cil ripped the head from another fowl. "Come out." He tossed its body to join the spasming pile. "Come out." Each final flight left a runnel of blood in the mud that curved and twisted and rose. Great butter-yellow eyes sought targets. Fangs curled open from gaping mouths, dripping hate.

The doors stayed closed. Ignored him. Scorned him. Discarded him like trash.

"Not for long," he told himself.

The road rippled as sinuous bodies, swollen and heavy, made their way to the buildings, wrapped themselves around pillars and beams, crept up walls and over roofs and always, always, pressed and squeezed and sought their way in.

Cil licked bloody lips and smiled.

The wagon left Meadton with the wounded young farmer sitting with Rid. The made-oxen would follow the road to Riverhill without guidance, but Domozuk was adamant they should show a face familiar to the villagers when they arrived. Nerves would be frayed. He wanted no arrows or pitchforks aimed their way.

Saeleonarial hadn't argued, grateful for the warmth and relative comfort of padded benches. Relative, for this final section of road was as poor as he'd feared. As the wagon jostled through deep ruts, the only way any of them stayed in their seats was by braced legs and a tight grip on a handhold. Despite the bounce and sway, he did his best to close his eyes and rest.

Seated across from him, Domozuk and Harn had already closed their eyes. A snore louder than the rattle of wagon and wheel drew the scribemaster's lips into a smile. His servant could—and did—sleep anywhere. Even knee-to-knee with the Designate of The Goddess.

"M-my lord Scribemaster."

One who couldn't sleep. Saeleonarial opened his eyes again. He couldn't discern more than the faint blob of the student's face. The lantern glow outside barely reached the windows. "What is it, Harn?"

"Wh-at happens? When we find the mage?"

Ah. Conscious of the silent figure sitting beside him, he waited to answer until the latest series of jerks and bounces stopped rattling his teeth. "First we must be sure that magic was involved. This is a wild land. There are—" he waved his free hand vaguely upward "—beasts in the mountains."

"But if it is someone from the school—what then, Scribemaster?"

Fear the loss of trust among common and noble alike. Learn first-hand how vulnerable we are to our neighbors and Her wrath.

Since none of that would comfort a frightened boy, he sighed. "Hope he's reached his last bell already, saving us the trouble."

And weep for an old friend.

The wagon lurched through another bone-wrenching series of holes. Harn bounced into Domozuk who grunted something unpleasant and curled deeper into his seat. Saeleonarial clung to the handhold, imagining how much worse it must be up front. But he didn't ask Rid to try and slow the made-oxen.

Get it over with. Better for everyone.

Almost.

Magic must be intended, directed, written by those with Her Gift and Words. Above all, it is limited by the willingness of a mage scribe to spend his life. Ordinary men, men who accomplish marvels with their hands and tools, who father children and build homes, fail to grasp their own superiority. There is nothing to envy. The best a mage can hope for is to acquire wealth for a comfortable death bed.

Those who'd captured him, who carried him, who whispered in fear and desperate anger—if they only knew, Maleonarial thought wryly, how much more life they had than he. From their deep voices, most were in their thirties or forties, prime years for an ordinary man. Full of future. Careless of it.

Could they believe the aged body they carried with grudging care was no older than theirs? That he'd been born a mere forty-one years ago, in a mountain village likely twin to theirs, that he had older brothers who looked like great-grandsons, that not even his mother had known him within the decay of a man almost too old to still breathe . . .

A shift of grip. They had him by the shoulders and legs. Downhill now, boots skidding over wet leaves more often than stone. Not murderers. That could have been easily accomplished with a rock to his head.

They knew what he was, or they wouldn't have feared his pen.

They knew what he was, but didn't want him for it. The rude handling, the sack stifling his face proved as much, even without the fearful whispers. Maleonarial couldn't believe they expected his willing cooperation, and torturers soon learned The Goddess would not permit Her Gift to be forced. With the first tainted word to parchment, She took what life remained to any mage scribe who succumbed to pain or threat.

The Deathless Goddess protected Her Gift, if not her mages.

Why? Who? Where were they taking him?

The closest village was Riverhill. Peaceful. Having more bottomland than most along the Terrhom, Riverhill's surplus grain found its way upstream and down. Welcoming folk, if reserved with strangers. He'd been there only a week ago. Traded wildberries for a day-old loaf and some honey. Followed the savory aroma of lamb stew to the inn's kitchen and coaxed a bowl from the kindly matron. Camped where he could see lamplight in windows and hear laughter from the wharves. Written his words and failed again. Left by dawn.

If these angry men were Riverhill farmers, they must think him someone else. "You've made a mistake. I'm Maleonarial," he croaked through the sack. "Maleon—"

"We know your name, Hermit."

"You'll pay!" From the other side, edged like a knife. "You'll pay for what you've done!" A hoarse chorus of agreement. The hands gripping his sore body tightened, as if ready to pull him apart.

Those carrying him moved faster, jostling any breath he had left to argue, to plead.

This was not good. Not good at all.

Made-oxen didn't falter or slow, even for a swollen bladder. Designate be damned, Saeleonarial thought, staggering with Domozuk to stand at the tail gate and send a companionable stream of piss onto the road.

The scribemaster clung to a handhold, swaying with the wagon. The world receding from them was gilded by early morning sun, drops sparkling along leaf edges, puddled wheel-ruts become flashes of light. Warm amber tinged the distant hills and the crisp air had a fresh-washed taste. Bird song—what could be heard over the huffing breath of the beasts, the slam of plate-sized hooves into mud, and the creak of wheel and wagon—rose from the meadowlands to either side.

The Deathless Goddess was in a better mood.

That couldn't be good. He scowled. "We're almost there."

Harn lurched between them, waving an apologetic hand. Domozuk caught him as a rougher jolt almost sent him flying after his piss. "Careful, lad!"

"Thanks." If the boy blushed a darker hue of red, he'd match his jerkin.

Saeleonarial leaned his shoulder into the side of the wagon, loath to return to his seat beside the Designate even though his legs shuddered in complaint and both knees ached.

Harn almost fell out again as he pointed urgently. "What's that?"

"That" was lying across the remnants of what had been a man. A lazy head, capped in horn, lifted as they passed, twisted to follow them. The motion pulled a pink loop of gut free, hooked on a tooth. The creature casually flipped the morsel down its throat, staring at the wagon until they turned a corner and were out of sight.

Not a bear. Saeleonarial's mind struggled as hard as his heart. What, then?

Nothing he knew. Nothing anyone knew. Which left only . . . "A gossamer."

"Gossamers are harmless," Harn protested, voice rising to shrill. "Harmless!"

Musk in the night. A dream of a dream. "So we believed."

"If that's—if they—what about the rest?"

"I don't know." Saeleonarial dug his fist into his aching chest and closed his eyes. How many? They'd no tally of the things at the school. Gossamers were mistakes; their creation cost a mage scribe without payment for the privilege. This—this mistake cost Riverhill its blood. Old fool. "I don't know," he sighed and clung with both hands to the holdfast.

"Enough." Domozuk pulled them both inside the wagon. The Designate turned from the small side window at their return, face raised, empty sockets bound by black tattoos. Beams of sunlight stabbed the gloom of the dark interior and picked lavender and gold from her silks, fingered the delicate ropes of jewels on her chest. No stains marred her clothing; the worms had been neat and swift. If it hadn't been for the screams . . .

No doubt the Designate had seen the gossamer. Saeleonarial let his servant ease him to the bench beside her and wondered if a goddess could be surprised.

"You should have brought the hunters," Domozuk scolded, half under his breath.

Sitting was its own joy. The scribemaster let his head fall back against the cushions and listened to his sputtering heart as it settled. "We can't harm The Goddess Blessed."

His servant gave him a familiar, dour look as he took his place beside Harn. "Tell that to our farmer up front."

Still, Saeleonarial cheered ever-so-slightly. A gossamer was never intended. This one, however grim, couldn't be blamed on its creator. "A mistake—"

"The intention was perfect. Despair. Vengeance. Perfect."

They all stared at the Designate, but she said no more.

Harn whimpered deep in his throat.

Saeleonarial was tempted to do the same. How could anyone imagine something so foul, let alone find words in Her language to form it.

Musk and laughter. Droplet-laced whiskers, glittering by moonlight. He hadn't imagined that either, nor intended to create it. He'd only wanted . . .

The scribemaster closed his eyes in defeat.

He'd wanted wonder.

Old fool.

And now a mage had wanted . . . what? Despair? Vengeance?

They were none of them safe, if those could be given life.

"It was me!" Cil grabbed a broken timber and threw it with all his might. It landed atop others. There were many others. Wood mixed with shards of bone and flesh and shredded cloth.

And everywhere blood. He stomped a puddle of it, squished it to warm mud between his toes, kicked it into the air.

His creations lay quiet, scaled sides heaving from their exertion, mouths agape. Spites formed tiny lines along what had been gutters, wings still, mouths closed. The first, the best, the biggest would be back soon. Someone had run.

Cil sank to his knees in the mud. "Silly-Cil," he sobbed. "Stupid-Cil. Couldn't do this. Couldn't be special."

Nothing answered.

There was no one left to know.

Then he heard the cries.

Cil looked up and smiled.

The body can only take so much. Maleonarial was half unconscious when his captors stopped, only dimly aware of being dropped to the ground. His hands and feet were numb; every joint on fire. He breathed in gasping whoops that burned the inside of his throat and raced his heart, but did nothing to fill his lungs.

The sack was ripped from his head.

Light and sound overwhelmed him. He curled into a fetal crouch, but they'd have none of it. With incoherent cries of rage, he was seized again, forced to his feet. When he couldn't stand on his own, they held him.

Rows of nodding heads, tawny brown against gold. They were standing in barley. Hairs from the ripe heads covered pant legs. Stalks lay trampled into mud.

Why would farmers trample their own fields? Maleonarial doubted he'd like the answer.

"Look, damn you!" Hoarse and distorted by passion. "See yorn bloody work!"

His work? What had he done? Maleonarial honestly tried to see what they meant, but something was wrong with his eyes—or with the world. Where was this place? What was it?

He must have whispered the questions aloud, for one of those who held him answered. "Riverhill." And spat.

The wet glob slid down Maleonarial's cheek, hot, then cold.

Riverhill?

The barley field swooped down to the river, dew-laden heads sullen and still. The river flowed past, dirty and swollen from the storm. All was as it should be.

Nothing was.

He swallowed bile, staring at the heaps of splintered wood lying between field and river. What could have done this to walkways and wharves, homes and shops, the friendly inn? Between the heaps, the sunlight struck red. Not blood, he told himself. It couldn't all be blood.

Thankfully, one of the Riverhill men blocked the dreadful view. Big, dressed as a smithy, fists the size of melons. His contorted features glistened with tears. "What did we do to you?" he pleaded. "Why di' we deserve this?"

The Deathless Goddess did, on occasion, clean house. Summoned by a hold daughter, or for reasons of Her own, Her Designates would appear to claim what life remained from any and all in a place.

Not this. Even if a simple village could somehow offend Her, this was not Her work. She dealt in life's start or its end, not wanton destruction.

Maleonarial looked from one face to another. All held the same question. Ten surrounded him. One more held him upright. Farmers, bearing pitchforks and spades, an axe. Tools, not weapons. All that remained of Riverhill. They'd kill him. How could they not? The disbelief that held them waiting for his answer would break with his first denial.

Maleonarial counted heartbeats, waiting for his last. Odd it would come like this and not be taken by The Goddess. Would She count that a trick on his part, to do Her out of Her just fee?

A dark cloud appeared behind the smithy, dissipating into hundreds of tiny black flies. From the decimated village, he guessed, confused between corpse and living flesh.

No, not flies. As the tiny things surrounded them all, one hovered before his eyes long enough to see it was nothing more than a tiny ball, a ball with wings and a gaping, toothed mouth.

"Look out!" he shouted. The made-flies—they could be nothing else, though he didn't recognize them—began to land on the farmers, attacking any bared skin. Tiny bites, but each tore away a bloody chunk of flesh. The men dropped their tools, frantically batting the creatures away.

A swarm headed toward him and Maleonarial tensed, but the made-flies turned at the last instant, going instead at the hands and face of the man who held him. With a startled cry, the man shoved him away and flailed wildly, trying to protect his eyes. Others covered their faces with their arms. One was too late, and cupped a hand where an eye had been, blood streaming between his fingers.

Maleonarial flinched each time one of the made-flies flew close, but they had no interest in him. Their intention was sickeningly clear—they'd been created to harm the villagers. But who would do such a thing?

Only a mage scribe could. No wonder the farmers had hunted him down.

"They're na bit'n him!" the big smithy shouted. "They're his work!" With a roar, he picked up a shovel and ran at the mage, made-flies a halo around his gore-covered face.

Something struck the smithy from the side, ripped off an arm, tore away his head with a casual snap and toss. Pounced on the next screaming farmer like a weasel among chicks. Playful. Dreadful.

Somehow Maleonarial stayed on his feet. The made-beast was—it wasn't anything he knew. Horny plates, claws, teeth come to life in some improbable body. Eyes that were slits of malice.

Eyes that never once looked his way.

Before the echoes of the smithy's scream died away across the river valley, every farmer lay dead. Worse than dead. They were hunks of meat, lacking any vestige of what they'd been. Fathers. Brothers. Husbands. Friends. Now only flesh, and the thing that prowled over it, tasted it with a purple tongue, but didn't eat.

As though already sated.

Maleonarial sank to his abused knees, supporting himself with his hands. The stench of new death choked his nostrils. "Gossamer," he named it, sure of only that. The monster didn't turn, deaf to his voice.

His?

He squeezed his eyes shut, but could still hear the dreadful beast as it walked and licked and purred to itself.

His?

No. He shuddered with relief. No. Strange, those gossamers that had come to life with his pen, but not fearsome. Some might have been beautiful, in their way, though he hadn't cared, too full of disappointment as he watched another scrap of his life fly or run or float away with a laugh.

Maleonarial opened his eyes to study the monster. This—this terrifying shape would have burned into his mind forever. Could it have come *from* one of his, then? Not by all he knew. Gossamers emerged as they would be—so he'd been taught, so he'd believed. Either the accumulated wisdom of the mage school could not be trusted or . . . something inside him eased . . . this wasn't from one of his intentions.

Then whose?

The dead deserved better than his fuddled reasoning. He'd find no answers here. Maleonarial assessed himself. Sore. Bone-tired. They'd been rough, but had done no more harm in their handling of him than The Deathless Goddess. She hadn't killed him yet.

An ownerless pitchfork became a staff to help him stand. He swayed for a moment, cursing the weakness of his arms, the treacherous wobble of his legs. The monster, now curled among corpses, paid no notice. The made-flies had settled like soot on the barley nearby, wings still.

The innocent.

Leaving the bloody harvest, he shuffled between rows of barley. The skin of his neck crawled to think what was behind him. His pant legs were quickly soaked by the wet grain but, small mercy, the sun warmed his cloakless shoulders, easing their ache. The village was an impossible number of steps, so he didn't look up after a while. Downhill, at least. If he fell, it would be in the right direction.

Though his fury ran so cold and so deep, Maleonarial knew he'd find a way to climb the tallest mountain of Her Fist if necessary. A mage scribe who could intend such evil was the true monster, whether gossamer or made.

He had the will. There remained one problem.

"I hope you've taken care of him already," he panted to the errant breeze that nudged rain-wet barley across his narrow path. "Because I have no idea how."

• ⁓ •

They were too late.

No one spoke the words. They climbed from the wagon to stand ankle-deep in blood-caked mud, surrounded by destruction. The accusing sun penetrated every shadow, revealed stripped bones and hanks of hair, rags and gauds, and ruin.

In their stunned silence, the Designate stepped forward. Her dainty pearled slippers turned red. Topaz glittered in the daylight as she lifted her face from side to side. The Deathless Goddess would see it all.

She might care.

She might not.

What he'd give for a trustworthy god . . .

The wooden beams. They hadn't been broken or burned. They'd been *squeezed* into splinters. Saeleonarial reached out blindly, found a shoulder for support.

Domozuk was quick to step close and wrap an arm around his waist. "You should sit—"

He shook his head. "No time. Nim. Nim. Are you all right?" Stupid thing to say. Of course he wasn't. But what else could he say? Be grateful you were away in Tiler's Hold, being dressed to suit Insom's foppish court, while everyone you knew and loved died by violence. Too late by hours, from the look of it. By meaningless, pointless hours.

The young farmer stood with Harn. At his name, he turned his bandaged face, exposed flesh the color of ash, his one eye dilated and wild. "Sir."

No mage scribe, yet with that one word, Nim Millerson said everything. Saeleonarial's heart steadied in his chest. Was he not the scribe-master? Was he not the hope this boy had brought with him? Had he not vowed to be responsible for all who intended magic? That he'd made that vow expecting his thorniest problem to be recalcitrant masters and arbitrating fees made no difference, standing in the blood of Riverhill.

Magic, used for good or ill, was his responsibility.

Saeleonarial found the strength to pull free of his servant, to straighten. "I'll find out what happened here. I promise."

"Look!" Harn shouted. "Someone's alive!" He began to hurry forward, feet slipping in the mud.

Rid grabbed him. "'Ware, lad!" This an urgent whisper, with a guarded look at the figure emerging from the shadows the scribemaster understood too well. "Na trust him."

The student was bewildered. "He's hurt—"

A bent body. Slow cautious steps. The movements of someone injured? Or of an old man, wary of the mud, a very dangerous old man?

"Think." Saeleonarial braced himself. "Who would have survived here?"

Nim's face was ash. Harn's suffused with blood. "Maleonarial." His mouth worked as if the word left a foul taste.

The worm eyes of the Designate now locked on the figure shuffling toward them.

Justice for the dead. Safety for the living.

Why did it have to be his dearest friend?

"I'll talk to him." As if there could conceivably be an explanation for what had happened here.

Nim shaded his eye, then dropped his hand. "It's na mage, sir. That be one o'mine. Cil. The knacker's boy." He drew himself up, jaw firm. "We tol' him t' hide, y'see. He's na right inna head. Simple. I'll tak'm wi' me." With a helpless shrug. "Tho' I dinna know where."

Young, this farmer, but already looking past his grief to care for someone else. Saeleonarial nodded to himself. "You'll both be welcome at the school, Nim Millerson. We'll find work for your hands. A home."

"Sir. Thank you." Nim ducked his head respectfully, but his jaw clenched. "No, sir. I'll na take poor Cil near magic or them as use it. 'E's seen 'nuf."

The figure lurched over a fallen beam, recovered his balance with practiced ease. Not a boy, Saeleonarial judged, his smile of welcome freezing on his face. Nor a man. He'd seen his share of twisted bodies, living by the bay. Fishermen lost hands, broke limbs, mended in crooked fashion if at all. Cil's body defied reason. His left side was larger than the right by half again. Hands, feet, limbs. One nostril gaped wide and red, the side of his mouth ballooned outward, revealing decayed and hideous teeth. His left eye was normal sized, but set adrift in a huge socket, lids drooping down. The left ear had suffered indignity after birth, the upper part cut away.

How could such a babe have grown to adulthood, let alone survived whatever had happened here?

Cil lurched to a halt. His good eye peered up at them, for he stood bent to his right. "Mine," he said, the word distorted by his mouth but clear. "My village. Strangers go 'way!"

Strangers? Did he not know Nim?

Of course not. Insom's fancy velvets, the bandaged face. The farm lad looked like some noble's brat, sporting a cut from a duel or tumble from a horse. The kind who probably laughed when they rode by the poor cripple. "Peace, my good man," the scribemaster said gently. "We mean you no harm. Do you know who did this?"

"I know." Cil made a hideous sound, a choking wheeze Saeleonarial belatedly realized was the only laugh possible from that body. "'Good man' knows."

Nim stepped forward, hands out and trembling. "Cil. Did anyone else survive? My—any one?"

"All meat. All dead. Only Cil." He tilted his lopsided head, opened the lids of his right eye to stare. "Know you!"

The piles of broken wood shuddered to life. Huge shapes emerged from the rubble, sinuous and long. Fangs hung from wide open mouths, dripping venom. Their eyes—

"To the wagon!" Domozuk shouted, pulled at him. "Hurry!"

Their eyes—

Topaz.

Resisting, Saeleonarial whirled to stare at the Designate. Silk flowed along her shapely limbs, caught by a breeze. Jewels took fire from the sun, including the gems that were Her eyes. Eyes that lived.

What did it mean?

Harn and Nim took Cil by the arms when he didn't move with them, dragging him toward the wagon despite his wild struggles to be free. "Mine!" he shouted. "Mine!"

"Riverhill's gone," Nim gasped out as they fought with Cil. "Come w'us, Cil. Easy now."

Saeleonarial half expected the made-oxen to be nothing more than ash by now, but they stood ready, oblivious to the massive horrors squirming closer and closer.

Cil, stronger than he looked or manic, broke free, pushing Harn into the mud before lurching away.

Nim chased after him.

The horrors, as one, turned to follow.

"Nonononono!!" Cil choked on bile and spat, but nothing lived, nothing appeared. Nothing was right.

"Cil, wait!"

Hands on him again. Strong hands. Hands always hurt. These hurt. "Mine!" he cried, twisting to bite.

The false farmer was too quick. They were always too quick. "Easy, Cil." One hand patted him. As if he was stupid. As if he was slow. Meat to walk stupid and slow to the hammer.

"Mine," he boasted as he stared past velvet at the death rearing to strike. "You be the meat."

Three hundred bells. A mage scribe who'd survived such accomplishment could command any price. All Maleonarial wanted was air in his lungs and the ability to move his aged bones faster.

He ignored the gem-eyed gossamers, except to avoid being crushed by their swollen bodies. They ignored him, intent on the pair of villagers clinging to one another in what had been the market square. Survivors! *Thump* went his pitchfork staff against a broken bit of plank. He'd reach them first. He must.

He might. His breaths were shallower now, despite the desperate need of his lungs, and whistled deep inside as though something had cracked. Shouting was out of the question. Three hundred bells. One decent brass gong, he railed to himself, shuffling toward the doomed men. One gong and a hammer to let them know someone cared, someone was coming.

For whatever good he could do.

Where was the mage? Sweat stung his eyes as he peered over the writhing gossamers.

There! A wagon. Figures beside it.

Wait.

He knew that brute of a wagon, those ornate lanterns and flags. It belonged to the mage school—to the scribemaster.

There were figures—five—they saw him. One gestured. He knew that beard.

Saeleonarial.

Consumed by hope, Maleonarial stopped and leaned on his staff.

He gasped a deeper breath. "Sael! Get the villagers!" Almost no sound came out. He coughed bloody phlegm and dragged in another breath. "The gossamers won't hurt you! Help them!"

The words were gibberish, impossible to hear over the grunts and slaps of the monsters as they poured onto what had been the road, as they closed on Nim and Cil.

But no mistaking the glint of bells knotted in that gray mane, more than any other mage. More than any sane man could bear.

"Maleonarial." The name hurt to say, but Saeleonarial was sure now.

There was only one thing left to do.

"Quickly! The monsters will only attack those from Riverhill," the scribemaster told the others. "Take the wagon. Save them!" This as Nim pulled Cil—who resisted, poor demented soul—out of reach of the nearest set of fangs.

He bowed to the Designate. "I will take you to the mage who has gone mad."

Who was shouting? Who was saying things? Cil shoved Nim to one side, trying to see the newcomer.

An old dirty man. Dressed in dirty rags. Bells in his dirty hair. A no one. A nothing, leaning on a funny stick.

Cil tilted his head to see better, squinted, strained. No stick. A fork. A farmer's fork.

Bells.

The stranger in the mountains. The one they said made what was his. His! The one they went to kill with their shovels and axes and forks.

They hadn't, had they.

His creations could kill him. Should kill him. Why didn't they kill him!? They passed the old dirty man. Went around him. Scared of him.

While he stood and stared at Cil.

As if Cil was nothing, unimportant.

"No!!! Kill him too!" Cil yanked free of Nim at last and ran among the monsters, pounded on their sides with his fists. "Kill him! Make him meat!"

They ignored him.

Ignored *him*.

As if he was nothing.

"MineMineMine!!" he wailed, betrayed.

Those with Her Gift know one another. It sings through the blood when the change from child to adult is complete, a song heard by any and all who wear the bells. The knowledge calls one to the other. There is no denying it, as there is no denying when a boy becomes a man. The Deathless Goddess thus anoints those who will sup on magic, and those who will, if able, return Her Gift with their lives. And only those.

Until now.

Leaning on the staff—without it he'd be flat on his face in the mud—Maleonarial watched the not-mage try to control his creations. Misshapen—by birth or disease. Older than a boy—not by much. Violent and dangerous—that, beyond doubt.

How. That was a question to ask. Among many.

Whether inspired by his pitiful shouts or not, the made-oxen and wagon had reached the villager who was the true intent of the creatures. As a rescue it was more a delaying tactic than of use, since the gossamers merely reared up and began to use their bodies to crush both the made-oxen and wagon and presumably all those inside. So many of them tried to do this at once, they interfered with one another, but it was, Maleonarial thought sadly, a matter of moments.

Then he'd be alone with the not-mage—who, if he stopped screaming in impotent rage at his creations long enough, would simply form a new intention and create it, aimed at him. Then go on to make whatever else came to his twisted mind, never, by the look of him, having to pay life for it.

And here he'd thought The Deathless Goddess played fair.

Not that magic would be required to end his life. Really, a rock or piece of wood in those powerful hands would do it.

Light-headed, he warned himself, gripping the pitchfork more tightly. Not good.

Though being light-headed explained what he now saw.

For tubby, sedate Saeleonarial was coming toward him, shooing monsters out of his way as though they were so many sheep, followed by a beautiful girl in lavender silk.

He couldn't help but wave his hands at the things, though it did no good at all. What did, he quickly realized, was the presence of the Designate. The monsters in her path moved to one side and lay still.

Once Saeleonarial realized this, he grabbed her arm and pulled her to the besieged wagon. Monsters peeled away.

The made-oxen were gone. Ash, he noticed with an odd relief, not flesh.

The wagon was a ruin, but those inside were not. So much for those who'd laughed at the massive thing. Domozuk held a cloth to a wound on his cheek. Rid simply shook his head at the bright-eyed monsters walling them on all sides. Nim helped Harn from the wreckage, the student cradling a wrist most likely broken.

No time to waste. "Stay with us," the scribemaster told them.

Then he pointed. "There, Designate." His heart shuddered. "That's the one. Maleonarial. Your mad mage."

"Wait!" Nim handed Harn to Rid, coming to Saeleonarial. "You're wrong," he said earnestly, tears streaming from his eye. "It's na mage at all."

"No," agreed the Designate, her eyes writhing. "It's not."

Worse and worse and worse.

The spites came back and ignored them. Ignored *him!*

His most and best and biggest lay stupid in the road like the rest. Cil kicked it and wept his rage, but it ignored *him.*

The old dirty mage had done it. He rose, wiped snot and tears from his face, and *knew* what to do about that.

"Make you meat. Make you nothing!"

He would, too. He was strong. He could kill a calf with one blow of his fist. He didn't need a hammer.

A fork. A fork would do better. Cil went close, closer. Raised his big hand and his small hand to take it, to use it, to stick it in the gut.

What was this?

The old dirty man didn't move, didn't run.

He *smiled.*

The monster from the meadow was as much under the Designate's whim as the rest. How long that protection would last?

How could there be magic without words? Without cost?

As scribemaster, he was appallingly uninformed. More time in the archives, Saeleonarial promised himself, fist against his chest. And in bed. No more time like this.

If there was time left at all.

Nim and Rid held Cil's larger arm, Domozuk the smaller. They'd stopped his attempt to attack Maleonarial.

While Maleonarial—

"Old fool." Saeleonarial feared to touch him, so frail he seemed, so worn.

"Nice hat." Little more than a hoarse whisper. The gentle mocking smile, though embedded in wrinkles and without bottom teeth, hadn't changed.

They were a year apart—a year! Friends since that first day at the school. How could he be so aged?

As for the obscenity of bells he wore . . . what had he been doing?

The shift in Maleonarial's eyes meant it was time.

"Designate." The bow was more a dignified stagger, knuckles white on the pitchfork Maleonarial used for support. Harn, after a glance at the scribemaster, offered his good arm.

Saeleonarial turned. He must witness this, though he'd take no joy from that duty. Nim, with every right to anger, was as gentle as he could be. There was no justice or vengeance possible here. Only the prevention of anything more.

Or anything, if he could imagine it, looking around at what had been Riverhill, worse.

Cil, who'd struggled frantically, mouthing incoherent threats and spit, closed his mouth and stilled at the approach of the Designate. When she stopped before him, he bent slightly, as if bowing to a great lady, then stared up at her. The uncanny eyes, topaz and moving as if to memorize his face, didn't appear to disturb him. Instead, he looked enraptured.

The Designate stooped to press her perfect lips to his.

Cil aged no better than he'd lived, his body shrinking in on itself, growing shriveled and more deformed, cheeks caving in, hands become wizened claws. The men holding him let go in horror, but only when the Designate ended their kiss did he fall.

What was this? Saeleonarial blinked. Had he seen a faint plume of ash as the sad corpse met the ground? Before he could be sure, a breeze danced through silks, tugged his beard, and whisked away any trace of glittering bronze.

The waiting monsters lifted their heads. The long ones closed their eyes and burrowed head first into the ground, debris and rubble toppling into the massive holes left by their bodies until nothing was left on the surface but the mud road, golden barley fields, and the river. The made-flies rose in a swarm, circled once, then rose to the sky to fly off in all directions, the sun sparkling on their tiny wings so it seemed for an instant that the air itself shimmered. The beast from the meadow rubbed its horn-capped head against one leg, then stretched like a cat. After a long and careful look at each of them, as if memorizing their shape, it curled on itself and bounded away, leaving no trail at all through the grain.

They were wonders again.

That's what they were. Wonders made the world deeper, wilder. As it was meant to be. Saeleonarial's heart burst with the joy of it. He smiled and took one last breath.

Musk.

Musk and laughter and droplets like gems . . .

All this. All this and the Ancient Hag stole the best of them. With a cry, Maleonarial dropped to his knees. He gently removed the belled hat, then flung it aside as he cradled his friend's head against his chest. The rest stood by; Domozuk silently wept.

"I am not done," the Designate said in her lifeless voice.

"I am," Maleonarial snarled. "Leave us be." Almost to himself. "Let me be." Hard to breathe. Nothing didn't hurt. Nothing hurt as much as this. All this.

"I cannot."

The voice . . . it wasn't the same . . . he looked up.

And saw . . . only the words of Her language could capture the face before him, and those words had no sounds to be uttered, no descriptions to recall. Only intention. Only magic. Only life. His mind could not encompass it . . . hold it . . . the face shimmered and faded and he didn't know if that meant he was dead or now wished to be.

"This was your doing." The voice became the clash of rock against ice. "Your intention. All this."

Saeleonarial chilled in his arms and The Ageless Bitch mocked him. She was destruction and death. "You lie," he croaked, and coughed blood.

"I cannot." The roar of wildfire across grass.

"Leave me be."

"I cannot." Rain and thunder. "You wrote that which could steal from Me. It was your intention that found haven in this shattered child. Your will that brought his fear and hate to life."

His gossamer, after all.

Magic without cost.

His triumph.

Empty of all but grief, Maleonarial closed his eyes and rocked slowly. "Let me die, then."

"I cannot." The crack of lightning through wood. "To reclaim what was taken, it must pass through My Gift to the world."

Lips pressed against his, at first dry and cold, then searing hot. He couldn't move, couldn't breathe, couldn't . . .

He tasted ash.

A dream. More vivid than most. Not so strange as some, especially after eating that rubbery shelled fish Sael's brother brought . . .

Maleonarial kept his mind at sleep's safe edge, unwilling to challenge, unwilling to know, not yet. He let himself feel nothing but comfort. Which was strange of itself. He couldn't remember the last time he'd awakened free of pain, rested and peaceful, without his bladder threatening to burst or his lungs itching to cough.

"I think he's awake."

"Shh."

"We kin na let him sleep the day."

The rarity of voices in his camp, let alone unfamiliar ones, pushed him from safety to the cold truth. No dream.

No Saeleonarial.

Riverhill. All of it. His doing. His intention.

Maleonarial lay still, feeling the cold trace of tears.

"Awake at last!" A known voice.

So much for peace. He opened his eyes to find Domozuk's pocked nose too close to his own. It disappeared before he could object, revealing a blue sky inhabited by one distant, soaring hawk.

He saw a hawk.

No, he couldn't see a hawk. Maleonarial distinctly remembered losing the better part of his sight two hundred bells ago.

But he saw a hawk. No, two hawks. A pair, lazily circling.

He sat up.

Another surprise. He hadn't been able to sit without propping himself with his arms for at least a hundred bells. At the thought, he raised his hands.

He hadn't had hands like these since his first bell.

A breeze slipped past his face, drying the tears. Maleonarial surged to his feet.

Rid looked up from the small fire he tended and grinned. "I na seen the mat'o'it."

Domozuk and two others—the villager and a mage student cradling a bandaged wrist—stood waiting. Maleonarial looked around. They'd moved away from the village. The only reminder of Cil's work, his work, were the shapes lying on a makeshift brier. One was wrapped in the robes of a scribemaster, the other, smaller and twisted, in strips of fine velvet. A tidy bundle of lavender silk lay at their feet, tied with jeweled ropes.

Ash on his lips. He'd never known her name.

The dead and the living. Himself, made new again. He'd need a mirror, but his hands, his stomach, most of all, the vibrant pent-up energy that had been the bane of lessons when he'd first come to the mage school, told the tale.

The Deathless Goddess had taken what remained from one life, and given it all to him.

"I wouldn't have believed it, sir, if I hadn't seen it." The bright-eyed student quivered like a coursing hound about to run. "They'll want to know everything. The other masters." A less bright glance at the briar. "My-my lord Scribemaster always believed you were innocent, Master Maleonarial. He always spoke up for you. You'll prove him right."

"Will I?" How peculiar, to hear a rich timbre to his voice again. "What's your name, lad?"

"Harn, sir. M-my lord." This with a crimson blush. "Harn Guardson. For now."

He remembered. To so badly want to be renamed. To no longer be Mal Merchantson, but Maleonarial. To intend dreams and write magic.

To begin paying life to The Deathless Goddess.

Maleonarial nodded a greeting to the villager, now clad in an assortment of clothing, including a weather beaten coat that must belong to Rid. "And you, sir?"

"I'm na 'sir.'" No blush here. The unbandaged eye held a glimmer of curiosity, though the face was drawn with grief. "Nim Millerson. I'm from—was from Riverhill. The scribemaster came w'me to—to end things, 's my guess. He was a good man. Brave."

A hint of accusation. Why hadn't The Goddess restored Saeleonarial, the deserving? Maleonarial nodded. "He was. This"—he thumped his now-solid chest—"is nothing I earned, Nim Millerson. The Deathless Goddess would have back what—" he didn't know the poor cripple's name "—what magic was taken and used here. She chose to give me his life so She can take it again, each time I use Her Gift. It's Her way."

So he could live, knowing what his intention had done. All this.

Why? he wondered for the first time. Why must it be through a mage scribe's intention? Why did She need to reclaim Her Gift at all?

Maleonarial felt his now-strong heart begin to race. She'd given him a second lifetime in which to stop it. To let young Harn learn magic without penalty. To keep men like Saeleonarial fit and well through their best years, instead of bleeding them dry before their time. All he had to do to release magic into the world, was bring death to She Who Couldn't Die.

As quests went, it had all the hopeless glamour a newly young man could ask.

"So," Maleonarial said cheerfully. "We need horses. Who has a pen?"

# Fundamental Lexicon

**The world was always thus.**

Those who sail from Her Mouth know certain truths. The sun rises in the east, winter begins with the solstice, and the jagged rocks of The Brutes crush any cast on their unfortunate shores, spitting the remnants back to sea as flotsam, feeding gulls or caught in nets, the cries of birds echoing those of grief.

Until Insom Fisherson, heir to Tiler's Hold, is swept overboard on a fine summer's day. Strong and determined, he clings to the rocks, drinks the blood of gulls, and waits. When he sees a passing fishing boat, he leaps into the waves and swims till eager hands heave him to safety. He is hailed a hero.

**We were the first here.**

Insom rejoins the living and if there's a strange look in his eye, if he refuses to sleep without a lamp burning near, none can claim to know what he's endured, for no one else has touched The Brutes and lived.

If, on his triumphant return to Tiler's Hold, the stones of the wharf shudder once beneath his feet, no one notices over the cheers of the crowd.

And if, a week later, a horse rears, frightened by something beneath its feet, and falls, killing the hold lord, Insom the First, none could claim it other than accident. All agree their brave new lord, Insom the Second, who'd been Insom

Fisherson and alone survived The Brutes, is the luckiest man
in Tiler's Hold.

*Magic, once, was almost lost.*

At that year's highest tide, in the dead of night, Insom
leaves warmth and light behind because he must.

Stands at the ice-slicked limit of the wharf, clothed in
bitter wind and sleet because he has no choice.

Stretches his arms to the unseeable horizon where vast
waves smite The Brutes, each larger and stronger than the
last. Waits till water surges up and over, water turning black
as the deepest depths—

Cries out in a voice that isn't his.

To his helpless horror, is answered.

# CONSEQUENTIAL PHRASES

# CONSEQUENTIAL PHRASES

Gray stone, some hauled and shaped, the rest gifted by cliffs to either side, filled the yawn of Her Mouth with a tower of unyielding might, its seaward side broken by the outpouring of Her Veil through a massive colonnade, emptying the Helthrom and thus the rest of Tananen's great waterways into the Snarlen Sea. The stone wore a slick of dark green in summer, glistened with icicles in winter, and at no point could it be climbed.

Where the thunderous cascade of Her Veil was little more than mist, a single broad gate had been cut low into the ever-shadowed northern cliff, the damp cobbled tunnel beyond well lit and wide enough for three freight wagons to pass one another without touching. More hospitable stone stretched along the curve of land and into the harbor as breakwater and wharves, offering haven to fishers and traders. Gulls cried above fish markets, and warehouses and inns crowded the lowest reach behind those, for nothing moved from ship to shore without intervention, and only here could shore be reached at all.

Leave Her Mouth and go west, past the rabid boil of waterfall, and you entered The Hunger, a treacherous narrow strait bordered to the land side by abrupt mountains and from the sea by The Brutes, a string of bleak rocky outcrops like the peaks of drowned mountains themselves. They could have been, for the roiling water of the strait was of unfathomable depth. The Snarlen Sea spent itself upon The Brutes, waves pounding day and night; at winter's highest tide, those waves grew high enough to crash over the outcrops to fill the strait with a terrifying roar.

Go east, staying close, and the curl of cliff provided sheltered water and safe passage to and from Her Mouth. Freighters flying the flags of Lithua and Ichep, or the fiery pennants of far-off Whitehold Isles, took the passage in their season, filling Her Mouth with their shouts and songs. At all times of year, save winter's high tides, fishers from Tiler's Hold eased their chubby craft past the larger ships, to go out and around The Brutes seeking the vast shoals gathered at their feet.

A noisy place, full of life and its boisterous rackets. Under it all, you wouldn't think to hear the stone. To catch it breathing. Hear it mutter to itself. Tell itself secrets.

Promise itself revenge.

But there are those, here, who can.

The tower and its surrounds comprised Tiler's Hold, Tananen's bastion and sole gateway to the world. One look at its seaward face muted ambition but in truth it mattered not who thought to conquer here, or sought to elude watchful eyes. The Lady waited beyond Her Veil, ever vigilant, and no one born outside of Tananen crossed into Her domain alive.

Kait Alder supposed that explained the lies on the map.

Leorealyon had brought word of this newest addition to the hold lord's collection, urging the three Daughter's Prospects to go and look at it. As that was the last request of a woman who'd become her friend, the last friendly smile and final twinkle of those wise-beyond-her-years eyes—

Kait'd come early, to see the map alone. Better than grieving in her chambers and far, far better than listening to those who viewed the sacrifice of the best of them cause for joyful pride.

Pride? How dare they. While a hold's acolytes stood ready to be spent by The Lady at Her need, these had escaped Leorealyon's fate by being less.

Not a truth to say aloud. Not by a newcomer here.

Belonging took work as well as tact. Kait refused to think of open sky, mountains, and forests; refused to summon memories of guile-free faces, shared work, and laughter. She learned what they taught, ate what they offered, spoke as they preferred. Would make this her home, should that sacrifice be asked—

Even if Tiler's Hold was as hollow as a rotten tree.

Oh, there were people enough. At times, she felt all Tananen crowded these halls. The Daughter's Quarters alone housed more than Woodshaven—

But where were its gossamers? She'd never been in a place without a shimmer of bronze, a giggle in the dark, some unexpected utterly distracting wonder—which gossamers were, after all. Everyone knew they were Hers and to be cherished, even the sly ones who pulled hair or tormented livestock or lured the unwary from their duty. Tricky to predict which, no two gossamers the same; once any gained such repute, the word spread where not to tread alone.

Or didn't. Woodshaven folk weren't above a trick or two themselves when it came to unwelcome strangers, and she'd watched for the same here. Then hoped. But she'd found none and she couldn't ask, could she?

Having lost The Lady, too.

Since the first spot of menses, Her Words had been part of Kait, Her Voice a constant gentle warmth. Guiding, reassuring, good. The Lady's Gift, that connection, granted to those few who would serve Her. Their duty, to hear what was truth. Preserve it. Share it, so Her magic continued.

Just not here. Kait closed her eyes. Her Words remained, she'd that much, but she'd neither heard The Lady nor felt Her Presence since entering these stone towers midsummer. What if Pincel Hopper, her fellow Woodshaven daughter, had the right of it, and she was wrong to abandon their people and her chores, even if the summons for prospects to be her successor-designate came from the hold daughter herself—

Even if Kait had felt, at that moment, swept up and bound to go and halfway down the mountain—

And hadn't it happened, just at that moment, Atta Moss, the third of them and her senior and more likely to go, cut her forearm open with an axe with unlikely carelessness?

A daughter might believe herself chosen.

A prideful one would, Kait snorted to herself. And yes, prideful, to take The Lady's silence here as disapproval, to believe She judged Kait's decision, to leave Woodshaven and those in her care, ill-made. The Lady had greater concerns than the choices of a single daughter from a humble village.

No, this lack was in her, a failing of worth she must and would confess today to Tiler's Hold Daughter, before heading home in disgrace to face those she'd abandoned. She would try and redeem herself. Try to regain what felt the loss of her soul, should The Lady be merciful.

Unless—she'd make one last attempt.

As she had each day and more since her arrival, Kait let herself be open and peaceful, listened with all her heart and soul—wished with every fiber of her being—

Feeling nothing. Hearing—nothing.

She squeezed her eyelids shut, waited till there was no chance of a tear. Fool, to hope The Lady would come when called, but hadn't she been one? No more. High time, as she'd tell her son, to pull the wool from her eyes, admit failure, and be done.

After this final duty to a friend.

Leorealyon's map hung in an alcove carved into the black marble of the wall, framed by delicate lamps burning scented oil. The hallways of the upper levels were studded with such displays, but Insom's finest treasures resided here, along the section of corridor all must pass to enter the audience chamber.

Unless you'd leave to enter the Daughter's Portion instead, in which case there were other passageways, alcove-free, and other doors. Where she should be, it being Kait's turn to breakfast with the hold daughter, then view today's audience—though she'd not stay any longer than it took to speak her piece.

The truth must be shared.

She'd time, yet.

This early, the hall held only the servants assigned to polish its gleaming floor. On knees and hands, they worked in triplets, pushing dampened wipes in great sweeps, humming together to keep a rhythm. One or more would nod in appreciation whenever she passed, for to walk here, Kait carried her shoes and wore warm socks.

Having spent days enough shooing Leksand and his little friends from her freshly sanded and swept floors. Her son cleaned those floors now, being almost grown and responsible for his aging great-uncle.

This morning, though, the servants let Kait pass without acknowledgment or grin. Their heads were down, shoulders hunched, and the hall echoed with a silence broken only by their soft huffs of effort.

Because of Leorealyon? Unlikely, as those Gifted by The Lady had fates separate from those around them. In Woodshaven, Kait would have asked what troubled them. Here, everyone had a role and station she was expected to know, insulated within walls of complex manners she most certainly didn't.

Back to the map. It was better done than most, the landmasses of Ichep and Lithua drawn with convincing detail, and she'd have been entranced by the intricate rendering of the coastline, from the rocks of the ominous Brutes to the open welcome of Her Mouth, but for the map's lies.

Where the rest of Tananen should be, where Woodshaven was and Leksand lived—the home of her heart? The mapmaker had drawn a loathsome monster sprawled across blankness.

Ignorance was unlikely. Maps of Tananen were easy to obtain; Kait had hung one in her chamber, bought in the same market that catered to sailors and traders from over the Snarlen Sea. The foreign mapmaker deliberately erased The Lady's realm, replacing its rich tapestry of mountains, plains, and canals—its people—with this foul misrepresentation.

Leorealyon had been right to alert them.

The mapmaker's message was plain: Tananen, forbidden and possessed of magic, was to be feared. As might anything unknowable be, Kait thought impatiently. Tiler's Hold didn't stop outsiders determined to explore beyond Her Veil, only insisted they first pay the set fee for the return of their corpse.

It dissuaded most.

Every few years, someone would mock the tales, ignore the warnings, and seek to pass Her Veil. They would drop dead, the breath taken from their lungs.

Common knowledge, but perhaps here with particular, sharpened point. Kait bent to memorize the name and the maker's place of origin, written in a bottom corner. Burgan d'Struth from the Whitehold Isles. She would check it against the identity of the latest to attempt Her Veil. A hold daughter must take heed of attitude and its changing tides.

Especially of the lord in her charge. What message did Insom the Second send, to display this lying map as if a prize?

The truth must be cherished.

Making his message a troubling puzzle. In Woodshaven, the most complex problem she'd faced was which stand of trees to log next— granted, a knowledge and responsibility none here could claim, but hardly of use within this stone tower and the wider world beyond.

Kait pressed her lips together, forbidding a sigh. Hadn't she'd taught Leksand to recognize the difference between needful humility and crippling self-doubt? Those with The Lady's Gift were few in Tananen; those She permitted to utter Her Words rarer still. However silent She'd become, the Blessed Lady worked in mysterious—

All at once, she felt a prickle of unease that wasn't the palpable weight of stone above, nor the chill air.

There. An echo to their breaths, mis-timed and deeper.

The servants continued their work, face-to-face with their reflections in the glistening floor. Couldn't they hear it?

The breathing became a mutter, distant and faint. The reverberation of the mighty waterfall outside?

No. This emanated from the stone itself and she wasn't hearing sounds. The mutters, the strange breathing, reached Kait inside as when The Lady spoke, Her Voice felt with the certainty of revelation.

Kait put an eager hand to the black gloss of the wall, only to gasp and draw back, fingers curled in revulsion.

This couldn't be Her. The incoherent mutter offered nothing of calm or comfort.

It promised horror—

Gone, the sounds, all at once, as if she'd been noticed in turn.

Gooseflesh rose on Kait's arms despite her warm cloak. No need to invent strange doings, she reminded herself sternly, shaking her head to clear it. Hadn't she fought her dislike of the stone walls? Done her best to find beauty in windowless halls and chambers? Made her peace with an ocean instead of sweet babbling brooks?

Refused to blame the foreignness of this place for The Lady's silence.

Strange doings were real. Villagers had been attacked. A mage scribe gone renegade and a precious acolyte claimed by The Lady to bear witness to his crimes. The hold lord had doubled the guards outside his chambers and halls even as the scribemaster himself, Saeleonarial, journeyed to Riverhill in search of the truth.

Truth? Kait's nostrils flared. The truth was she'd wish she'd never set foot here, had it been her wish to make, but Tiler's Hold Daughter, though in robust health, had summoned her possible successors from across the holding. Whatever Wendealyon knew, whatever was happening here, was that perilous.

The stone remained mute, if it had been the stone at all.

"Prospect Alder. Why are you not in the Daughter's Portion?"

The dour note in Ursealyon's voice was familiar. In Kait's opinion, the senior acolyte delighted in finding everything a disappointment, from those she helped teach to the splendid food they were served, as different as winter and summer from Leorealyon. Who'd learned each prospect's name and heritage when the rest of the acolytes couldn't be bothered. Who'd smiled even when sweat-soaked and exhausted from training, for Her acolytes lived to serve and would defend the hold daughter—whomever she was—with their blood.

And be Designates of The Lady, should She ask, and die.

An oath Ursealyon had taken, so Kait composed her face and turned with a respectful bow, raising her gaze. Everyone here was taller, especially the acolytes. "I'm on my way." She lifted her shoes in evidence.

"What—show some dignity in public," the other snapped. The black curls tattooed beside each eye added weight to her scowl. "This isn't some mountain hovel. You're Kaitealyon."

As well as the tattoos, Ursealyon wore the pearled slippers that were the mark of her office. They'd left scuffs Kait could see a servant hurriedly buffing clear.

She'd not be here much longer, but that didn't mean accepting a pompous "ealyon" to her name, or rudeness to those unable to speak for themselves.

"Aie. It's nayh 'at," Kait replied agreeably, dropping into the rolling accent of Woodshaven. "We do 'r own mop'n."

The acolyte regarded her stonily for an instant, then gestured down the hall. "With me."

Kait padded alongside Ursealyon, silent in her sock-covered feet. She'd have felt a cheeky child caught stealing berries, if not for the map.

If not for Leorealyon and what she must confess.

If not for what she'd heard, that wasn't there at all.

Maleonarial tossed aside the blanket, too restless for sleep, and stood. Stars crusted the sky but the moon had yet to rise.

Too dark to walk. Not that they traveled on foot. A group of madehorses, four suited for riders and two more, larger to carry what was needful, waited like statues at the edge of their small camp. They could see in the dark; he'd written them to be tireless and easy of gait as well, for none of their company were riders. Hard enough, riding without saddles.

Harder still, riding with grief.

Domozuk and Rid served the scribemaster; they would learn who he'd be, and if they'd be welcome, when they reached the school. Maleonarial had no counsel to offer; he'd lost interest in the politics of the place the day he'd left it.

The capable pair had been his servants before being Saeleonarial's.

Whatever they thought or felt about him now, they kept to themselves. With Nim's help, they'd salvaged what they could from the wreckage of the great wagon. Shreds of draperies secured Saeleonarial to a made-horse.

They'd buried Cil with his victims, Nim staring down afterward as if the loose soil might hold answers.

Maleonarial having supplied none.

The clothing and jewels worn by Her Designate had been tied on the second beast of burden, along with what else they'd scavenged. Some was useful. A kettle, the remnants of tents to use for bedding. Some, like Sael's ridiculous belled cap, was not, but he wouldn't argue with them. Harn's wrist was broken. Domozuk's cheek would scar and Nim's eye, a ruin. None of them would forget what had happened in Riverhill.

They slept like the dead themselves, tonight; muffled shapes at a distance. They kept apart from him, consciously or not, and he didn't blame them.

He'd lived alone for twelve years. Alone with neighbors felt little different.

Maleonarial sat on a log. He stirred up the embers of the dying fire and forced himself to watch the glow. Still new, this burn of impatience. The pointless twitch of muscle and nerve. Being young again was, in many ways, a nuisance.

A danger, that too. The lust? To pick up pen and find ink, to write *anything* to release the damnable magic boiling inside of him?

Masters like him conveniently forgot how overwhelming their early urges had been, losing the memory in the years spent to gain control until fear of the consequence—of aging—gradually won. Forgot why even the most diligent students broke the rules and desperately wrote whatever they'd learned, groaning with relief as their magic spilled like seed on dry ground. Successful results ranged from tiresome to dangerous. Made-mice that sang one note. Made-spiders that spun webs over the cutlery. Made-fish that tried to walk, stumbling through the galleries. Made-moths that sent forth sparks and occasionally—he poked the embers—set fires, which was why students were to keep buckets of water in their rooms.

Masters forgot their youth.

Here he was, once more afflicted by it. The Deathless Hag must be laughing—

Something snapped within the blackest shadows. Maleonarial ignored it. The heartlands were well farmed and hunted. There'd be nothing larger than a fox watching him. Curious about a man who couldn't rest.

Closer, eyes caught starlight and ember glow. Rabbit, perhaps. Gossamer?

Perhaps.

Whatever it was took risks in his company, he thought dourly. Poor Harn's eyes had nearly popped from their sockets when he'd borrowed the student's pen and inks, of the lowest quality, to write not one, but six made-horses with a single sure intention.

A master's skill and knowledge, in the body of a student.

The only thing more dangerous in Tananen had made him into this and She wanted Her magic back. Wanted him to use it. To spend his new life as quickly as possible and he didn't believe for an instant the consequences to those around him mattered to Her at all.

An ember popped, releasing a gout of flame.

A good thing he'd other plans.

Pylor Ternfeather, a damesen of Tiler's Hold and, by virtue of being cousin to its lord, highest of that rank, pressed her tongue into her cheek as she decanted bubbled scum from atop the crucible. Despite the mask over mouth and nose, she held her breath to avoid inhaling corrosive fumes. Having poured off as much as she could, she skimmed the rest using a spoon made to her specifications, porcelain and impervious.

"Hold it still," she ordered.

Her apprentice, Tercle Kelptassle, grunted a rude acknowledgment through her own mask. Both knew whose callused hands were steadier. Both knew they were equals, colleagues and friends, but outside this private space and their shared work, "apprentice" it was. That, or be called a servant and thus subject to the rules of a hierarchy Pylor didn't control and Tercle wouldn't abide. Besides, as her friend gleefully pointed out, she could go where a damesen could not, including visiting her old haunts in the fishmarket.

Pylor leaned over the crucible, her critical gaze reflected in rich emerald green. According to Saeleonarial, not a tint sought by mage scribes, but as a base for other, deeper inks, it would do well. Possibly for her ledgers. Now to—

"Py?"

She turned her head to glare accusingly at the other woman, her eyes green as the ink. Tercle's grimace showed over her mask. The door had been locked, then. Pylor returned her attention to the crucible and snapped, "Who let you in?"

The owner of the deep male voice chuckled. "I am lord here."

By traditions brought to Tananen by their forebears, older than holds and courts, female descendants could own but not rule, while the male could rule but never own. The same traditions named her for the first living thing she'd touched as a child, while Insom had been Insom Fisherson, named for his family's role in the community.

Until her father died last year, putting Insom, the eldest male eligible, in his place.

A lordship temporary, should The Deathless Goddess decide him unworthy or flawed. Unlikely, Pylor thought comfortably. Her cousin made a good lord, possessed of caution and compassion.

If poor timing when it came to her experiments. At her nod, Tercle put the crucible on a stand to cool. Only then did the damesen pull down her mask and dip her head in acknowledgment. "Welcome, my lord, but you're premature. I don't have an answer for you."

An eyebrow rose, creasing the rank tattoos across his forehead.

"The scribemaster's request. An alternative source for their inks. Aren't you here for that?"

A man of action and decision, it was rare for Insom to hesitate. Rarer still to see a look of—was that confusion?—cross his strong features. It vanished beneath a frown as Insom waved at her waiting apprentice. "Leave us."

Tugging her mask to hang around her neck, Tercle wiped her hands on her well-stained apron and looked pointedly at Pylor.

"Fetch more potassium salt from the stores, Tercle. If you please," when she didn't move at once.

The while, Insom stood like a rock, watching the apprentice leave, the door close behind her. He didn't stir when the latch dropped with a loud clatter, Tercle tending to opinion.

Only once sure they were alone did his shoulders slump. He half-staggered, as if the effort to stand had been exhausting. He rubbed a now-trembling hand over his face. "Oh, Py—"

At once she stepped close to catch his hand in both of hers. "Cousin. What is it? What's happened?"

"I—I've come to wit's end. I can't take any more," he told her, his voice distant, eyes downcast. "I need help. Your help. Will you help me, Py?"

Never had he seemed weak. "Of course. In anything. Name it."

"It's—it's—" He choked, as if the words turned themselves in his throat to gag him. Muscles clenched along his jaw and Py held tight. They were the same height but Insom was half again as broad and thick with muscle. He was her hold lord and ruler. Never had his voice grown faint or failed.

Insom drew a long, shuddering breath. "Forgive me, cousin," his voice smooth again. "It's this hermit mage, Maleonarial. I need you to go to the scribes' school and question the masters about him and his magic."

It wasn't what he'd started to say. She was certain of that as of the formula giving her ink its hue. They'd grown up together, close as siblings. Yes, he'd changed of late. Who wouldn't, being lost at sea, then thrust young into a lordship and its heavy responsibilities? She'd been proud— "But cousin," Pylor said uneasily. "What of Saeleonarial—"

"Did you not see it? Were you not in the hall? He knew something he wouldn't admit. Conspired against me. I cannot trust him. I must know of this mage!" Now, at last, Insom looked up—

There was something horrible in his too-wide eyes, a writhing shadow crossing the whites like black lightning, and she would have backed, would have fled, but he clenched her hand in a grip like stone and pulled her to him till their noses touched. His breath stole the moisture from her mouth and his voice struck her ears, raw and piercing and strained, like no voice could be. "You will do this. You will do this. You will—"

"Stop!" Pylor cried, tearing herself free. The crucible smashed to the floor as she spun away and landed half across the table, emerald splashing the tiles. She hung there, numbly aware a finger—or more—felt broken, staring up at her cousin.

Who once more ran a trembling hand over his face. As it passed, it left his face normal again, if bloodless; his eyes clear and full of remorse. "What did I—? I'm so sorry, Py." Anguished and low. "Forgive me, please. I can't stop—I haven't—I can't sleep."

"That's no bloody excuse." She pushed up, faced him, shaking with what she told herself was fury, not fear.

"I know. You have to un—understand. It's the shadows, Py. They've spread everywhere. You've seen them." Words spewed forth, heaved like vomit. "They wanted to come here. Couldn't until I touched—I touched—I didn't know. Couldn't know. No one knows—"

"Make sense!"

"It's hungry. It made me bring the rest. I couldn't help it. I try to resist. Climb from the well. Always, I try, I swear it, Py. Light hurts them. Fire they hate. Nothing I do is enough. They're too hungry. They want—I don't know what they want. Who can know—I have to save the hold. I can only do it with your help."

A fever dream. It had to be. "You're ill, cousin. The help you need isn't mine."

"And I will seek it, I vow." Insom's hand reached to her, withdrew at her flinch. "First, do this. Go to the school, Py. Learn all you can of this mage. Please. Call it my crazed folly if you will. Do it to ease my troubled mind."

Never had she pitied him, till now. "I don't know—"

"Py. Cousin. Please, I beg you. By what we mean to each other. For the love we share."

Had he ordered her, as hold lord, she could have refused. But this was the Insom who'd been like a brother, who'd taught her to fish and swim.

As for whatever else he'd become?

"I'll go."

Call her a coward, but she wanted to be as far from that as possible.

Stone couldn't breathe. It most certainly couldn't mutter to itself.

A gossamer after all? They'd been told of the village and the hermit mage. The hold daughter shared his name and past: Maleonarial, once scribemaster, now renegade. If any mage scribe was capable of perverting Her Gift into deadly creations, it would be this man. Thus the command to send forth Her Designate to witness and mete out justice.

But they didn't know, did they? Kait would have argued Her Blessed Gossamers couldn't be made to kill and they should leave matters of this mage to The Lady, had she been asked, as she hadn't been nor deserved to be.

As for what she'd heard? If something of Hers, magical and wild, roamed the hall where Insom kept his treasures, no one had spoken of it.

Kait would have asked Ursealyon, but the acolyte appeared in a great hurry to whisk her out of sight.

Or her sock feet.

They passed the grand doors to Tiler's audience hall, presently closed, taking a branching corridor. After a short distance, Ursealyon took Kait through what appeared a servant's access, and her first impression of the famed Daughter's Portion of Tiler's Hold was the homely smell of breakfast.

It waited on a table, fare identical to that served in the Daughter's Quarters: cooked eggs in half-shells, fresh bread and apples, bowls of the ever-present dried fish those who grew up here relished, brittle and over-salted to Kait's inland taste, and a thick-walled crock of porridge steaming in the chill.

Regardless of season, cold emanated from the stone—walls, ceilings and floors. She'd learned to don an extra layer under the usual tunic and pants. It gave her a thickened look and she couldn't bend gracefully, but better warm, in her estimation, and what use was grace?

There were carpets, but Kait paused to put on her shoes, grunting with effort, using the moment to compose herself. Disturbing, whatever she'd heard, but surely—surely harmless.

If she'd heard anything at all.

They'd arrived first. Ursealyon took up station by the food, arms crossed, head lowered to glare. Kait wandered the novelty of the Daughter's Portion, doing her best to ignore the other. What did the acolyte think? She'd fill her stomach before the hold daughter? Word was Ursealyon favored Ella, the prospect from Meadton, a village so large, it boasted two inns. Woodshaven could be dropped into its weekly farmers' market and vanish.

Bigger, Kait reminded herself, was no guarantee of better, be it manners or ought else.

The space was longer than wide, separated from the main audience hall by a screen from floor to ceiling. The screen's woodwork was exquisite; each complex piece of interwoven lattice hand-polished and oiled to a warm honey glow. It could have been lace. To her exploring fingertips, it felt like porcelain.

It might have been hers one day, had she been worthy and The Lady willing, though Kait supposed regret wasn't worthy at all.

Nor was judging the ornate screen ostentatious, however true. It was what it was and as it needed to be. Ursealyon scorned her socks? No one here had believed her when she'd told them the Daughter's Portion in Woodshaven was distinguished by a fragrant bough of fresh-cut cedar, ideally but not always free of perturbed spiders or moist slugs, the bough plopped on whatever table in the village inn was vacant at the moment.

However true. Woodshaven being a peaceful little village, beyond Her Veil and three days' climb into the mountains distant, reasons to invoke the authority of The Lady were vanishingly few and predictable. Within living memory, only once had there been need to gather and pronounce Her Doom, and that on a fool who'd felled a tree home to a Blessed Gossamer.

The pronouncement came after the fact, the tree having fallen on the fool and smashed him flat. The gossamer having moved to another tree, deeper into the woods, that might have seemed the sum of it, but Kait and the others had heard Her Words. The Lady's penalty for working evil on the land was death.

A truth must be shared.

Pincel, Atta, and Kait had summoned all of Woodshaven to hear, crowding into the inn. There'd been nods of somber agreement, the fool in question having been warned on several occasions, then a shared feast, it being rare the entire village stopped work at the same time, and why waste the chance?

Kait doubted those in Tiler's Hall feasted together, unless to a purpose. As for a simple summons to share Her truth?

There were politics, here. Nothing could be simple.

This hall was where those attending—other than the lord—would stand for the duration of the day's audience on the well-polished marble floor, having first entered through the paired massive doors at the far end so all came and went in full view, including the lord. They stood, Kait had been told, in order to be counted among those who were important to the hold.

In her opinion, anyone with a day to spare to stand in a hall should find themselves an occupation. Maybe polishing the floors. Then they'd be important. Not, she supposed, an opinion Tiler's Hold Daughter would express.

At least on this side of the barrier the arrangements were practical. An array of comfortable seats and tables faced the screen. Four narrow doors, plain but solid, with strong, well-greased hinges, lined the back wall. Those here could come and go without notice.

Ursealyon noticed her interest. "Near door's the privy if you need it."

Practical indeed. Kait half smiled. "Handy."

"Far door's Her Promise." A long, scarred hand raised to point. "The hold daughter bears the key at all times."

Kait's smile vanished. Her Promise: safety for a hold daughter who called the wrath of The Lady down on her lord. A way to flee, leaving the rest to die. For that was Her charge upon all hold daughters, to judge the actions of their lord and restrain any that might threaten the land. Fail to do so, and The Lady must be summoned, Her Doom pronounced, and those Designated would "clean house."

After the daughter and those She would spare were safely away, through that one, seemingly innocuous door.

To the credit of Tananen's Hold Daughters, and the relief of everyone else, such a cleansing hadn't happened in their lifetimes. All were taught of Xcel and Aote. How their hold lords ignored the warnings of their daughters and seized control of the canal flowing through their lands. How they declared war upon one another and prepared to attack.

How, in a single night between one moment and the next, everyone still within those hold walls was visited by Her Designates, to receive Her Kiss and die, corpses aged beyond recognition.

Better a tree fall on a single thick head, Kait shuddered. She was grateful Woodshaven's cedar bough most often marked a sharing of knowledge, the daughters asked for advice on logging matters, or how much water to apportion to the mills in dry years, or on anything else the village might need. Grateful custom, outside the great holds, held that all of those Gifted with Her Voice act together, none above the rest.

Why, Woodshaven's three daughters took turns baking for their meetings, it being polite to compensate the innkeeper for their use of a table. Atta's biscuits were a favorite.

Nothing so common here, where the Tiler's Hold Daughter ruled an extensive court and oversaw the entire holding in Her Name. Laws affecting everyone, from the wharves to Woodshaven and beyond, were passed in this hall. Here, as in all the holds across Tananen, such an elaborate barrier must separate the Daughter's Portion from the hall of the hold lord, so that those who watched and judged were not themselves observed.

Not that any outside Her court had witnessed what had happened to Leorealyon, two nights past. Corridors cleared by the Daughter's command.

A life ended. That command too.

Turning away, Kait sucked in a breath, settling herself. She'd no right to judge the hold daughter. One unimaginable day it might be her turn to order such a sacrifice.

On this, she'd begin her journey home. Her fingers gripped the lattice. Home. Erased on that map, locked behind stone, Woodshaven's sun-kissed meadows and bright flowers seemed more dream than real; Leksand—she'd promised him more shells for his growing collection. Would they grant her time to shop or throw her out the gate—?

"Tell me."

Kait looked up at the tall shadow now beside her. "Tell you what?" She wasn't about to confess to anyone but the hold daughter.

"You fuss over footprints." Eyes glinted within their daunting black surround. "Why mar the wall with your hand?"

Nor was she about to admit hearing stone breathe. "I was there to see the map—grew careless—"

"The truth, in Her Name." A hand like a claw gripped her shoulder, drew her close. The acolyte leaned down, lowered her voice, and said what sent Kait's blood pounding. "Tell me, Kait. What did you hear?"

And Kait knew, with that, Ursealyon hadn't come to the hall to find her. "You were there listening for them. For the—stones." The final word came out a whisper, but the other released her with a grim smile.

"Then you did hear. Good."

Which it hadn't been, in any way. "What was it?" Kait demanded. "Was it a gossamer?"

"There are none within these walls."

"Why?"

"No one knows. There were. Then there weren't."

Hairs rose on Kait's neck and she dared ask, "Could you make out what they said? The stones?"

A stare, then a hand lifted, palm flat and forbidding. "No more questions, Prospect Alder. The hold daughter will be here shortly."

Along with the end of mysteries, fell voices, and her future here. She would confess, then be sent home as undeserving. With a nod, holding in a sigh, Kait turned to inspect the lattice, this being her last chance.

A third of its openings were filled with squares of glass, each suspended within an intricate weave of wire she puzzled at briefly, then dismissed. The remainder were crisscrossed with thin slats, leaving deep shadowy gaps too small to offer more than a glimpse through to the other side. She bent to peer through the nearest.

The grand audience hall of Tiler's Hold was deserted, as she'd expected. The big rectangular room was crossed by a line of thick carpet from the doors to Daughter's latticework and was otherwise furnished only with the lord's chair, set against the lattice slightly to the left of center.

So the hold daughter could prod her lord from behind?

Another question to put aside. Within the hall, braziers weren't yet lit, but flame burned in every sconce and chandelier. Kait pinched her nostrils to hold back a sneeze. By the cloying thickness and smell, they'd done so through the night. Woodshaven could be lit for a year. There were rumors but, "I hadn't known Insom was this afraid of the dark," she murmured. "Poor man."

"Mind your tongue," Ursealyon snapped. "A hold's lord must command respect."

"I meant—"

"Outside the Daughter's Portion." A tight smile. "Here, we maintain a clearer view of our lord and his court." Ursealyon selected a fine strand of wire, then plucked it with two fingers as if playing an instrument. The nearest glass square turned and tilted, edges taking fire from the lights in the hall. "See for yourself."

Kait obeyed, lips parting in wonder. Through the glass, the hall jumped toward her; she could discern individual knots in the hall's lush carpet as clearly as if she'd put her nose to it. She glanced at Ursealyon. "How is this possible?"

"The glass is a modification of the lenses used by mariners." The smile vanished. "Be aware, prospect, ours do more than see. Their use betrays the daughter's interest to those in the Hall."

"To our gain, oft as not."

Kait bowed low with Ursealyon as Tiler's Hold Daughter approached, careful to wait until she could see the tips of the older woman's shoes had stopped moving before she straightened.

"Stop the damn bowing, Urse," ordered the woman who controlled the fate of Tiler's Hold and beyond. "You look ridiculous."

Ursealyon stiffened, shoulders back. "It is my role to instruct—"

"A role you take too seriously at times, old friend. Alone, let us be as sisters. I insist"—with a daunting gleam in her pale eyes. "You too, Prospect Alder."

As if it were possible. Nonetheless, Kait straightened, giving a small nod to say she'd understood. The hold daughter, like the acolyte, wore layers of beautiful silk, this being a day of official business. On Ursealyon's tall athletic frame, the multicolored fabric draped from shoulder to floor in orderly flow. On Wendealyon, the tunic bunched over ample breasts and hip, the pants billowed wide, hems caught in the tops of her slippers, and the magnificent jeweled ropes both bore around their necks were, on the hold daughter, tied into a loose knot, the bulk shoved inside her bodice.

Unlike the acolyte, her rank tattoos were faint and blue, like a trace work of fine veins framing intense eyes. There was no doubt who ruled here in Her Name.

Armored in work-ready brown wool, the daughter from Woodshaven clasped her hands at her waist so they wouldn't shake. "I regret to say I cannot continue as your prospect, Hold Daughter Wendealyon."

Thin lips quirked. "Wend, together and private like this."

Had she not heard? "Hold Daughter—"

"Sit a moment, Kait. You too, Urse. You'll stand enough later." The hold daughter filled glasses with pressed berry juice for the three of them, then settled into her chair, drink cradled in both hands. "Now, what's this about?"

"I no longer hear The Lady." There. Kait remained standing; waited to be shamed.

"She hears the stones," Urse announced, taking a seat.

"Ah." Wendealyon's expression—how could it be relief? "Better news at last."

"I don't understand." Kait looked from one to the other. "What does that—" She knew what was right. What had to be done. "I can't stay. I'm unworthy."

"Are you?" Wendealyon's now-stern gaze impaled Kait. Her mouth opened. "ᛈ≈ᚷᛤ᠋ᚾᛥᚼᚤ"

The Words sent the lights blazing. Stole the air. Kait fought to see, to breathe. Her Words, aloud. Such consequential phrases were not uttered casually.

Nor could they be spoken by men. Should one try, the air left his lungs with the Words and didn't return.

Spoken or written, each had no discernible meaning. No congruence with any language or sound of the world. Mage scribes long past had given up the effort, saying Her Words couldn't be understood by mortals, only used to create intentions. Magic.

That the phrase made perfect sense inside Kait's head was further proof of Her Gift. She could understand The Lady's Words, write them—though not with magical intent—for it was only through daughters that Her Words could be returned to the mages should their knowledge be lost. She could speak them aloud. At dire need.

The phrase uttered by the Hold Daughter was: *Have you walked with Me?*

It commanded truth.

"Times without count," Kait answered. The Lady would appear as a swirl of dried leaves or the glisten of a dewdrop. She announced Her Presence with the abrupt singing of a lark, or by the soft patter of rain. The world grew larger, warmer— "Always, in the woods. Until—" her voice broke and she collected herself. "I don't know what I've done to lose Her Voice, but it does not excuse my fault in it."

"The fault is ours, Kaitealyon." Wendealyon's lips turned down. "I hope you come to forgive us. Forgive me. We brought you here without warning of the cost."

"It was necessary—" Urse began.

"Pain never is. We should have told you when you arrived, Kait. You and the other prospects."

"To no gain." The acolyte waved her glass dismissively. "Had we, would any come through our gate? Would we now have Kait, at long last another to hear what only you and I have?"

"The others do not—you're sure?"

"I am." Cold eyes regarded Kait from head to shoe. "Also, of them, Kait alone has had the courage to admit The Lady's silence."

"As you predicted, Urse." The hold daughter gazed into her glass. "Take Ella and Mish aside. Tell them Kaitealyon of Woodshaven will be Tiler's Successor-Designate, but they aren't to leave."

They spoke as if she didn't stand before them. Said what she didn't understand, but did, suddenly. And it wasn't hope filling Kait, nor triumph.

It was dread. "The Lady—She doesn't come into the hold."

"She did. No longer."

The grief in that, the loneliness—she'd felt both. Still did, but with a rising flood of outrage. "Now you've talking stone in Her stead? Yes, I've heard their foul voices. There's nought o'good innit—nought o'reason."

"'Voices'?" The hold daughter gave Ursealyon a startled look.

"Well?" Kait demanded fiercely. Her hands became fists. "Wha' ill ha ye brought here?!"

"Not our doing, I swear to you, Kaitealyon, by The Lady's Gifts." And such was the earnestness in Wendealyon's face and tone, such was the potency of that oath, Kait felt her anger slip away and fear rise again. "Where did you hear it?" the hold daughter asked them both.

"On this level," Urse said grimly. "It's climbing again."

"What is? What's happening here?"

"We don't know. Sit with me, Kait. Please. We've too little time before the audience begins." When she had, the hold daughter put down her glass and reached for Kait's hand, taking it in hers. They were cold and strong. "Understand, Successor-Designate, there can be no speaking of what I tell you next outside the three of us. Not yet."

Kait pulled free. "There are no secrets among those with Her Gift." How could anything get done, if some knew a thing, and others didn't? "The Lady doesn't permit it."

The acolyte lifted a brow. "You know The Lady's not here—"

"Enough." Wendealyon regarded Kait with fond exasperation, as if she were Leksand come late to supper with another of his strange tales. "Very well. You will hear the truth, Kaitealyon, and decide for yourself, even as I had to, who else should know."

Ursealyon's lips locked in a disapproving line.

Kait's heart fluttered in her chest, but she gave a grave nod.

"I'll begin with The Lady." The hold daughter's pale gaze was haunted. "Like you, each of us believed we'd transgressed unknowingly and lost Her Voice. Then I asked my court, my sisters."

"She'd abandoned us all," Urse said quietly. "When we compared our experiences, The Lady last spoke in Tiler's Hold the morning of the second of Darksmeri. The year's highest tide."

Tides. A villager from the mountains went to Her Mouth, climbed over rocks to gaze in equal wonder at exposed seabed and stranded fish. Could be excused for being confused now. "How is the tide important?"

"It meant no ship came or went that night."

Ships being what exposed Tananen to the wider world. Think, Kait told herself, not ready in any way to contemplate succeeding Tiler's Hold Daughter however distant that future. To earn the role, perhaps. "You must have sent acolytes from the hold. To see if—"

"If this was the end of all things?" Wendealyon finished, her face grim. "Yes, we feared that. How could we not? To our relief, The Lady continued to speak elsewhere. And our dread. What had we done to lose Her Grace? I went myself, disguised, to offer myself as sacrifice, hoping it would be enough."

Kait nodded in unconscious agreement. This too, was being a hold daughter.

"But when I passed through Her Veil, The Lady spoke to me thus: ''"

*Defend Me!*

Her Words sank into Kait's bones, leaching away safety, stripping any certainty she possessed, wiping clear the world she'd known with a power the mapmaker would have envied.

Irrefutable truth.

But what could threaten a goddess?

***

"Here. I meant to give this to you yesterday." Domozuk held out his hand. On the callused palm glittered a tiny round bell.

Maleonarial dug fingers into the thick locks hanging past his shoulders, hearing the sullen chime of hundreds. "I've enough, don't you think?"

"Not for me to say, sir. You're the mage. A bell for each intention. That's the rule."

Did he still abide by any? That was the question in the other man's troubled look. Without argument, Maleonarial took the bell. "Thank you, Dom." He gave a helpless shrug. "I'm not sure what to do with it." His hair was as tangled and fouled as it had been before the village.

"Forgive my saying, sir, but a bath would be a good start." Features twisted in a grimace, the servant gestured. "And clothes that aren't filthy rags."

He hadn't paid attention. Hadn't cared. Suddenly, Maleonarial twitched, new skin prickling at the feel of soil-stiffened material.

Warming to his subject, Domozuk went on, "I put soap and a brush on a rock. Downstream. You'll foul the creek, sure as can be. And I should bury those rags of yours. Burning them might choke us all."

Maleonarial hid a smile.

Ursealyon was first to move, going to the breakfast table as if stocking up on food would help. Perhaps, to someone trained for battle, it might.

Wendealyon sipped on juice, wincing and probing her cheek with her tongue, as if Her Words left scalds in her mouth, but spoke nonetheless. "We first heard the stones this spring, late one night. The twentieth of Lightsmeri, to be exact. Urse and I were walking along the wharf. The air was heavy with storm and at first we dismissed it as the sound of thunder rolling in—but this was nothing natural. Nothing safe or good. Evil itself. You judged it so?"

Kait nodded, mute.

Wendealyon nodded to the acolyte. "When we realized only we were able to hear the Fell—for so we chose to call it, between ourselves— I decided the burden of The Lady's silence sufficient for my court to bear, and neither issue the business of those outside it." A challenging look. "Would you do differently, Successor-Designate?"

She'd taught Leksand secrets were poison. Believed it, with all her heart. But this? "I see no other course," Kait admitted reluctantly. Tell Atta or Pincel of talking stones called the Fell? They'd offer her tea and kindly suggest a nap.

"The Fell's moved up from the lowermost level since then. Slow at first. Quicker once you lot came." Ursealyon touched the hilts of her blades. "We'd worried none of you could hear it. That we'd be on our own still. Glad of your help, Kaitealyon."

Ludicrous. Of what help could she be? "Surely you've contacted the wise—other hold daughters—"

"Let the rest of Tananen know Tiler's Hold can't be trusted?" Ursealyon replied, quiet but cold. "How long would we last?"

"If we fail, they'll know soon enough. Peace, Urse." Wendealyon's hand gestured, sweeping from the acolyte to Kait, coming to rest over her own heart. "We must contain the Fell here. Thwart this evil, whatever it may be. The Lady has chosen us as her bastion. We will not question Her Will."

Prideful, to name the three of them The Lady's defense. Rank folly too, Kait would have judged, but she met the other's eyes and read them as if looking into a mirror. Fear, yes. But also a defiant courage.

The Lady was more than the embodiment of magic; only Her Will kept it in balance. If, however inconceivable, She could be harmed, Tananen would suffer the consequences.

Kait bowed her head under that truth, then raised it, her voice calm despite the hammering of her heart. "What must we do, Hold Daughter?"

"Discover what lurks in our hold. Learn the Fell's true nature—its vulnerabilities. Protect Her. Tell me what you heard from the stone, for you've heard more than we."

Without thinking, Kait pressed a hand to her heart. "I heard breathing. Like cows in a barn, but not—not natural. Then muttering." She moved her hand to her forehead. "Vile, it was. Confounding, as though several spoke at once, or one spoke in many voices. I'd nought of sense from it." She dropped her hand, firmed her resolve. "But purpose, aie, that was plain to me. What's in the stone wants destruction and death."

"Of The Lady?"

"Of everything."

Their faces mirrored the horror Kait felt, but she'd given them the truth.

"We begin in a few moments," Wendealyon said at last. She nodded to the lattice and hall beyond. "Listen with more than ears, Kait, to today's audience. For what shouldn't be here. What it might say. Anything you can tell us."

"Breakfast first," Ursealyon said grimly. "From now on, we stay battle ready. Treat each respite as your last, Kaitealyon."

So the three resumed eating their porridge and salty bits of fish, the humble daughter from Woodshaven doing her best to chew and swallow despite a mouth dried by fear.

Long shadows flowed over the cobblestones, shifting with each passing moment like something alive.

Insom's nonsense. Pylor avoided the shadows nonetheless. She'd arrived to find the courtyard empty save for those assigned to see the hold lord's cousin speedily on her way. Two freight wagons, with drivers. The hold lord's gaudy carriage, with its driver and groom. A small harried troop of guards trying to deal with real, not made, horses. They should have asked the scribemaster for more before he left.

She could have waited to be summoned. Instead, she'd abandoned Tercle to pack what samples they'd been able to prepare; no doubt the scribemaster would want his answer, if not her cousin. Blurted instructions to a servant to arrange suitable clothing. Shed her mask and apron, grabbing a cloak on the way.

That she felt safer, here and outside the walls, disturbed her.

That Insom anticipated her haste disturbed her even more. His gift had been waiting for her, delivered by a guard at the courtyard door.

With her good hand, Pylor fingered the handle of the cane. Silver, it was, fashioned as the humped back of a whale, leaping from the waves that formed the collar. The wood of the shaft was finished in a deep blue that darkened to black toward the tip, a reminder of the vast depths beyond Tiler's Hold's safe harbor. An heirloom and treasure, this. The mark of her authority as Tiler's Hold Lord's appointed representative outside the holding.

They whispered about her, within it. Spread wicked little tales why she—unquestionably brilliant and accomplished—hadn't been selected by The Lady for Her highest service as hold daughter instead of Wend Sharktooth of the docks. Why she—of noble birth and useful connections—had yet to seek a marriage to better the hold.

Let them whisper. Pylor was well content. Could others say the same? Those few granted Her Gift were obliged to enter the shadow court; a commitment, however worthy, reducing their options in life. Without that calling, women of rank were expected to enter a profession and, yes, obtain worthy partnership.

Pylor had no interest in the latter. Her—and Tercle's—work with inks was of such renown the scribemaster himself, Saeleonarial, had come to Tiler's Hold to consult her. The mage school made its own inks, as did its masters, and traded for crucial ingredients. Saeleonarial searched for a reliable supply of the rare gemstones that were ground into a rich blue pigment. Presently, these were obtained from Icot Holding, but that hold's lord had abruptly raised the price an outrageous amount. It might be time, Saeleonarial had proposed, to look outside Tananen. Could she identify the best source?

A man of accomplishment, refreshingly humble and open to ideas, even if Saeleonarial was too canny to fully disclose his school's needs. She'd been close to identifying the right markets to approach—the hinterlands of Lithua offering the greater quantity, but not every mine's product was equal—when Insom and Wendealyon sent the scribemaster chasing after the hermit mage, frustrating her efforts.

As he sent her.

Restless, Pylor wandered to the first freight wagon. She kept her left hand tucked inside her cloak, the thumb hooked in a belt to prevent jarring. The pain rose and fell in queasy waves, but the damage appeared minimal. A finger bent, not broken. Tercle's hasty binding would do for now.

Guards stood at the covered back of the tall wagon. Guards who didn't shift aside at her approach. Pylor tapped the cane suggestively.

"I'm sorry, Damesen Ternfeather," one said, staring past her shoulder. "No one is permitted access to the cargo."

Whatever it was, she'd be delivering it to the mage school. "It's my cargo," Pylor told them.

Both stiffened. "Hold Lord's orders," said the other guard.

So. Insom hobbled her from the onset. She tapped the tip of a green-stained finger on the silver handle, her only outward sign of frustration. Under other circumstances, she'd have been delighted to be sent to the school, the one place in all Tananen where The Blessed Lady granted Her Words be taught to students.

The one place outside her laboratory where minds of equal skill labored over inks and parchment with justly famed diligence. Their records alone—

Knowledge must be pure.

To arrive burdened with secrets? The Goddess take her cousin—

Pylor's attention shifted to the carriage where her apprentice, newly arrived, stood vociferously defending the case of samples in her arms from the over-helpful servant trying to take it.

Before she could move to take charge, the courtyard door opened and Insom stepped through, dressed for court. Guards and servants snapped to attention.

Tercle grabbed the sample case, triumphant.

Her cousin didn't wait for her to approach, his great strides covering ground as if it was all he could do not to run.

Strides that avoided the shadows. A face as grim as she'd ever seen it, and cold thrilled through Pylor even as her injured fingers throbbed with heat. Which version of Insom was this?

The public one, she realized when he stopped short of a collision and bowed graciously to her. "My dearest cousin," he began, then stopped, gaze transfixed by the nearest covered wagon. As abruptly, his face cleared and he smiled broadly. "Excellent. Your gifts for the school's masters are ready."

Fair enough. Mage scribes weren't above bribery. Still. Pylor lowered her voice. "Surely I should know what they are, my lord."

His smile became fixed and unnatural. "You will." Before she could argue, Insom seized her elbow and drew her to the carriage, too quickly and rough. Tercle dared scowl but edged out of the way. "Leave as soon as your companions arrive," he ordered, pushing her at the steps.

Companions explained the too-large carriage.

If nothing else.

Pylor hesitated. "Cousin, remember your vow," she urged so only he heard. "Seek help, please."

For an instant, an eternity, his face softened. "Py—"

Black lightning flashed across the whites of his eyes and she flinched, scrambling into the carriage, the cane awkward and smacking the side.

Huddled inside, Pylor feared any help would come too late.

Hanks of hair came loose when he dunked his head in the chill stream. Maleonarial tried to catch them before they floated away, but they squirmed like eels through his fingers. What remained attached was cleaner, if not yet clean. Dutifully he rubbed the bar of soap between his hands—for horse leathers, by the nose-burning smell—till he'd a lather, then attacked a smaller section of scalp.

Meanwhile, a coil of dark smoke rose from Domozuk's fire. His clothes—his rags, the mage scribe corrected—set free too.

Freedom. He felt none of it, nor need. It was enough to be consumed by purpose, cleanliness a step forward, nothing more. To slip through Tananen unnoticed would be impossible. Those with Her Gift would recognize his. Whether they knew him as Maleonarial the former scribemaster or the scandalous hermit mage was irrelevant. The tinkling bells in his hair proclaimed his mastery.

His youth, well, that would puzzle them.

Puzzle, and entice. He possessed what they all wanted, and there was nothing a mage at his desperate hundred-and-fiftieth bell would hesitate to do in order to reclaim his own life.

Maleonarial grabbed a fistful of wet hair and bells. He could shave it off—or most. Pretend ineptitude. Claim to be a student, tossed from the school. There were a few such.

None with ability. The masters at the school knew better than set those loose on everyone else. Besides . . .

The truth must be told.

He applied more soap, unable to tell if the words were his or whispered by the coy breeze, newly sprung up to chill the bare wet skin of his back. "Enough, Hag," he grumbled. "I'll not lie."

With any luck at all, he'd end Her before the need arose.

If they entered in preset order, Kait couldn't discern it. The grand hall of Tiler's Hold filled with the shuffle of slippered feet and attendant whistles, throaty warbles, and chimes, for most chins, male and female, bore a complex artifice. While some were dainty, others were too large to be reliably attached by glue, requiring chains and wires of gold to hold them to their wearers. The fashion had arrived from the Whitehold Isles, to be modified by those with access to the services of a mage scribe.

Through a lattice lens, Kait saw each artifice contained life, none of it real, much of it grotesque. Made-birds with two mouths to sing. Made-toads with tongues like flickering rainbows. Made-lizards with gems for eyes. Her magic, squandered on ornamentation. Mages presumably well-paid, given the life they'd spent.

The display of heedless wealth wasn't for mages or the likes of her. The courtiers preened to impress one another, like birds themselves. Kait didn't believe for an instant the soberly dressed groups of foreign merchants settling to one side cared a jot.

They were here for the hold lord.

Breakfast had been whisked away, replaced by pitchers of water and cups. Through the door leading to the Daughter's Quarters had poured those trained in business and languages, arranging themselves in chairs, a couple at tables with parchment and pen poised to make notes and calculations. Tiler's shadow court didn't, so the prospects were told, overtly communicate during the hold lord's audience, meeting afterward in private session to approve, modify, or deny any particular dealings. Acolytes, including Ursealyon, stood with fingers on the wires, ready to focus on whomever caught the hold daughter's attention.

Wendealyon sat brooding, her chair centered on the hall, chin in hand as she watched the assembly form on the other side of the lattice. If she paid attention, Kait thought it to what couldn't be seen, the peculiar charge set on her as well.

Yet there were ordinary matters amiss, of import to her as successor-Designate. Over porridge and bitter fish, Kait learned the hold lord had orchestrated the villager's report about the hermit mage as a public display to force Wendealyon's hand and the scribemaster's.

This very morning, they'd a report Insom ordered his cousin to the mage school, ostensibly on a trade matter, but the acolyte bearing the news added the damesen had orders to question those at the school about this mage and his magic.

The hold daughter didn't dispute Damesen Ternfeather's qualifications to represent the hold on a trade matter, particularly one involving the inks used at the school. What toppled the apples, in Woodshaven terms, was that matters of Her magic—including questions to any studying and teaching its use—were the rightful concern of the hold daughter, not lord.

Appalling secrets to add to breakfast.

This growing fixation on the hermit mage was of a different nature than Insom's compulsion for light and maps. It risked a perilous trespass. Should Insom the Second perish of The Lady's displeasure, his heir would be selected from the courtiers milling before the lattice.

Kait had her doubts about the tall one with toads hanging from his chin. While there were a few more seriously garbed, none, according to

Wendealyon's biting assessment, were a better choice. They must support the lord they had and guide him to prudence.

While the stones muttered.

She'd good ears—could catch the morning lark's lilting voice before her young son and be ready with his breakfast. Larks and sons being far from this place, Kait listened, straining as she was certain the others did to catch what weren't sounds amid the cacophony of the hall. There was, in Ursealyon's chilling words, no place more vulnerable in the hold. They were to be aware. To bear witness.

Kait's fingers wanted to clench the wool of her cloak.

Insom arrived, walking the carpet patterned like a desert, courtiers bowing like waves. As much as their artifices allowed, that was, and Kait found herself hoping one would topple forward, a lesson in excess for his fellows. None did, implying practice.

The hold lord wasn't alone. Or was, since those with him had been made, not born, and thus were what they did, nothing more. Two were bulky mauls, armored and drooling, creatures more dog than man who existed to attack any physical threat Insom might face.

She'd heard these weren't as terrifying as he'd like, the mage scribe responsible for these having been fevered at the time and obsessed with dappled rabbits or some such.

Four made-servants, attentive and well-groomed. At a guess, they'd been modeled after sheep, having broad backs suited to carrying a tray around a room. They dispersed through the hall, tentacles, six in number, appearing to proffer a selected item. The tentacles whisked away debris too and she'd have liked a peek underneath, to see where it went, but the made-servants were robed in the hold colors.

Insom the Second gathered attention as he approached, a large and brawny man, muscled and sun-scoured from a life on the water. He walked with the roll to his step Kait observed in others along the wharves. The rich red velvet of his jerkin, the white silk of leggings and gloves, the crafted leather boots struggled to fit, as though he couldn't be bothered to sit still for his tailors.

Beneath dark tattoos, keen pale eyes, alike enough to Wendealyon's to suggest a family tie, swept over the lattice and Kait flinched. Never would Insom have set foot in the Daughter's Portion, but he knew well who watched him.

Or believed he did. Feeling a fraud, Kait eased left, out of line with the nearest lens. Ursealyon, at the farther end of the lattice, noticed and gestured sharply for her to return to position.

Reluctantly, Kait obeyed.

Under other circumstances, such as innocence, she'd have been fascinated. Insom's steward introduced the waiting delegations, this one with a trade proposal, that one with a dispute. If not for the scale of their commerce, the different accents and unusual dress as those foreign to Tananen approached, what transpired wasn't much different from the business of Woodshaven. Goods to be ordered. Those received to be paid for, fairly but not always in coin. Explanations for delays offered and exceptions made—or not. Through it all, Insom sat at seeming ease, his back to the hold daughter and her court, giving prompt and reasonable responses.

No mutters or breathing other than from those gathered. No sign of the Fell. Kait found her attention wandering to a pitcher of water, temptingly near.

"—Woodshaven."

Startled, she grasped the wire and turned the lens, trying to focus on the speaker, forgetting only acolytes were to do so, and only then at Wendealyon's behest. A hand closed on her wrist and Kait met a tattooed frown. Denial.

"Approach," Insom ordered whomever it was, his deep voice carrying the word to every corner.

Like an echo rose the horrible muttering from the stone. This time it traveled and Kait's head spun to follow what rolled like thunder along a wall, to the ceiling. Went over the lattice to enter the hall.

What wasn't sound at all yet shouted inside her head until she felt dizzy.

Worse—much worse—a shadow went with it, sucking away the light, or was it a dark fume drifting sideways, as if the stones exhaled what was foul and dire—

The hand on her wrist released but she couldn't move. "What is it?" Urgent that whisper, but she couldn't answer.

The fume moved on, sank, split into black smoke-like streams that billowed among those courtiers nearest the lattice and wall, passing through the filigree and bars of their artifices. Made-beasts became ash in their cages, gems dropped to the floor like rain. The robe of a made-servant collapsed, spilling delicacies from a back no longer there, and commotion sped through the hall, courtiers shouting in surprise and outrage.

Seeing the result, if nothing of the cause—

"What do you see, Kaitealyon?"

As if no one else could, and wasn't that a nightmare—

"ENOUGH!" Insom roared, thrusting out his arm.

The courtiers fell silent.

The fume vanished.

And the sound from the stone was no more.

His arm lowered, Insom's voice calmed, became bizarrely jovial. "Come now. The makings of a mage don't last. I am disappointed to find this many in my hall so lax in their deportment. You receive what you pay for, is that not true?"

Kait could see uneasy looks. A few appeared taken aback, but none dared show offense.

"Now!" The hold lord threw up his arms. "Welcome our honored travelers!"

As curious murmurs broke out in the hall, every lens whispered and clicked into place, bringing the two who approached the hold lord into focus. An elderly man, travel-worn and weary; though his hand was on the shoulder of his companion for support, there was a proud lift to his head.

His companion was but a boy, though as tall as she since midwinter and with the hint of whiskers on his still-soft cheeks.

The muttering from the walls burst forth again, louder, more agitated. Kait covered her ears, but it wasn't sound and she couldn't block the Fell, only endure.

What brought her son, with her uncle, to the audience hall of Tiler's Hold, Kait couldn't imagine.

What made the stone—what was in the stone—take notice?

She didn't dare guess.

As the others readied to leave, Maleonarial harvested galls from a strip of wildflowers by the roadside, habit and need in one. Harn's inks were the commonest sort. To do what he planned would take the most exquisite craft.

And materials he couldn't afford, so galls it was. He'd boil them tonight when they camped. Begin carving a pen. Scrape his own parchments. No time to waste.

He'd spent years, lost more, in search of an intention to stop The

Deathless Goddess. The problem was, he'd succeeded. Something he'd done had produced what gave the village boy the ability to steal and use Her magic, without cost. She'd come to collect, but it was a starting point.

If only he knew which intention of the many it had been.

Domozuk had insisted on dealing with his now-clean hair, Nim and Rid enlisted to hold the locks while the servant's experienced fingers twisted lengths together. The result was a thick but tidy mass down Maleonarial's back, with a braid on either side of his jaw.

Heedless of dirt or order, the bells rang as freely as they had before.

A breeze tickled his face, tugging hairs from the leather strip he'd tied around his forehead, blowing dust in his eyes.

It would take far more to distract him.

The galls went in a pocket of what had been Sael's work jerkin. A belt snugged the soft ink-stained leather over one of Domozuk's shirts. Rid had donated a pair of leggings to his attire; the faint aroma of horse hardly mattered, given they'd be riding all day. They'd no boots to fit. Domozuk having burned what remained of Maleonarial's footwear, there'd be a stop at the first village or town to make that purchase.

Becoming young again had robbed his feet of their useful calluses.

Rid and Nim helped Harn mount. Despite being told the made-horse couldn't let him fall, the student clutched its mane with his good hand, already looking green.

Domozuk was already mounted, the made-horses with burdens waiting beside his with tree-like patience. As they'd wait till dissolving to ash, a span he'd set at four days. Sufficient. "Ready when you are, sir."

Maleonarial grabbed a hunk of mane and swung himself up and over in one easy move, a feat he hadn't been able to perform since his third year at the school. He glanced at Harn as he settled himself. Did the lad see it yet? That what The Hag took for each use of Her magic was as intimate a theft as it was inescapable?

For now. West by south would take him to Aote, though he'd avoid the hold itself and keep to farmland, then overland to Her Tears—

The nuisance breeze became pressure against his skin, as if to discourage.

Or warn—

"Tiler'old." Rid spat in that direction, sharing his opinion of the lord who'd sent Saeleonarial to his death. "Bould'rt'n's north."

The intersecting roads offered other directions—and closer towns—but Boulderton lay on the route to Alden and the mage school. "Our path," Domozuk declared.

Maleonarial opened his mouth to say it wasn't his, to bid them farewell, when the servant lifted high a slender branch. From it fluttered a ragged pennant, a bold black stroke across white. The scribemaster's sigil. Saeleonarial's. Saved from the wagon's ruin, hidden till now.

With stick and scrap, Domozuk made them a funeral procession as official as any in Tananen.

Without comment, Maleonarial set his made-horse to the northern road, kicking it into a lope. The others followed, Harn giving a squeak of dismay.

He'd accompany them as far as Alden Hold, see Sael home, if only to spite Her. Barter an intention or two for supplies, and be gone before the masters of the school were aware of his presence.

For all their sakes, before they learned what he planned.

※

Her feet were on the floor. Her breaths came steady, after one betraying gasp, but she was entitled to that.

Her son being here, instead of home.

"This way," the acolyte whispered, taking her hand.

So much for steady, Kait realized. She was grateful for the anonymity of the lattice as the acolyte drew her through the others, grateful no one on this side looked at her. Their attention was for the hall and those in it.

Leksand. With her mother's brother, Ferden Haulerson, who'd retired from logging under protest when his eyes clouded—and continued to split kindling, despite the times they'd hide his axe. Ferden was not a person able to travel, but had.

Coming here.

The acolyte brought her to the hold daughter, bowed, then left. Wendealyon beckoned Kait close, so she knelt at her side. The woman leaned down, fish-scented breath warm against Kait's cheek. "You heard the Fell."

Kait nodded. "I saw—"

The hold daughter stiffened. "Later."

For Insom was speaking. "Hold Daughter. Will you grant the boon these two ask?"

What boon? She'd missed what was said before. Kait turned to the lattice, stunned to find Leksand's face sliced across dozens of lenses. In some, only an anxious brown eye. In others, the nose he'd inherited from his father; the wide cheekbones and generous mouth so like hers.

Wendealyon lifted her right hand and acolytes spun the lenses, then stopped them.

Another quick bend and whisper. "Your son."

Kait gave another nod.

"As I too shall gift these important travelers," the hold lord declared, rising to his feet amid a stir from those assembled. The surviving madebirds shrilled. Something shrieked. "They shall continue their journey speedily and in comfort, with my trade caravan."

Cheeks blushed. Eyes widened, their pupils dark holes. Leksand, understandably, flattered by the lord's attention, and it was all Kait could do to keep her mouth closed, because nothing Insom offered was safe, not for her son.

A hand gripped her shoulder. With her other, Wendealyon stuck a long thin rod, painted black, through the lattice to give the hold lord a firm poke in the backside.

The man sat quickly. "I but offer my assistance," he added in a calmer tone. "Those The Lady claims are the business of the Daughter's Court."

Good thing Kait was kneeling, for the floor seemed to move beneath her. A hold lord's assistance for a lad from Woodshaven? Who shouldn't be here at all, and she'd have harsh words with her uncle, she would, as soon as they were alone. Because it couldn't be right, what Insom the Second said.

The Lady couldn't have claimed her son. Wouldn't steal him from her. Mustn't fill his beautiful mind with Her Words and make him a mage scribe, to age and die before his time—

Like his father before him.

Hands clapped in applause on the other side of the lattice, for a mage scribe was a valued commodity and rare.

On this side, hands found Kait in her huddle of misery, and held her tight.

"Don't you 'be patient' me, Dolren Keeperson. It's bloody shameful your damesen waits in the courtyard with the horses. Move your smarmy ass and find out what dung heaps are wasting our time and hurry them up, or I swear I will!"

In full agreement, Pylor didn't hush her irate apprentice. Especially with Dolren, Insom's own man, clinging to the carriage doorway like an obsequious leech. He'd bad teeth and fouler breath, and, according to Tercle, an outstanding ability to shirk responsibility while licking the right boots.

Maybe that's why he always stared at the ground when dealing with nobles, Pylor thought uncharitably. Assessing the flavor.

The man did have a talent for organization—and for annoying others until they did what he wanted—of use, she supposed, in whatever arrangements must be made to expedite their travels.

"They'll be here soon," Dolren soothed, though he knew nothing of the sort. "We're ready to go at once."

Unlikely. They'd tarried in the courtyard so long everyone from guards to herself had made a quick trip indoors to relieve themselves, no one about to use the so-called convenience of travel pots before forced on the road. A second trip was imminent, let alone the frustrating effort to calm horses removed from stables and food sooner than necessary. "We should have made-horses," she murmured to herself.

"Worry not, Damesen." Dolren's other talent, depending on who you asked, was superb hearing. With a lack of understanding when his opinion wasn't wanted. "I'll arrange those once we've crossed Her Veil, then again after the barge—"

How curious. "Why then and not now?"

The man visibly squirmed. "I really can't say—"

Tercle squinted at him. "Why not? Everyone knows—staff knows," she corrected, meeting Pylor's gaze. "There's nought made-stock left in the hold but for what serves the lord's court. We'd all hoped the scribe-master was here to restock."

Because made-beasts assisted throughout a hold, saving work for its inhabitants—or had. She hadn't noticed. Why would she, there being no place for magical creations in her lab, and abhorring the contraptions of her peers. As for Saeleonarial, he'd escaped lightly. No one mage could replenish an entire hold and survive.

No hold could afford his price were he willing to try, not even theirs.

"How long has there been a shortage?"

"Since the twentieth of Lightsmeri, just shy of midnight."

Pylor blinked. "Impressive precision." Implausible was another word.

With a gratified nod, Dolren settled himself on a narrow step, still gripping the handle. "It happened there was a caravan of freight wagons—thirty of them, with cargo from Ichep, some of it perishable—taking the tunnel to Her Veil. All at once their made-oxen just—" He made a throwaway gesture. "It took the next day and night to clear the mess. And some bribes to quiet tongues, believe me."

She hadn't heard. Again, why would she, locked in her pursuits? Little wonder her cousin had grown strange, faced with such doings.

Or were such doings because her cousin had grown strange?

Those with Her Gift knew one another. There was a draw between them. Recognition of a higher purpose. Respect.

It made being a mother confusing. Leksand's scarf was askew and Kait's fingers itched to fix it. She'd bought it for him in the market by the sea, along with luminous shells and a pot of spiced jelly.

As if sensing her attention, he pulled it from around his neck and shoved it in a pocket. "I had to see you, Momma," he said with quiet urgency, each word carefully pronounced. Kept up his lessons, he had.

"Great-uncle said I could write a letter, but"—brown eyes rose to hers, their expression pleading—"I couldn't. I couldn't go without telling you myself."

"Aie, lad," she murmured, plucking the poor scarf and rolling it properly. She returned it to his pocket, then flattened her hands briefly on his chest before stepping back. "Aie. Nought's to be changed, but a proper start, that matters. Well done."

"You taught him," Ferden said from where he sat cradling a hot cup of tea. He looked gray under the dirt, and Kait spared a moment to worry.

She'd no more. They'd been given this much grace. The hold daughter and Ursealyon waited in Wendealyon's chambers for her to say good-bye—the daughter's boon. Both doubtless burned with impatience. What mattered to them wasn't her family or even a new student for the mage school. They wanted her report. What she'd heard.

What she'd implied she'd seen.

An acolyte had brought her tiny family to the Daughter's Quarters, to clean the travel grime before whatever came next. Insom had sent an offering of clothing.

As if she'd dress her kin like one of his courtiers. Having intercepted the delivery, Kait waited for the door to close before she dropped the pile on the floor. "Hang your cloaks here."

Under those admittedly stained and dusty travel cloaks, the pair wore their best. Kait felt a rush of pride. She'd embroidered the Woodshaven crest—crossed axes and a crock of honey—on the right breast of both jerkins. Those were of fine elk leather, supple and etched with leaf designs, dyed forest green. Beneath were the red shirts of the village. "Wash now," she ordered gruffly.

There was a bowl of warm water. Combs and towels. She passed each a damp rag to polish their boots as best they could when done. Finally, they stood for inspection and she ran a critical eye from head to toe. As usual, Leksand blushed; he did so easily, cheeks aflame, and she managed not to smile.

Ferden took her face in his hands and pressed dry cracked lips to her forehead. "We're tidy as we can be, Kaitie-dear."

She searched his face. The maze of soft wrinkles didn't hide once-handsome features, nor the kindness there. His eyes? Milky centers obscured the bright blue they'd had, though her mother's brother could see, still. Large shapes. Bright lights. The edges, if not the whole.

Then there was his heart, strained from hard years and weakened by the ague last winter, making it flutter under stress. "You should be home," Kait chided fiercely. "What were you thinking?"

He smiled. "That if I let my great-nephew travel alone, you'd have my ears."

"Aie," she agreed, the word a breath, no more. "Did you ride at least?"

Leksand shook his head. "Pincel couldn't spare the mules," he explained earnestly. "She's clearing another field."

"The hold lord's offered you transport," Kait told them, though she'd no idea if that meant horses, made or real. The distance to Alden was something of a mystery to her as well, though once in the rich heartlands didn't everyone go by barge? She'd ask. Anything to see them safely away from Tiler's Hold and its stones.

"Will we see Lord Insom again, Momma?"

Knowledge has no pity.

"From now on, you must call me Kaitealyon, as I soon will surely call you Lekeonarial. Unless we're alone," Kait relented, seeing rebellion brewing in her son's eyes.

"I'll stay yer great-uncle, lad," Ferden promised, clapping the boy on his shoulder. "Nought fancier than that."

Ursealyon opened the door, nodding respectfully to Leksand and her uncle. Another, younger acolyte stood behind her. "You're to come to the hold daughter, Kaitealyon." Her eyes flicked to the discarded heap of velvet; they returned to Kait, their expression unreadable.

"Now?" Kait couldn't move, wouldn't. She looked to her son, then to Urse.

"Bettealyon will escort your guests to the courtyard." The acolyte paused. "Take those," gesturing to the cloaks, speaking to her family. "You leave for the mage school immediately."

She'd counted on tonight, perhaps a tomorrow. First The Lady, stealing her son's future, and now to lose these last precious moments for she knew—if Leksand didn't—the next time they met he'd have left her behind. Not just in the distance brought by teaching and expectations such as he'd never known—that they could bridge—but time. Depending on how many intentions he created, The Lady would age him by years. Her boy would be gone.

Soon, to be older than she—

"We canna—can't go," Leksand protested, proving he did know, after all. He confronted Ursealyon, straight and bold despite having to look up. "We just arrived. I came to visit my m—Kaitealyon," he corrected himself. "Surely another day—"

"You'll have what the journey takes," the senior acolyte pronounced, and was that the ghost of a smile? "By the hold daughter's command, Kaitealyon travels with you to the mage school to represent her court, as Damesen Ternfeather represents Insom's. Unless you've objection?"

The three from Woodshaven shook their heads in joy-filled unison. Kait jumped for the door. "I'll get my things."

"They await you in the carriage. Come with me to the hold daughter, then you may join your son."

This being impossibly more than Kait had hoped, she clasped

Leksand's warm hand in hers, then her uncle's in a hurried, not to be farewell, and followed Ursealyon through the door.

Magic must be intended.

Maleonarial watched the newly birthed gossamer scamper up the tree, its huge topaz eyes agleam with mischief and life. Like a squirrel, if the animal were almost transparent, winged, and cast the scent of baking bread through the air so a hungry man might drool and swallow with regret.

Harn slumped in a ball of woe, pen clenched in his shaking hand. "I didn't mean—I wanted—"

Ah, the young. To want desperately. To have the power to reach.

And lack the discipline and training to grasp.

"It's never happened to me before. Her Words just came and they were in order—I thought they were—and—you won't tell, will you?" This with woe.

Domozuk tapped his shoulder. "Here, lad." A calloused palm held a bell. "No harm done."

Which wasn't true.

The young farmer watched the gossamer change its hue to that of the leaves and vanish. He turned to them, his face grim. "S'at's how h'did it? Cil?"

Harn looked horrified, Rid and Domozuk distressed. "No, Nim," Maleonarial answered. "This was an honest mistake. Harneonarial paid Her fee."

The student brightened at the name, an eager hope in his eyes. The aging was almost imperceptible. The loss of some freckles. Perhaps a shade less red in his hair. Nothing a young man would notice.

It was how She seduced them all. Take My magic. Create and amaze. Pay Me with your future.

You aged not as if you'd lived the full time She stole from you. Nails, hair, and beard remained their length. Belly, bowel, and bladder remained as full or as empty as before the intention came into being— though their ability to hold their contents weakened. You aged as though seeing your future in a mirror, then found yourself become it.

Explain such matters to Harn, flush with his first success? Gossamer or not, success was how it felt, and Maleonarial restrained the master's itch to demand what the student had intended to make, then point out what he'd done wrong.

"We've rested long enough," he said. "I'll carry your bag from now on." Being master enough to want temptation out of the boy's reach.

He rode well to the back of their little troop to avoid road dust, letting the others set the pace. They weren't comfortable in his presence. He couldn't change that. Couldn't recover in a day skills neglected for a dozen years.

Little eyes glinted bronze in a shrub as he rode near. Twigs shook at him. The mage grinned. "Spent most of my time talking to you, didn't I?"

Twigs shook again. Gossamer. The Deathless Goddess. Rabbits. He'd never lacked for company in the wilderness, only intelligible answers.

Domozuk claimed Saeleonarial had brought Harn with them to Tiler's Hold out of pity, the student incapable of keeping Her Words straight in his mind and driving his masters out of theirs.

How had Harn been able, suddenly, to write a complete, living intention? And no mere made-moth or mouse, but a full-fledged gossamer?

Maleonarial eyed the shrub as he passed it. "Hungry, Hag?"

Twigs shook a final time, whatever that meant.

If it meant anything at all.

Tiler's Hold Daughter's chambers were cluttered and small. A cot against a wall, identical to Kait's own save for a tapestried cushion, well worn, depicting some sort of undersea life. With tentacles. A clue to the made-servants? She knew nothing of what lived in the sea, other than what appeared on her plate. The back wall held narrow shelves crammed to the tipping point with objects. Sharp ones. Hooked claws arranged by size. Jars of tiny teeth. Rows of triangular serrated nightmares longer than Kait's palm, not that she'd touch them. Betwixt and between were little statues. Cats in various poses, of varied materials, their teeth showing.

Wendealyon sat in an armed chair, framed by that collection, and showed her teeth in what wasn't a smile. "Insom waits in the courtyard and threatens to have them leave without you, Kait, if we delay. Quickly now. Urse and I heard the Fell take a deep breath. You?"

"The stones spoke to themselves. As before. No," Kait corrected herself. "Their voices were louder. Excited or agitated. Then I saw something move—"

"You saw the Fell?" Ursealyon interrupted, eyes on fire. A warrior, given a target.

Kait shook her head. "I don't know. What I saw traveled along the mortar, wiggled through cracks as lightning might cross a sky, were it slowed enough to see, but this—this wasn't light but its opposite." Words. She needed better words. "What I saw drifted—no, oozed out from the wall. Like onto smoke, but heavier. Thicker. Darker than any shadow. Intent."

Wendealyon caught the word. "Intent on what?"

Her son.

Which couldn't be true, mustn't be, so Kait stuck to the truth of what she'd seen. "The Fell went for the small made-creatures, in their cages. When its darkness touched them, they turned to ash. As if— consumed." She paused, prepared to say the rest and the worst, that the darkness vanished, ceased at Insom's command—

Or had it? Insom's shout was to silence his hall, his gesture to gain courtiers' errant attention. She couldn't assume the cessation of the darkness other than coincidence. The Fell had been satiated, in some foul way. Or frightened by the shout, if such felt fear.

Who was Kait Alder of Woodshaven, to doubt her hold lord? Not Tiler's Hold Daughter, not yet, able to summon the wrath of The Lady—

"That we saw too. 'Consumed,' you say." Wendealyon's eyes narrowed. She looked to her acolyte. "Did it seem so to you?"

"Like our lord, I assumed they'd expired," Ursealyon admitted, her tone reluctant. "To the chagrin of Insom's bootlickers, mage work has limits. Remember the mess in the tunnel? The lead drover swore she'd paid for made-oxen to last a fortnight, more than needful to reach their destination, but clearly hadn't."

"I remember." The hold daughter pressed a finger's tip to the arm of her chair. "I remember it happened the night after we first heard the stones. Perhaps now, we know why. The oxen were consumed."

Kait's pulse hammered in her ears.

"By smoke from the walls?" the acolyte replied darkly. "Do you hear what you're saying?"

"That we've been under attack since then. The Lady has, and Her magic. We just didn't know it."

"Blessed Goddess." Ursealyon's hands reached to the crossed blades at her waist, then fell away. "What's to be done against stone?"

Brave, the acolyte, braver than she'd ever be. Hearing despair in her voice, Kait felt her own.

The hold daughter's face might have been carved from stone. "What we must. We keep this evil from devouring the rest of Tananen." She held the arms of her chair. "The Lady came when summoned—despite Her silence. And yes, Kaitealyon, I spent the best of our sisters to test that She would. Not for one hermit, but for this. To know I can still call on Her to cleanse this hold, if I must."

And if she took that dreadful step? Be it their shared Gift or something in Wendealyon's eyes, Kait knew in that instant the hold daughter would not unlock Her Promise to let any escape.

The acolyte was first to stir, lips twisting in a wry grin. "Let's hope for another answer."

"Agreed." Wendealyon's hands released their grip. Her gaze rested on Kait. "I believe it's no accident you've come to us, Kaitealyon. In you, The Lady gives us a way to track this evil—discover if the Fell has moved outside our walls. A scout."

The mere thought of the black fume spreading through the woods, the muttering inside in homes and inns, froze Kait's blood. "Yes, Hold Daughter."

"To stop it, we need to learn if this has happened before. If it was stopped, before. Question the master mages. Loremasters. Historians. Anyone who might have that knowledge."

"I'll go," Kait said. She was, after all, already bound for the mage school. The hold daughter left nothing to chance.

Yet, "Be sure," Wendealyon told her. "This is your choice."

There was none, but the words were kind. Kait bowed. "It is. I'll go."

A brief approving nod, then an assessing look. "Urse will provide you the means to make reports. Once you're away, our messengers will go to Tananen's other hold daughters, asking they spread the warning further, but that will take time. If matters here grow worse?"

Wendealyon showed her teeth in her fierce not-smile. "In Her Name, by force if necessary, I will seal the gates to Her Veil."

This was larger than woods and inns. By so doing, the hold daughter would cut Tananen off from the outside world. "I understand."

"Then, Kaitealyon of Woodshaven, on behalf of Tiler's Holding, I send you forth. ⵙ≈ಖ≋Oⵙⵕⵥⵙⵖ"

Teeth bared. Claws gripped. Kait's heart thudded wildly in her chest, the chamber going gray and distant, for what Wendealyon uttered was a call to arms, Her Call.

*Defend Me!*

*Be My Designate, should I ask it.*

*Preserve Tananen.*

"I will," Kait gasped.

A claw rattled along its shelf, falling to the floor. The words echoed, deeper and deeper, as though traveling a tunnel. Stone shifted in answer.

The three having clasped each other in a final, heart-felt good-bye, none noticed.

# Fundamental Lexicon

*The world was not always safe.*

Magic is perilous. Those come new to Tananen succumb to it as tinder to flame. Those who survive take stock and make choices.

Magic belongs here, not there.

Magic is Hers, not theirs.

*We were not alone here.*

Those who survive know this. To grasp the incomprehensible, make it small, make it fit, those who survive give the other shape and name. The Deathless Goddess, The Lady, She who is and always was. Those who survive write themselves in Her story. Feel safe. Forget, in time, it's a story at all.

She does not.

*Magic, once, was untouched.*

Now magic is not, for those who survive have added themselves to what magic is. They take it in. Spew it forth. Change what was. Create what's never been.

Only She remembers the truth.

And weeps.

# Fraught Passages

# FRAUGHT PASSAGES

"Kin'ye do sommat o'the flies?" The driver used his hands to shoo a growing cloud of insects from Saeleonarial's wrapped corpse. "Well?" Rid demanded, his eyes red-rimmed and angry. "Kin'ye 'r no?"

The warm sun, welcome on shoulders and backs, didn't help. Soon it'd be the stench of rot and Rid wasn't wrong, to want dignity for the scribemaster's return.

Another intention. So be it. Maleonarial sat cross-legged in the dust of the road. The others, curious perhaps, stood in a circle around him. They blocked his light, but no matter.

Preserving meat was one of the earliest learnings at the school. If Harn hadn't created a gossamer already today, earned a bell with nothing to show for it, he'd have used the opportunity for a lesson.

Had he been a master still.

Maleonarial opened Harn's bag of supplies. Spared a moment to regret Saeleonarial's doubtless fine pens and inks, ground into the dirt by Cil's gossamers, but these would do.

He set to work. First, to concentrate. Find the words he needed, Her Words, arranged in the correct sequence. An unexpected struggle, finding the discipline to check each.

More so, to resist the pounding urge to hurry and do this. To call forth magic. To have the surge of satiation nothing else gave.

He owed Harn a certain sympathy.

Magic requires purity.

Maleonarial focused on his purpose. Saeleonarial didn't deserve to hang over a made-horse, his corpse plagued by hungry flies and beetles. His fault.

Her doing.

The nib drew up ink. He stroked the tip over a scrap on his knee, each move sure and complete. Word over word, none legible, all of power.

A breeze tugged, a line shifted, and magic spun and spilled across his hands, consuming the parchment. Drew breath. Grew shape and size. And even as exultation rocked him, so did fury as the gossamer, for it was that, rose and spun and laughed in his face.

Topaz eyes. Pearled skin. Whiskers or feathers or both, the thing was a shimmer of wild poetry, soaring higher and higher into the dull leaden sky, taking into itself all color from the world.

When at last it plunged beneath the road, to go wherever it chose, Maleonarial heard the others sigh with wonder and regret.

Hag. Silently he cursed Her meddling, his carelessness. He'd no life to spare, not from his hunt.

He dipped the pen once more and wrote his intention on a fresh scrap. Out of it came what he'd intended, a flesh keeper. Maleonarial poked the end of Harn's pen into the palm-sized red ball, hooked it, and rose to his feet. A flick, and the ball sailed to splat against the rump of what had been a man. A friend. Wise. Kind. Good.

The keeper spread on contact, becoming a patch, then a sheet, widening and wrapping until the corpse was bound within a shroud of red.

Meat, ready to transport. Those who'd sighed at the wonder of a gossamer looked askance at him for this.

Anger wanted a target. They deserved none of his and Maleonarial found himself saying calm as could be, "Let's get him home. It'll last till then."

Two more bells.

A shame they weren't enough to cool his blood.

Travel where she'd never been. Ask learned scholars about what most likely none knew, while—according to Ursealyon—being careful to avoid the topic of how a lowly daughter from Woodshaven, Tiler's Holding, could see what no one else had.

They mustn't spread fear, the acolyte warned. Mustn't permit doubt.

Unless they were too late, the Fell spread everywhere and their efforts futile—

Kait refused to believe it. The phrases still throbbed along her bones, commands to offer strength, give purpose. *Defend Me! Be My Designate.*

What matter the opinion of others? The Lady needed help.

Improbable as it seemed, that's what she was. At least, Kait reminded herself, she was good at asking questions.

Ursealyon escorted her to the door to the courtyard, doubting her resolve, perhaps. Once in sight—and in smell—of the bedlam outside, the acolyte stepped aside, leaving Kait alone at the top of the stairs. No acolytes would travel with her. There were no seals or documents in the small pouch at her belt.

Her Gift must be the bond to open doors and unseal secrets.

First to cross the courtyard. Below Kait was a daunting forest of beasts and people, encircling hills made of freight wagon and fancy carriage. Everyone was shouting instructions; few were being heeded.

She couldn't spot Leksand or her uncle, surely already here. Though unlikely their transport, the fine carriage was closest, a point of stability in the mass confusion. Kait headed briskly down the stone stairs, aiming for that.

No one let her through, being preoccupied with their own feet and business. Being smaller, she ducked under elbows and flailing whips. Not so easy to dodge horses who, not being made, had every right to tense and kick if a stranger hurried too close. She needed to dodge what such horses left on the cobbles too, something Kait realized when she stepped in a hot fresh pile.

Having but two shoes to her name, Kait kept her head up and pretended her left foot didn't squish and slip as she continued. The smell she'd worry about later.

A wall of shoulder-to-shoulder velvet stood between her and the carriage. Having come this far, Kait tapped the nearest.

A head turned. Eyes squinted down a long nose at Kait. Their gaze fixed on her soiled shoe. "What do you want?"

"To get through, if you please," she said firmly. "I'm expected."

"I hardly think so. Move along." Fingers flicked.

By the ceremonial key dangling from the chain around his neck, the man was the hold lord's major-domo. Kait didn't know his real name. Acolytes referred to him as "Squid." Whatever one was, he'd earned the name by, so she'd been told, an ability to claim credit for work done by others.

Ignoring him, Kait put her fists on her hips and bellowed. "You want this caravan out of here, let me pass!"

She'd good lungs. Even so, it was a surprise when the bodies in front of her parted as though blown apart by a wind and she came face-to-face with Insom the Second.

Who stood with his arm around her son.

The carriage lurched forward. They were underway at last and Damesen Pylor Ternfeather kept her hands atop the handle of her cane as she regarded those seated across from her, imposed upon her, concealing her dismay. The boy and old man were well dressed, after the fashion of mountain folk. She knew what they were and dismissed them.

The woman—clearly the mother—looked a servant but wasn't. She'd fooled Insom, who'd treated her with absent courtesy, his attention lavished on the young mage-to-be.

The conveyance settled into an easy rock from side to side, the horses stretching into their travel gait. "We weren't introduced in the haste of our departure," Pylor began. "I'm the hold lord's representative, Damesen Ternfeather. And you are?"

Large brown eyes, a match for the boy's, gazed back serenely. "My name's Kait Alder, late of Woodshaven, Damesen Ternfeather." Her accent was barely perceptible to the discerning ear, a polish requiring study and effort. "This is my son Leksand and my uncle, Ferden Haulerson. We're grateful to share your transport to the school."

"It wasn't my idea."

"Then even more so, please accept our thanks." A slight bow: courtesy between equals. This was a woman whose voice mattered—in her village, perhaps in Tiler's Daughter's Portion as well. "We'll do our best to be no burden to you or your staff."

Oblivious, the boy clutched the black gleaming box Insom had bestowed on him, his eyes still round with delight, but the older man nodded a quick agreement. "Aie, your graciousness. I kin help—"

A shoeless foot nudged his shin. "I'm sure the damesen's staff have no need of it, Uncle. We'll care for ourselves." With a lift of her head that, yes, held authority.

Did Insom know Wendealyon sent her representative to the school with his? Pylor doubted it, though by rights, her cousin should have made that offer directly to the hold daughter.

Were their goals the same, to learn of the renegade and his magic?

A question she would have answered before reaching the school. Meanwhile, Kait's shoes were with Dolren, who'd been ordered to ride with the driver and be sure they were cleaned. A bright point in an otherwise tedious morning and Pylor allowed herself a smile. "I won't hear of it. Ask whatever you need on our journey. My staff is up to any challenge."

Tercle made no comment, disapproval radiating from every pore, as it had since the strange confusion of their departure.

Her cousin's doing. Insom wanted them gone.

. . . then didn't, lingering to put his arm around the boy.

Brought the boy his gift.

. . . then walked away with it under his arm.

Turned back after a handful of steps, his movements jerky and odd, to thrust the box at the boy, bending to whisper in his ear.

. . . then shouted they were to leave, smacking the side of the carriage with a fist, swearing in dockside fashion at the guards when they didn't hurry to his satisfaction.

To stand abruptly still, hand over his mouth, as if wanting to call them all back.

Pylor'd stayed in the carriage, watched this play past a curtain she'd held half-closed. A coward, unwilling to face this man she thought she knew.

Afraid she wouldn't know him if she did.

The carriage rattled through the gateway and tunnel, tilted as they turned onto the so-called Easy Road. Pylor eased her sore fingers from the cane, gesturing to the box to hide her discomfort. "Feel free to open it. My cousin is known for his generosity. I'll admit I'm curious what he's given you, young mage."

Sock toes poked when the boy didn't answer. His gaze shot up, face turning red. "Whaddaya say?"

"You kin open yer present, laddie," Ferden urged with a gap-toothed grin.

"Oh no." Arms gathered the box close. "I'm not to look until we've passed Her Veil. Lord Insom's command."

His mother's frown was quick and gone, but Pylor caught it.

Shared it. Insom provided freight she wasn't to see, now a gift to be kept hidden. She was tempted to insist.

The carriage and occupants lurched sideways. Her guests looked alarmed and Pylor didn't blame them. "Hold on," she advised, taking hold of a strap herself. "There'll be several more switchbacks as we climb."

They followed her instructions. As the man and boy settled, eyes closing in exhaustion, Kait twisted to press her face to the window, looking up and down, forward and back.

What could she hope to see? The cliff obscured one side, the mists of Her Veil the other. But the woman stared out nonetheless, so Pylor felt compelled to do the same, eyes straining in search of what she didn't know.

Loath to ask, and find out.

Knowledge is magic.

Mage scribes study Her Words, rehearse the proper combinations in their minds, never commit those to pen and parchment until certain. That is how an intention comes to life.

And the mage lose some of his.

By his two hundredth bell, Maleonarial could write every known combination of Her Words, certain and sure. By his three hundredth, or thereabouts, he'd stopped caring about certainty, sure only of his purpose.

As for gossamers?

He'd lost count. It was possible he'd created more than any before him, being heedless of anything but severing the link between The Deathless Goddess and Her magic.

And their lives.

He'd tied the new bells in his hair. He hadn't made a mistake, hadn't been careless, yet a gossamer he'd made. Something had moved the scrap the tiniest bit as he wrote upon it. Enough to distort a word—he couldn't be sure which—

—or what—

"—barge."

A blink reset the mage among his weary companions. The road had left the hills to meet the lowlands, turned north to follow the first canal they'd encountered. The head-high coil of silt left by last night's dancers steamed, ripe in the autumn nip. Farmers would be along to take their share. Trees marched the other side. Their bare branches framed scudding clouds and long v-shaped strings of geese heading south and Maleonarial could almost taste snow on the wind.

"Stink'n barges." Rid spat. "Why n'ride t'Alden?"

"I'd have no backside left?" Harn muttered, squirming with a wince.

Domozuk pointed the pennant at the made-horse and its sad burden. "By barge, we could have him to the school tomorrow."

Too soon. Too late. Both were true and could not matter less. There were other reasons for a change in travel mode. Tough, Domozuk and Rid, but older; Maleonarial knew full well the misery of cold ground on aging bones. The farmer, Nim, could handle it, but he and Harn were injured and deserved proper care. Add the strain of riding—even his renewed body felt it. The mage gave a slow nod. "The closest port is Nor Holding."

"Aie. If we push hard today, we should make the russet barge." Domozuk noticed Nim's questioning look. "I was in charge of the scribemaster's travel. There's not a schedule in Tananen I don't have in here." He tapped a thick finger to the side of his head. "Saffron, Blue, Brown, and Russet. Four a day leave from Nor, first at dawn, last at dusk. To Alden? Ten gils each of us, fourteen for the livestock."

"A fortune—" Nim protested.

Rid's thumb jerked at Maleonarial. "H'kin pay."

With an intention? The mage let an eyebrow drift upward, but Domozuk was already shaking his head. "We want passage, not to buy the barge. The Designate's jewels will do. If that's proper." The scribemaster's servant looked to him for assurance.

The Deathless Goddess had consumed the young woman, Her Witness, even as she'd restored Maleonarial. His memory of those moments? Shards of glass, cutting deeper and deeper. Lips like fire. A voice of thunder and ice. Words vanishing before they could be grasped.

As for who this woman had been—he would learn her name and honor it. Beyond that, her sacrifice had been the fate expected of her calling and his pity unwelcome. "Use them to pay, but keep an accounting for Tiler's Hold Daughter," Maleonarial ordered. "The gems were hers." As the life of the acolyte had been.

A needful reminder. It wasn't only mage scribes who paid The Hag's terrible price.

Kait held tight to the strap to one side of the carriage door and poked her head through the opened window. Mist kissed her face, dewed her lashes and lips. The rumble of the mighty Helthrom receded with each greedy stride of the team and they couldn't go fast enough for her. Almost there. She'd seen nought but plain rock along their road. The Fell, whatever they might be, hadn't spread beyond the hold walls. Soon, any moment soon, she'd hear Her Voice again. Relief bubbled in her chest.

"Have a care! You're getting us wet!"

Sliding shut the window, Kait sat back, pushing damp hair from her forehead. Droplets splattered on the glass, obscuring the view. "We're passing through Her Veil."

"We noticed." The damesen's apprentice, Tercle by name, glowered. Her feet protected a square case of dark wood with brass corners and she pointedly pushed it deeper beneath the seat she shared with Pylor.

On the seat Kait shared with her kin, Ferden snored in his corner. Leksand, between them, looked up eagerly. "How far now?"

Tercle closed her eyes in disgust.

The damesen answered. "Barring delays? Alden is a full day's travel, scribe-to-be. We'll arrive tomorrow." Pylor looked nothing like Insom, other than being as tall. An aquiline nose thrust from a narrow oval face. Her eyes were a vivid green and what showed of her thick hair beneath its dark wrap was as red as the threads on Leksand's jerkin. Eyes edged with fine lines, as were her now-curved lips; older than Insom, those said.

Leksand ducked his head, giving his mother a worried glance. Kait carefully didn't smile. "Go on, then," she advised her son. "It'll be a longer trip if you don't talk."

"Thank you, Damesen Ternfeather," the boy said shyly, then, being young, went on in a rush. "Will we ever stop? To look around?"

"We'll stop as needful."

Without opening her eyes, Tercle elaborated, "Hard to take a piss while this thing's bouncing about."

Oh, how he blushed. Kait took pity. "What is our route to Alden, Damesen? So we may know what wonders to anticipate." Play the mountain villager. It was nought but the truth.

Lips pursed unhappily, then relaxed. "I didn't ask. Tercle will inquire at our first stop."

Kait had been grateful for their rushed departure, glad to avoid Insom and leave the hold behind. Perhaps she hadn't been the only one.

Light and shadow took turns filling the carriage. The scents of pine, then wet autumn leaves, then harvested fields entered the slotted vent, marks of their journey down the mountainside. The Lady remained mute, try as Kait might to be open to Her Voice. She remained hopeful, hard as it was as the hours passed.

Perhaps The Lady wasn't fond of carriages.

The monotony was broken only twice, first when Tercle produced a welcome basket of tidy little meat rolls and a jug of water shared by all but Pylor, who claimed no appetite and gave Leksand her portion. Then again, too briefly, when the horses were changed for the made sort with a great clatter and commotion.

They went faster after that, and though the road from the mountains was well-maintained and smooth, the carriage swayed in a new, heavy rhythm Kait feared would cost her the meat pie before too long.

"Who are you, Kait?" Insom's cousin asked abruptly, a brow lifted.

"The lad's mother—" A second brow rose to join the first. Well then. "I am that, Damesen, but also am I called Kaitealyon." The temptation to impress, to add "successor-designate" was easy to resist. She scarcely believed it herself. "One of Woodshaven's daughters, visiting Tiler's court."

"Ah," with satisfaction. "Tell me, Daughter Kaitealyon, do you come to learn more of the hermit mage or to be sure I do not?"

The damesen knew full well the line between courts, acknowledged it, yet crossed without hesitation. A refreshing bluntness, after weeks in the hold, and Kait answered in kind. "Kait, if you please, and neither, Damesen Ternfeather. The hold daughter kindly allowed me to accompany my son to the school." Kait patted the leather seat. "Lord Insom is generous indeed. We hadn't thought to ride in such comfort."

"I'm glad of company." A small, knowing smile invited her to share secrets. "But surely you—and by that I mean Wendealyon—are curious about this mage."

"It appears you weren't informed, Damesen," Kait said coolly. "The Lady's Witness accompanied the scribemaster."

"I was not." The smile dropped away; the grave intensity left behind more natural to this face. "I understand what that means and grieve with you. An acolyte's sacrifice is—oh—" A gesture begun stopped, a flash of pain crossing her face as she cradled a clumsily wrapped hand against her chest.

Kait shifted forward. "Let me see that."

Leksand sat straighter, familiar with her no-nonsense tone.

"Tercle's cared for it."

Badly, by the discomfort. "I've some skill." She took hold of Pylor's wrist, easing the hand into a stable patch of sunlight. She looked into the other woman's eyes. "May I?"

A terse nod, the arm no longer resisting.

Freeing the knot, Kait unwound the strip of cloth, careful not to jar the hand. When the last came free, Pylor hissed between her teeth.

The middle finger was the worst, awry and discolored at the second joint, the whole swollen like a sausage. The others were straight and undamaged, but a pattern of purple-black bruises marred the back of the hand. She'd seen the like before, Linnet's drunken brute of a husband having used his timberman's grip on his wife.

The husband had been shamed and run out of Woodshaven. Tiler's

Hold Lord, for Kait had her notion who'd done this, wouldn't be as easily brought to account.

First things first. Thank The Lady, Pylor wore no rings. Kait indicated the rest of the finger. "The color's good. A physician can reset the joint, but now we must ease the swelling and your pain. The guards should have a suitable ointment."

At "your pain" Pylor gave a wistful sigh, but shook her head. "It'll have to wait. I don't—"

Ferden, who'd awakened during this, grunted. Removing a boot, he pounded it fiercely on the roof of the carriage.

The damesen slid as the conveyance lurched to a stop, but Kait had her arm, kept the hand still. "I'll get what we need."

A relief to be outside, despite the carriage's generous upholstery, but Kait didn't linger. A guard had bandages. A driver of a freight wagon had the rest. The Squid hurried after her as she collected these items, bleating about schedules and consequences, though from the number watering the verge, a respite was overdue.

She ignored him until he blocked the steps into the carriage. "Go take your piss," she advised. "This won't take long."

He managed to look offended and comically desperate at the same time. "What's all this?" Bird-like, he dipped his head, eyes fixed on her hands as if the roll of linen and leather bag would give a more reliable answer.

"I've a minor injury to tend," she said firmly. "Then my own piss. Unless you want to take over?" She offered the items.

He stepped aside hastily. "Be quick about it."

Her menfolk must have heeded nature's call, for on the Woodshaven seat resided Insom's gift to her son, red lacquered wood with brass at corners and latch. He'd left it covered by his folded scarf, as if too precious to leave unguarded, and Kait worried, seeing that.

"Go, Tercle," the damesen ordered. "Make yourself comfortable."

The apprentice lowered her brows but obeyed.

"She worries," Pylor said as Kait sat beside her.

"No need. I've done this before. Raised a son." The explanation would suffice. She opened the leather bag, scooping two fingers' worth of salve, then held out her free hand for Pylor's. The truth. "It's for treating horses."

"Tincture of Arnica, then." The damesen half-smiled. "Inks are my passion, but I'd be a poor chemist not to know potions and medicinals. A—" A hiss as Kait began to stroke the salve along the damaged finger. "Your Leksand seems a fine boy."

Even a noble needed distraction. "I think so," Kait agreed, spreading salve over the bruises as well.

"His father? If you don't mind my asking."

"I don't. I accepted The Lady's offer—" Kait stopped to grin at the other's appalled expression. "The mage was willing and kind. I wanted a babe." Rogeonarial hadn't returned to meet the result.

He'd been close to a hundred n'fifty bells, had whispered his despair in her ear at growing old before his time, had vowed to resist the call to write magic.

By now? Surely dead of it.

The fate ahead of her son—Kait focused on her patient. "You'll feel relief soon," she promised. "It must be reapplied several times each day. Until you have a physician reset the joint—" This sternly as she secured the dislocated finger to its neighbor with some of the fine linen, testing it wasn't too tight. She looked up. "—or it will stay crooked."

"I'm no fool, Kait. I'll have it done. Thank you." Pylor reclaimed her hand, gingerly flexed the rest of her fingers and thumb. "Leave me the salve, please. Tercle will tend me."

The carriage shook as Ferden climbed in, with Leksand's help.

"My turn," Kait declared. "Damesen?"

"I'll remain."

Kait found the driver checking the harness. "Good sir, I need m'bag, please." She waved a vague hand downward then scrunched her face. "It's m'time."

Being an older man, from country not court, he gave her an understanding wink. "I know the one. Came last. I'll fetch it down."

When she'd the bag, Kait headed for the nearest unoccupied stand of shrubs, clambering into the ditch to be sure she was out of sight. Then she sat on a boulder and put the bag on her lap. Ursealyon had promised a means to report.

Kait opened the bag.

Three sets of bright black eyes looked up at her. Unremarkable, ordinary birds. They appeared to be thrushes, in their drab fall plumage. Not that real birds would sit on her clothes—

—fouling them. She grimaced. A shame the mage scribe had to write them so real.

Kait picked one up. It stood placidly on her palm, tiny claws digging in, eyes rapt on her face. "What do I do with you?" she whispered, and hesitated.

Its beak opened. The senior acolyte's voice said, "I will deliver," and away the made-bird flew, straight for the mountains.

Well, now she knew how to use the dratted things. Kait picked up a second, speaking to it clearly and without pause. "I saw and heard nothing of the Fell once through the gate out of Tiler's Hold. Nor have I yet heard The Lady. We travel in haste, but the damesen hasn't explained why or doesn't know. Courage to you both." She stopped.

"I will deliver," and away it flew, fluttering after the first.

Maybe it wasn't her place to wish the formidable pair courage.

Kait closed the bag.

She'd a feeling they'd all need it.

Magic serves a purpose.

Tananen's people take it up and discard it, of less import than the shoes they wear, confident it will always be there. That mage scribes will write what is needed. That The Lady will provide, as She always has.

For how else could the world be?

Tercle had brought news: there'd be no more stops. They traveled in such haste to catch a barge. Her companions were pleased. Barge or carriage, Pylor cared not, but who wouldn't smile at the boy's excitement? For the first time since her lab, her hand didn't throb. "That's right," she told Leksand, answering yet another question. "The wagons and this carriage will fit on one, with room for the guards and drivers to pitch tents."

"The horses too? Damesen," he added politely.

"Na." Tercle snorted, easy with them now. "They'll be left for the next to use them. More'll be waiting for us at Alden's port, you'll see."

Grief, fleeting—kept from the boy—crossed the mother's face. Her gaze met Pylor's, held in a moment of understanding. Some might celebrate a mage scribe in their family. Kaitealyon knew the cost too well to be among them.

Share her own burden? To what end. There was nothing to be done but obey Insom's command. Or was there?

"My cousin's gift." Pylor looked to the boy. Everything about this journey troubled her; the box alone in reach. "Would you like to open it now?"

He swallowed. "May I?"

"It's not from me." The words came out harsher than she'd meant. She gentled her voice. "It's yours to do with as you wish, Leksand.

You've no need of permission. Please yourself. It's what my cousin would want."

Kait frowned.

"Aie, laddie," the great-uncle said, blissfully unaware of troubles or fear. "I been wait'n patient as can be. Not get'n any younger." A gnarled finger tapped the box.

And it wasn't that he'd done harm—there was no reason at all—but Pylor watched Kait's eyes widen then narrow, staring at the box. Saw her face grow pale and felt afraid, all at once, to see what was inside. "Stop—"

Too late. With an eager smile, Leksand undid the latches.

And took off the lid.

Saeleonarial's funeral procession, pitiful as it was, arrived at the east side of the port of Nor Holding in time to join the queue of those awaiting the final barge of the day. Wooden docks lay tilted up on both shores, crews sitting by with their hooks. Once the barge arrived, the docks would be pushed into the water and linked together for as long as the barge lingered.

The shadows were lengthening, the air adding chill to the damp. On the far shore, a matching line snaked down to the canal along the cobbled laneways of Nor Hold's market. Buildings rose between, most brick, for the bottomlands held clay, none taller than the hold itself, rising on a distant hill.

Smoke curled from chimneys, promising hot suppers and warm beds. Maleonarial heard a wistful sigh. Harn, no doubt. For his part, he was glad to avoid entering the hold proper and delay the inevitable. The first to spot him. See what he'd become.

Domozuk dismounted, steadied himself, took up his stick and pennant. "The rest of you stay with him," he said gruffly. "I'll find Nanse— the bargemaster—and arrange passage."

He forged into the line, pennant lifted high.

"Wa'appens now?"

Maleonarial turned to regard Nim Millerson. "We travel to Alden."

"No need'o me, then."

Ah. He'd wondered where the anguished young man would decide to leave them. When. Not while they were alone on the road, Nim too responsible a person for that, but now?

He was in too much pain to be left on his own, without help, and too proud to accept it. "There is, Nim," Maleonarial said gravely. "A great need."

Nim twisted to bring his surviving eye to bear, full of distrust. He lowered his voice. "What need?"

"To speak for the fallen. For your village."

"T'mages," with disgust. "Why'd such care 'bout us?"

Because they'd learned a terrible truth, that magic could create not only from Her Words but from spite. Magic to cause harm, harm The Deathless Goddess couldn't prevent or gladly allowed, and Maleonarial hadn't decided which, but it didn't matter, in the end.

"Because what happened to Riverhill mustn't happen again."

Nim turned away. He didn't leave. Satisfied, Maleonarial waited with the rest and watched. Time later to confess he very much doubted the masters at the school would be other than intrigued by such magic, and care nothing for its dire impact. So long as they didn't bear the cost.

Domozuk moved through eddies of the curious, men and women who listened to what he had to say, then looked up the rise toward the body in its shroud. They moved apart, then, granting the road, standing alongside in grief and respect. Saeleonarial had been that rarity among mages, a man who never forgot his origins, a man cherished by Tananen's people.

As he was not. When Maleonarial would have hesitated, Domozuk waved them forward and that was that.

He dismounted, to avoid being even more of a spectacle; the others did the same, Nim helping Harn.

He walked to the canal beside the corpse of his friend and refused to flinch even as eyes widened, at the gasps and gossip, as he was spotted and the rumor of who he was—who else could he be?—spread like wildfire and raced ahead so the road widened as those they passed stepped as far back as they could.

To avoid him. The hermit mage? Or Maleonarial the renegade? He'd have asked—had any been willing to talk to him.

At least he'd one answer. There was no traveling Tananen unnoticed.

The tap of Ferden's finger had spawned a dire echo. She'd heard it.

Hadn't she?

Or she heard an odd rattle from the carriage. The springs made their own music as it bounced along the roadway. At times they couldn't talk over the din without shouting.

. . . *Stop* . . .

Kait shivered. The word—had she heard it from more than one voice, or heard Her, at last?

Was she so desperate for Her Voice she now imagined it?

Too late to obey regardless, Kait made herself sit quietly and watch. What harm could be in a box no longer than her forearm nor wider than her hand?

Held her breath and tensed, for harm there could be in stone. What if the Fell had come with them?

Blissfully unaware, Leksand's voice cracked with excitement. "There's a pen, Momma. Of glass." He removed the glittering amber and cream object from its black silk bed. "See, Damesen?"

Pylor leaned forward in answer, eyebrows high. "A treasure, Leksand. This isn't any glass. It's Surano, crafted solely on the island of that name, deep within the Whitehold Isles. You might," she added dryly as she sat back, "want to gain skill before attempting to write with it."

"I'll take care. I promise." Leksand lifted the pen, tilting it this way and that to catch the sunlight, then replaced it reverently. Next in his hands was a curious bronze object, a little tub with a lid, set into a base like an opened flower, with four flat petals. The lid was worked into a design of leaves, exaggerated and flattened in no style Kait recognized. The petals of the base were edged in curlicues. Two opposing petals were crowned, with holes as if the base were to be attached to something else.

Three dollops of bright red wax sealed the lid. As if entranced, Leksand shifted his grip, fingers going to break them.

"Na do that, laddie," Ferden advised, hanging onto the strap as the carriage hit a bump, jostling them sideways. "Could make a mess."

"It might be full of ink," Kait clarified. She wiggled her fingers and Leksand put it back in its place within the box.

"I'm sure it is." Pylor's face was unreadable. "This inkpot was one of our grandfather's most prized possessions. My father used it often."

Poor Leksand was mortified. "Then it's yours." He caught it up again. Went to offer it. "Please, Damesen Ternfeather. Take it—"

She forestalled him with her good hand. "It was Insom's to give. May it bring you good fortune."

Left in the box, last of the gifts, was a small scroll of parchment, the sum a most appropriate gift for a student heading to Alden's mage school, if one so far beyond the means of a student from Woodshaven her son could have no idea the value of what he held. Nor could she, for that matter, except it was too much.

And too soon. A master's tools. What was Insom thinking? Still, nothing of it appeared more ominous than over-generosity; the echo, Her Voice, products of a weary mind. She'd speak with her son when they were alone. Be sure he understood the difference between decent gratitude and indecent obligation, in case Insom sought to lay the latter upon him.

Leksand must have judged the scroll safe to handle as they rattled and shook, for he plucked it from the box and slipped off the ribbon. "It's a letter," he exclaimed, then fell silent, eyes scanning. His face turned serious as he read.

His great-uncle nudged him. "Will you be tell'n us what it says?"

"It's from the hold lord himself." Astounded, he looked from one to the other, even Tercle, his eyes wide. "In it, Lord Insom says I must use his gifts for my first writing at the school, to show to the masters I have the support of Tiler's Hold and holding. He ends with the hope I'll return to be his court mage scribe."

A future that hadn't existed the instant before The Lady's Gift, now twisting around her beautiful boy, consuming him like tendrils of black smoke. And why did she think of smoke, Kait chided herself, but she knew the answer full well. Anything of Insom's—everything of Tiler's Hold—

Might be tainted by it.

Ferden gazed fondly at his great-nephew. "M'guess'n it'll be a while some, laddie, 'fore yer a master mage."

"Aie," Leksand replied, blushing. He rolled up the letter to return to the box, latched that, then tucked it carefully by his side. "Would there be more of those wonderful meat pies?" he asked, a boy again and hungry.

"Haven't you noticed? We've slowed down." Pylor's apprentice pulled back her curtain. "There'll be a proper meal soon."

Seeing buildings, not trees or fields, Kait and Ferden did the same, staring out as avidly as Leksand. They'd slowed, if not enough to make it easy to see details. Kait gained a blurred impression of brick walls and busy walkways, of lights in windows and the smell of fish. The carriage wheels rolled gaily over cobbles, in tune with the urgent clipclop of hooves.

"Nor Hold." The damesen left her curtain drawn. "You'll see little of it. To reach the canal, we turn into the market."

Explaining the fish.

The barge coasted to a stop with a final surge and suck of water that added to the ever-present stink. Pylor Ternfeather pressed her square to her nostrils, drawing breath through its pocket of finely crushed carbon. Fresh, they called the water of Tananen's canals and rivers. She'd no idea why. The greasy opaque stuff was rank as any swamp, befouled and bordered by piles of dung and smothering green.

"Not long now, Damesen," Dolren promised. He lifted his gaze to her midriff, then dropped it again.

Unreassured, she looked to where the captain of Insom's guards stood arguing with a group of locals over passage. Her cousin had insisted on his show; here was the consequence. No one was impressed by her rank or his caravan. People inland considered those from Tiler's to be merchants, corrupted by the outside and greed. They'd be taxed at every stop and receive no courtesy for the trouble.

Docks were being linked to the barge from both shores, creating a bridge. Not long now. Around her people stirred, preparing to cross once the chains were secured. Wagons with children. Flocks of sheep. Those on foot and those on horseback. Chaos, albeit a practiced one, though there was no telling who else wanted to be on board when the barge went on its way.

Insom would have sent an ample purse; the captain should prevail. "Do what you can to hurry this up, Dolren," she ordered wearily. Anything, to gain a moment's peace.

Alone, Pylor walked to the edge of the cobblestones, separated from the drop to the canal by a hedge, bare-branched with hairy little buds. A stunted tree fought to hold onto the bank. Abandoned bird nests clung to its forks. Gulls cried and circled overhead, drawn by the bustle, and she gazed up, grateful for their presence though these inland birds were lesser and soiled, their voices foreign to her ears.

One caught her eye, larger and bright. As if her attention was a summons, it swooped lazily down to land near her feet, then waddled bold as could be toward her as if expecting scraps.

She readied her cane to fend it aside.

Its bill gaped, mouth wide and red-lined, and words came out. "Cousin. Listen to me. Do not make a sound—"

Insom's voice. Pylor closed her eyes and the illusion that he stood here, speaking to her, was perfect.

"—until I say. Only then answer me. This is our chance. They ignore me now. I've done what they wanted. I pray this is the end of it—"

Blessed Goddess, the end of what? What new madness was this?

"—I never wanted you part of it. Forgive me, Py. Soon you'll understand why—why I did—why I had no choice. My gifts. The boy. They must reach the school. You must see to it, at any cost. They ignore me for now, but they watch you. Tell me you'll do this. Promise me, Py. Say it!" And the voice changed, became strange and shrill. "Say it! Say it!"

Her eyes shot open. "I will. I promise."

The bill snapped shut, as if swallowing her vow. The gull waddled away a step or two, then opened its wings.

And the darkness beneath was no proper shadow, but moving, twisting streams of black.

Her cane dropped from numb fingers.

With a flash of an evil yellow-ringed eye, the gull lifted into the air with great beats of its wings. Turned, heading for Tiler's Hold.

Who awaited her answer? What?

"Cousin," she whispered, tears in her eyes. "Foolish dearest cousin. What have you done?"

The clouds thinned, afforded a glimpse of the waning sun. Lower than he'd thought, but that was the way of fall. It crept up, stealing the light. A bit more each day until you forgot what it was to feel warmth on bared skin, until you huddled close by the fire, too cold to sleep, afraid if you did the fire would go out and you'd die, frozen in place, a forgotten fool to be found in spring and scare the children.

Maudlin, was he? Grimacing, Maleonarial put his thoughts and newly strong back into his task. "Leave be. I've got him."

"As do I," Domozuk insisted, though he struggled with his share of the weight as they lowered their charge to the deck. "Gently!"

Maleonarial did what he could, Saeleonarial being uncooperatively stiff, as corpses were wont to become, and worse, bent at the middle as though still over a horse.

Once satisfied, they covered the body with more seemly blankets, among the gifts from those gathered to watch. They hadn't included supper and the mage had his doubts the barge crew was prepared to feed them, quick as they'd been to take the jewels.

Then again, "What about them?" He aimed a thumb at the caravan just arrived on the hold side of the floating bridge.

Domozuk glanced over his shoulder, then stared. "How—that's the hold lord's carriage. From Tiler's." His voice turned rough. "What's he doing here?"

Insom the First, he'd met. Maleonarial had no idea who led the hold now, nor cared. His stomach growled. "They'll have food."

"We've no room." Domozuk swept up his trusty stick and pennant, striding forth into battle. "No room!" he shouted, waving the pennant furiously. "Go back!"

Harn came up to stand beside Maleonarial. "Sir. Should he do that?"

The mage shrugged. "A scribemaster's funeral procession takes precedence over hold business. A lord's," he qualified. Never over the daughter's. Not when She could choose to act through Her Designate.

A sidelong, too wise look. Grown, had Harn. "We're hardly a procession, sir, are we."

Maleonarial put an arm across the younger man's shoulders. "What we are, my good Harneonarial? Tired and hungry. For our stomachs' sake, hope Dom doesn't scare them off. The right company could have provisions to spare."

"Yes, sir. It's a big barge after all."

"N'big'nuff," Rid grumbled. "N'f they bring teams."

"Compromise," Maleonarial replied. "We left our stock, they leave theirs." They'd sold the made-horses before boarding. Unsaid, he'd have to create more at Alden.

The Hag kept winning.

Like the rest of Tananen's barges, this was a massive rectangle, walled waist-high, with gates on both sides and added rails to bow and stern. Barges were constructed of wood written to resist damp rot, though no magic appeared able to prevent the growth of slime below the waterline, resulting in laborious maintenance come the freeze. The barge's crew of four lived in a shed to the stern.

The gates were presently lowered as ramps. Cargo, under canvas, filled a third of the deck, leaving a wide center aisle. There were rings to secure tents, if desired, after the deck was hosed clean of the leavings of bridge traffic.

Traffic that had to move quickly. A barge's schedule was unalterable, being set by those who cared nothing for those using it.

By custom, passengers ready to disembark and any freight destined for a hold moved first. It wasn't unknown for the crew to toss a sluggish passenger over the side. Once the deck was clear, those on shore coming to the hold rushed to be across docks and barge before the bargemaster's flag lifted.

Being the signal for those leaving the hold to cross next, a line ended when the bargemaster's flag dropped, turning bridge back to barge. New passengers and any freight then promptly loaded, having paid the fee in advance.

Unless you arrived with the body of the scribemaster. The bargemaster had allowed their procession, humble or no, to board ahead of all else. They'd kept to the right of the bow, out of the flow of those crossing.

Seen by it. News of his return—of a mage crowned with hundreds of bells, yet possessing the face of a young man—would speed across Tananen. What they'd make of it, and him?

He couldn't begin to guess.

"Time to find a hood," Maleonarial muttered, then shook his head.

Bells laughed.

As if that would be enough.

Saeleonarial was dead.

Kait sat in the carriage, hands in her lap. Did the news warrant her last made-thrush? No, she decided. However grievous, the scribemaster's death was of less import to Tiler's Hold Daughter than knowing his replacement, and far less than whatever she might learn of the Fell.

The death announcement would reach Wendealyon regardless, Insom's troop being sent back. There wasn't room on the barge for them, not with the scribemaster's procession and cargo already on board, and the damesen had been adamant. She would accompany Saeleonarial to the school, along with her carriage and the freight wagons, servants, and drivers. They'd arrange for new made-horses at Alden.

Anyone else at Nor's Hold who'd thought to take this barge could, in Tercle's triumphant summation, "Spin on their thumbs till tomorrow's."

Bribes? Having watched Pylor, Kait doubted any were necessary. She'd been shaken by the news. Had clung, briefly, to the servant with the pennant, who'd stopped shouting at the sight of her to hurry over and bow low. Her discourse with him and the bargemaster had been brief.

Setting all in motion. "Might we go out, Momma?" Leksand asked, eyes pleading.

The carriage gave another lurch. Someone shouted. "Once they're done," she replied rather breathlessly. It shouldn't take much longer to secure the vehicles, then remove the teams. Mustn't.

For barges don't wait.

Magic is everywhere, but not everyone sees.

Watch the barges ply the waters crossing Tananen's heartland. Pay attention. Dismiss the cries of gulls, the shouts of those at work, the smells and works of people—

For the canals are the dancers',
And what travels them has wings.

Her heart thudded in her chest and Pylor refused to look into any face, certain hers would reveal the dreadful truth.

That she obeyed a madman and no good would come of it, nothing good at all—

The rail at the bow stopped her. She clutched it with both hands, though her wounded finger protested, and leaned forward, staring down, seeing nothing, not even a future.

She heard gulls overhead and shuddered.

Was another his?

Now, the scribemaster dead. Insom's fault. And who'd be next? She should have ordered those in her care to stay behind: her people, Tiler's people, Tercle, odious Dolren, the elderly uncle, even Kait. Would have, but for the sickening certainty they'd be no safer at home. What was she to do?

"You're just in time."

Pylor froze at the unfamiliar voice, then straightened to regard the stranger beside her. One of the crew, by his slovenly garb. A hood shaded his face and paired black braids hung over his chest. "In time for what?"

A hand, cleaner than she'd expected, swept out in invitation to the canal.

For the singer was rising.

Sheer, singers were, so if you didn't look at the right time, by the soft light of sun's rise or set, you'd miss the delicate amber tracery of vein and cartilage, and notice only the burst of expected color. Russet, for this barge, filling the way ahead like an enormous flag, announcing a departure that wouldn't be stopped.

As great wings rose into the air.

Then drove down.

The barge quivered to life. Chains dropped away and gates slammed shut. Pylor held on.

Russet rose again.

Drove down.

Water pushed aside, cleaved by the bow as the ungainly barge leapt forward against the current. Air billowed to either side, trembling empty twigs, rattling bare stems. She'd always stayed inside a carriage or tent as the barge moved. Missed this—

"Such power," Pylor exclaimed, forgetting her worries, that she wasn't alone.

"Look down. To the water."

She did. Dark waves rolled up against the wood, breaking in creamy foam laced with debris. At that edge, a series of large metal rings protruded. Gripping those, huge black—

"Are those claws?"

"That's how they tow the barges."

"Then they could let go. Why don't they?"

"No one knows. Like the dancers, singers suit themselves." Within the hood, a square chin showed. She glimpsed curved lips and a dimpled, clean-shaven cheek. "To our gain, so long as we keep to their time, not ours, and are willing to stop where they decide."

"Now you speak nonsense," she bristled. "Barges go from hold to hold, and stop only at ports."

"True," he replied easily. "No less true, ports and holds were built where the singers stop. Does it matter which?"

Ports dictated by wisps. Schedules by whim. Her cousin—Pylor felt undone, her world tilting on a skewed axis, and grew angry at it all. "Of course it matters. What you're saying—it's unmanageable. Out of control." Like Insom.

"Most magic is." He turned away, leaning on the rail to gaze through sheer wings into a russet-tinged distance, revelations done.

Pylor collected herself; considered him. A cultured voice. The ease, talking with her. This wasn't a member of the crew, but a fellow passenger, making this man part of the funeral procession. "Your pardon, sir. May I ask you about Saeleonarial?"

A nod.

"I'm Damesen Ternfeather of Tiler's Hold. I counted the scribemaster my friend, as well as colleague." She tried in vain to find eyes within the hood's shadow, an expression to read. "Saeleonarial left my company in good health, I swear it. Please, the truth of this. How did he die?"

Silence stretched, filled with the lap of wave and slough of air through uncanny wings; convinced he wouldn't answer, she prepared to excuse herself.

Then, "Sael died as does every mage, Damesen." Hands gripped the rail beside hers. "The Goddess took her fee."

"And—" Didn't she know already, by Leorealyon's absence? She had to be sure. "Her Witness? Tiler's acolyte?"

"Her life was forfeit before she left the hold." He turned and walked away.

Pylor stared out through wings that owed nothing to any mage, that pulled a barge for reasons no one knew, and wished she were done with Insom's bidding. Done with magic.

She welcomed the return of anger. Putting her back to the singer, Pylor headed to the freight wagons.

The tail gate of one was lowered. Inside was an impromptu but effective kitchen as well as supplies and extra harness. On the gate, travel trays were being filled and distributed, steam rising from mugs and reheated soups. The rest was cold fare, but ample.

Dolren Keeperson lurked nearby, his attempt to look too busy to help fooling no one here.

Pylor smiled to herself, then put on a stern expression. "Dolren."

He whirled around, bowed clumsily. "Damesen. I was seeing to your supper."

She didn't need the cloud building in Tercle's face to know the lie, but the man had his uses. "I thank you for your concern, but I've a more important task for you. Please see to it, personally, that those who accompany the scribemaster are fed first, and well, then the barge crew and our guests from Woodshaven."

"But—"

"Without the guard, we've rations to spare."

"Twice over, Damesen," crowed the driver turned cook; Bense Groomson was his name, she recalled. He and his sister drove the freight wagons, their brother indeed a groom. All three were cheerful and boisterous people, willing to do other jobs when they'd no teams, as now. Bense handed Dolren a full tray, stacking another on top. "Careful—"

The unfortunate Dolren having staggered.

"—and come back quick for the rest."

"Thank you, Dolren," Pylor said warmly.

He squinted at her through the steam, as though suspicious of approval, then gave a wan smile. "My pleasure to serve, Damesen."

"Then get to it," Tercle suggested pleasantly, scowling till he left, then gave Pylor a keen look. "No need for you to wait around, Damesen. I'll bring ours to the carriage."

She nodded and walked away.

Supper was the least courtesy deserved by those escorting Saeleon-arial's body home; feeding those responsible for their travel, a prudent generosity.

Enlisting Dolren? Other than the pleasure of watching the man forced to labor greater than his tongue and ears, he was the only one left of their company who might know Insom had ordered her kept from his cargo.

Pylor didn't intend to be stopped again.

Nim Millerson was his name. How Ferden found the young man was anyone's guess, but the pair arrived with Leksand, carrying supper trays, and Kait helped the barge crew—two brothers, a wife, and son—willingly make room for more. They'd barrels and planks, good solid seats and tables. She doubted any but the damesen in her carriage would eat in greater comfort.

Or better company. Farmer. Forester. Barge crew. Field, mountain, or canal. They worked for themselves, lived with the land and in The Lady's grace; Kait was touched to be asked to bless the meal in Her Name, but not surprised.

Nim watched her, most of his expression hidden behind a bandage, but his one eye glistened, perhaps at the homely blessing, perhaps simply worn from travel. He sat close to Ferden, as if finding a haven, and put his head down to eat. Slowly at first, as though he'd forgotten hunger, then more quickly, for the damesen had provided well.

The crew were like as peas in a pod, weathered, broad, and good-natured. The bargemaster, Nanse Heronsbill, had a mass of gray curls tied atop her head with a yellow bow and an embroidered patch over one eye she lifted companionably when they'd reached the stage of black tea and whiskey. Empty socket and sharp blue eye leered at Nim. "Lessee yers, lad."

He shot her a startled look.

"C'mon w'yer. Dun b'shy."

Nim undid the rag covering the left side of his face, and plucked free the oval pad of clean linen where his eye had been, his remaining eye defiant.

"Huh," Nanse declared. "Mine's better. 'Ere." With a wicked grin she topped up Nim's mug and her own. "Ta'the one we got!"

An angry gash shot from chin to eyebrow, shocking on an otherwise comely face. It should, Kait judged, familiar with injury from axe and branch, fade to a roguish scar. The eye, well, there was no help for that, but a surgeon with skill had stitched the worst of the injury and the skin would mend. Ointment such as she'd left with the damesen might ease the redness and puckering, soothe the pain. She'd obtain some in the morning.

Nanse's son, Arnsey, leaned forward to study Nim's face. He gave a satisfied grunt. "If ye like, ye kin ha m'ma's glass eye. She dunna use it."

"N'so fast." His father, also named Arnsey but referred to as "Bitters" for no reason Kait could discern, cuffed his son's head fondly. "M'beaut saves it f'parties."

Senert, the father's brother and twin, burst out, "Afer a sup like this'un? A party's wha we need, f'sure!" Lurching to his feet, he pulled a pair of throwing axes from his belt, pointing their gleaming heads at the shed wall beyond the firebowl. "Less h'a game!"

"Sit n'drink," Nanse advised. "It's t'dark f'yer fool'n. Ye'll hit our guests."

"Will not!" The big man straightened to his full height, axes wavering. "I n'r miss!" An axe aimed at Nim. "Can ye say t'same?"

Fireglow distorted friendly features, turning smiles into hungry grimaces. It picked out the innumerable gouges and pits marring the shed's wooden planking, most but far from all clustered toward a prominent knot near the center, head-high, and Kait recognized the signs of a favored pastime, probably one the crew used to part newcomers from their coin.

Leksand's expression of polite curiosity was a feint; he'd be aquiver with joy, being Woodshaven's up and coming champion.

The current and longest with that title sat beside Kait, gnarled fingers clasped around a warm mug, milky gaze vague but attentive.

Nim busied himself retying his rag bandage, but his eye shone. "You'd take a friendly wager, n'doubt?"

With that, Leksand's box prudently disappeared from view.

Nanse chuckled. "We dinna rob t'poor."

A sudden grin. "I've anothern bet in mind." Nim curved an arm, smacked its muscle. "Any job needs do'n?"

The barge crew, it turned out, had a plethora of tasks waiting, each dirtier than the last. The young farmer, unperturbed, rose to take the offered axe. "If'n I win," he announced, "I get your fine boots." His feet, puzzlingly, being in worn court slippers.

Ferden smiled into his drink.

And the game was on. In his cups he might be but Senert lifted the first axe in his massive hand and threw, the axe spinning once in midair before burying its head half into the wood; his family crowed with triumph.

Nim's first throw, to Arnsey's outspoken glee, bounced and fell.

"Giv'm another," Kait urged, despite Nim's dismayed look. Boys and their pride. "It's fair. He's new to your axes."

"Aie," agreed Bitters. "Canna ha' it said we took advantages. Not that m'bro won't crush ye, Nim," he added kindly. "Sen 'ates hos'n down t'decks."

Now aware his remaining eye couldn't be trusted, Nim took longer lining up his next throw. The crew called out advice he ignored. This time he sent the axe to strike with an authoritative thud, blade biting deep. Wide of the knot, their erstwhile target but, Kait observed with satisfaction, closer than Senert's.

"Best tree o'five!"

The whiskey a pleasant burn in her full stomach, Kait crossed her ankles and relaxed. The dark crept close; the comforting dark of night and peaceful rest. Somewhere on the barge, music played softly. A fiddle and flute, presumably the drivers and grooms relaxing. Did canal dancers listen?

Nim lost, if you counted throws and who'd be hosing decks come morning; won, if the cant of his head and rise of confidence mattered more, as Kait firmly held to be true. Leksand, though sorely tempted, begged off a turn.

She was sorry to see they thought less of her son for it. Did they judge him already more mage than commonfolk? Kait was half inclined to have Leksand show the bargeman what skill was—but it was his choice, not hers.

"Thankee f'the game." Senert raised his drink to Nim.

Ferden stirred, aiming his face to the voice like a flower to sunshine. "Ye canna be done yet."

The son looked askance at his parents but the uncle roared with laughter. "Ye canna see the bloody shed. How're ye go'n hit it? Wi'yer face?"

Leksand ducked to hide a smile. Nim flushed with anger. "Mind! Some respect—"

Ferden's hand closed on the farmer's arm. "Too dark f'ye, issit?" he asked gently.

"Aie," Bitters chuckled. "'E'd hit us, most like!"

His brother's face clouded and he set down his mug. "I kin see, ol'man." He rose, axe in hand. When he drew back his arm, Arnsey, being in its path, scrambled clear, but the throw was more than assured, it was Senert's best of the night. The handle quivered, blade lodged a hand's breadth from the knot. After a stunned pause, his family leapt to congratulate him, slapping his shoulders and sitting him down again with a brimming drink.

Ferden stood. "Laddie."

Leksand jumped to his feet and went to the shed, pulling free the bargeman's axe. He leaned head and shoulders against the splintered wall by the knot, as if taking his ease. Nanse's one eye squinted at him then at Kait, who merely smiled. "Ready, Great-uncle."

"Wassit a good 'un?"

Leksand fingered the gash left by Senert's axe, the closest of any mark to the knot. "Missed the target a smidge."

"Best shot o'me life!"

"If'n I best it," Ferden proposed, "I get yer bed t'night."

"If'n y'it the wall ye kin h'ours," Bitters said. "Move aside, boy."

The wide smile on Leksand's face was, to Kait, a thing of beauty. "I'm fine here."

The silence thickened when Ferden plucked a worn-handled axe from inside his tunic. He slipped the leather guard from the head. The metal was black with age, but the blade splintered the firelight. This was a tool used over a lifetime and too sharp, by the concern on their faces, to be tossed in the dark by anyone, least of all a blind man.

Muscle honed by a lifetime felling trees and trimming bush flexed. "Laddie?"

"Sir." With a gentle hand, Nim turned Ferden to face the shed.

Nanse glared at Kait, who shrugged.

"Great-uncle." Leksand rapped a knuckle against the knot, once, twice, then moved his hand away.

Before anyone but Kait could prepare, Ferden's axe tumbled handle over head through the air, as if drawn by the sound. The blade split the knot, plunging so deep the handle vibrated. "Do I get m'bed?" Ferden asked with a smile.

They all burst out clapping. Nim shook his head. "I could ne'er do that."

"Jus'a bit o'practice," Ferden assured him, sitting back down. "I'll kin show ye, if ye like."

Kait smiled to see Leksand the recipient of his share of awe, his face aglow with pride, and wished with all her heart she could pretend, for another moment's laughter, another drink, that this passage wasn't fraught with perils to threaten them all.

"You should know who's there, sir."

There were others with Her Gift on the barge. A daughter. Another mage. The feel of them made Harn sweat, but they weren't who Dom meant. Maleonarial slipped another bundle of sticks, by the pungent scent waste from a lumber mill, into the metal bowl, watching the dry tips smolder, then catch. "Do I?" he murmured.

Domozuk shook his head. Whether at the obtuseness of mages, him in particular, or the placement of the sticks, Maleonarial couldn't tell. He sat back to make room in case. "They'll want answers," the servant said after a moment.

"I have none." He hadn't twelve years ago, only the glimmer of a possibility. They'd have judged him mad.

Nothing in that was likely to have changed.

"When I arrived," Harn volunteered, "no one spoke of you except in whispers. Except the scribemaster."

Maleonarial lifted a brow. "I trust I was a cautionary tale."

Rid grunted something noncommittal.

"They said there'd never been a scribe with your skill. There never would be again."

"Distrust absolutes, Harneonarial. They have teeth." Their regard was a weight; he shrugged to shift it. "Very well. How many masters will be home?"

"T'was fourteen when the scribemaster left for Tiler's."

"Twelve," Harn said at the same time, then stared at Domozuk as if he'd grown feathers. "There were more? Who? Where?"

Rid spat to the side. "W'yer t'ink's inna cellars?"

The student brought a hand to his mouth, his eyes big as saucers. Maleonarial didn't know if he should take pity or not, or if it was pity at all.

And not cowardice. Students weren't told until ready to be masters themselves, something Harn was unlikely to be.

Yet hadn't Harn witnessed more of magic's toll than most ever would?

"They aren't in cellars," Maleonarial said at last. "There are rooms in the attic, decent ones, above the dining hall and kitchen. If a master can no longer be trusted with Her Gift, he's moved to the upper floor."

As were dangerously talented students unable or unwilling to control their magic but this Harn didn't need to know. Though surely even he suspected. There were those students who just disappeared one day and though the masters might say they wandered off, no one believed it.

Alden's mage school was as much prison as it was school, and its purpose as much to protect Tananen from those unable to safely use Her magic, as to train new mages to do so.

That The Hag approved was evident from Her inattention.

"What of Pageonarial?" he asked abruptly.

"Sorry to say, sir, he's been on the upper floor a few months now.

Comes and goes. Seems happy." Domozuk forced a chuckle into the appalled hush. "Attends all the gatherings."

That much at least was good news.

"And Alden's hold daughter?"

"Affarealyon still builds and bothers and keeps the masters on their toes. Her cousin Nedsom's hold lord. Does a good job, by all accounts."

A lad he'd taught a nice flourish for his signature, and how to catch carp from the school ponds. Not the only one to age honestly since he'd left. Rid had lost hair and gained a wreath of wrinkles around his keen eyes. Dom—"Your nose is bigger."

Domozuk tapped the offending organ with a fingertip. "Sign of wisdom, sir," he opined.

"Sign o't'bottle, mor'lik, y'fool."

Familiar once, if no longer, their companionable banter, and Maleonarial let it wash over him. Of those he'd abandoned, these two had deserved better from him. "I didn't think it would take this long."

The pair gazed at him, knowing what he meant. "To do what, sir?" Dom asked, softly.

"What I've yet to do." Something cold followed the words, spun embers from their homely little fire. A beat of the singer's wings, he told himself.

Or opinion.

"We'd Sael," Domozuk offered. "He was a fine scribemaster."

Rid spat over his shoulder. "A right good boy."

"Kind," Harn added.

The mage nodded. "Better."

"No," Domozuk objected, bushy eyebrows knotting together. "Sir."

Rid lifted his mug. "Aie."

They tried to rewarm his heart, restore him in their lives, thinking they recognized this younger self.

Unaware how much he'd changed. How impossibly distant from friendship and hope he'd gone. Seeing no way back, Maleonarial said helplessly, "I'm not staying."

"Xareonarial."

He blinked, remembering sharp features and a slim build, brilliance along with a self-conceit rare even among those who thought of themselves first as a rule of survival. A cruel streak—

"What of him?"

"He made master soon after you left. Made a name in Xcel. Came back fuller of himself, if you can believe it." Domozuk added another bundle of sticks. Renewed, the fire lit his cheeks and reddened his nose. "Saeleonarial refused to make Xareonarial his successor. He said a scribemaster should care more for the students than the robe."

"I'm not staying," Maleonarial repeated. "The masters able to focus will elect whomever doesn't run fast enough. If Xareonarial wants the job, there's nothing to be done about it."

"M'gonna 'ead back 'ome." Rid's expression was stark. "Y'ought." To Domozuk.

Harn, forgotten, looked up. "What of tomorrow?"

Dom shrugged. "Tomorrow is what it is. We'll take the scribemaster home. We'll see what our places will be soon enough."

Maleonarial wanted to tell them. That if—when—he ended The Hag, mages would lose Her Gift and if that meant the end of magic, so be it. Harn could sing for his supper and be happy. There'd be no masters or students. No hapless captives in attics.

Once-powerful mages like Xareonarial would find themselves judged for their real worth, as all should be.

But he couldn't tell them what might be a hollow dream, any more than give them what they thought would help.

The rest of the meal the four sat staring into the fire and it wasn't a mutual silence of trust or comfort.

It was the silence of those unsure of a future.

If The Lady was anywhere, She must be here, on a canal in the heart-lands of Tananen, Her domain.

Yet remained silent. Why? Kait would be back to her first assumption, that the flaw was in her or her actions, save for her growing suspicion Insom's caravan wasn't what it appeared.

Nor was everyone on the barge.

Those with Her Gift know one another.

Pulling her fingers inside her sleeves, Kait worked her way to the front—the bow. Feeling the draw himself, if not yet understanding why, Leksand would have come with her. She'd prevailed on him to stay with his great-uncle, truly blind come nightfall despite their clever trick with the axe, and with Nim, who seemed a good person and lost. Bitters, Nanse, and Senert vowed to enlighten and inform their visitors from far off wee Woodshaven with stories. Ferden had laughed and offered to trade eerie tales from the mountains.

New to them, all this, but her kin weren't overwhelmed. She took pride in that.

Overwhelmed summed her feelings. By day or night, the world stretched to the horizon on every side, its immensity plain, and a daughter from Woodshaven could be forgiven for feeling smaller than a fly's speck.

And no more significant. Who was she to defend The Lady? To ferret out the truth about muttering stones? About this caravan?

The fool too far from home, that was who.

You did your duty and prayed it was enough. The Lady was silent, but Her Gift was not and since coming on the barge Kait had sensed those others, as they would sense her and her son. They hadn't come to her—

With Leksand safely occupied, Kait let herself be drawn to them.

The crew distributed firebowls and fuel as the sun set; meal done, the drivers, and Dolren, huddled around a pair. Pylor had retired to her carriage with Tercle, drawing the curtains. Presumably Kait and her kin were welcome to sleep beneath it.

Kait exhaled, saw her breath. She'd find blankets.

She wound her way among goods wrapped against the weather, stepping over tiedowns and flaps. Clearer, the aisle between the freight wagons, but the tall conveyances cast disquieting shadows.

And looked too much like stone.

Better the open sky, however dark and cold, and ordinary things. What people made with their hands and machinery. What was needful to make what they made. Odds were some cargo came from across the sea, through Tiler's Hold. Some might be from as close as Woodshaven, there being a strong demand for fine lumber.

Kait rested her hand on a likely pile, then shook her head. Too early to be shipping. Last year's walnut and cherry would be dry and ready midwinter, no sooner.

A rail atop the side wall marked the bow. That, and the end of what light the firebowls cast, for beyond the night was overcast and black as pitch. She ran knowing fingers along the wood. No magic in this piece other than straight good growth. Woodshaven's own, perhaps, though the northern holdings boasted forests of their own.

She looked over the rail, but couldn't make out anything but a line of creamy froth in the black. She'd return at dawn, maybe see the fabled singer—

Something drew breath.

A long indrawn breath greater than any to fit within person or beast, and Kait gripped the rail, not knowing if she was in danger or—

The something exhaled, and sang.

It wasn't music. Wasn't meant for her. Wasn't heard, as sound would be, but felt, as Her Voice should be, and Kait dared not move, this time in case she startled the singer and it stopped.

For the song held the flows of water and eddies of air, the rhythms of what lived. Kait listened with her entire being, so close to comprehending—

Too far from understanding, for this song wasn't meant for her, and with regret, to save her sanity, somehow she pushed it away—

A daughter from Woodshaven, serenaded by a canal singer. Kait blinked away tears and swallowed laughter, happier than she'd been for too long. If what muttered in Tiler's stones was evil, what sang out here in the night was—not.

Nor was it good, nor had to be. The singer belonged in the world, as what muttered did not, and to hear its song was a privilege as well as joy.

Surely now, The Lady would make Herself known.

But though Kait listened with mind and heart, of The Lady she heard nothing. Nothing yet, she reminded herself.

She looked toward the small group sheltered against the far wall. A firebowl lit their faces and knees. Two mages were among them, this Her Gift confirmed.

Kait walked briskly toward the group. One—

Her steps slowed. One was . . .

"Lass, ye come f'r y'trays? Thank—"

"No, Rid." The one stood, a tall shadow, and she heard bells. "She's come for me."

Too many bells, and too strong, Her Gift. Kait reeled inwardly, as if she stood in the presence of The Lady Herself at last, even as She poured the glory of Her magic forth.

The others rose to their feet, looked at one another uneasily. The second mage, Her Gift a distant echo, said a name. "Maleonarial—?"

"It's all right—"

"No, it isn't," Kait assured them, certain of that much. "You. Hermit mage. Come with me."

For a second time he stood at the barge rail with a woman he'd just met, but this was no casual encounter. The feel of Her Gift was introduction and warning, for if one of The Lady's commanded an intention, a mage had no choice but to obey.

He could hope she was here for a different reason. "Daughter," Maleonarial began respectfully, pitching his voice for her ears alone, "Her justice was done and witnessed. Why do you seek me still?"

"M'name's Kait Alder, I'll thank you to use it, and I don't seek you at all," she replied, as low but blunt. "Last I heard you were hid'n in the hills. Now we're on the same bloody barge? Have you no sense, mage?"

Baffled, he blinked down at her. "I don't underst—"

"Bah." A palm thumped the rail as if he weren't paying attention. "Insom the Second's sent his cousin to the school to learn about you and your magic. He believes you made gossamers that can kill."

"I didn't," Maleonarial said heavily. The truth had to be known. "But they can."

He was prepared for disbelief and argument, not her swift grab of his wrist and upper arm. She squeezed those as if testing the ripeness of fruit, then let go, taking hold of his chin, her other hand tugging a braid so bells jangled. Appalled, Maleonarial shook free. "Stop that!"

"You're young again," she accused. "How?"

"You know how. She did it."

"Why, then."

To punish him, he almost answered, but that asked for pity and Her Daughter would have none. "I—"

"Wait," she interrupted. "We should move from the others. There's room to sit over by the cargo. Do you have an extra blanket?"

The abrupt practicality stunned him. "Pardon?"

"Three, actually." He couldn't see her face in the dark. That didn't mean he couldn't hear a smile. "It's grow'n cold, young-again mage, 'n I dinna wan't'freeze m'buttocks. Do you?"

She put on the accent, coddled him as if he were as young as Harn, and Maleonarial wasn't sure if he should be amused or offended. "I'll get the blankets. Is there anything else?"

"Aie." The word was the saddest sound he'd ever heard. Then, briskly, "But nought to be done about it. Let's have our chat."

Wrapped in blankets so only her nose peeked out, Kait listened to what chilled her beyond warming again.

"I made mistakes," the strange mage said, his cadence measured, almost slow. Even if she hadn't been told Maleonarial lived as a hermit, this would have informed her. Woodshaven had its share of folk who preferred to be alone, their home in the forest. Their voices too were thoughtful, not worn slick from overuse.

By "made" Kait understood he meant a living creation, for that was a mage's portion of Her Gift. "Gossamers."

"Yes. I lost count," ruefully. "I believed their existence mattered only to The Goddess and my creaking bones. Then a gossamer I brought to life entered an angry man and gave him magic without cost. With it, he brought his spite to life, creating terrible, beautiful gossamers he set on his own people. Only one from Riverhill survived."

Nim Millerson. It had to be. Kait pushed aside her pity. "Just his people?" she asked.

"Wasn't that enough?"

Another full of anger, she judged, despite his careful words and distant manner. "A tragedy, aie, and my heart aches for them."

"If The Deathless Goddess had a heart, She'd have stopped it. Saved them."

Kait squinted at him. "A master like you, thinking The Lady's everywhere at once, seeing everything? She's not some myth, like the godlings of Ichep or Whitehold." Had Her attention been pulled elsewhere? Tiler's perhaps? "It's good to know such gossamers have limits, even if they are those of malice." She licked her lips, then dared asked, "What else could have stopped them?"

"What?"

Mutters in stone. Made-beasts turned to ash. A hold without gossamers or The Lady. A world empty—

Kait drew the blankets tighter. "You heard me, mage. Do you know what could harm a gossamer—or scare them away?"

"Nothing. They do as they will. That's what a gossamer is." He straightened a leg. Bells whispered at his every move, each a mark of magic.

More than any sane mage would have dared. Remember that, she warned herself, knowing what it meant, him again young.

She felt hope too. Maleonarial was a loremaster, or had been. He could have the answers she sought—but where to begin?

They leaned against what felt to be bags of grain, as if taking their ease. Private, this spot, though light spilled over their faces from the fires burning elsewhere. Those fires flickered with the beat of wings unseen in the dark, and Kait asked abruptly, "The singers. The dancers. Are they gossamers?"

"No one knows," he said. "Every master has an opinion."

"And yours?"

"That you're full of questions, Kait Alder."

"Aie. So I've been told," she replied absently. She peered at him. "The singer didn't seem a gossamer to me. Her song—" How to describe it? "—was like hearing the heartbeat of everything wild at once."

"You heard a singer." It wasn't disbelief, it was awe. "That's—that's remarkable, Kait."

She had to ask. "How remarkable?"

"I can't say. Only that neither I, nor any mage I know of, has heard a singer sing. There's no record of it. Every once in a while, someone grows curious why we call them singers at all."

"Because they sing," she countered dryly.

"I believe you. It's been a day of revelations." A chuckle. "This morning I was assured by my colleagues dancers do indeed dance, especially to a cheery dockside ditty." He spread his hands. "I swear it's the truth, if one I didn't expect."

She regarded him. "Then what are they?"

"Ancient." Maleonarial paused a long moment, then went on, his voice filling with wonder. "Perhaps as old as the world. When people arrived in Tananen, for yes, we weren't always here, they found the canals, dug by dancers. When they put their boats into that water, singers took hold and towed them."

"Not gossamers," she concluded. "I wouldn't call them normal beasts."

"On that even masters agree."

"Then they're Hers." A satisfactory answer, for once. "Her magic, made for us."

His bitter laugh wasn't that of a young man. "'For us'? That I doubt. Now, Kait Alder. My turn for a question, if you will. What else do you alone hear?"

She'd the choice. To answer or no. The humblest daughter stood foremost in Her regard over a mage, even one such as Maleonarial. Some took that regard to believe themselves superior and demand favors; they'd be the same sort who'd no idea how food came on their plates, or what happened to their tidy pots of shit.

To Kait's way of thinking, the two of them, daughter and mage, were Hers. Be it chance or The Lady's need brought them together, together they were.

"I've heard evil. That's why I've come. To find help to fight it."

"'Evil'—" He might have scoffed. Dismissed her words. Instead his voice turned grim. "Riverhill taught me evil can walk like a man. Where have you heard it?"

"From the stone of Tiler's Hold. It breathes. Mutters in a dire voice, or voices. I—as do the hold daughter and senior acolyte—can hear it. We couldn't make out words." She swallowed. "Feelings, yes. Horror. Destruction and death. We call it the Fell. I saw it—" Kait stopped, having not meant to go so far.

Bells chimed as if alarmed. "Saw what?"

"During the hold lord's audience, the Fell flowed from crevice and mortar like smoke. I saw it move outward, spreading as might lightning, or as water seek its channels," she added, thinking that was apt too. "There was evil purpose to it, Maleonarial. It went toward—" her son "—the made-beasts in the hall. No one else saw, but I did. As the Fell passed over them, they were consumed."

"Leaving ash or not?"

Kait took heart. She spoke to a master of magic, of such creations. "Yes. Ash."

"That suggests the magic within them, giving them life, was taken." He studied what he could see of her face. "Are you certain it wasn't The Goddess?"

"The Lady isn't evil!"

Relentless. "Does She not reclaim what is Hers?"

As life, from the mage. Kait covered her mouth with her hands to keep the terrible words unsaid. Was this why The Lady refused to speak to her? Because of her weakness, to be horrified Leksand, her son, her heart, was now promised? Would now give his life, for magic? Did She know Kait would give anything to have him back again?

"Who is the boy?" Gentle. Implacable. "I can tell his Gift is new. Untried." A heavy pause. "Your son."

She lowered her hands. "His name is Leksand. We're taking him to the school."

"Kait. I am so sorry." The profound regret, from a master mage, from someone full of Her magic and all it granted, jolted her.

She recovered with a sniff. "Aie, well, there's nought to be done 'bout it, is there. My task is to learn what's to be done about the Fell, for Tiler's and The Lady."

It seemed, all at once, as though he moved away from her. "Are you Her Designate?"

She was tired, cold, and losing patience. "I'm Kait Alder. If you're a master mage, can't you tell?"

"The Deathless Goddess has her guises." But Maleonarial settled, seemed again at ease in her company. "And makes Herself known in the least convenient way possible," he complained. "A page shifts. A breeze when the air's still. Things tumble—She's taken my socks." With affront.

Kait had to laugh. "A game we played each washday. I'd pin socks on the line and one'd be gone from a pair, sure'nuf. To turn up in my basket, or up a tree."

They found themselves in a companionable silence, contemplating a deity who hid socks. Then Maleonarial said, without expression or warning, "I plan to kill Her."

"Do you, now," she murmured, somehow not shocked. "Why?"

"Why else? To stop all this. Stop The Hag taking our lives—your son's life. I've dedicated mine to it."

"Hid'n in the hills. Making gossamers."

"Do you mock me, Daughter?"

"Not at all." Though truth be told she thought him most likely as mad as rumor said. Still, what he wanted to accomplish—

*Defend Me!*

From this mage? No. However strange and powerful he was, The Lady played with him, stole his socks, restored him. Something more was going on between the two, whether Maleonarial knew it or not. It wasn't her place to decipher what. Kait stifled a yawn. "Seems a bit drastic, by my way o'thinking. Killing. Should be another way, surely."

"Ask Her for me."

"To stop claiming mage lives?" Oh and there was a question no daughter would contemplate. Unless it was a fool, too far from home, who found herself in waters deep as the Snarlen Sea and alone. A mother, with a son—

"Even if I would, I can't." Kait rolled up the blankets as she stood, tucking the bundle firmly under one arm in case he thought to reclaim them. "The Lady hasn't spoken to me since I came to Tiler's Hold. I'd hoped She would once I left, but no. Not yet."

Maleonarial rose with her, stood with inordinate patience for her to say more, but she'd nothing left. "We'll talk tomorrow, mage, if you're willing," Kait told him. "I can't see anything changing afore that."

"Agreed." The tinkle of his bells subsided until all Kait could hear was their breathing, the lap-lap of water, the whoosh of air across an unseen wing. The hoot of a distant owl. Muted voices. Good sounds, belonging here.

Her head snapped around.

That didn't.

Curtains drawn, supper done, Pylor and Tercle each took a bench seat for their bed. Pillows helped, as did thick blankets, but they'd a long habit of napping on cots or tables during experiments. This was luxury by comparison.

In short order, a melodic snore filled the carriage, her colleague wrapped from head to toe. Tercle always could fall asleep at will.

Pylor listened with envy, unsure she'd sleep again. She stared up, eyes open and dry, feeling the dark press against her and she wasn't lighting a lamp. Wasn't giving in—

With a soundless curse at her own weakness, she reached for the coach light and ran her thumb across its knurled flint.

The wick caught. Warm golden light poured over her, soothing and safe. It took several moments before she could bring herself to turn down the lamp to a minimal glow, shielded from her companion.

She cursed her cousin for good measure.

What was he up to?

The freight wagon had been loaded with fourteen porcelain urns, presumably one for each master at the school, though she'd not thought there were so many in residence. Each urn was a work of art and rare. Insom must have stripped his collection to provide them. The urns were individually wrapped then secured to one another and the wagon sides by rope and strap, the mass supported on thick netting to absorb the bounce and shocks of travel.

As if what was inside were more important than the urns themselves.

Unfortunately, short of smashing one, she couldn't see inside. Each bore a lid comprised of a unique and beautiful brass clockwork, locked in place by hinged clamps. A small etched plaque named the intended recipient, but the styles were strikingly different, implying the masters would recognize their gift among the rest. Here a cluster of paper-thin frogs, there a waterfall flowing upward, some had pens, others stars, no two the same.

Except in what they lacked. She'd found no keyholes or dials; no moving gears or clue how the things operated.

Pylor had known better than touch one. Those from Ichep were known for their clever devices. Some were mysterious enough to appear magical, unfolding in intricate shapes at a musical tone, or themselves making music. There was always a mechanism to prevent tampering; poisoned needles weren't unknown.

Easy to surmise Insom had had them made. Less clear was why. Gifts shouldn't be impossible to open.

Unless—unless mages could open what those without Her Gift could not. Was that it? Did Insom want some display of magic to acknowledge his generosity?

What was in the urns?

In other lands, they worship gods or goddesses, ancestors or fire-eyed birds. These hear prayers. Offer comfort. Grant sweet respite at the end of life. Or hell's fury, depending on your life choices.

In Tananen, The Deathless Goddess neither listens, nor comforts, nor grants anything but Her magic, now, in return for certain death later.

Little wonder She isn't worshipped at all.

Maleonarial perched on a crate, safely out of range, as this surely the oddest of Her Daughters he'd encountered tore a verbal strip from her son for sneaking up on them in the dark. Kait's accent thickened with her fury. "I left ye car'n f'yer uncle! Count'n you, m'lad—n'this?"

He clutched a small box as though for courage. "Momma—"

"Kaitealyon to you."

"Ye canna mean that," the boy protested, voice threatening to crack. Not so old as his height suggested. A growth spurt.

"Don't mean," she corrected icily. "Oh, but I do."

"Y'me Mom!"

"Wha'a y'uncle, y'blood, who took ye t'raise as h'own—"

"I did not abandon him, Momma. The crew gave Great-uncle their nicest bed. He's already asleep."

Her Gift boiled beneath the righteous anger. This boy wasn't a Harn, to struggle throughout life to achieve a reliable competence. This would be, in Maleonarial's trained estimation, a very dangerous student indeed. Rewarding, yes. Should Leksand survive his early lessons, he boded well to achieve mastery at a young age.

Should those around him survive too.

An intriguing pair. As a mother should be, Kait Alder was worried and anxious. These were nothing compared to the dread in her tone when she'd talked of hearing evil. This Fell. And that she'd "heard" a singer too?

Maleonarial had no intention of leaving her company. Kait could be the help he needed; a truth felt in his bones.

"Well." She dropped the blankets to the deck as she took hold of her son's shoulders, giving him a shake that became a hard, quick hug. "And well done. Other than interrupting a private conversation between your elders." Stern.

His eyes shone as he gazed up at Maleonarial. "But I had to meet him, Momma. Her Gift—in him it's—"

Kait shushed him. "Don't talk about someone here as if they weren't. This is Master Maleonarial, once scribemaster at the school. Mage, my son, Leksand Loggerson. Who usually minds his manners."

His cue. The mage jumped lightly down from the crate where he'd been sitting, out of range, offering a hand with a bow. "Student Leksand."

The red lacquer box glittered as the boy shifted it beneath an arm, brass fittings and silken edge caught by torchlight; a curiously rich item to be in the possession of a rural villager. Perhaps he minded it for the damesen. The boy's hand was strong and callused. Unused to writing at a guess. Ordinarily a disadvantage but there were clues the lad had received a broader education than most from his village. A credit to his family and mother.

Who would lose him.

Making the daughter an ally. Perhaps.

None of this explained why the daughter—and Tiler's—had lost Her Voice; The Hag had been nuisance enough on shore.

Quiet since, come to think on it.

He'd take Her neglect as a boon. "Come to our fire," the mage urged. "Harneonarial will be beside himself wishing to meet you both. A brief courtesy," he added, reading the weary slump of her shoulders. "No more."

"Aie, then." Kait bent to pick up the blankets.

Leksand had them first, using their closeness to plant a gentle kiss on his mother's cheek and see her smile.

Maleonarial hid his. Ally indeed.

The others were nodding around the firebowl when they approached, too comfortable to seek their bedrolls, or too weary for the effort. Domozuk squinted across the flames.

Harn's startled leap to his feet sent Rid toppling into Domozuk, who steadied him with a quick hand. "A Daughter! I—" The poor student brushed at his clothes. "Forgive me, I—"

"Forgive us, my good mage, for disturbing your peace," Kait said pleasantly, offering her hand. "We wished to greet the others blessed by Her Gift, and to express our sorrow at the loss of Scribemaster Saeleonarial. I'm Kait. Kait Alder. This is my son, Leksand Loggerson. Of—what's wrong?"

Harn shied from her hand as though it might bite. He looked to Maleonarial for help, then, with sensible concern, stared like an owl at Leksand.

"You're his first Daughter in the flesh," Maleonarial told Kait. "They won't eat you, Harn." Chuckling, the mage sat on the deck, crossing his legs, even now taking the time to enjoy the renewed flexibility of joints once gnarled and contrary. "Sit, everyone. We'll be back to tiresome formality tomorrow."

Harn dropped more than sat back down on his barrel. Leksand arranged the blankets for his mother, then copied Maleonarial's position. He looked up at Harn. "Are you a master too, sir?"

Domozuk snickered. The fire's glow hid the blush the mage was certain lit Harn's face. "I'm a student."

"Momma, did you hear?" Leksand's delight was infectious. "Good sir, I'm to be a student—I hope to be," he added. "What's it like? Do you wear robes? Is there chanting?"

Kait ducked her head to hide a smile.

Harn appeared to grow. "Neither. We memorize Her Words," he declared. "We try," he confessed, gaze sliding to Maleonarial. "And we practice writing. A lot. And learn to make our own parchments and pens. Ink—I haven't started that yet. It's harder than it sounds," he finished lamely, as though worried he'd said nothing to entice his fellow student.

"A mage scribe's work is complex and difficult, Leksand," Kait said. "Years of careful scholarship are required to attain mastery."

Years of life, that too. Maleonarial saw no need to say what she knew full well, grateful for her kindness to Harn, who visibly blossomed.

"Years and years, Daughter Kaitealyon," the student replied honestly. "But worthwhile. To watch your intention come to life, feel the magic work through you is—it's incredible." His face filled with bliss.

Leksand's eyes widened.

Domozuk coughed. "I'd not brag about a gossamer."

Once more, Kait came to Harn's rescue. "You've pleased The Lady, Harneonarial, I assure you."

Every time they bled life pleased The Hag. Still. "A mage scribe does his utmost to write the intention required," Maleonarial pointed out, lest Leksand—or Harn—arrive with any other notion.

"About writing," Leksand said eagerly. "What will I be asked to write when I arrive? Our gracious hold lord, Insom the Second, gave me this." He put the box across his knees.

"Unless matters have changed?" Maleonarial smiled at Domozuk's snort. "A formality, Leksand. You write your name in front of the assembled masters. Tradition holds this to be the last time you sign your birth name, but it's more about assessing your skill." The Deathless Goddess had a penchant for rural lads; few arrived able to read, let alone write. "Based on that, you're assigned an appropriate mentor." A task senior students loathed, regardless how many received that help themselves.

"I can teach you how," Harn offered generously, if without tact.

Leksand's eyes glinted. "Thank you, but I've a fair hand. Kaitealyon taught me well." The lad missed the shadow crossing her face. "Here. Let me show you what I'll use." Clasps flipped and the lid lifted before Maleonarial could utter a word to stop him.

Firelight traced the exquisite shape of a pen, drew sparks from the gild of the inkpot, and even as Maleonarial heard Harn's helpless gasp of longing—

Lust for both items—for the magic he could write with such glorious tools—burned through him.

He heard a voice, hoarse and ragged, order the boy to close the lid. Recognized it for his own only when the daughter snapped, "Mind yourself, mage."

Came back to himself only when the pen was out of sight.

He'd thought The Hag distant.

Here was proof.

She remained all too close.

Mages. Cantankerous, self-centered, and peculiar, the lot of them, and that was being generous.

As for Maleonarial? Kait had never heard the like of him: old in magic; young in years. Though she knew full well how it had been done.

Leorealyon, as Her Designate, would have been the conduit. Spent, at The Lady's need.

Not Maleonarial's fault. Or was, if she counted his reckless use of magic in this quest of his. To end The Lady?

To end Her toll, by whatever means. On the surface, who could argue? Not a mother, given who slept beneath the carriage, wrapped in two of their three blankets, dark lashes curled over still-soft cheeks.

A daughter must. For magic filled Tananen, and only The Lady kept it, tamed it, made it serve Her people. For all their sakes, She must be defended. Kait was ready—would strive to be, with body and mind and heart—to be spent as Her Designate.

Against what might have come with them?

Unwilling to risk sleep, Kait sat against a wheel, blanket around her head and shoulders. She wasn't convinced Leksand's arrival had been what she'd heard, or all, not when she continued to be rocked by sickening dread. Were the Fell here?

Another had their doubts about this night or what roamed it. Lamplight limned the carriage curtains; the vehicle creaked every so often as if someone moved restlessly inside.

Someone not to take lightly. The damesen was under Insom's orders—full, in Kait's opinion, of his secrets. Could Pylor be trusted? Oh, how she missed her fellow daughters, Atta's good sense and Pincel's steadfast lack of imagination. Together they'd been more than three, they'd been Woodshaven's heart and soul, and if with her now—

Her lips quirked. Used to her fancies, they were. They'd believe none of this one, and ply her with wine till she slept it off.

The sisterhood of the Daughter's Quarters of Tiler's Hold hadn't been the same. There were too many of those raised there who looked askance at a stranger in homespun; too few among the prospects, vying for position. Mish, maybe.

Who wasn't here, was she? Kait gave a silent, impatient snort. She wasn't alone. She'd her family. She'd met the hermit mage, and while Maleonarial had perilous notions—was perilous, no doubt, himself— he'd knowledge and an open mind. Mayhap more than any she'd find at the mage school.

Where they'd arrive tomorrow. Domozuk had set out the details during their visit by the fire, stepping in with practiced ease to settle nerves frayed by the mages' reaction to Insom's troublesome gift. There'd be a brief stop in Alden Hold while teams were obtained—or rather made.

Hadn't Leksand's eyes lit at that?

Maleonarial had stared into the fire, his mouth a crooked line. He expected to write that intention; would do it, Kait guessed, however unwilling he appeared. Though from what Rogeonarial had whispered to her in the warmth of their bed, magic was its own reward, the euphoria linked to a successful intention greater than sex or love.

From the hold, they'd travel as one, the damesen having decreed Saeleonarial's body be carried with respect and thus accorded space within a freight wagon.

The wagon presently loaded with food and supplies, goods the damesen had ordered offloaded for the use or profit of the barge crew. A loss Kait wouldn't have thought acceptable even for a rich lord. By the grimace on Rid's face, Saeleonarial's former driver had agreed with her, but it was Pylor's decision to make.

The firebowls had been replaced by torches at the corners of the barge. Warnings for any small craft in the canal, Kait supposed. If other craft used it. Frustrating, to have nothing but questions.

What filled the other wagon, that it couldn't take more cargo?

Kait shuddered. By daylight, she'd have dared a look inside. Not now. By torchlight, the shadow between the two wagons looked like an opened black mouth, waiting to close.

Not a thought Pincel would have. Kait had always been the flighty one. Always the one who lost socks to The Lady and herself in the woods—

Who'd have guessed she'd wind up here and now?

"Wake up, Py. There's a bloody great bird on the roof."

Pylor cracked open an eyelid. She'd slept after all, if not comfortably, by the soreness of her head and neck. She tried to focus on Tercle's face. "Par—Pardon?"

"It's crapped on the luggage. I told the crew to shoot it for their supper but that fool Dolren is bleating we leave it be in case there's gore and guts. Are you awake?" With suspicion. "Did you sleep at all?"

Another of Insom's gulls, it had to be. She could hear it, feet waddling overhead. Almost feel its black stare.

"Not enough." Pylor swung her legs over the bench, sitting up. She drew the coverlet close. "Tell them to leave it alone. It's just a bird." Would it were true. Yawning, she rubbed her eyes with the back of her hand, winced at the throb in her finger. Less, though.

Her apprentice, her oldest friend, noticed. "You need fresh ointment. I'll put it on after you eat—"

Pylor waved fitfully. "Do it now. I'm not hungry."

"You barely touched supper—"

"Leave be."

"Bullocks, Py." In private, Tercle took such liberties. "You're churned up tight as I've ever seen you." She sat on the other bench, eyes fixed on Pylor. "Over what?"

"I want—I—" Say her cousin's been possessed by a dark force from The Brutes? That their hold lord obeyed this force in some scheme requiring she deliver fourteen sealed urns and a student mage from Woodshaven to Alden's school?

By the light of day, it sounded foolish, even to her. "This news about

Saeleonarial," she replied, which was true and more than grief. "I'd counted on his support to clear up this hermit mage nonsense."

"You won't need it. Here, now. Give me your hand." As she unwrapped the bandages, Tercle leaned forward and lowered her voice. "I've learned a mage travels with Domozuk. A mage with hundreds of bells who looks no older than Insom himself."

"That's imposs—" the rest a hiss as Tercle applied the ointment. Pylor waited impatiently until she finished. "Did you get his name?"

"Aie. Maleonarial. You'll remember it. Despite his look, they swear he's the same mage as was scribemaster before Sael. Best of all? That he's lived on his own for the past twelve years—and was found in Riverhill!" She tied off the bandage and leaned back with a triumphant, "Your hermit mage is here, Py, with us. You can learn what Insom wants from him, then we'll head home."

Triumph didn't lurch inside her chest as if her heart tried to escape. Success didn't fill her ears with the frantic pound of blood.

Foreboding did.

The urns. The boy and his gift. Now this mage and his magic, all going to the school.

Was this what Insom wanted?

Or what lived inside him.

"No."

Sweat beaded Harn's forehead despite the chill air; though daylight, the pupils of his eyes were dilated. If Maleonarial hadn't known full well what ailed him, he'd have worried the student fevered from his broken wrist.

"Sir. Please."

Magic must be used.

Her Gift arrives, opening the world. The mage-to-be gains a new, richer sense, but it is potential without purpose.

Knowledge must be acquired.

Learning the first few of Her Words is a revelation, for they feel familiar, as if always known. Tempting, to sort them into meaning, but pointless, for there is none to find. Only Her Daughters comprehend a language and that is their portion of Her Gift.

For mages, Her Words are puzzle pieces, some fitting together better than others, patterns flowing from experience. The more Words learned, the more a mage can do.

Must do.

"Please, master." The fingers of Harn's good hand, his writing hand, twitched.

Magic must be used. Students are taught the easiest Words first, so they might form an intention and create only what is small, short-lived, and harmless. That first intention, if successful, changes the student to mage. Someone who has tasted the exultation of creation, paid Her price, and will henceforth seek the former and pay the latter till death.

Harn's gossamer hadn't been harmless. With its creation he was afflicted for life with the longing for more. Maleonarial had expected this moment sooner. Had hoped it'd be later, within Alden's school and safe.

Leksand's pen had tipped the scale.

"You'll not put hand to pen or ink, Harneonarial, till at the school," he ordered. "If you can't control this, I will have you bound for your good and ours—funeral procession or no. Do you understand me? Is that what you want?"

The student gave him a wild look, then shuddered and wrapped his arms around his middle. "I do, sir. I swear." He sank down on a barrel, rocking back and forth. "I didn't know it would be like this." With pain. "Will it always be like this?"

No, it would be worse.

"You've done well," Maleonarial said quietly, hating himself in that moment as much as The Hag. "Saeleonarial would be proud of you, as am I. You'll be at the school and settled before the masters take their afternoon tea."

"That's not long, sir, is it. Not long."

"Shorter if you keep busy." Without temptation of ink or paint. "Dom-ozuk's preparing the wagon for the scribemaster. He and Nim could use help."

Color came back to his cheeks. Harn took a steadier breath. "I can do that, sir. Thank you."

"Go on then. But Harn," as the student stood to leave. "Come to me, if the urge grows unbearable."

Sweat-damp ringlets bobbed with the vigor of his nod. "I promise, Master Maleonarial." He dashed away, clumsy with hope.

Rid, a silent witness, spat eloquently over the rail. The mage raised a brow. "You'd have done differently?"

"Aie. Tied'm up proper," with a scowl. "N'tell'n h'notions."

"Harn isn't a threat," Maleonarial disagreed. "Whatever notions he gets."

The older man studied him. "Wha'a'yorn?"

The mage half smiled. "Fear not, Rid. Mine will leave with me. Now, tell me more of Sael's favorites."

Distanced from the sea and Tiler's Hold, Kait refused to add dried fish to her porridge, though she thanked the one who offered it. She was more grateful for the mug of hot sweet tea. Her mouth felt like caterpillars had spun webs in it.

Teach her to pretend to sit a watch, like a guard at a wall. She'd fallen sound asleep against the carriage wheel; startled awake when Tercle emerged with a cheerful "Breakfast's waiting." Gone to get her own and come back amid the general stir of people.

Her son remained a peaceful lump within blankets, oblivious. Kait made herself comfortable against the low barge wall, sat where she could watch him, sipping her tea, as she'd done mornings without count. She supposed she could wake him. Have more time together. Talk.

Try to wake him, more like. Stirred too early, he'd rouse a grump. Better this. A mother's moment.

Her last—

"Arrk arrk!"

Far from the sea, yet afflicted by a noisy gull. Kait eyed the creature. Perched on the carriage roof, it tilted its head to aim a yellow-ringed eye at her. Tercle had waved her hands at it, to no avail. Bold creature. Maybe it wanted the little fish provided for porridge. "You're in for a disappointment."

The head tilted the other way, then the bird fluffed itself in the fashion of annoyed fowl everywhere and settled with its tail to her.

Kait resumed her tea and son-watching, unnoticed by anyone else. A small parade began, the sleeping gull apparently cause for concern. Bitters and his son took turns flailing at it. First a broom. Then rags. Having kept geese, she'd have told them the bird knew full well it was beyond reach, but their attempts were entertaining as they tried not to make undue noise.

Not that they'd have disturbed Leksand's healthy slumber, but she supposed the damesen might be asleep, having been restless in the night.

Tercle returned with a breakfast tray and growled at the gull before climbing into the carriage.

Finished her tea, Kait put the mug aside. She'd get another when he awoke—

The carriage door burst open, Damesen Ternfeather taking the stairs at speed. She wore yesterday's travel clothes and her red hair stuck out in a sleep-tousled mane. Tercle followed behind waving an impotent hairbrush. "Wait!"

The damesen spotted Kait. "You. Take me to Maleonarial."

"Mmph—ma?"

"ARRK!"

Kait found herself on her feet. As was the gull, waddling to the roof edge to peer down, the damesen now staring up at it, and Kait earnestly hoped the bird didn't aim a stream of its crap at the noble's face—

Snatching the brush from her apprentice, the damesen threw it. Whether by skill or fury, it caught the bird square on its snowy breast and sent it flapping off.

As it disappeared from view, its screech of rage sounded like a man's impassioned shout—

"Py, you can't go out looking like that!"

"Momma?"

The damesen's eyes found Kait's; Woodshaven's daughter knew desperation when she saw it. Knew what she'd heard, she thought uneasily, looking after the gull. "Back to sleep with ye," she assured her groggy son, giving him her blanket.

While the damesen swept her errant hair back and tied it in a quick knot behind her head, gesturing angrily to Tercle to stay with the carriage.

To the mage it was. "This way, Damesen," Kait said, heading toward the bow.

The damesen had longer legs. Most did; Kait was used to half-running to keep up, but the other noticed and slowed. "I need to see for myself," subdued, troubled. "See him."

Not how things were done in Tiler's Hold; Kait had learned as much. "I could bring him to you—"

"He shouldn't expect me. Surprise is best." The damesen's steps slowed nonetheless. A darting glance. "Unless he's dangerous."

Was he? Kait thought even Maleonarial didn't have the answer. "He's unusual," she chose to say. "The Lady restored the life she'd taken from him. Made him young again."

The damesen halted, so Kait must. "To what purpose?"

They'd stopped in the midst of the barge, subject to curious looks from nearby crew, stripping canvas from cargo in preparation for today's landfall. Nim was helping. There were the drivers too, taking notice with their tea, and didn't the Squid appear from behind a wagon, the man immediately taking interest—

The truth must be shared.

A worthy sentiment but not, Kait decided, with Dolren at any time. No one in Tiler's Daughter's Portion had had a good word to say about him, which she might take for spite and status talking had she not seen for herself how he snuck about the barge, avoiding work while prattling how others, such as Bense who'd fed them all, did too little. Dolren'd avoided her, till now, likely considering her and her family beneath such a fine and important servant as himself.

Showed some sense, that did, for Kait was ready to introduce the Squid to the canal if he picked her kin for his gossip.

Not now. Grasping the damesen's good arm, Kait pulled her along briskly. "Over here."

The closest privacy was behind the freight wagon not being prepared for the scribemaster. The damesen stopped short of its shadow.

The sun being warmer?

Or the shadow a threat.

"The Lady's purpose," the damesen repeated. "Why restore this mage and no others?"

She hasn't told me—which wasn't an honest answer, however true. Kait sighed inwardly. "I don't know, Damesen. It concerns me too. As does this." She put her hand on the tail flap. "What's in here?"

"My cousin's gifts for the masters." Lips twisted. "No more games, Daughter. You aren't here as a mother. Something's amiss at home. Now this mage." The damesen leaned close, green eyes intent. "Tell me what you do know. Please."

A plea, not order, from someone as worried as she. Kait didn't hesitate. "Amiss it is, Damesen. There's evil at work in Tiler's Hold."

"'Evil.'" Unlike Maleonarial, it was as though she tried the word for fit. The damesen shifted uneasily, glanced at the closed flap. "This isn't—we mustn't talk here. Come with me."

This time Kait followed as the damesen led, moving between cargo to the front of the barge. The damesen put one hand on the rail, gazing out over the canal.

She did the same, squinting, but it was already too bright to discern the singer's wings. Mayhap a warm rosy glow—

Erased by words, soft and horrible. "My cousin's no longer himself. Some thing lives inside him. Controls his actions. As you said. Evil's entered our home."

The wind, of wings and nature, bit to the bone and that's why, Kait told herself, she shivered. It wasn't thoughts of Wendealyon and her sisters, of the people of Tiler's being ruled by the Fell. Doubt felt an ally. "You distrust him because he hurt you."

"This?" The damesen flicked her bandaged hand. "No. I say it because the voice from Insom's lips isn't always his, even when sent through his messengers." A nod to the flock of gulls flying over the barge. "That's the voice ordering me to see his gifts—and your son—delivered to the mage school."

Her son, again? Kait's heart hammered. What could Leksand have to do with the Fell? "Go on."

"Insom told me—in a moment I believe he was himself—that some thing came back with him from The Brutes. He's forced to obey it. Them. Claims he resists. That he fights back with lights and strength of will, but—Kait, I don't think he's winning. This evil in him is desperate to learn of the mage and his new magic. Worse of all, I've seen—" She closed her lips, head raised in challenge. "You won't believe me."

"You'd be surprised what I'll believe, Damesen, but hear this first." Kait reported what had happened in Riverhill, as might a daughter to her hold lord, for how was this different? The damesen listened in shocked silence.

Kait finished with, "As for Tiler's Hold? I've seen shadows move between the stones of its walls like lightning turned black. Venture forth like groping hands. I've heard their mutters, if not understood, and yes, Tiler's Daughter sent me forth to do more than be a mother to my son. I'm to seek answers to this enemy we've named the Fell. Learn what we face and how to stop it."

She left it at that. Wendealyon and Ursealyon. The Lady's silence and Her exhortation to *Defend Me!*

Matters for those possessing Her Gift.

The damesen nodded, eyes now fierce and bright. "You give me my first hope, Kait. I too have seen this black lightning. It stains my dear cousin's eyes when evil—the Fell—speaks with his mouth. Do you see what this means? We've a sign. A way to tell if this Maleonarial has been corrupted."

Why—"You believe the Fell's come with us." On this now-tiny

barge, afloat far from any help—Goddess save them. "That it's here, now. Following. Watching." She'd hoped to be wrong.

"Don't you?"

A gull cried in the voice of a man. Or what passed for a man—

Now she feared it was true.

After Alden Hold, the barge would travel deep into the foothills to its final port, the junction of the canal with the mighty Helthrom River. There its singer would abandon it. The barge would tie up, ready for miners from holdings in the mountains beyond to load their metals and gems. Cast into the current, tillers manned day and night, the barge would drift, making its way south again and east until swinging into port at Nor.

There, claws would grasp its rings again, russet wings rise, and the barge once more be towed upstream, whether by the same singer, come to retrieve it, or by another of that color, no one could say.

Making the morning a busy one, for any passengers and cargo not meant for the northern holdings must disembark at Alden. Busier than usual, as willing hands applied paint to cloth so that pennants with the scribemaster's sigil proclaimed the barge his funeral procession by the time the red spires of Alden Hold rose in the distance.

They'd painted the sigil on the sides of the wagon as well. Within, Saeleonarial reposed in gleaned splendor on pillows, blankets, and sleeping pads. The preserving shroud over the skin couldn't be helped, but Domozuk had brushed and oiled the wiry beard into a semblance of order, then put the damned travel cap on his former master's head, bells gleaming.

Maleonarial leaned his chin on his arms, folded atop the gate, regarding his old friend. Sael had liked his comforts. He'd approve. He'd have liked this Kait Alder too, and her son, not that Sael hadn't been willing to like most people on sight. Everyone had their decent side, he'd argue. With some, like Xareonarial, you had to root around a bit to find it, but he'd insist it was there.

Maleonarial remembered taking the opposing view, to claim everyone had a nasty streak, simply to extend the debate. Once masters, both teachers, they'd talk through till dawn, most nights, intoxicated by scholarship and conversation. Sael's wisdom—

Stolen by The Hag when he needed it more than ever. "You'll pay," he vowed under his breath.

Bells tinkled as he straightened and turned, Her Gift serving notice he wasn't alone. "Daughter."

"Mage."

"Maleonarial." The damesen towered beside Kait, frowning and pale. Her eyes glittered. "Hermit mage. Come with us."

Kait he trusted. Insom's cousin called herself Sael's friend but, apologies to the late scribemaster, those were legion. He closed a hand on the gate. "What's this about?"

"We'd rather show you," Kait urged. "It's not far. The other wagon."

To be tied up and tossed inside, no doubt. "I've been kidnapped once lately," Maleonarial informed them. "I think not again. Lord Insom will have to wait—"

A gull called out and both women looked up with fear on their faces. The daughter from Woodshaven seized one arm, the noble damesen the other, and he was too startled to resist as they pulled him along.

Their destination was, indeed, mere steps away, being the back of the second wagon. As it proved reassuringly free of surly men with ropes, he relaxed on that score, if no other.

"Quick. Get inside before anyone sees." The damesen led the way

with the alacrity of practice, climbing over the gate to disappear between the flaps.

Kait eyed the height dubiously. Without a word, the mage offered his
cupped hands. She took off a shoe, tucked it under an arm, then put her
little socked foot into his hands to be boosted up. Once astride the gate,
she disappeared inside with a whispered, "Hurry."

Shaking his head, Maleonarial stepped up and over, slipping between the flaps with care lest he step on her toes.

A flint rasped. Light flared.

The front half of the wagon was filled with tall ceramic urns, se-
curely fastened for travel. Their tops reflected the light, casting myriad
bright little spots over the wagon's cover. Fascinated, he went close.
They were stunning clockworks, elaborate and costly. "What's all this?"

"A test." The damesen stood by the coach lantern she'd lit, arms
tight around her waist. "Check his eyes, Kait."

"I told you," the daughter said. "If he were tainted I'd know."

The evil Kait had sensed in Tiler's Hold. The Fell. She could mean
nothing else and Maleonarial stared at the nearest urn, skin crawling.
"What are these?"

He was ignored. "You promised. Look, Daughter."

With a huff of impatience, Kait came to stand in front of him. "Show
me your eyes, mage," she ordered. "Nought less will satisfy her."

He bent to meet her searching gaze, face aimed toward the light.
"Tell me," he breathed.

Kait waved to the damesen as she stepped back. "His eyes are clear.
Tell him."

"These are gifts for the masters at the school. One for each."

Too extravagant to be mere gifts. Too many to be just for the masters able to return a favor. "What does your cousin expect in return?"
he asked.

"I don't know. They aren't from him." With something ominous in her voice.

He looked to Kait. "What did you seek in my eyes?"

Kait's lips were shut. The damesen answered. "Proof you could be trusted. We'll explain later. Do the urns mean anything to you?"

Maleonarial examined those in reach. Of the names he could read, six had been masters under his leadership. To still be able to receive gifts, they'd stopped doing magic, voluntarily or otherwise, when he'd left to do more. Three he'd known as traveling Tananen: mage scribes for hire. Daveonarial had retired in Aote to avoid teaching; maybe he'd returned to the school to avoid the greater danger of magic.

With a shrug, Maleonarial admitted defeat. "Nothing. Except the lids—" he held fingers behind a pyramid of glittering frogs "—would be gift enough. Each acknowledges an accomplishment. One of which that master would be proud." Painfully so, for the oldest mages clung to past successes as if they'd help resist temptation instead of fuel it, regaling students and fellow masters unable to avoid them, mouthing the words of past intentions as if any but a daughter could utter them aloud. "I don't see how they open."

"Nor do we," the damesen admitted.

Kait balanced on the netting between two urns, busy prying a gap in the straw mat around the nearest. Once through, she rapped her knuckles against the porcelain, frowning at the dull sound. "It's full. Sand, for packing?"

Maleonarial leaned into the frog urn with a shoulder, gave it a solid push. The contents sloshed. "More likely wine. If so, Insom doesn't know much about mages. We don't care for drink." Didn't dare, was the truth, the longing to do magic difficult to resist sober and the ability to hold an intention fading with every glass.

Cruel Hag, refusing those She afflicted the comfort of oblivion.

He looked at the two who'd brought him. "What am I doing here, Damesen? Daughter? What's this about?"

"Later, I promise. First—Kait."

"Aie, Damesen. I'll listen."

"Wait. To what?" She'd heard the singer. Evil in Tiler's stone. If whatever they sought here was the latter— "What do you think is in these?"

"Hopefully nothing," Kait assured him, but her round pleasant face was grim. She went to press her ear to the side of the urn.

Froze before she touched the smooth glaze.

Eased back with lips set in a bloodless line, and only when she'd backed away from any urn, did she turn to them and speak.

"They're here. The Fell."

The whites of his eyes remained clear, his voice steady. Was that enough?

A mug of tea found its way between her palms. Kait, wordlessly taking care, though her eyes were haunted. Pylor thanked her by taking a sip when she wanted none at all.

"Insom had the urns sealed. To keep in the Fell and protect us?" Maleonarial said at last. "Or to keep us from discovering them?"

If it wasn't enough, they'd given an enemy all they knew or guessed, for Kait had insisted she tell the mage everything. Pylor took another sip to hide how her hands wanted to tremble, measured him over the cup's rim. "I say throw the damned things from the barge. Let Her beasts—the singers and dancers—deal with these Fell. Be done."

"We don't know what would happen. Not even The Goddess controls those in the canals. Though She has other means at Her disposal. Daughter?"

"The Lady remains silent." Kait had gone pale. "It's up to us. We canna let those seals break and free what's inside, be it by dancer or rocks." She looked to the mage. "Ye could warn the masters. H'them help keep the urns safe till we know what's to be done."

How could anything—anywhere be safe? She hunched, letting them talk.

"I could try. One or two might listen. The rest? Will only see priceless gifts, no matter what we say. The life of a mage foments greed, not forethought. And, with respect to you both, we've no proof without opening an urn—which we can't and mustn't do." A shrug set his impossible weight of bells in motion. "My return will preoccupy the masters, for a time. I suggest we keep the urns concealed as they are until we learn more. Damesen, if you'd order your people to keep silent?"

Pylor looked up. "I'd order them far from here, if I could."

His face softened. "Have them wait for you in the hold, Damesen. There are good accommodations and Alden will be agreeable. The fewer outsiders approach the school, the better."

"Is that all you can say?" She found herself on her feet, cup rolling along the deck. "All you can do? You're the great Maleonarial. The hermit mage! Use your magic to help us. Save my cousin. Protect us! Or do you require payment before you help others?"

"Damesen. Pylor—Sit." Kait retrieved the cup. "Dinna insult him again." And there was no missing a command issued by one of Her Daughters. "We're in this together. We'll survive or not, together."

The mage gave Kait a considering look, before holding out his long-fingered, graceful hands to Pylor. "With these, The Goddess lets me create with magic, and yes, I've the skill—and life left—to do more than any living mage. That's the easy part. The hard, sometimes impossible, part?" The fingers curled into empty bowls. "Knowing what to create. I don't."

"Then what good's magic?"

Maleonarial ducked his head, bell-riddled braids restless. Lifted it, eyes clear, voice steady. "A question I ask myself every day."

The little snort from Kait signaled her belief they wasted time. She wasn't wrong. Pylor gathered her sorely scattered wits—and courage. "I'll do as you say. Hide the urns. Keep them secret. But make no mistake, by taking them to the school, by bringing the boy there, we continue to do what the Fell wants done."

Kait's eyes flashed. "Until we stop it."

A lust for destruction. No, a hunger for it—

Overpowering, those feelings. Their voices. She'd heard the Fell, in the urn. In all the urns, their inchoate mutters filling the wagon like doom itself.

Would hear them still, Kait feared, if she hadn't learned from the singer how to push away what wasn't meant for her kind. The dark wet hunger was hardest—

She stared down in stark horror, for an instant convinced her hands and arms had been consumed—but no, just lost in the suds—

"Momma? Are you all right?"

Leksand. Part of this madness, but how? Hiding a shudder, Kait made herself look up. Smile brightly. "There you are," she said, as if surprised. Drying her hands, she let herself fuss with his scarf. "I'm fine, m'lad."

His hands caught hers. "You aren't. I can tell." Peering into her face, his dear eyes warmed with concern.

"Aie, and how could I be," she told him, letting her voice shake, knowing her eyes were moist. "My wee babe, off into the world."

"Oh Momma." Leksand gathered her in his arms, his chin on her head—as he could now. "It's your footsteps I seek to follow. To be a good person and honest. To serve The Lady and Tananen, as you do."

"Proud I am." And was, yet for the first time she wished Leksand born a girl instead, able to serve, if not in guaranteed safety, then at least through a natural whole life.

Better still, been among the twain, those born owning neither sex or both or somewhere between. The Deathless Goddess left such children in peace, choosing those at the first bleed or whisker to receive Her Gift—why that was so—

—was piss under the barge. Kait sniffed and pushed them apart, aiming an eyebrow at the waiting piles. "Proud, aie, yer in time t'do some work."

His eyes shone as he stripped off his best jerkin and folded it carefully, then rolled up his red sleeves.

"Here now." Bense bustled toward them, flapping a towel as though to shoo Leksand away. "I'll not have a mage clean dishes."

"I'm no mage yet, sir," her son replied with a cheeky grin, snatching the towel. "And excellent at dishes. Ask m'Mom."

"A'times," Kait agreed, pretending to cuff his ear. "When he minds what he's at."

Later, she would remember standing at the wagon gate, washing trays and cups and spoons with Leksand, joking and chatting with Bense and the others who knew nothing of the evil brooding nearby.

Remember it as the moment she made her commitment with body and mind and heart to defend them from it. Became Kaitealyon, "Promised to the Lady," in truth.

Willing, should The Lady ask, to relinquish all she was.

"Master?"

Maleonarial cracked an eyelid to find Leksand gazing down at him. The boy looked vaguely disapproving to catch him in a nap. "Old habit," he explained, rolling easily to his feet. "What can I do for you, Leksand?"

Warm brown eyes, so like his mother's, shifted to look toward the funeral wagon and his skin paled beneath its freckles. "I came to—I mean I—" Leksand visibly settled himself, then spoke with quiet dignity. "Harn told me, sir, you and the scribemaster were close friends. You must be very sad to lose him. I came to say I'm sorry. As I should have last night, when we first met."

"Thank you." Empathy, manners, as well as Her Gift. The masters, those few who valued such attributes, would be pleasantly surprised. But nothing about Leksand explained what Insom—or what the damesen claimed possessed her cousin—wanted with the lad.

Nothing about Kait explained The Lady's continued distance from such a fair and true daughter. Darkest thought? For he'd plenty. The Hag bided Her time, intending to unleash Kait as Her Designate at the school, to end them all in order to deal with the evil in the urns.

The Deathless Goddess not known for restraint.

"Sir?"

The mage shook off his mood. "Shall we see if Alden's in sight? Your new home? We must be almost there." Another habit of his hermit days, to pay attention to the sun's path across the sky.

"Yes, sir. Master, sir." With the hint of a grin, "M'lord former scribemaster, sir."

He laughed and resisted the temptation to ruffle the lad's hair. "I'm none of those now. 'Sir' will do." He grinned. "Unless you're willing to try 'Mal'?"

Leksand raised both eyebrows in feigned shock. "M'Mom'd clip m'ears. Sir."

"And mine. Let's not risk it then."

Together they went to the front of the barge, joining those gathered to watch their arrival. Maleonarial was unsurprised when a wide gap opened to grant them the rail. The wind. Servants' gossip. As easily slow the singer as stop word of him spreading.

For a wonder, the sun had broken through the clouds of the past days in time to add welcoming sparkles to the water and brush warm bronze over the low rolling hills of Alden Holding. The canal bent ahead, on its way to meet the headwaters of the Helthrom, disappearing be-hind rows of planted forest on the far shore. Alden Hold stood a dis-tance from its port on the canal, a wide boardwalk connecting the two across a vast expanse of marsh.

One of Alden's hold lords had tried to dredge a channel to solid land. Dancers filled it each night until he stopped.

The hold itself was a whimsy of tile and brick. Small towers capped with spires marched along its wall and grew like a forest within, no two the same shape or size. To the center of the hold they rose in modest extravagance, affording a view for the courts of hold lord and hold daughter. Without, tile-roofed cottages clustered tight to the wall like bees to a flower and it was said most had cut doorways through to save steps to market.

Alden Hold being a peaceful place, of special interest to The Death-less Goddess and thus decidedly of no interest to anyone else.

"What do you think?"

"It's—nice," Leksand announced after a moment's study. "Not grand, like Tiler's Hold, but nice."

The faint praise of the young and impressionable. Maleonarial chuckled. "Don't let appearances fool you. Alden Holding is smaller than
most, but richer than any, even Tiler's. Its wealth comes from us. Mage
scribes."

The boy's mouth rounded in an "oh" of thought. "But—that's it?"

Best not swell his head too soon. "It's sufficient." Alden provided what
physical necessities the school and students required beyond inks and
parchment, from clothing and luxuries, to servants and groundskeepers.
In return, the masters paid a pittance from their earnings to the hold lord,
amounting to a truly stunning sum, and for their part did their best to
keep students out of Alden's pubs and gossamers outside its walls.

Magic not welcome in the hold. Long and hazardous familiarity
with the school had taught its neighbor magic was best kept away from
their homes and families.

Another service Alden Hold provided the school was to be its gate-
keeper. Students' relations and friends said their farewells to their
mage-to-be within the hold. Those come for the services of a mage
scribe were informed a message would be passed and request recorded.
They were welcome to wait for the result.

The foolishly curious or recklessly bold were sent on their way.
While the merchants and innkeepers of Alden might lose some business, no one argued. Better that, than needless risk.

There being no place in Tananen as perilous as where magic was
taught to those not yet able to control it.

"Once we enter the hold," Maleonarial informed Leksand, "we'll be
introduced to the hold daughter, Affarealyon. You too. She'll ask your
business on her land. By your answer, she'll decide if you may pass
through or be sent home."

"But, sir. Everyone's said I can't go home. Can I?"

Would he have sounded this wistful, had he not come from a dreary place? Where the only question was how soon his father's scant patience would wear thin, and the only defense to outrun his brothers, which he'd refused to do.

Brothers who might recognize this renewed version. A thought—

—to be put aside. His family—his father—had demanded a share of his supposed wealth. As a student, what his magic earned went back into the school. As a master?

By then, he'd learned a mage has neither family nor ties, only magic and The Goddess and the ever-shrinking remnants of life.

"The truth, Leksand?" The mage put a hand on the lad's shoulder. "No. Once we receive Her Gift there's no home for us in Tananen but here." A nod to the waiting dock, the boardwalk beyond, and the hold. "No place Tananen will be safe from you, young mage—" with a press of that hand, "—but the school."

If there.

A sober look. "What's the school like, Master Maleonarial? Like my village—or Tiler's Hold?"

The mage school was nothing so simple and in no sense kind, but some lessons had to be learned for yourself.

"Better than either," Maleonarial promised, gaze rising to the familiar smudge on the distant hill.

"There'll be magic."

# Fundamental Lexicon

*The world was ever thus.*

The mage school, and there is but one, lies in Alden Holding because it can be nowhere else in Tananen. Those who tried, failed, The Deathless Goddess making it plain where She wished mages to learn Her Words, and where She did not.

Mage scribes, being contrary, claim their school is where it is because of a central location, moderate climate, and Alden Hold being amenable to their presence.

Loremasters and historians point out the school has been rebuilt following catastrophe on the selfsame spot since records began. Again, mages have an answer. Or rather, a question. Why change?

*We were left alone.*

And yet have never been, for should the mage school be destroyed, as has happened over time, there is always a new one. Always new students and masters, however reluctant, to teach them. Always daughters to restore any of Her Words lost. Always magic, demanding to be written.

*Magic, once, was not written at all.*

Now it is, by mage scribes trained at the school, the only school there is, in the only land with magic left in all the world, and the real question to be asked, that no one ever does?

Is why.

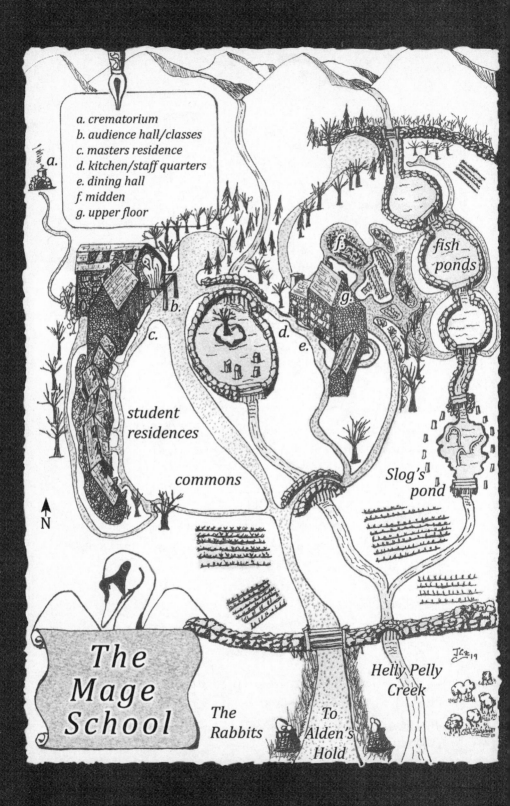

a. crematorium
b. audience hall/classes
c. masters residence
d. kitchen/staff quarters
e. dining hall
f. midden
g. upper floor

a.

b.

c.

d.

e.

f.

g.

fish ponds

student residences

commons

Slog's pond

N

The Mage School

The Rabbits

To Alden's Hold

Helly Pelly Creek

# DREADFUL
# SYLLABUS

# DREADFUL SYLLABUS

Axe-throwing at dusk, then dreaming through dawn had cost her chance to glimpse the singer. Now they came into port at Alden Hold and try as she might, Kait couldn't discern if the haze across the oncoming sky was wing or chimney smoke.

Smoke, she decided, as the barge lost momentum and coasted shoreward, and found herself relieved. The song continued its seductive thrum deep inside her, if she let herself think on it, and when she did think on it, because how could you help it, it was all a daughter from the mountains and forests could do not to long to stay on this barge and travel the canal through these languid heartlands, ferried by slow beating wings, for the rest of her life.

Then, because she did think on it, up welled the echoes of the Fell's dark mutters and dire hunger and nothing was right. Her mouth turned sour. Her skin burned. Kait gasped—

"Best we be off," her uncle stated, rubbing a hand over his face, and didn't know he'd saved her. "Canna recall t'last time I slept inna t'day. Shameful."

"It's done you good," Kait assured him, catching her breath. She slipped her arm through his and pulled him close. Felt the real of him and the love.

What seethed inside the urns hated both.

Ferden let out a sigh, milky eyes aimed at the sun. "I'll mis'im, Kaitie. Won be t'same. Won be home."

"I know." She rested her head on his shoulder, took in the comforting scent of leather and wool and family. Too soon to talk of arrangements and plans, but Kait vowed Ferden Haulerson wouldn't make the sad trek back to Woodshaven alone. Perhaps the young farmer, Nim, who needed company and a place, or one of the damesen's staff, ready for a quieter life.

She refused to think of her own journey, if she survived to make one. First see Leksand to the school and safely in the care of its masters. Deal with what snuck along with them, as she'd sweep soil from a floor.

Then—

She'd left her son before. She'd pretend this was the same, that was all.

All at once, here he was, his gift box under one arm, face glowing with excitement. Kait smiled. "You look fine. Just fine."

Leksand gave a proper little bow. "My thanks, Daughter Kaitealyon."

Making it not the same at all. But Ferden, wise in good-byes himself, pointed to shore. "D'ya see t'logs, laddie? Those came fr'm our forests, th'did."

A distraction, but Ferden could be right, Kait judged. The wooden dock was massive, supported by whole logs driven deep below the marsh. They'd not shipped any in her time, but trees that size? Woodshaven was renowned for them.

The dock, Alden's port, was broad enough to house buildings that had the look of warehouses, with a covered area for those waiting to board. Empty now, but she'd been told at dawn tomorrow the blue barge would arrive. Abandoned by its singer, it would fill with those willing to drift all the way south. Anyone in a hurry or heading in other directions would travel the road west, to the canal on the far side of Alden Holding, where orange and yellow singers plied courses opposite to their brethren here.

Did the singers ever meet?

Their barge eased close, reeds clattering as the hull rode over them.

If their singer clung underneath, did the reeds tickle it?

Or did the singer let go and sink to the bottom of the canal, leaving mere surface dwellers to their busyness until ready to move again?

Kait kept asking herself such innocent questions, pushing aside all else.

Workers waited with hooked poles to guide them to a stop, then hurried to attach ropes at front and back. The gate dropped into place with a thud that made Leksand jump, which made Ferden chuckle. Only one gate, the canal too wide here to bridge, and by the haste of the crew, they'd even less time before the singer took hold again.

"Dolren, where are our teams?"

Kait looked over her shoulder. The damesen stood by her carriage, cane tapping the deck as she confronted Insom's servant. Who, by his downcast eyes and hunched posture, hadn't an answer, there being no horses or oxen waiting on the dock. Though there remained a gull on the carriage roof—

"Momma—" Leksand's voice trembled. "Do you feel it?" He took her hand. "Do you see?"

"Aie. I see."

Together, hand in hand, they watched horses grow from the barge deck, each white and more beautiful than any horse, made or not, Kait had ever seen. Necks curved with pride as willing brown eyes regarded their new world. The creations of a master.

Maleonarial.

Fitting, the respectful, nay, awe-struck silence attendant their departure. The wagon carrying the scribemaster's body went first, its driver replaced by his own and the younger mage, his companions riding alongside. Pylor held to a strap as her carriage began to move, but these weren't any made-horses. These were exquisite, with a pace smooth as glass, and eerily familiar.

Saeleonarial's wagon had been pulled by such a team; no doubt Maleonarial had known or found out.

What skill he had, to craft these. What license, to spend magic for friendship's sake, for Tercle said he'd accept no payment.

The wagon with Insom's dreadful urns would follow behind. It should, by Maleonarial's plan, arrive at the school before any word of the contents. She'd done what she could. Rather than order secrecy, she'd offered her people a bonus, from her own purse, if the lord's gifts inside remained a surprise until presented, counting on self-interest as well as courtesy to close mouths.

The gull rode atop the carriage, a spy, uninterested in conversation. If the Fell wanted the pretense of a real bird, they should have had it fly off, but it remained, despite determined efforts by driver and groom to shoo it away. Pylor let them try, so long as they didn't harm it.

She wasn't sure they could.

Problems for later. To brighten the gloom within the carriage, Pylor opened curtains with a determined flourish. "I'm told Alden's border marsh is a sight not to be missed."

When no one else moved, Kait drew back the curtains on her side. Obediently, they peered out.

The boardwalk, a wooden road wide enough for wagons to easily pass, meandered like a stream through the marshlands. Reed grass, tips curled by early frost, stretched in a great arc between canal and the rise of drier land. Cattails, their neat brown heads nodding, marked shallower pools. There were occasional lumps of greener stuff. Bare branched bushes here and there. No birds—

It was late fall, Pylor reminded herself. In the rest of Tananen, away from the sea, birds left before the water froze. Were there not thin rings of ice clinging to the cattails?

"Excuse me, Damesen, but what aren't we to miss?" Leksand asked. "This looks like any bog back home to me. Just bigger."

The uncle chuckled. "Glad ye said it first, laddie."

While she knew more of oceans than bog, Pylor couldn't see anything special about the place herself. "I've no idea."

Tercle gave a smug little grunt. "Gossamers."

As the others in the carriage pressed noses to their closest window, Pylor lifted an eyebrow at her friend. "'Gossamers'?"

"Dom told me, the scribemaster's man. He said the marsh is full of them. And yon hills behind the school. You don't go there." Tercle made a whirling motion with her fingers. "Might not find your way back."

"Why so many?" Leksand asked.

Kait's eyes narrowed.

"Mistakes." Tercle grinned at Leksand. "Years and years and years of them. The kind that don't die or go away."

"Gossamers aren't mistakes," he retorted hotly, looking to his mother for support. "The Lady loves them."

"Mages don't—"

Pylor shook her head. "Tercle. Leave be."

"Kaitealyon. Momma!"

"Aie. Aie. The Lady cares for them." Kait closed her lips, making it plain she'd not add more.

Satisfied, the boy twisted to press his face to the window again. "I don't see any. Do you?"

"Might be shy," his great-uncle ventured when no one else answered. "Ours ha' great trees to hide'n."

Pylor met Kait's troubled gaze with one of her own. The daughter claimed Tiler's gossamers gone, something, in hindsight, she'd realized she could confirm. Years without count, a gossamer shaped like a blend of owl and spider and sunbeam had taken its ease on the windowsill of her chambers, overlooking Her Mouth with its cluster of gem-like eyes. A familiar presence, absent since summer. She'd assumed it had finally grown bored of the view. Or the smells of brewing inks.

Instead, had her window gossamer fled the evil Insom brought to the hold? Or, the thought neither of them dared utter, but both, Pylor was certain, shared—

Had Tiler's gossamers been consumed, like the mages' creations, by the Fell? An evil presence now riding behind them, secured in nets and straps.

If so, Alden's were right to hide.

If so—Pylor closed her eyes—something far greater was wrong. When any of Her Blessed Gossamers were in danger, The Deathless Goddess struck without hesitation, ending whomever threatened them.

Opening her eyes, but refusing to look outside, Pylor took hold of the strap.

Where was She now?

Magic serves a purpose.

A mage writes in answer to a specific need, frivolous or dire, his intention clear and direct.

Sael's matched made-horses being a case in point. Rid had sat so stiff at their reins he seemed paralyzed with joy. Domozuk had openly wept. Nim been unimpressed. Harn envious.

Regardless, Maleonarial hadn't spent some of his life for them. He'd done it for no greater or lesser reason than to bring Saeleonarial home in a way to impress those waiting. His friend deserved respect.

Unlike Sael, who'd made a team that outlived their creator and might them all—it being possible to make beasts able to consume nourishment and need care, if the mage were willing or extravagantly paid—his made-horses would conveniently turn to ash in four hours, give or take.

Out of habit, the mage used his tongue to test each tooth. Still tight in their sockets, as were his limbs. If anything, Her toll for this intention left him more comfortable, stripping away youth's burning impatience.

Some of it.

Maleonarial looked between the pricked ears of his mount, this bend in Alden's boardwalk facing southwest. At this distance, the mountains bordering that side of Tananen appeared a low bank of cloud, their stark bleak slopes blurred into soft folds. The impassable range was called Her Left Arm and where it bent, like an elbow, cradled Her Tears, the trackless fen surrounding the tower where The Deathless Goddess lived when not tormenting mages.

Her Soul.

He'd been to Her Tears, once. Each new scribemaster made the journey, to stand at the end of solid ground and gaze into thick everpresent mist until patience failed and damp won. He'd stayed that day and night, and through most of the next morning, surely longer than any of his predecessors, in hopes the sun would burn off the fog, or a breeze blow it thin so he could see Her fabled tower for himself.

Why? Because that Maleonarial had believed in curiosity for its own sake. Had trusted the way the world worked to be fair. Believed in the grace of The Lady, and longed to view Her sacred place.

The mist refused him, or She did, though once, in the eerie quiet between night and the first hint of dawn, he'd thought he glimpsed something tall blocking out stars, and imagined a shape that might have been a tower—

Or a hand.

To this day, Maleonarial couldn't be sure what he'd seen, or dreamed. It didn't matter. To him, The Deathless Goddess had become The Hag, graceless and foul. He'd stayed as far as possible from Her Soul while searching a means to end Her grip on magic and mages. Though nowhere in Tananen was hidden from Her sight, distance had seemed—prudent.

No longer. Her Soul would be his destination once he made sure those with him were safe from the Fell.

He'd burn Her tower down, if that's what it took.

"Ye be leav'n again."

The mage turned to look at the farmer. Nim sat twisted on his madehorse to glare at him and Maleonarial told him the truth. "Not yet."

"M'Mom fed you." Hot and low. "You ow 'er. Owe all'o'us. To stop this." A too-hard slap on the pristine white of a hide that neither felt nor responded. "Not anothern Cil, mage. Not anothern village gone by magic. Swear't."

A breeze ruffled through the stands of cattails to Maleonarial's left, as if hunting a rabbit. It flowed up and over the boardwalk, strong enough to shake bells and make Nim squint, bitter enough to numb fingertips and noses. Gone, as quick as that, and he'd have thought it a gossamer—

But his blood was young again, his heart full and sore, and if She was listening?

"I swear," Maleonarial vowed, to more than the grieving young villager. "By Her Gift and on my life, I'll put an end to it."

If there were no gossamers, there'd be no Lady, but she wouldn't know for sure, would she, unless she listened with her heart.

What if she heard the Fell?

Kait leaned her head against her uncle's shoulder, pretending to look out the window.

Pretending they were safe. On a trip into Meadton to market, though their wagon was a flat with wheels and the mules weren't smooth travelers, being inclined to balk at hills or loads or rabbits so instead of riding, she and Leksand would walk by their heads and tell the silly beasts stories to pass the time.

If she didn't listen, what if an urn bounced and cracked, or a rat chewed off the seal, not that she'd seen one, but rats did such things, so that the Fell were even now flowing like smoke through the wagon, and onto the seat, reaching for—

She'd know if she listened, wouldn't she? Be able to give warning if nothing else.

Kait closed her eyes.

Nothing, at first. No sense of Her Presence. The singer was too distant, or not singing at all. The mutters of the Fell were memory, not fresh, and Kait pushed them aside. Well, then—

She felt pressure, as if her insides resisted the push of a wind that wasn't there, then realized it wasn't a feeling but another unheard sound, and it was wind—

—but wasn't.

Because it was the soft, endless susurration of air moving through the needles of the old pines about their home—

—but wasn't.

It was breathing. Not like the Fell or singer. This was as if the past inhaled the future, then breathed out the present, and she was too small to hear it, too small to survive hearing it.

"Kaitie." A nudge. "Sorry to wake ye, but we're 'ere."

She hadn't been what slept . . .

The thought drifted, with nothing to attach to it; gone as Kait turned to look out the window.

An empty bog. A sky turned to dull metal.

A heart—Kait ignored, busying herself with what was needful and could be done. "Put on your scarf," she told her son. She brushed a nonexistent crumb from Ferden's beard and eyed the damesen's bandage.

"I took care of it," Tercle informed her, catching the look. She'd shrugged on her cloak after helping the damesen adjust hers and now sat with both arms around her wooden case. On the opposite seat, scarf donned, sat Leksand with both arms around his box. Ferden still cradled a mug of what might be tea, though the bargemaster had slipped it to him with a wink.

The damesen rested her hands atop her cane.

Bereft of duty, Kait tucked hers inside her cloak.

The teams might have trotted on air, by the lack of hoofbeats, but wheels that rattled over wood planks clattered suddenly over cobbles as if to say "We're here! We've come!" They passed through the chill shade of a brick-lined tunnel, Alden's hold wall much thicker than it seemed from outside, and into a yard full of waiting attendants.

No, not attendants, Kait realized. Residents packed the immense space, spilling into the wide streets as far as she could see. They stood on the great tiled stairs leading up to the wide open doors of a hall, itself full, and crowded the modest doorways of homes, business, and stables.

More looked down from windows in the wall and towers until Kait had to believe everyone of Alden Hold watched them arrive.

"We'll get out here," the damesen ordered, her hushed voice loud in the silence.

Kait moved first, climbing down from the carriage. She stepped sideways to stand by the rear wheel and make room for the others, though Alden's folk didn't crowd close. The drivers had drawn their teams to face the stairs, the made-horses become statue-still.

The people she could see were dressed in what looked to be their best jerkins and tunics, most brown, livened with green and yellow wool cloaks and bright woven sashes. Each adult bore a twist of sweet hay on garment or hat. Children stood in front with bundles of the stuff in their little arms and the aroma gave the yard the unexpected warmth of a fresh-cut field.

For Saeleonarial, returned home.

Every eye snapped to Maleonarial when he slipped a leg over his mount to jump lightly to the cobblestones. The bells sang with every move, but this was more. Recognition. The children wouldn't know the former scribemaster but it was plain the adults did, sufficient to duck heads and share soft whispers. Fear?

No, the faces Kait could see showed astonishment. A few, curiosity. The rest, welcome, and she realized that from student to master, Maleonarial had been as much of Alden as the school. Despite the solemn occasion, as he walked forward hands reached out to clap him on the shoulders or brush his arms.

He looked astonished himself, gravely nodding to those he passed.

"They liked him here," Leksand whispered to her. "Missed him."

"Aie." Mages weren't likable, as a rule; what they could create was missed, not the person or the charge.

Tercle leaned toward the damesen. Whatever she said, Kait missed for two were coming down the broad stairs to meet Maleonarial, the crowd parting. It didn't take Her Gift to know Alden's hold daughter and lord, though they were dressed as any of their subjects.

Slight, the lord, and dark, with a neat black beard and glossy hair pulled back in a braid. He'd a pleasant face with lively brown eyes and his curious gaze touched each of them. The corners of his mouth turned down when he looked to the wagon with the scribemaster's sigil, curving up in a glad smile as Maleonarial clasped his offered hand.

But it was the hold daughter who claimed Kait's attention. Wrinkles couched her features and her hair, shaved close to her scalp, was white; nonetheless, she took the stairs with the vigor of someone half her age and Her Gift blazed forth—

Kait felt the pull and resisted, taking her son's elbow lest he move out of turn, this being neither the place nor time for those from humble Woodshaven to seek notice.

Instead, with the others waiting, she bowed her head to Alden's Daughter and Lord, pleased Leksand and Ferden quickly did the same.

Unknowing her bow was that between equals.

"Your pardon, Daughter." One of Alden's people approached them. If the earnest young woman was an acolyte, there were no obvious marks of her calling. There needn't be. Kait could sense Her Gift, if muted. From Leksand's widened eyes, he did too.

"Come with me, please." The acolyte smiled at Leksand. "And you, student-prospect. Your audience with Affarealyon shall be private."

Making this public moment when they'd be separated. Kait looked to her uncle, not hiding her dismay.

Ferden put his hands on Leksand's shoulders. "Mind y'teachers, laddie," he ordered gruffly. "Remember where y'come from."

"I promise, Uncle." Then the boy broke and threw himself into his great-uncle's arms, holding tight; his fervent, "I'll come home soon as I can. Come see you," muffled against the other's tunic.

"Lady Willing." Over his head, Ferden's glistening eyes searched for Kait. "Now go w'yer Mom. I'll b'fine."

Another's gaze found her. Nim Millerson's face was set in determined lines. "I'll see him home." The farmer almost smiled. "Ferden's t'teach me ta throw."

Her uncle's chuckle was the bravest sound Kait had ever heard. Gently, he eased Leksand from him. "Tol'him it's 'ard work, but Nim's will'n t'stay t'winter." He pressed his lips to the boy's forehead. "Go on, laddie. Find yer magic."

Leksand took Nim's hand in both of his, nodding his thanks as if he didn't trust himself to speak.

"This way, please," Alden's acolyte said, with the impeccable timing of someone who'd seen such a scene many times before.

And what kind of place was this, Kait thought, after giving her uncle and an abashed Nim farewell kisses of her own, that it was true?

Pylor Ternfeather's knowledge of the wider world surpassed most. However large Tananen seemed to her people, how complex and vast with its nine holdings and myriad canals, in reality the realm of The Deathless Goddess was smaller than a minor province of Lithua and held fewer inhabitants than called the barrier islands of Whitehold home.

Still, Tananen was large enough for diversity. Customs varied from holding to holding. Styles and ideas spawned in one traveled, or didn't, to others. Most noticeable was the gulf between those of the heartland and those from a holding nestled in one of the valleys of the surrounding mountain ranges. "Of the hills" referred not to distance, but to the likelihood the individual spoke a dialect nigh incomprehensible to counterparts from anywhere else. It was said only those with Her Gift truly understood one another, Her Words immutable by time or place.

Pylor hadn't heard of spreading cut grass as a symbol of respect, but that's what Alden's population busied themselves doing, children dropping their bundles on the cobbles of the street leading through the hold. Marking it as the one along which they'd take Saeleonarial and the damned urns to the mage school, and nothing about the stink of dying plants improved the damesen's opinion on how terrible an idea this was.

First, they must receive the hold daughter's permission. Dare she act on her own? A hold of Alden's fabled wealth must have secure storage— vaults, perhaps, underground. As Pylor climbed the stairs into Alden's audience hall with the rest, she focused on the click of her cane's metal tip—her authority—on each tiled step. Could she prevail on Alden Hold to be a repository for Insom's gift? Find some excuse. The urns had been for the dead scribemaster, not the living. They'd been brought by mistake.

She kept her head up and eyes ahead, her face composed in the needful somber dignity, and hoped no one could hear the pound of her heart.

The flow of solemn people leaving the hall passed them to either side, exiting through a sequence of six tall doors supported by pillars. Not all could be nobles, but their clothing provided no clue as to social status. They must have attended a funeral service of their own for the scribemaster, for each held before their breast a small handled tool, its paddle-like metal blade chalked with his sigil, and most wept.

Pylor felt shamed. Her hold would do nothing but gossip about the next to lead the school and govern Tananen's magic-users, their true concern whether fees would be raised or some new opportunity for profit arise. The man she'd known deserved better.

Deserved this.

She welcomed the distraction of the building itself. Accustomed to the austere magnificence of stone and marble, she found the hall entrance bewildering. It lacked any effort to impress or solemnize or keep out the unwelcome. Instead, pillars and arches were coated in tiny gleaming tiles, the resulting colorful pattern turning the former into tall twists of growing grass, while the arch over each door vanished into a dome of open blue sky. The tedious work of many hands, simply to make a pretty illusion. Why not use magic? Was the school not beholden to Alden?

When she said as much to Tercle, her friend shook her head. "They don't allow magic here."

"Why?"

"Who knows? Will you look at that," Tercle murmured as they stepped under sky and through grass to enter a hall—that wasn't one.

Oh, there was space to gather, tiled underfoot in elaborate whorls and sunbursts, but where there should be a ceiling was actual sky. A great swath of it, from the far end of the long hall to where they stood, letting the natural light indoors.

Along with a cold breeze to flutter cloaks and disturb hair. Metal shutters lined the opening, presently folded like misplaced fans; Pylor supposed they'd be employed to keep out storms. Here and there figures stood waiting, a white cup in hand, towel over an arm. Shadows brewed and shifted along the plain brick walls, making her glad their path—on the heels of the hermit mage and Alden's hold daughter and lord—lay within the sun's reach. Behind her and Tercle came Domozuk, Rid, and Harn. Kait and her son had been taken aside, but the old man from Woodshaven, the young farmer, Dolren, and the drivers and grooms followed them into the hall, as they wouldn't in Tiler's. There, business of the Daughter went to her Portion, of staff below, and Pylor began to despair of a chance to plead her case in private, if this was the manners of Alden Hold and rank accorded no special courtesy.

They were stopped by a rope of gold braid, looped from stands to separate the very back of the hall from the rest. The hold daughter ducked beneath it and went to perch on a stool behind. The hold lord remained on their side of the barrier, turning to face the hall, and Pylor was forced to believe the rope was, in fact, the sole division between their courts.

What sort of hold was this?

Narrow banners, inscribed with words, depended from the wall behind the hold daughter. So many, they extended from side-to-side, ceiling almost to floor, layers upon layers, and rustled like leaves in the breeze from above. Some were curled and yellowed by time, their letters faded; others, new. As Pylor stood waiting, good hand tight on the reassurance of her cane, she realized they weren't words at all.

They were names.

Sael Fisherson. Mal Merchantson. Buried within a staggering multitude of other names, each left by a boy who'd arrived with the hint of whiskers and throb of Her Gift, displayed here for all to see as long as there'd been an Alden Hold to part son from family. In the otherwise immaculate hall, beneath the banners lay a line of fine brown dust and the tiles themselves were stained. The decay of names from generations untold, reverently swept up and stored, though sometimes the dust was stirred by errant breeze or motion, making new visitors sneeze.

Each banner, each speck of dust, marked more than a new mage scribe striding across Tananen, writing intentions to create what he would. This dreadful syllabus taught any who stepped in this hall the true measure of The Hag's toll. Children who might have become other than mage; lived a whole life.

Could no one else see it?

"Maleonarial. Welcome back," Lord Nedsom said. "I wish it had been under other circumstances."

Under other circumstances, he wouldn't be here, so Maleonarial smiled. "As do I, Hold Lord. Hold Daughter."

However much he hated The Hag, She chose Her Daughters well, making those ruled by Her choices fortunate, especially here. Affarealyon, the woman before him, had governed Alden and influenced doings at the mage school since he'd first arrived, and looked fit and able to continuing doing so after the last of his new life was sucked away.

Governed well, influenced wisely, and now regarded him down the length of her nose as if he'd crawled from under her boot. "Left without farewell. Snuck through our gate in the night."

They'd been close, once. Friends. Confidants. Not in this, but he offered a repentant bow. "To avoid debate, Hold Daughter."

"On what you alone decided," she admonished. "I want an account of what you've been up to, Maleonarial the Young-Again Mage. A thorough and detailed account."

"Affar," Nedsom pleaded out the corner of his mouth, giving him a sympathetic look. "We can't delay Sael's procession."

One, in the scribemaster's honor, all of Alden had turned out to watch. Maleonarial tried a second bow. "I promise an account before I leave, Hold Daughter."

Her eyes doubted him. It hurt more than he'd expected. A curt nod. "Continue, Lord Nedsom."

"We thank you for accompanying Scribemaster Saeleonarial on his final journey," the hold lord proclaimed in a strong ringing voice, even though those to whom he spoke stood in a polite row steps from him and a couple winced at the volume. Seeing, he flushed and lowered his tone to normal. "Those granted permission by Affarealyon may continue from here."

She lifted two fingers, swept them to the side. "Harn may return to his classes. Maleonarial—to whatever you'll face."

Attendants appeared at their elbows. "This way, sirs," one said. Harn went without a word. Maleonarial stepped back, gesturing to indicate he'd stay a moment longer.

Affarealyon gave him an inscrutable look, then nodded to Domozuk and Rid to approach. "We grieve with you," she told the pair. "Take your ease here."

"By your leave, Daughter, we'll see our master home," Domozuk said. Beside him Rid Smithyson nodded, hat in hand.

The hold daughter shook her head. "You no longer have a master."

"They do," Maleonarial spoke up. "I've need of them both. Rid to drive the team. Dom to assist me at the school." He made a show of brushing dust from a dead man's clothes. "Unless you think I look ready for the funeral?"

Wrinkles deepened at the corners of her mouth. Instead of commenting, the hold daughter lifted two fingers, and swept them to the side.

Another set of attendants came to guide Dom and Rid. They'd be taken to join Harn in the next chamber off this one, offered the use of privy and washstand, then given a ceremonial quaff of Alden's famed mulled wine before being hustled back to the wagons.

The damesen took their place, impatient or fearing Alden would deal with her servants first. "Hold Lord and Daughter." She lifted her cane, pressed the handle briefly over her heart, then held it out for inspection. "By this, know me as the authorized representative of Tiler's Hold Lord, Insom the Second. I am his cousin, Damesen Pylor Tern-

feather, come on urgent business with the school's inkmaster. I respectfully ask your leave to conduct it, and that Alden house my staff and
property until my business is complete. At my expense."

"Our business." Her apprentice, having come forward with the
damesen, lifted the lid of the box she'd brought into the hall. "Here are
the samples we've prepared." Emphasis on the "we."

Maleonarial leaned close to inspect the contents, ignoring the hold
daughter's quelling stare. Inside the box were six clear vials, each half-
full of a powder of unmistakable blue. Lapis pigment. There'd been
hints Icot's mines were nearing exhaustion in his sojourn as scribemaster. Jowen Hammerson, Tankerton's inkmaster, hadn't seen the pigment in years.

"We were aware the scribemaster went to Tiler's Hold to consult
with you, Damesen," the hold lord replied. He looked over his shoulder
at Affarealyon.

Whose hand remained still.

Behind that life-weathered face was a mind Maleonarial knew well.
The hold daughter would judge the business of ink supplies and samples
likely to tarnish the dignity of Saeleonarial's funeral, distracting the
school's masters from their duty. She'd keep the damesen in Alden
Hold until the funeral was done.

Affarealyon's gauge of the masters' flighty attention span might be
correct, but to get the urns out of Alden—for the mage was in no doubt
what the damesen had meant by "property" and he'd let The Hag have
them all before he'd leave the Fell behind in this innocent place—the
damesen and her wagon full of urns had to go. Now.

Maleonarial moved to stand by the damesen. Dared put his hand
over hers on the cane while keeping his attention on the hold daughter.
"Damesen Ternfeather doesn't speak of her friendship with Sael, so I
must. She is a friend who should attend his funeral."

He pressed lightly. *Understand why I do this,* that pressure asked, as aloud he continued, "As well, the damesen generously loaned her caravan's second wagon to convey his belongings. Those must go to the school with her."

Feeling her hand tense, he removed his, but the damesen made no other protest.

Affarealyon glowered at him. "Has the great Maleonarial decided on the rest for me too?" Without waiting for an answer, she swept two fingers through the air. "Go then. But the rest of your staff remains here in the hold, Damesen. At your expense."

"Thank you, Hold Daughter." The damesen's nod was stiff but gracious. "Dolren, see to our people." Without a glance his way, she left with Tercle and their attendants.

Insom's servant bleated a hasty acknowledgment, forced to scamper to catch up to the caravan's drivers and grooms, the group only too pleased to be led out the main doors and on to whichever inn was next on the hold's roster to house guests.

The older man Kait had named her uncle paused to bow toward the lord and daughter. Beside him, Nim stared at Maleonarial, his good eye eloquent. *Remember your vow,* that look said. The farmer took the man's hand, guided it to his shoulder, and led him from the hall after the others.

Alden's remaining attendants fell in behind, leaving mage, lord, and daughter alone. A gust of wind through the opening above set the banners aflutter and stirred the dust of the forgotten. There'd be a bright new banner hung later today, in memory of a boy named Leksand Loggerson.

Doubtless where Kait and her son were now, Alden's unmagical scribes making sure of the spelling.

*Another life to consume;* The Hag would persist in the habit forever unless stopped. Firming his resolve, Maleonarial bowed. "The teams are mine and expire this afternoon. By your leave—"

"A moment more." The hold lord's brows knitted together. "What haven't you told us, Mal?"

Quick as a lad, Nedsom. No surprise now he sensed a hidden current to their words and actions and Maleonarial hesitated, tempted. They were alone. Every master still alive had left their name in Affarealyon's care; Nedsom would have been her selection, trained by her to be Alden's hold lord. No one could know the school or the twisted nature of its masters better.

No one feared magic more, or for better reason. Alden insulated itself from the mistakes of students by forbidding intentions, purposeful or otherwise, be written within its walls. No sons of Alden received Her Gift and even Her Blessed Gossamers stayed outside, in what masters suspected was a rare bargain with The Deathless Goddess. Not that any Alden's hold daughter admitted such.

"Only that I've lived alone too long to be easy in company. Accept my apologies." With a deeper bow, he turned and strode away before they could stop him again.

No more free to debate his purpose in this moment than all those years, and bells, ago.

⁂

A hold run like a village, free of segregated courts and courtiers with pretentious beards. A daughter from Woodshaven should approve.

A hold that offered well-practiced condolences over wine warmed with costly foreign spice. A name taken to be hung in their audience hall as if decorating Alden Hold healed a village lost a son. A hold grown rich on the magic mages spent their lives to create.

Kait Alder most adamantly did not approve a whit, but the face she showed those offering words and drink, and the scribe carefully copying letters, was composed and pleasant.

Not fooled, Leksand kept giving her worried little looks.

"When do we speak with the hold daughter?" she asked when the scribe finished, packing away her pens and parchment.

"Only the student-prospect—"

Kait raised an eyebrow. The acolyte closed her lips and nodded. "Affarealyon awaits you."

They were escorted to a plain chamber and left, the acolyte closing the door behind them. There was a narrow table along one wall, a tray with an ewer of wine and cups centered on it. Beyond, another table with a basin, jug, and a tidy pile of towels.

Beyond that, the door to outside, closed.

They were alone but for the hold daughter. She stood by an open window, running a fingertip along the gap between bricks as if the aging of mortar held her fascinated.

How old she was, Kait couldn't guess and didn't much care. "I'm going to the school with my son."

Affarealyon didn't look around. "A daughter may go where she chooses."

Good. Had a message from Tiler's reached this far? Had Alden's Daughter's Portion been warned of the Fell?

Before Kait could decide, with Leksand present, how best to broach the subject of evil within the mortar of walls, her son spoke. "What of me, Hold Daughter? Am I to go to the school?"

"That depends." She faced them, a presence solid as brick and as immutable. "Tell me, Leksand Loggerson, of your first morning."

"I don't understand."

Her frown matched Kait's, who turned to her son. "The morning you woke and felt Her Gift, Leksand." It arrived thus for them all, daughter or mage: a dream as though the world fell away and you rose within the sky, gathered in gentle hands; the opening of eyes to find you weren't the same and would never again be alone.

A mother knew that lip, taken between teeth. The whitening of fingers around the precious box. The effort to stand tall while not offering defiance. "Laddie? What ha' ye done?"

He gave her a wide-eyed look. "I meant no harm, Momma. I wanted to serve, as you do. She said I could."

Alden's hold daughter surged closer. "Who said?" Affarealyon demanded. "What is all this?" directed at her. "His Gift is real."

"Aie," Kait nodded, eyes on Leksand. "Tell us."

"I took a sock, a clean one, and tucked it in the old pine tree—the one where The Lady puts yours on washday. I stood underneath and prayed to Her. I promised to serve with all my heart if She picked me. To do my best to help you. That you'd be so proud." His voice trailed away as he looked from one of them to the other, seeing their incredulity. Leksand flushed. "It's the truth. The woman of the woods came and gave me her hand. When she touched me, that's when I first felt Her Gift." His face filled with wonder. "I had to come to you, right away. I knew She'd answered my prayer, that I could serve—"

"Mages don't serve The Lady, child," Affarealyon snapped. "They take from Her and pay the price." She glared at Kait. "Who is this 'woman of the woods'?"

"A legend." Kait fought to keep her voice steady. "The loggers speak of a mysterious woman who sometimes appears in the depths of the forest. She doesn't speak, but her presence is a warning of a branch overhead about to fall, or of a gossamer in a tree they thought to cut. They don't claim she's The Lady."

"They believe it, as does your son." With scorn. "Is this what you teach where you come from, Daughter? Such dangerous, foolish lies?"

Where they came from, evil didn't ooze from stone. It didn't seal itself in jars or utter commands through the mouths of lord or bird.

Lies . . .

Blood pounded in Kait's ears, every thought darker than the one before, as if she tumbled into a well and watched the light recede beyond reach.

Had The Lady taken her sweet son for no greater purpose than to ensure she, Kaitealyon and willing Designate, would go with Insom's caravan? So she would discover the Fell? Be in place to thwart their plan for the school, whatever that was?

Was that why the Fell paid attention to Leksand? Did they sense that in him Her Gift was a ploy?

Was this why she no longer heard Her Voice?

Could a goddess feel shame?

"Well?"

A shadow crossed Leksand's face. Kait shot him a warning look, then turned her attention to her counterpart. "Before you make accusations, Affarealyon, know that Leksand's father possessed Her Gift too."

"You're far from the only daughter to lie with a mage." A dismissive flick of fingers. "It makes no difference."

It made every difference. Had Rogeonarial been her decision—or Hers? How far must she fall? The well was walled in slime-covered stone. From every crack spewed doubt—

"Momma. Kaitealyon!"

"What's wrong with her?"

From below, a fume reached up for her, to seize her and pull her down—

"I don't know. Momma, please!"

Anguish, in her son's voice. Pain. They shouldn't be there, not in her son, and Kait began to struggle. She flailed with what weren't arms, called with what wasn't a voice. In Her Words. "ᏕᏮᏗᎤᎷᎷᏕᎤᏒᎤᏕᏮᎷᎾ"

Their shape scalded her mouth and tongue, but this pain was real and good. It burned out the fume and brought light.

*Tananen is in danger. Defend Me!*

It felt like a mother's cry.

No, she was crying. Great wracking sobs blinded and choked her, even as arms held her, eased her to sit, even as hands dried her face and warmed her fingers with their own.

"Drink this, Daughter. Slowly." Kind, Affarealyon's voice. Shaken, that too, and Kait blinked her eyes clear. Opened her mouth and swallowed gingerly.

"I'm here," Leksand said and she realized his arm was about her shoulders, his hand holding hers. The box lay abandoned on the floor.

Alden's hold daughter knelt before her, cup in hand. "Forgive me. I presumed to know what none of us can. To know all the forms The Lady chooses. All the ways in which She acts. Today, from you both, I've learned the depths of my ignorance and am grateful, Kaitealyon, Leksand, truly, for that."

Kait twitched and Leksand freed her hands. She took the cup and swallowed again. Not wine but water, cold and real. When certain she could speak again—that she dared—she looked up at her son. "You serve The Lady. We all do." He'd saved her from the despairing depths the Fell had planted inside her and she no longer questioned why he was here.

Or what she must do. Kait sat up straight, offering a hand to Affarealyon, the other to her son.

"The Lady's enemy is called the Fell."

They left Alden Hold chased by heavy fat snowflakes, the sort that melted before touching the ground but found their way under scarf and hood. Spots of cold damp misery they were, the turn of autumn's chief mischief; more familiar to him now than riding this road.

Home, once.

To another Maleonarial.

Not that he didn't recognize the low hedges to either side of the road, clipped as much by roaming sheep as groundskeepers, and the glisten of Helly Pelly Creek to the east as it slipped past on its way to the marsh. Free of made-fish; perhaps, the school's grates weren't foolproof. The road he knew too, its surface of black fitted slate impressive to those who didn't have to deal with sleet or freezing rain. Or walk barefoot in summer. The roll of sedge-covered hills conjured memories of their fulsome carpet of yellow in spring, tiny blooms the joy of bees and butterflies, made or otherwise, and the way leaves gone crimson swept over the slopes like strokes of flame in autumn.

Brown now, and done. Even Alden's gossamers tucked themselves below ground once the cold came in earnest, though there were always those ready to pop up to surprise passersby.

Except between the hedges, on the road of slate—

—usually. There were, with gossamers, no guarantees.

Most familiar of all, the heady lure of those with Her Gift, for nowhere else in Tananen were so many in one place. It mattered not if some were mad and others inept, most selfish and precious few kind; only what The Hag had slipped into each of them in their dreams, without consent or recourse. Magic.

Harn sighed. "Feels good, doesn't it, sir. To be nearing home."

What could he say to that? Maleonarial settled for a grunt. Though it gave him a question for Kait Alder. Did those of the Daughter's Portion take comfort in living together for the same reason mage scribes, no matter how wealthy and successful, found their way back to the school before the end?

Even he wasn't immune, drawn like a hapless fish upstream—

"Look! The Rabbits, sir," Harn exclaimed with relief. "Praise The Goddess, we're almost there."

Ancient pedestals tilted from the hedges, one to either side, tall as a man on horseback, which Maleonarial was not, having elected to ride with Harn and drive the team pulling the second wagon. Atop the leftmost perched an eroded stone statue that might resemble a rabbit with its nose to the ground and tail up. Or a gourd. Its partner on the right could be taken for a rabbit standing on hind legs, ears down its back, or an owl. They were older than hedges or road, and were rumored to date from the very first mage school. They'd escaped whatever destroyed the ones since.

Owl, gourd, or shapeless lumps of rock, students had always called them rabbits, so The Rabbits they were, with eyes, or dimples where eyes should be, aimed as if watching uphill.

The important thing about The Rabbits was they marked the boundary past which students were forbidden to do magic. Unless you were coming from Alden, as they were, meaning The Rabbits marked the boundary past which magic was encouraged and taught. Not hard to know what Harn was thinking.

"Almost," Maleonarial cautioned, "isn't close enough, Harn. You'll wait until in the care of a master. Harn!" When the student didn't answer at once.

"But mightn't I—"

"No. You've waited this long," the mage added more kindly. "You'll last."

Harn slumped in the seat, useless wrist cradled in his other arm, his solitary bell caught in a ringlet. "If you say so, sir."

They followed Tiler's fancy carriage, driven by Domozuk, which followed Saeleonarial, that wagon driven by Rid. He'd have preferred to keep Harn as far from the urns as possible, but there was no other order that wouldn't raise more questions than they wanted to answer.

Maleonarial gave his head a small shake, listened to the restless bells. A good bet those waiting ahead would take one look at him and forget the wagon he'd brought. As for the rest? Questions remained.

"When we get to the school, Harn, the masters will ask you about Riverhill and what happened to Saeleonarial."

"Me, sir?"

How best to caution without alarm? "They'll ask us all, and I want you to do as we will. Answer honestly, with what you yourself witnessed. The damesen's cargo—whatever you might have heard on the barge—is none of our business. Speak of it to no one. She will deal with it when ready. Is that clear?"

Sweat beaded Harn's forehead, sticking down his usually tousled hair. His eyes were dull and desperate, but he nodded dutifully. "Yes, Master Maleonarial."

"Good lad."

As to how they'd deal with her cargo? He stared out at the road, seeing the urns with their glittering mechanical tops. Kait and her son had come last from their meeting with Affarealyon. He'd hoped the daughters would confer, but seeing their wan faces, how tightly Kait held Leksand's arm? If they had, the result hadn't been good.

A relief to learn Master Pageonarial remained at the school. Of them all, the historian might have the answer.

If his failing mind remembered where he'd left it.

"One problem at a time, Harn," Maleonarial declared.

A mumbled, "Yes, sir."

Insom's caravan, so grand and bold leaving Tiler's Hold, guards clattering alongside, halted to let sheep cross the road. Pylor and the others took the moment to open the carriage windows for a glimpse of the famed mage school.

She blinked, wondering if they'd taken a wrong road. Enclosed by low, bare hills dotted with sheep, the few connected structures, none over three storeys tall, seemed at best to comprise a tidy little village. At its center, like any village, was a pond set amid a grassy commons, splitting the road around it. The buildings themselves were gray stone, as were the plentiful chimneys, while their gabled roofs were tiled in red. Those not covered in moss.

Such an ordinary place, home to Tananen's greatest—and most expensive—magic users, where legends were made and debts collected?

A low gated stone fence, also moss coated, surrounded the school, presumably to keep sheep from the vegetables for it had no conceivable value in defense or status.

To be fair, the red-tiled rooftops with their hint of snow frosting made a pretty sight, and the abundance of windowed dormers thrust to their edge promised bright airy rooms. The doors were inset and of carved wood, framed by mature plantings. Sturdy. Comfortable.

Row houses, the first line anyway. Residences for the students or masters? Past those rose something taller, at an angle, but she couldn't make out much more. Pylor slipped over to Tercle's side to see. So encouraged, Kait and Leksand, hitherto silent, switched places. The first building here, though again of stone and tile, appeared to be a barn, or livery. There was a larger building past it—

Something flew in the open window and brushed by her hair. Pylor threw up her hands to fend it off.

It wasn't the cursed gull. Tercle reached out a finger, and a tiny made-bird settled on it, sleek jewel-bright feathers catching the light. Its long bill opened, releasing bubbles that floated through the air. As they watched in fascination, a young voice began to speak. "Welcome to the school. Be aware students may be creating at any time. Should anything appear that poses a hazard to belongings or person, take shelter at once. The school assumes no responsibility. Please proceed directly to the main hall."

The bill closed, wings moved in a blur, and the messenger zipped out of the carriage, stirring the bubbles so one drifted into Leksand's nose. He went cross-eyed trying to see it, then it popped. "Oh."

"Welcome indeed," said Kait with wondering smile. "Did you notice the sheep?"

Pylor frowned and looked out again. The last of the flock was moving off the road.

Did you call it a flock when the creatures in it walked on twigs, not legs, and had bodies like the fluff from a seed pod?

The carriage rumbled through the open gate, students with crooks standing guard to either side against the perils of wandering fluff. As they passed, Pylor noticed a metal grate where a large culvert released the stream's flow beneath the stone fence. A grate with back-pointed spines and a lock the size of her head.

The wagon with its secret and perilous cargo came last. By arrangement or some signal from Maleonarial, a student waved it onto a side road by the barn. After watching it disappear behind the building, Pylor dropped her gaze to her fingers, unsurprised to find them clenched on her cane.

Would it be safe?

Would any of them?

When she looked up, Kait was regarding her. By the lip between her teeth, the daughter had the same doubts.

Pylor gave a little shrug. They were committed to Maleonarial's plan, that said, such as it was. Stay the course, hide the urns, hope for answers before the Fell made their move. Pretend they hadn't brought evil here, at evil's behest.

Kait nodded and looked outside.

The wagon with Saeleonarial went ahead, white made-horses prancing, and their carriage trailed it through the school commons. Add the students in their brown robes, scurrying about like disturbed ants, and the occasional master in blue—those not moving quickly at all—and Pylor found herself charmed.

A reaction she distrusted. It was her nature to appreciate scholarship for its own sake. Nothing so innocent happened here.

The row houses lined one side of the road, the long oval pond to the other, and Pylor frowned, noticing the pond was bordered by massive stones and another grate guarded its outflow. Why?

In the middle of the pond was a normal-looking island with a straggly tree and some shrubs. A rowboat laid pulled on its shore and there were what she took for ducks sleeping nearby. There were also pillars sticking up from the water which didn't look normal at all, having thick chains depending from them as if they secured something unseen below. As they passed, she saw a brown-robed student sitting cross-legged on a floating platform, his attention on a board across his lap. A pen glinted in his hand.

Pylor looked away. She wasn't ready to watch magic practiced. Not like that.

Across the pond were larger buildings, a set of three with a shared roof, but she'd no time to inspect them more closely, for the carriage drove beneath a roof of its own, to stop before what weren't doors.

A student opened the carriage door and dropped the stairs. Pylor rose, cane in hand, and allowed herself to be impressed as she stepped down.

The mage who'd written this had created a made-swan two storeys-high whose brilliant white wings cloaked entrances on either side of its torturously up-stretched body. The head was magnificent, with liquid black eyes and a noble beak, dipping on its long neck to regard her. Perhaps part of its role was to scrutinize visitors.

Case under one arm, Tercle hurried ahead. "This is the Damesen Pylor Ternfeather of Tiler's—"

"Welcome." A head popped out between flight feathers like a cygnet's, only this was a mage, his silvered hair sparkling with bells. He smiled toothlessly at Pylor and Tercle, then sneezed and disappeared. "Come out of the chill. Come come."

With that repetition, the wings folded up and away in invitation.

Pylor understood Tercle's frown. No guards, no defenses. No one checking she was who her apprentice claimed nor questions why she'd come. Did the school rely on the value of those it taught for protection? If so, as well unlock the coffers of Tiler's Hold and rely on the gold to object to theft.

Unless the masters relied on The Deathless Goddess. Everyone knew She tolerated no harm to those who used Her magic.

Pylor walked inside, feeling a breeze from behind as the made-swan lowered her wings, and wondered if what everyone knew could be wrong.

Wendealyon had threatened the drastic measure. Affarealyon had taken it. Every gate, every door and window, was shut and secured behind them. Nothing and no one of Tiler's Hold or the mage school would be allowed to pass in or out until the daughter from Woodshaven assured Alden's the threat of the Fell was over. If that assurance didn't arrive soon?

Kait drew her cloak tighter, hardly able to believe Affarealyon's shocking ultimatum, that Alden could and would destroy the school and the Fell with it. Such pronouncements were The Lady's to make, not those who served. Weren't they?

If not, how many times had the mage school come to grief in generations past not by accident or greedy hold lord, but because an Alden hold daughter lost trust?

What sort of hold daughter could ignore the pull of Her Gift many times over, as she felt here, in order to destroy it? Or was Her Gift concentrated here, in one place, so a hold daughter could?

Maleonarial. Did he know? He'd been scribemaster; she supposed he must.

Timber and water rights. Whose turn to bake for the innkeeper. Missing socks and snow-draped mountains. Had that ever been her life?

Leksand sat by her side, silent and still since leaving Alden. He'd feel the draw of those in the school too, yet hadn't remarked on it. He missed Ferden, but this was a different quiet. He mulled over what she'd told him and Affarealyon, what they'd decided. Who, as she did, should know. A burden on still-growing shoulders, but he was a thinker, her son; much as she'd prefer to protect him, ignorance wouldn't.

Besides, who was she to argue with the woman of the woods?

Leksand had received Her Gift. *Tananen is in danger. Defend me!* Her throat still burned, but surely there was comfort to be had. If The Lady spent her son to bring Kait here, it must mean the Fell could be defeated and they were part of how.

Unless, as the damesen feared, they were doing evil's bidding, The Lady helpless. In which case, Kait thought grimly, let Affarealyon do her worst.

In one way, she had. The hold daughter's parting words disturbed her and contributed, she knew, to Leksand's quiet. *"You don't know what they do up there. You think they teach magic. What they really do is to keep desperate lads from wasting their lives. Stop them filling the world with useless things, dangerous things. That's the purpose of the school."*

A tactful knock. Domozuk, suggesting they not tarry.

Kait leaned over to plant a solid smack of a kiss on Leksand's cheek, smiling at his feigned grimace. "Kind a'ye t'let y'mom h'r mush'n," she teased, heart-heavy.

"Always." He cupped her face in his hands, brown eyes searching as if to memorize it. He pressed his lips to her forehead, staying close to murmur, "You'll always be m'Mom."

Then there was nothing for it but to step outside.

Domozuk waited by the front wheel. Worn to the bone, he looked, as well as troubled, and Kait shook her head in denial when he would have climbed to retrieve their belongings. "Let younger legs do it."

"My pleasure, Dom." Giving her his box to hold, Leksand clambered up with a will.

"Good lad," Domozuk said awkwardly.

"Aie." Kait found a smile.

"Kait, I've—" He hesitated, looked around as if to see they were alone, then went on in a rush. "I need you to take care of my master. His funeral." Grief deepened the lines of his face.

"Won't you be there?" She read the answer in his eyes. "You aren't welcome. Dom, that's not right."

"I've other duties," with an accepting shrug. "Besides, they'll listen to a daughter. More than they'll mind Maleonarial, matters as they are."

Kait doubted her sway over master mages was as profound as the man believed, especially newly arrived and dusty from the road, but nodded. "I'll do m'best. What do you want me to do? Say?"

"If you could make sure they don't rush—that they give the scribe-master his due respect, I'd be grateful."

Kait nodded. She glanced at the giant white feathers draped over the doors, daunted by what might lie beyond. "How do we—are we to pluck them?" she asked dubiously.

Domozuk's expression eased. "Daisy'll let you in. She's more pet than—" His eyes widened at something he saw behind her. "Usually."

"Momma?"

Kait whirled to find the made-swan's vast black and gleaming beak moving toward Leksand, atop the carriage. Before she could blink, the beak changed direction, a ponderous yet graceful movement that brought one great black eye to bear.

Her son put down the bags in his hands, then reached out to press fingers into the white down of the door's guardian. Kait held her breath.

"Blessed Goddess. I've not seen her do that before," Dom whispered.

The impossible neck curved, withdrawing the eye and beak. Leksand picked up the bags, face split with a grin.

With a motion that sent air swirling around them, the head lowered to regard the daughter from Woodshaven.

Kait could see herself reflected in the gleaming depths of the eye; watched astonishment, then awe fill her face. Hard to remember this was a made-bird, created to serve a purpose. It—Daisy—appeared curious. Might some creations exceed the intention of the mage?

Or a mage intend what almost lived. "You're Maleonarial's," she told it, somehow certain.

The guardian laid its great head at her feet, wings rising to open the doors.

If Maleonarial had thought to delay recognition by driving the freight wagon to the rear of the kitchen, he should have remembered what lived there.

Stone-like lumps clung to the walls, most under eaves and windowsills. Round beady eyes shot open as the wagon passed beneath, then each lump began to shake vigorously, producing a loud chorus that sounded exactly like the ringing of mage bells.

Made-toads, they were; a practical student project to reduce the number of flies and other bothersome summer visitors entering windows left ajar at night, and they weren't supposed to ring like bells. Nor were they supposed to ring a warning of the imminent arrival of a master mage.

Needless to say, the more talented students, including a young Maleonarial, found adding those features irresistible.

More on the wall than he remembered, implying an exceptional class this year. The poor masters. These made-toads would expire in the cold to come, making it easier for the masters to move around without being "rung."

Today, however, he was and thoroughly. Students working at the fish ponds looked up. A window above the dining hall was thrown open so someone could look down. By the time they reached the kitchen, its back doors stood wide, staff waiting on the stoop, and he might as well have asked for trumpets.

Harn choked on a giggle.

"Dom and Rid will be here shortly," Maleonarial reminded the student. "Let's get this out of the way."

With a polite nod to the kitchen staff, he sent the team past the buildings, the midden, and pools to the beaten circle where wagons bringing deliveries turned around. The circle was surrounded by a hedgerow wilder than most; no one cared for appearances here. Maleonarial backed the team until he heard the snap and crack of the wagon meeting the hedge and the rubble at its base. He set the brake and tidied the reins. "There."

Harn craned around. "Sir? Shouldn't we move up?"

"No." Maleonarial jumped down to take a look. The wagon was well and truly stuck in the hedge, branches smothering the tailgate and canvas flaps, a wheel lodged between rocks for good measure. What snow had been in the shrubbery made clumps on the ground. "This'll do."

Maybe not to keep in the Fell, should their urns be opened, but idle students? He couldn't see one forcing a path through the hedge just to snoop.

Harn climbed down one-handed. He staggered before catching his balance, and it would have been a kindness to send him to his room to rest, if not for the reception Maleonarial knew was waiting. "Not much longer," he said instead.

The six made-horses, mud splattered up their perfect legs, stood waiting, their patience endless; they'd not exist much longer. He cast an anxious eye on the road, hoping Dom and Rid weren't delayed. Lord Nedsom would have sent word ahead. There'd be a gathering underway in the main hall, more precisely a table of what the cooks had ready along with pots of the ubiquitous tea, but the combination should draw a sufficient number of masters and students to supply Saeleonarial's corpse with a worthy greeting.

A funeral was nothing unusual here. Masters wrote their final intention, to wither and die of it, and the only hope left was they'd do so where their remains wouldn't rot before being found. The school had a wheeled trolley covered in cloth ready to go, and go it would: out the rear door of the hall to the tidy little crematorium set into a hill—it being less than politic to leave corpses about to remind living masters of their fate, and efficient to use made-salamanders to burn bodies to ash.

Unless there was some grieving to be done. For Sael, there might be. Should be. He'd insist—

"Sir? Here they come."

Dom and Rid brought their conveyances in line with his, though clear of the hedge. To forestall comment on his driving skills, or lack thereof, the mage gathered the three of them and pointed to the kitchen. "Make sure Harn's fed and his arm tended. And your cut, Dom. Stay with staff, you too, Harn, till I'm back."

None of them moved. "You're not going to meet the masters like that, sir," Domozuk said stolidly. "Rid?"

Rid reached up and behind the driver's seat of his wagon, producing a roll of blue fabric. "'Er y'go, sir."

A master's blue tunic and pants, complete with warm cloak. Maleonarial stood speechless as Domozuk and Harn stripped him of his borrowed rags with practiced speed, right there between wagon and carriage, only moving when he could help don the new, clean clothing. "Now these," Dom ordered, producing a pair of polished boots as if a mage himself.

Once those were on, the three regarded him critically. Maleonarial wondered with some amusement when he'd entered their care, instead of the other way around. Dom nodded brusquely. "Loose the braids. There's no hiding your bells, sir."

Quick as that, hair, and bells, flowed over his shoulders and back.

Harn's eyes shone. Maleonarial frowned at him. "What?"

"Pretty as 'm nags," Rid declared, spitting cheerfully. "Now g'on."

Dom put a hand on Maleonarial's shoulder, gripping tight. "Say good-bye for us."

And a mage with more bells than ever before, younger than any master could be, a mage who'd left friendship and duty behind?

Found he'd no choice but to bow before both.

The swan doors had promised splendor. Inside? Trestle tables and well-worn benches had been stacked to the side, suspiciously bright and un-soiled carpets laid over floors past due for polish, and the main hall of the mage school prepared for an event. It was unclear what event the organizers had in mind, though possibly this was how they prepared for any gathering at all. Certainly the long table set in the center of the room, loaded with platters of meat pies and an uncut wheel of cheese, had a rugged, impromptu air about it.

Which, Damesen Ternfeather thought, begged several questions about the supposedly luxurious lifestyle of a master mage scribe. From what she'd seen so far, they lived hardly better than their students. Here, at least.

Students thronged around the food, loading their trenchers. Each had a metal cup hanging from thumb or finger, and a spoon tucked in their belt. More were coming down the staircase at the back of the hall and through doors to either side, and masters were part of the flood, as eager to eat as their charges.

"Is this a funeral or supper?" Tercle muttered.

The sole indication of the former was the long wheeled trolley, draped in blue, left before a cold fireplace. The drapery rose at toe and gut, a mannerless reminder what—who—rested beneath.

They knew Saeleonarial's body was there. Masters and students alike assiduously avoided that side of the hall, crowding elbow-to-elbow. None looked toward it.

Nor at them. The silver-haired master who'd welcomed them had joined those seeking food.

"They'll settle soon." The aproned woman had a giant teapot in her gloved hands and a cheerful face. "Most forget to eat, you see. Don't know they're starving until we remind them." This with a wicked little wink.

"How?" Tercle asked.

"We hide their pens." She hefted the teapot. "Have some tea and make yourselves comfortable. Might take them a while to notice you." Another wink. "They forget we're here too. Those of us without magic," she clarified, then went on her way.

Pylor and Tercle looked at one another. "I've had enough sitting," the latter hinted, tipping her head to the staircase. "We could explore, Py. Maybe find the inkmaster's rooms. Doesn't seem anyone would mind."

It didn't, but Pylor felt uneasy. "Go if you wish. I'm staying." She looked toward the trolley with its lonely inhabitant.

Tercle sighed, but nodded.

There were chairs against the wall by the fireplace, dusty as if rarely used, and they sat, alone despite the crowded room. Her friend touched her arm, nodding upward. "See the lights?"

She had not, the late afternoon sunshine slanting through large windows. She looked up, immediately puzzled, for there were no fixtures or lamps as such, only ugly balls of wire. In each was a bright spot and she squinted, trying to discern the source.

"Wait. Here's one." Tercle got up and reached under another chair, producing a hand-size silver ball. She quickly passed it from hand to hand. "It's hot."

Pylor took off her scarf, and they rested the ball on its folds. Though dented from its fall from the ceiling, there was no mistaking it was a cage. Inside was a large moth with a fat body and small wings, curled as if dead.

Tercle poked the cage.

Wings beat frantically and the body became flame, scorching the fabric and sending up smoke. Snatching up scarf and cage, Tercle tossed the mass into the fireplace. The two stood staring at where it burned white hot, safe in the hearth, but the walls were paneled with wood, beams supported the floor above, and every scrap inside, from chair leg to clothing, might have ignited.

What was wrong with oil lamps?

"Just as well I stayed, Py," Tercle said finally. "Goddess knows what else might be roaming around."

A thought to chill the bones. Where did the school keep those made-beasts that didn't conveniently turn to ash? Chains in the pond, cages, fences of stone and metal grates. Precautions implying such weren't always harmless, that the students deliberately or by mistake made dangerous things.

Insom had worried about deadly gossamers. About some new magic. What was here all along, she decided, was bad enough.

It explained Alden's prohibition on magic, the school's reluctance to host visitors, and Tercle was right. They'd not explore, not without a guide. Otherwise, Pylor couldn't see how the knowledge helped, unless those dangerous things could be used against the Fell and not simply feed them.

They needed help. Had come for it, but what help was there in masters and students who must be forced to remember to eat? Two in blue robes argued over a trencher, neither letting go, so food spilled around them. Another stood staring at a wall, as if he'd already forgotten why he was there. A student came up and tried, gently, to put a spoon in his hand.

These were Maleonarial's source of knowledge?

The swan wings parted again, admitting chill air and new arrivals.

Everything stopped. Trenchers slipped through fingers. Spoons and mugs clattered to the floor, servants throwing up their hands in dismay.

Every head, every eye, locked on the pair who'd entered. Proving the tea server's point. The only ones noticed here were those with magic.

Kait Alder took in the scene—and mess—with one scathing glance, then turned her back to the masters and students, walking directly to the wrapped form of Saeleonarial.

Her son followed, though he glanced twice over his shoulder at the mages as if drawn, and Pylor's mind filled with questions for which she'd no answers, about The Deathless Goddess and those she picked—and those she didn't.

Questions of no import now. She stood to greet Kait, waving to a nearby padded bench.

Kait didn't sit. "This is their idea of a proper funeral?" Pitched to be heard through the hall. "You allowed this?" As if a damesen had authority here.

Tercle's grin wasn't friendly. "They don't see us. They see you."

"Her Gift," Leksand replied in a quiet, miserable voice. "That's what they see."

Those he'd come to live with and learn from were setting a poor standard. Pylor wasn't inclined to sympathy.

"No. That's their excuse." Kait spun around, fists on hips. "All of you. Clean this up and be ready to honor your scribemaster."

She should seem ridiculous, a small daughter from a smaller village, but wasn't. Seem powerless, but then Kait from Woodshaven uttered incomprehensible Words. Windows rattled. Furnishings shook. The trolley rolled and Tercle grabbed for it, because Leksand—all the masters and students—were bent double, hands over their ears.

Nothing would keep them from hearing. Whatever she said insisted on it.

When the Words stopped, the world held its breath, then a student vomited and another sat abruptly on the floor.

"Well done, Kaitealyon," said the tall master in blue, stepping through a door by the fireplace where Pylor could have sworn there hadn't been one. Hundreds of bells sang in his now flowing hair, a sound in its way as profound and terrifying as the Words.

The master who'd been staring at the wall blinked and beamed and came back to life.

"Maleonarial!"

The language of The Deathless Goddess was not to be used lightly, for uttered aloud it seared the throat and shook those who heard. Instead, it must be memorized, letter by strange letter. Written with intention by those with Her Gift. Only thus were Her Words released safely into the world of mere flesh and bone.

The daughter from Woodshaven didn't appear unduly worried or in outward anguish. He couldn't deny the result was laudable. Mages might not understand Her Words when spoken, but Kait—Kaitealyon— had used them with undeniable intent. Masters and students busied themselves retrieving utensils and cups, moved before their astonished staff to scrape the worse messes from the floor. If he hadn't seen it with his own eyes, he'd never have believed it.

Two weren't so occupied. Xareonarial, face suffused with resentment, paced on the other side of the table, eyes locked on Kait.

The other hurried toward him as quickly as he could and Maleonarial closed the distance between them with long strides, ignoring the would-be scribemaster and the rest as their hands met. No more than fifty, Pageonarial, in years. Thanks to The Hag, he appeared twice that, wizened and so frail Maleonarial might have gripped a flower. His friend and mentor.

Their hope.

He'd take him aside, give him what little they knew. Help him to the archives. "Pageonarial. We must speak."

"Look at you," the aged master crowed softly, eyes shining. "Look at you."

More and more were. "We need your scholarship, my friend," Maleonarial said quickly but quietly. "We face an unknown threat—"

"Look at you. Look at you." A gnarled hand reached toward his hair, the bells. Dropped short, limp as if the effort were too much. The shine in the eyes receded, their focus lost. "Look . . ."

Maleonarial felt his heart sink in his chest. "Page—"

"Don't waste your time." Xareonarial beckoned and two students came rushing up. "Return Master Pageonarial to his room. Bolt the door this time." He grimaced once they'd walked away a few steps. "Mind's so addled he's forgotten how to use a pen."

"Inconvenient," Maleonarial said, knowing the other would nod and believe he felt the same, that the least Pageonarial, once one of the best of them, could do was write a last intention and rid them of his care.

"But you, Master Maleonarial, are worthy of a great deal of time and interest." Cold eyes considered him, from boot to bells. "Tell me. Why are you back? Why like this?"

Greed. He could almost smell it on Xareonarial's breath and it wouldn't be long before they were all at him, desperate to restore their own youth. Not one would have believed he'd left in the first place to try and save them from The Hag. That he planned to do it, would do it, no matter how unworthy a master like Xareonarial might be.

Having first dealt with the Fell. Was The Hag as perplexed as he felt, constrained to defeat Her enemy before returning to Her destruction?

Darker thought, had She arranged for Kait Alder to be who she was, a daughter able to convince him the Fell were the immediate threat?

He could turn himself inside out trying to decipher the mind of a goddess. The Fell had invaded Tananen by sea. Taken control of a hold lord. Wished death and destruction to all. If he had to take the word of a stranger those things were the truth, he'd take Kait's without second thought.

After all, hadn't she made masters and students tidy up?

"Why am I back, Xar?" Though the master before him was the least likely to care, he'd promised Nim and it was a start. "To warn the school of the existence of gossamers able to take life." To swim in blood and gore, crush a village to tinder, all the while gazing placidly from glorious topaz eyes. "But first, to honor Saeleonarial."

A smooth bow. An artfully stricken face. "Such a shock. A loss to us all. I will strive to do my best in his place."

A young man's impulse, to curl fingers into fist and contemplate the satisfaction of bloodying a nose. "You aren't scribemaster yet," he said instead.

"Good, you're here." Kait glanced up at Xareonarial, the remnants of Words swimming in her eyes like chips of ancient ice, and Maleonarial caught his breath, trapped by a question whose shape—

The master took a prudent step back and bowed. "Daughter."

Leksand, no longer smiling, stood at her shoulder. "Harn's come."

"Are you ready to begin? Maleonarial?" Kait asked gently.

—faded from thought. "I'm ready," he told her.

*Tidy your mess. Show respect.* She'd used Her Words to scold a roomful of mage scribes as if they were a bunch of drunken loggers causing a ruckus. The loggers she knew by name and family, Kait thought wildly, men and women rightfully abashed—later the next morning—to have misbehaved.

She'd yet to have names for any here but Maleonarial. Who now wore master blue, had decent boots, and proved by his means of arrival an intimate knowledge of this place. Most likely he knew all their names. She'd ask, later.

Anger was no excuse, not even if most of it had been seeing Leksand's dismay at the spectacle greeting them, when they'd expected a solemn funeral.

Which they'd have, by The Lady, or she'd pin back their ears again.

Not, Kait decided, wincing as she swallowed, that she'd invoke Her Words. Though to be honest, she hadn't expected them to react as they had, to obey as if they'd understood.

Something else to ask. Or not.

Something of obedience lingered, or their startlement at Maleonarial's appearance did the trick, for in short order he had everyone standing in respectful silence before Saeleonarial's body. Dom would be gratified.

Mostly silent. Kait noticed a trio of students gawking at Leksand—or was it the bedraggled Harn, standing with her son, who had them whispering to each other? Harn, she decided, and what they whispered wasn't kind. A mother learned the signs. Kait stared back at them until one noticed her attention. When she raised an eyebrow, he paled, nudging the others. They fell silent.

Good.

The master who'd spoken to Maleonarial kept looking at Leksand. His regard reminded her of the cunning fox who'd gone after their hens until meeting Ferden's axe. Lacking an axe, Kait nodded congenially at him, before going to stand with the damesen and Tercle.

To hear Maleonarial say good-bye to his friend.

"Sael came to us as Sael Fisherson . . ."

Pylor'd thought the Fell terrifying, until Kait Alder spouted gibberish and the world danced in answer.

". . . leaves with a brother here, good Braneonarial, but Sael treated all as family . . ."

She'd believed The Lady had chosen a humble, unimpressive vessel for Her Designate, until sixty or so mage scribes, from master to student, jumped to obey.

". . . as Saeleonarial, represented the school to the rest of Tananen with grace and compassion. Those beyond these walls grieve his loss with us . . . ."

They'd had no choice. Resentment and fear filled in their eyes when they risked a glance at the daughter and she sympathized. Who was Kait? What was she?

". . . went to Riverhill to help those without magic, who were being attacked with it. Saeleonarial gave the last of his life to The Deathless Goddess not for profit, but so She could end this tragedy. Hear the name of Her Designate, Her Witness. Leorealyon of Tiler's Hold. Honor her sacrifice."

Pylor risked her own glance. Tears slipped down Kait's face, leaving tracks in the dust on her round cheeks, and no longer questioning why or what, Pylor reached for her hand, feeling hers taken in a warm, calloused grip.

The trolley, with its fancy wheels and blue drape, with its lost friend and scribemaster and family, was rolled from the hall by Braneonarial, who cursed any who offered to help like the fisher he'd been born. Like his brother, he wore a belled wig, having lost his hair too since he'd arrived and Maleonarial left. Lost hair, and gained a belly. There were spots on the backs of his hands.

He'd been fifteen, twelve years ago. To look at Bran now, he appeared older than the damesen. Was older, the mage reminded himself. Hadn't he lived the truth of The Hag's toll?

Harn stayed with Leksand, who remained beside his mother. Kait, with Pylor and Tercle, sat by the fire, nursing cups of tea. The rest of the students slipped away, seeing their masters preoccupied.

Preoccupied? Maleonarial found himself the eye of a storm. The masters—the nine who remained, for two more had been "sent to their rooms" after Pageonarial, and the remaining pair had never left confinement—shed their awe of him and wanted answers. Wanted a great number of things, from their bellowing, including to be rid of a daughter from their midst, and weren't slow to object to the very notion of anyone not with Her Gift staying the night.

Not, he noted, that any volunteered to write the intention to make it possible for the damesen, Tercle, and Kait to return to Alden for the night, the latter hopefully not to return.

Teacups rose and lowered with studied calm, the individuals in question leaving him to sort this out; fair, though he'd begun to think fondly of resuming life as a hermit.

As for the student-prospect? To no surprise it was Xareonarial who broached the subject, arguing a boy whose Gift was potent enough to distract must sign his former name promptly and be admitted to the school—once his mother left.

Which wasn't about to happen, Maleonarial pointed out when those swarming him stopped for breath. Their guests could house for the night with staff and tomorrow morning would have to do.

Tomorrow, because if this many overstressed mage scribes, presently deprived of pen and ink, saw what Leksand carried? One or more would lose the battle for self-preservation. They already had to worry about students set loose to write The Hag knew what. At minimum, firemoths to light their way—

And what of Harn—

He wasn't scribemaster.

Xareonarial drew breath for another round of argument. "But—"

"We've more important matters to discuss." Maleonarial took a fistful of hair and bells, shook it at them. "Unless you aren't interested?"

"We're interested," Braneonarial said grimly.

"Good." Catching the eye of a server wiping the table, Maleonarial beckoned him to approach. "Please escort our guests to the kitchen and ask the cook to take care of them. They'll be staying the night."

The man grinned. "Happy to, sir." Kait had made some friends today, if not among the masters. "And yourself, sir?"

A tactful question that covered another: did he plan to take back the scribemaster's quarters?

Maleonarial considered those who stood in expectant silence around him and what he had to say.

"I don't think I'll be sleeping."

⁂

The sun sank toward the hills behind the school, surrounded by in-bound cloud. Late afternoon, but the air already had an ugly chill that encouraged quick steps. Pylor stopped at the top of the little bridge, in no mood to be rushed off by weather or mage. "What's going on?" she demanded.

Kait tipped her head to the servant who stood waiting. "Eaple's kindly taking us to quarters. Domozuk will have your bags. We've ours." She lifted a small black valise. Leksand had his sack over one shoulder and the damned box under an arm.

Of course Kait knew the servant's name. Pylor tapped her cane. "What's the mage up to back there?"

"Who cares?" Tercle shivered, shifting from foot to foot. "C'mon, Py. It's been a long day. We could use a hot supper."

Of course they were ready to settle for the night, to eat and rest and sleep. Think themselves safe.

"Cook'll have one waiting," Harn promised.

"Don't you have a place to be?" Pylor snapped.

He hung his head, that ridiculous lone bell waving with his hair, and his, "Yes, Damesen," was more subdued than its ring.

"The rest of you go ahead," Kait said, as if she were in charge. "We'll be right behind."

Her son hesitated. His mother nodded meaningfully at Harn, as if the mood of a student mattered among all else. "G'on with ye."

Pylor waited impatiently for the four to enter the building on the other side of the pond, but before she could speak, Kait turned, her face shadowed. "Alden's closed her gates. Affarealyon won't open them till I send word the Fell are no longer a threat."

"I—" She collected herself. "Thank you."

The daughter gave a surprised little huff. "Why? It's hardly good news. None of us can leave till we're done, not even your friend."

"I know." Pylor let out a long breath. "But something's being done. Others know. I was afraid—" She stopped there.

"Aie." Soft, understanding. "As am I, Damesen. By The Lady, how can we not be? But for right now, the best we can do is rest. Make ourselves eat, to keep up our strength. The mage will come to us once he has any news."

Pylor looked toward the hall. "He's with his own now," she said, uneasy. "Can we still trust him?" When Kait didn't answer at once, she stared down at her. "Do you?"

The daughter nodded. "I've no doubt of Maleonarial. Only of whether he'll find any answers." She shook herself. "C'mon with ye," she finished briskly. "We're like t'catch our deaths out're." A wave to the black waters of the pond. "'Nd no tell'n what's swim'n."

As if in answer, there was a large splash.

Pylor found she could take quick steps after all.

The cook's name was Nelisti Barnswallow, her kitchen spotless, and whatever Eaples had told her of them made her snatch Kait up in a giant's hug. Her face mushed to an apron that, frankly, wasn't spotless, the daughter managed to squeak, "Thank you—"

"NARRR!" the cook exclaimed, thrusting her back. She rounded on the damesen who dropped hastily into the closest chair to avoid the same fate. A pleasant "Harrr!" came next, with a gap-toothed smile and wave of a spoon with a handle longer than Kait's arm.

"Supper's coming," Eaples interpreted.

A plank worktable, well-sanded, formed the center of the kitchen, pots, hams, and skinned fowl swaying above. Caged firemoths illuminated the back counter and sinks, where staff were busy washing dishes. Double doors led into the dining hall, presently dark, while a plainer open door showed the way to the larder.

The brick bread oven and immense fireplace were aglow, heating the room to summer. Like the others already here, Kait shed her cloak as she joined them at one of three smaller tables.

Leksand leaned forward conspiratorially. "Harn warned me new students tell the cook their troubles, believing she can't tell the masters. He said she writes just fine."

At the furthest table, Dom and Rid sat with tankards of ale, deep in conversation with two others. Eaples dropped into the remaining seat, greeted warmly. Old friends, that said, and Kait was glad. She looked around. "Where's Harn?"

"You sent him off." Tercle scowled at the damesen. "That wasn't right, Py."

"I didn't mean—" The damesen's eyes were haunted.

By more than one regret, Kait knew, so she interceded, "The lad should be with his friends." Remembering the students she'd seen, she added, "In his own bed."

"He won't sleep. Harn needs to write magic. Has to." Leksand patted the box he'd set on the windowsill. "He wanted to use these so badly it hurt."

Her son, who'd known nothing of mages and their magic a day ago, looked older and serious, as if he'd learned his own future.

The damesen looked up. "I suggest you not judge the masters or school by what we've seen today." She managed a smile. "Other than Maleonarial."

Leksand's face brightened. "He was the best. Is the best, isn't he?"

"He's something," Tercle commented dryly, being innocent of the Fell and their hopes for the mage.

Would Pylor tell her tonight? Warn her? The two were close, Kait thought, meaning she should, unless it was a kindness not to add that burden—or Pylor knew Tercle wouldn't believe her.

Aie, Kait decided.

"Harrr." The cook set a long tray on their table. Kait's mouth watered at the loaf of steaming bread, the slices of fruit—though too late in the year for peaches and melon, so she had to assume magic was involved—and crock of cheese curds. There were curls of crisped bacon wrapped around tiny onions and a bowl of cooked eggs sprinkled with fresh pepper.

A smiling younger woman added plates, cups, and a pot of tea. Another used a hooked pole to place a caged firemoth on a waiting stand, for the light coming through the window was waning.

"This is most kind and appreciated," the damesen said for them all. She bowed her head to the cook. "Thank you, Nelisti, for your hospitality."

The cook bared crooked teeth in a fierce smile. "Naarr."

The sun set before they emptied the tray and second pot of tea. Leksand alone went for dessert, gobbling the baked pudding with appetite. The cook knew what to put before a growing boy; reassuring to a mother.

If nought else was.

Stairs inside the larder led to staff quarters above. Eaples showed them to rooms doubtless vacated for their arrival. Leksand, not yet a student, would share with Dom, who had his room still. They'd given Kait her own, housing the damesen with Tercle; not an arrangement Tiler's Hold would find acceptable for the hold lord's cousin and representative, but Pylor merely asked Eaples convey their gratitude, thanked Dom for bringing up their luggage, and went inside without another word.

Exhausted. They all were. Kait lingered to watch her son disappear into his room, by his yawn probably to drop to sleep at once, then stepped inside and closed her door.

Stood, bag in hand, knowing what she had to do. Afraid to do it—

They were all scared. Here she was, useful as teats on a tree. What would Atta and Pincel say?

Do what needs doing.

Someone, likely the room's rightful inhabitant, had turned down the colorful quilt and fluffed the pillow. Thoughtfully left a proper lamp burning on the nightstand and curtains drawn, as well as started a cheery little fire in the black heat stove that filled a corner and sent its pipe through the ceiling to a chimney above, and none of it would do.

Kait dropped the bag on the floor. No point looking inside for clean clothes; the remaining made-thrush had had ample time to soil what was packed and normally she'd be curious what the bloody thing found to eat to produce so much. She pulled on her cloak, putting her arms through and digging her fingers into the thick wool for courage.

Then got to work. She moved the chair near the window. Doused the fire and turned the key to shut off the lamp, grabbing the quilt on an afterthought.

Once sat in the chair, wrapped as best she could in quilt and cloak, Kait opened the curtains. The window was deeply set on its stone sill, so she had to stand again to reach its lock, then push it ajar. Cold air rushed in.

Nought wrong with that. It'd clear her head. Keep her awake.

Being staff quarters, this side of the building overlooked the midden and fish ponds. Past those, Dom had told them, they'd left the dame-sen's carriage and wagons.

Kait stared out into the night. Gradually, her eyes grew accustomed, letting her pick out breaks in the cloud overhead. Stars, distant and unhelpful. Closer, lower, what might be fireflies on a summer's night, dozens of them, moved across the hills, if fireflies were large as a horse or woman. Gossamers.

They weren't dancing or whatever gossamers did at night. Those she could see, that let her see them, moved in one direction, steadily and with purpose. Away from the school.

She wished them well.

Putting her hands on the stone sill, Kait let down her guard and listened. Nothing. The Lady was silent, but Her neglect had grown to an accustomed loss, like the scab over a wound she must carry.

She listened harder, half-closing her eyes, then stiffened. There.

Wind—

But wasn't.

It was—breathing. Like to that she'd first heard in the bog, each breath steady as stone and slow as seasons. Each enormous, greater than the singer's, impossible, as if the world itself drew in, let out, what wasn't air at all.

Not the Fell. Not—not like anything else. What took these breaths slumbered. How could she have forgotten?

Forgotten. Overlooked. Safe—

But wasn't.

Had she lost her mind? Kait opened her eyes, shivering. How could there be anything safe about whatever terrifyingly strange new thing she could hear? Whatever it was, if one and not, Goddess help her, two, the sleeper didn't belong under the same stars as the likes of her or anyone of flesh and blood.

Nor did the Fell.

She took a steadying breath of her own. Insignificant, that breath, barely moving the curtain. A drop of cream in a cup of tea.

Everyone here was in her care tonight, whether they knew it or not. Guarded by a daughter from Woodshaven, sitting huddled in the dark by an open window, growing colder by the hour.

Should have brought tea.

She would listen. If the Fell escaped their prison, she would hear.

And if they did, Kaitealyon would speak Her Words and sound the alarm.

# Fundamental Lexicon

***The world has one shape.***

Babes resemble their parents and their parents' parents in a lineage stretching back to the cessation of ice, or fire, depending on your belief.

Mage scribes create what never before has been seen, though some would point out the requests they fulfill most often resemble what has. Made-oxen. Made-fowl. Made-roses. Practical intentions, to improve or entertain. A prudent lack of imagination, to stay close to what works.

Even gossamers, unpredictable and unique, remain as they are once created, forever. Or not. Impossible to prove one way or another, for a gossamer reveals itself at its own whim and will.

Only those who were here, before the cessation of ice or fire, take any shape they please.

***We are who we are.***

Until we contain what is not us, but has, shall we say, an interest. Mages host what they call Her Gift and give life for magic, but theirs is a slow trade and might seem a choice, if it were not.

Daughters and acolytes host what they call Her Gift and choose to offer their lives, having faith The Lady acts for the good of Tananen. If claimed, their life ends, to become Hers. Her Designates complete Her acts, their emptied flesh become ash.

There were once those far less merciful, whose arbitrary claim on a body included the host's delectable awareness and delicious despair. Whose actions had nothing to do with the good of anything but the unending appetite for everything.

Eaters of life. Eaters of hope. Eaters of magic.

**Magic must be defended.**

Or magic will be lost. The Eaters are coming and it is a simple choice.

What would you sacrifice, to keep magic alive?

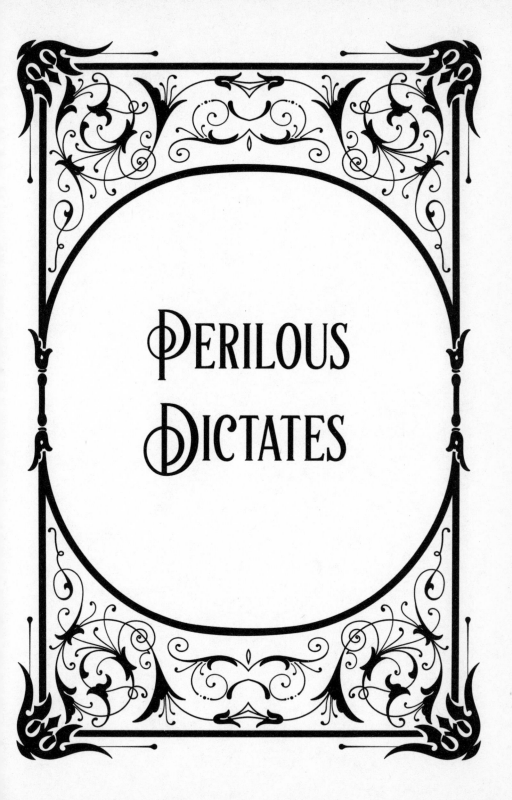

# Perilous Dictates

# PERILOUS DICTATES

Every so often, the question is asked. To preserve a mage, keep him from writing magic and expending life, why not cut off his hands?

As The Deathless Goddess cares enough for Her mages to take immediate vengeance on those who harm them, vanishingly few are the number who'd risk severing hands or any other part. And to what end? Mages without hands—and there'd been some in history—find other means. Any means. Her Words demand to be written.

But if a mage must write, and can't be stopped, what happens when his mind loses the discipline to form an intention? When his reality breaks—yet, being still a mage, he must write—what does he loose upon the world?

What hasn't been requested, paid for, and needed by anyone. What rises from some fantasy within. Most, to the relief of all, are gossamers and harmless.

Some are nightmares.

Maleonarial's footsteps echoed down the long narrow corridor of the upper floor. The light of his lamp chased his shadow and shuddered with the breeze of his steps. He didn't look up. It was best not to pay attention.

The high peaked ceiling was the underside of the roof. In a bargain renewed each time Alden's workers marched up the road to rebuild the school, the means of its future destruction was left behind when they were done. In his time, a netting of twisted rope impregnated with flash powder was affixed to roof planks, with sacs of more powder interspersed with oil bladders suspended from the joists, in every building. Though it seemed redundant in the student residences; those learning magic needed no help whatsoever to destroy their own quarters.

The masters confined here were left the means to write, being the way mages came to their end. As for their creations? Any gossamers written on the upper floor soared to freedom, neither roof nor Alden's bargain an impediment.

Things kept in, things best ignored, slithered along ropes and between sacs and bladders. Added their glues and dreadful mementoes. Remained high above and harmless, unless noticed.

Usually.

Busy with his own thoughts, Maleonarial had no trouble ignoring them. The masters hadn't liked what he'd told them, that magic's toll couldn't be escaped despite what they'd heard of Cil's gossamers. All would comply, for he'd provided a graphic description of Cil's demise, and who'd want to end life with Her Kiss? As for his restoration—

He'd suggested they pray.

Not that The Hag listened, but the ploy proved an admirable distraction, Xareonarial the first to depart on urgent business he'd forgotten, the rest following behind like a flock of made-sheep.

Leaving him free to come here.

The floor was metal, as were the walls and doors. Nightmares down here too, giving way, their eyes hot discs in the lamplight. More rooms stood open and vacant than closed. Things slithered in them as well. A good sign, Maleonarial supposed. The empty rooms, not the slithering. Fewer mages and students in confinement.

Or lately most had written their last flawed intention and died of it.

Gifted student, bent of heart. Eccentric master, ill of mind. Innocent or evil, those held here were incredibly dangerous, sequestered by the mage school to live out the rest of their lives, hopefully short ones, where they could harm no one but themselves. Where what they created, whether it lived a flicker of time or endured, remained.

Another hope not always realized, hence Alden's bargain. Alden Hold guarded the rest of Tananen from the school's creations, despite most masters' fond belief the hold existed solely to shield the school from intrusion and provide staff.

Had he not sought the wilds and lived alone, far from here, Maleonarial was well aware his actions would have seen him in one of these rooms.

He passed three closed doors, raising his lamp to read the name chalked on each, before finding the one he sought. Gave grief time to wash through him, for this was no good end for anyone, least of all a friend, before he knocked once.

Then drew aside its bolt.

Not vacant, this room. Books lined two walls, a tapestry another. A pair of leather chairs and small table waited on a thick carpet. A desk stood ready for scholarship. Another door, this with a curtain swayed to the side, showed a luxurious bed chamber. A tub sat on clawed feet, bubbles heaped as if he'd interrupted a bath.

He stepped in quickly and drew the door closed behind him, for none of it was real. The chairs opened big brown eyes and wagged as if encouraging him to sit. What appeared books on shelves quivered, as if uneasy to be noticed, then suddenly broke apart, each tome sprouting sticky feet and fleeing to cluster on the ceiling.

Little wonder Pageonarial had aged, if he'd made this and who knew what else. The greater amazement? That he'd lost the ability to write in time to survive it.

Maleonarial took a quiet step back. He'd leave his friend in the peace he'd created.

A faint but cheery, "Look at you!" came from the tub to stop him.

And there was nothing friendship could do but walk into the other room, dodging the eager chairs, to answer. "Hello, Page."

Pageonarial's smiling face and knobby knees poked up from what weren't bubbles of soap, but living bubbles with tiny eyes, mouths, and hands. Those in the air giggled. Maleonarial sank on his heels where the other could see him without twisting, his hair falling over a shoulder with the tinkle of bells.

Rheumy eyes glistened. "Look at you!"

Maleonarial put out his hand. A made-bubble landed on it, proceeding to scrub with ardent attention between his fingers. "Is there any of you left, Page?" he asked, wistful.

Those eyes sharpened. "Just enough." A trembling hand rose. "Help me up."

Before Maleonarial could try, the bubbles lifted Page from the tub and floated his wizened naked form to the bed, his white hair, dense with bells, chiming like a song. Task accomplished, bubbles flew back to the tub as a thick red robe purred with joy, rushing to wrap itself around its creator and help him sit.

A not-mage might feel this a paradise of care. Knowing the decades lost to achieve it, Maleonarial felt the stir of fear. The bolted door lied. These were reasoned intentions. Purposeful.

Once slippers put themselves on Page's feet, he rose. "Sit with me." The leather chairs tried to squeeze through the doorway at the same time. "Out there," the master commanded testily. The chairs paused, brown eyes blinking in confused woe. "Out!"

They wiggled backward, setting themselves on the carpet in the outer room with unhappy whoofs. "They're new," Page explained, shuffling after them. Seeing him, the books hurried back into place, muttering titles at one another as they sorted their order on the shelves. The desk gave a resigned sigh when the mage sat in one of the big chairs and not at it.

Maleonarial sank into the second chair, doing his best to ignore its welcoming hug. This wasn't confinement to the upper floor. This was a sanctuary, one for which Page had paid his health and future. "How long?" Despite the warmth of the chair, a chill went through him. "Why?"

The historian's lips were colorless, his sunken cheeks spoke of teeth lost, but the wise little smile, full of secrets, that was the same. "When and because someone touched The Brutes and returned to Tananen, alive."

"Insom the Second. Then you already know what came back with him."

"I suspected. Feared. And, now, look at you, Maleonarial." Pageonarial raised a finger. "Ottle's Memoirs. Ban's footnotes." A made-book on the top shelf squirmed free with a popping sound. It ran down the wall and across the floor, leaping for the side of the chair. An anxious brown eye formed to watch it climb. "Steady," the master said, and the eye closed. The made-book turned around on his robed lap until satisfied, then flounced flat and opened.

Maleonarial swallowed and looked at the shelves. "The archives . . ."

"Are here, yes. As are you, at last." Said without warmth. "Caton wrote of the possibility of a mage being restored by The Goddess, if She'd some great need." Three made-books by that author eased out, to sheepishly reshelve themselves when not summoned.

He put a hand to his chest. "Her need's for me to return this." Maleonarial let himself say the truth. "It should have been Sael."

Cold keen eyes regarded him, summed the bells. "Sentiment, of which The Lady has none. Our good scribemaster was careful of his life. By your count, you'd spent enough to be dead."

"You're one to talk."

"This?" Page wagged his finger. "I calculated precisely what I'd need in order to be here and hidden if—when—the Eaters reached us. By your arrival, in a caravan from Insom? I take it they have. Chair, trap!"

Leather turned hard and tough, encasing Maleonarial from neck to foot. He didn't attempt to struggle. "What's this?"

The finger stabbed at the made-book lying on his lap. "Ottle writes of a man washed up on The Brutes, four hundred years ago, who then tried to swim to shore. Those who pulled him from the water cut off his head and threw his remains into the sea, because he'd swallowed evil and become it. Ban's footnote adds 'other accounts of that time list be-heading as the only defense against possession by an Eater, a being of evil whose goal is to destroy Tananen.' Desk, release the blade." There was an unpleasant buzzing noise.

A huge made-fly zipped to the ceiling, circled the room, then stopped midair, hovering by Maleonarial's ear. After a sidelong glance to confirm that yes, its razor sharp mouthparts could sever a head, if not quickly, he focused on Pageonarial. "You're right. It's true, Insom's possessed. I'm not, Page. You can see it in my eyes. There's a black lightning—"

The old master snorted. "If I come close to you, what's to stop you from changing hosts and taking me?"

"They can do that?"

A finger twirl. "Farid." A book scampered to obey. "Anecdotal, but reliable. 'An Eater will exude from its host to enter another or to feed.'"

Page had knowledge they needed; was surely the help they'd come to find. "If you want proof," Maleonarial said eagerly, hearing the chair growl. "Kaitealyon can hear the Fell—these Eaters. She'll vouch for me."

"The daughter is irrelevant here. Urray." Another tome scampered into place, fell open. "'The Deathless Goddess does not arbitrate between mages.'"

He'd like to see Page try to tell that to Kait. More urgently, how to get Kait here? "In this She does," Maleonarial insisted. "The Eaters are Her enemy."

A stark look. "Nonsense. She has none."

The archives—he'd spent his own years nose in books. Knew, all at once, the only way to convince the historian.

"Corvinas, *Fundamental Lexicon of Tananen Vol. 1*, the arrival." To Maleonarial's delight, a volume larger than most popped free and ran down the wall. It hesitated on the carpet as though conflicted, then climbed to the arm of Page's chair, oriented so Maleonarial could read the text. "'The world was not always thus.'"

"Pssh. Garrod and Nabo dismissed Corvinas as a writer of fiction."

"What if she wasn't? 'We were not the first here.' Corvinas wrote that before ice or fire, there was a struggle between magic and what would destroy it. Sound familiar?"

"Fujin!" Pageonarial half-shouted. The made-book wasn't halfway down the wall before he quoted angrily, "'When people arrived in Tananen, they received Her Gifts and lived in peace and magic within the arms of The Deathless Goddess.' No mention of a destroyer. None."

"Gudrun." A made-book budged.

"No!" A scowl as the book pushed itself back. "A flawed source that shouldn't be in the archives. I've no idea why I've tolerated it."

The book whimpered. The chair rumbled happily until Maleonarial said, "It's here because unlike my predecessors, I was willing to consult my counterparts in the Daughter's Portions. Gudrun and Urray, now!" Both raced to obey, this time crawling on the leather of his chair as if afraid of being summarily discarded, stacking themselves close to his nose. Maleonarial didn't dare sneeze. "Gudrun's accounts are based on generations of verbal records, passed down with exceptional accuracy within Xcel's Daughters." He stopped. Waited.

The historian's lips worked a moment, then his finger bent, conceding interest. "Your point."

Kait had said it. The Hag wasn't omnipresent. "According to Gudrun, the first settlers to Tananen met but a tiny portion of The Goddess, the wounded remnant from the battle that threw up Her Fist and Veil against the world. There was almost no magic to be had."

"Tales."

"Accounts," he retorted. "Those first daughters were tasked with helping The Goddess recover. The first mages, with channeling Her magic back into the world and replenishing Her life. If She depended on us then and since, what's to say we don't act for Her now, daughters and mages together, against the Eaters?"

"Fantasies."

The book shifted as though to argue; admittedly, he'd taken certain liberties with Gudrun's text. Was the leather tighter? Had the blade's wingbeats grown louder, as if closing in on his neck?

Ignoring those as best he could, Maleonarial tried once more. "You've always said scholarship is the hunt for truth. That however buried or distorted by time, truth remains to be found by those who reject their own prejudice."

A suspicious look. "I said that?"

Maleonarial dared wink. "Maybe I just did. Does it matter? We believe in the truth. Strive for reason. We always have."

"Humph." Almost a smile. "Go on, then. The Urray? What will you cite from it to impress me?"

He grinned. "You know how it is. The more books, the better-sounding the argument." Before the hint of goodwill could fade, he turned serious. "Kait will tell you the truth about me. Call for her, Page. She's staying in the staff quarters. She's come with me and the damesen to find a way—"

"Insom's chemist. I saw her." For the first time, Pageonarial looked uncertain. "We corresponded for a time. A formidable intellect, not that I would share the inkmaster's secrets, but the history of our ink-making, yes. What does she have to do with this? Is she possessed too?" With renewed alarm.

"No. Pylor discovered Insom is possessed. He—the Eater in him—ordered her to ask questions about me and to bring his gifts to the school. Through Kait, we know there are Eaters sealed inside those gifts. I said you'd know what to do, how to defeat them." And been right, he thought with rising triumph. "Call for Kait, Page," Maleonarial urged again. "After what happened at the funeral, you must believe in her. That she's sent by The Lady, not this evil."

Hands clenched on the made-books, which wriggled in protest. "I believe," Pageonarial said after a moment's consideration. Another of his wise little smiles that neither reached nor warmed his eyes. "We will have Kaitealyon here. And you will wait as you are, Master Maleonarial, to learn if she believes in you."

"Sorry to wake you, but it's your turn to keep watch."

Pylor rubbed sleep from her eyes, endeavoring to focus on the earnest figure at the door. A servant stood behind Kait, who'd draped a quilt over her cloaked shoulders and whose cheeks were as crimson as if she'd been outside. "It's all right, Tercle," in response to a muttered question from the dark room behind.

Though how could it be, if the daughter asked her help? Now wide awake and concerned, Pylor kept her voice calm, wary of the servant. "Where?"

"Keep an eye out the window. For any signs the owls are about," Kait said with inane cheer, as if it weren't the dead of night. "I'll be back to take over soon."

The servant covered a yawn, suitably unimpressed by visitors to a school of magic who watched for owls. Pylor, having seen only the moth-eaten stuffed specimen in the storeroom she used for her chemicals, would have enjoyed watching for the living version. For anything but the Fell, but she knew what the daughter asked. Still, "But Kait, you've the best eyes," she protested. "Shouldn't you do it?"

Eyes that rolled meaningfully at the servant. "I've been summoned to a master. I may have overstepped in the hall," Kait added.

Or Maleonarial had urgent news to share, for the daughter's ears only. Nodding, Pylor pulled her wrap tighter. "I'll keep watch."

"You can't be serious," Tercle said a moment later, sitting up in bed. "Bad enough you've kept the damn lamp burning."

Because shadows were the enemy, the dark its home, and Pylor contained a shudder, saying bravely, "Once I'm settled, blow it out." The pillow on the chair, blankets to wrap around herself; Kait's quilt and cheeks ample proof the window had to be opened in order to stand watch. "It's stuffy in here." She threw the latch and pushed.

"It's bloody cold out there. Py!" A wail.

She tossed one of the blankets to her friend. "Go to sleep."

"Damn right I will," Tercle muttered, blowing out the lamp. "Owls."

Shadows pressed close. Outside was black without so much as a star and the air blowing over her was every bit as bitter as Tercle claimed, stealing moisture from her nose and mouth. Pylor was accustomed to waiting long hours for an experiment to finish; took pleasure in patience and persistence, rewarded by result.

Now, if anything happened, if anything finished, if the result she awaited was the Fell showing themselves free, what did Kait think she could do? Cry out? Do as her pathetic cousin and light every lamp? Pylor's bones itched and her eyes burned, until it took every bit of will she had left to sit there, afraid to so much as blink.

"Move over." Tercle's shoulder bumped into Pylor's as she dragged the other chair close and sat. Her friend shifted with an annoyed grunt, pulling a blanket over the top of her head. "Bloody owls."

Pylor stared out into the night with eyes no longer dry nor burning. Blinked, surprised by a trickle of icy moisture down her cheeks.

Amazed how warm she felt.

The servant's name was Hardly Bakerson, he worked at the school to put aside a smidge extra and when not working here he helped his grandparents with their shop in Alden which would be his eventually, and wherever he was taking Kait made him less and less comfortable by the stair step.

"It's the upper floor masters," Hardly blurted when they reached the top landing. "They don't—I was told they can't ask for things. Or visitors."

"One's asked for me," Kait concluded. She'd presumed it was Maleonarial till now. She eyed the door. Unlike the others she'd encountered, this was of sintered metal. A once-red sash came through a small hole in the door frame, tied with a bow to a large rusty bell hanging from a hook; an arrangement presumably to let someone on the other side pull the sash and sound what, an alarm? "Should I worry?" she asked, judging the baker from Alden kind and truthful.

Hardly frowned at the door with her. "I've nought been past here,

Kait. Senior students bring up trays from the kitchen. Eaples does the rooms with the masters out. He never says a word about them, mind, but I met him once, coming down these stairs." Hardly licked his lips and swallowed. "There was no color to his face and his hands—his hands shook so hard, I had to help carry his buckets."

Which, no offense to Eaples or Hardly, might simply mean a messier room than usual. In her experience the infirm struggled to hit the pot with their piss, let alone anything else, and cleaning the result part of their care. Babes were no different.

Were master mages? Kait stiffened her shoulders. She was about to learn who the school kept hidden from the rest and why, though from Affarealyon's warning, magic would be part of it. Still, however dire the reasons, for Leksand's sake, she had to know. Even if it left her with nightmares.

"Thank you, Hardly. I'll keep that in mind."

"It's the fourth door to the right. You'll need this," passing her the lamp he'd carried. "I'm not to go past here." He lowered his voice. "I will, if you like."

At possible cost of his position, upon which Kait suspected his grandparents relied too. "No need. I walk in the steps of The Lady," she reminded him. "Thank you again."

He wasn't happy, but couldn't very well argue. "Good night, then."

Kait waited, holding the lamp high, until he'd descended past the next landing to where caged moths lit the stairwell. "G'night?" she echoed, almost amused. It seemed there were as many awake now, as in the day.

She wrapped her fingers around the door handle and pulled, stepping through promptly to let it close behind her, in case a dottering wanderer stood ready to escape and likely tumble down the stairs.

Kait found herself isolated in the rectangle of yellow light cast by her lamp. She tapped a toe, confirming the floor was metal. Unattractive and hard underfoot. Did those confined here tend to set fires? Raising the lamp, she saw the corridor continued into the dark. She'd tread softly; most here should be asleep.

She paused at the first door. Bolted, so perhaps she'd been right to imagine the stairs a hazard to whomever lived in these rooms. Metal, with a name neatly chalked on it: Esteonarial.

Was one Rogeonarial? She'd believed Leksand's father dead years ago, but it wasn't as if the mage school sent out notices. He hadn't returned, that was all. Eaples should know the names of those here.

To what gain? Might as well ask an acorn attach itself back on the oak, and that after the wood was made into furniture. Kait resumed walking, counting doors as she went; she no longer read the names.

As she passed the second door, something brushed her leg. She couldn't help but jump, though she managed not to make a sound. She turned to see what it was, half-prepared for a rat.

It was not. Perhaps its creator intended a cat, but this was no fluffy pet. Closer in size to a dog, its back covered in plates like armor, the made-cat's enlarged eyes were white discs in the lamplight. Sharp, long fangs dripped with venom that steamed as drops hit the floor.

Explained the alarm bell, didn't it?

It blocked her way to the stairs. Kait took a step back. Another. The creature followed, slow, sinuous, and ready to pounce. It had only to decide in which fleshy portion to sink its fangs.

She'd open the next door and wake its occupant before that moment arrived.

Something else entered the light. Smaller, without eyes or fangs, but needles stuck from it like a pincushion. More of them, piling into a pursuing wave, and what was that sound from over her head?

Time to be elsewhere. Kait whirled to run, only to freeze in place. In the light stood more of the made-cats, with more pincushions behind, and hanging down, glistening mouths level with her face, things that shouldn't exist—couldn't—

A door flew open down the hall, warm bright light streaming forth. A white-haired head peered out. "Don't just stand there. We're waiting."

As if she wasn't surrounded by salivating venomous made-monsters. Which she obviously was, Kait thought, becoming rather cross, but the speaker's head disappeared, his door left open with its promise of safe haven and two choices.

Either she could walk through what crawled and slunk and prowled, ready to tear her to bits. Or he'd made them and was impatient to see her in bits.

Well, the night wasn't getting any longer. With an irritated snort, Kait raised her lamp and eyes, and strode toward the door as if not surrounded at all, resolutely ignoring the snarls and growls from the shadows. Harder not to react when something squealed and crunched underfoot, and what jumped into her hair?

Fumbling to pull whatever it was out with one hand, Kait half-stumbled into the room, recovering her footing as the door closed. She found herself blinking at Maleonarial.

Who'd been swallowed, except for his head, hair, and bells, by what looked like a very comfortable leather chair. The mage gave her a wry smile. "Kaitealyon."

"Free'm at once!" Kait demanded fiercely, whirling in search of the "you" in question.

The subject of her ire stood no taller than she, weighed half as much, and wore a fluffy red robe. And slippers. Old—she'd no idea how old, but a wealth of bells, almost as many as Maleonarial's, clung to his white hair and she didn't care for his faint little smile that judged her in turn.

Kait half-raised the lamp in mock threat. "Free—"

Something stabbed her scalp.

"G'me a moment." Putting the lamp on the floor, she felt until a pricked finger located the culprit. Wincing, Kait ripped the pincushion-thing from her head, along with some hair. She searched for a place to toss it and her eyes found the old master. She gave her own humorless smile. "Free Maleonarial," she ordered, waving the thing by her hair.

He didn't appear concerned. "Greetings, Daughter. Mal claims you can detect those possessed by an Eater."

The truth of that name shivered down her spine. Not the Fell. Eaters— and what they consumed was magic. She'd seen it. "How do you know of them?"

"Pageonarial's the historian I told you about. Unfortunately, he suspects I've one in me." Maleonarial grimaced. "It's getting warm in here, Page."

"You're being digested," the old master said offhandedly, his attention on Kait. "Well? Does he?"

Though tempted, she lowered the writhing pincushion. "I swear by The Lady that Maleonarial is himself. Alone in his body. Unpossessed. Now set him free."

Pageonarial's relieved sigh improved Kait's opinion. "Chair," he announced firmly, "I fear you'll have to wait for supper. Release him."

Large brown eyes blinked in reproach. A giant made-fly that belonged in the corridor with the other monsters zipped from its hiding place behind the chair to be snapped up by the desk.

Was any furniture to be trusted?

"Now," insisted the master.

The leather receded from the mage. The instant he could wriggle free, Maleonarial did so with a will. Standing, he ran his hands over his clothes, lifting away fingers covered in clear goo. "Page?"

"Oh." With that little smile, the other settled himself on the chair that had spat out Maleonarial. "Jump in the tub. We'll wait."

There was, indeed, a bubble-filled tub, the most luxurious Kait had ever seen, in view through the door to a bedroom. Which made no difference, to her mind, given the hour and their fear. "We've nought time for bathing."

"Quite right." Pageonarial whistled through a gap between what could be his only teeth. Bubbles rose in a sparkling cloud, then flew to engulf Maleonarial. For an instant, he was obscured from view, other than waving arms as he tried to keep bubbles from his face.

Did the bubbles giggle?

As quickly as they'd come, the bubbles zoomed back to the tub, leaving Maleonarial dry and freshly cleaned from hair to gleaming boots. Recalling the drudgery of a laundry day back home, particularly in spring when mud found its way everywhere, Kait almost asked how much the intention would cost.

But wasn't it before her, in Pageonarial's shrunken face and frail body?

"Y'pardon." Kait went to the door, tossed the pincushion into the corridor to join its kind, closed the door firmly again, then turned. "Do you know how to stop them?"

"I might have information of use. Please. Sit."

Not on anything with eyes and appetite, she wouldn't. Kait took the quilt from her shoulders, overwarm anyway, and spread it on the carpet in front of Pageonarial. Seeing her sit on it, Maleonarial did the same. "How do we stop the Eaters?" she asked, barely containing her impatience.

That's what she felt, she assured herself, so tired her legs wanted to twitch, yet so awake it was as though she knew better than to relax. It wasn't the feeling they were already too late.

"How do we stop them other than cutting off heads," Maleonarial qualified. The desk, or what was in it, gave an enthused buzz. Seeing Kait's shocked look, he shrugged. "Apparently how one deals with the possessed."

They were not cutting off Insom's head, she vowed then and there. Poor Pylor.

"While we waited for you, Kait, I told Pageonarial what's happened. What we know—what we fear," the mage went on. He bowed his head to her. "Because you can hear and see the Eaters, you came from Tiler's to warn the rest of Tananen of this dire threat and seek the truth. Because of you, Kaitealyon, we three have a chance to defeat the Eaters who've come to our school to destroy the heart of magic."

A fine and loquacious storyteller he was, of a sudden, as good as any at the inn; Kait narrowed her eyes at Maleonarial. Why?

"'A chance,'" echoed the old master, eyes gleaming. "I've waited these months. Spent these years." His lips worked. "Hidden myself and what I know."

"Your wait is over, my friend." Theirs wasn't, and Kait resisted the urge to poke the mage's ankle with her toe. "By the will of The Deathless Goddess, we've come together and it will be in time."

"Yes!" Pageonarial quivered like reeds in the wind. "It will! It will! I've been afraid—once I knew an Eater had come ashore, I knew they'd be coming here. Might already be here—how could I be sure? How?" His voice faltered.

"You made the courageous choice, Page," Maleonarial praised. "You told no one. Pretended to lose your wits so the masters would confine you here, where you could work in secret. Sacrificed—" He stopped, shaking his head as though overcome with emotion.

Ah. The winding tale was for her benefit, as well as the old master's. Maleonarial wanted her to understand why they were here, why this was their only ally.

Who couldn't be rushed, for he was truly frail. How young would he be otherwise? A gift for scholarship, nurtured and given focus, and the historian could be her age. Should be. Kait bowed her head in respect. "The Lady's Blessing on you—"

"I couldn't trust anyone, you see." As if he hadn't heard. "Then Sael—" A stricken look to Maleonarial. "I tried to warn him not to go to Tiler's Hold." Tears fell. "I'd hidden myself too well. He couldn't believe me. I couldn't explain."

Pageonarial jerked back, hands held as if to fend off an attacker. The eyes on the chair opened wide and it snarled. "And now the Eaters have come—they're here!"

"Here, aie, but not free." Wary of the chair, Kait rose on her knees to take the distraught historian's hands in hers. Chafed them gently, for his fingers were like ice. "The Eaters are imprisoned—"

Pageonarial pulled back his hands. "How? Where?" Fretful. Querulous. Kait looked to Maleonarial, trusting he'd reassure the poor man.

"In sealed urns, in a wagon tucked behind the kitchen," Maleonarial said, as if making a careful report. "There are fourteen, Page; one for each master in residence, labeled by name and the artwork of the seal."

Not how she'd have given the news.

"Fourteen, you say." Kait was astonished to see Pageonarial's agitation vanish, his demeanor grow confident. "A tally absent our late scribemaster, but including those confined to the upper floor. Ah!"

"What are you thinking?"

That they should thank The Lady the Eaters hadn't prepared an urn for Maleonarial too.

"An attack, in force." Crisply. Pageonarial steepled his gnarled fingers. "The number of urns suggests the Insom Eater believed Saeleonarial wouldn't return before these urns arrived and, like the rest of Tananen, is unaware some of our number are not, shall we say, functional. Indeed, Est and Arco are within an intention—at most two—of their end. Imperfect information. No master has been possessed," with satisfaction. "We are safe from spies."

"We can't be sure," Kait cautioned. "Insom warned Pylor she was being watched. He—the Eater sent a made-gull to communicate with her. It might have come with us."

Maleonarial shook his head, bells chiming softly. "Most of what takes place at the school is under a roof. A made-gull would be remarked; the active masters keep watch over whatever's not real."

She'd have found that more comfort if the masters then dealt with it. A good start would be clearing up the corridor. Little wonder Eaples occasionally looked green.

"The first question to answer is why aim this attack at us? We must consult—" The historian rattled off what sounded like a string of titles, fingers parting to wiggle in the air.

Books raced down the walls to stack themselves beside the chair, by Kait's feet, which she tucked hurriedly aside, and in front of Maleonarial, individual tomes shoving and pushing to establish their order.

"With respect, I disagree." She put a quelling hand on the nearest pile, feeling the made-books grow still. "The question that matters, the only one, is how we destroy them." *Defend me!* "And quickly. Before the Eaters destroy Tananen."

Pageonarial's gaze locked with hers. "How do we prevent that destruction, Daughter, without first knowing how the Eaters could accomplish it?" Before she could respond, he continued grimly, "I doubt you've come with assurance of divine protection. Balfour!" A book not under her hand scampered up the chair to fling itself, open to a page, on his knee. He quoted without looking away from her: "'Lest later generations forget this truth, it shall be recorded and taught by every hold daughter. Tiler's Hold was built not to protect the people of Tananen, but its Goddess.'"

*Defend me!* Kait let out a slow, less than steady, breath. "Aie, it's been forgotten." Along with how much else? Which didn't matter now. "The Lady no longer comes to us in Tiler's. She's commanded we defend her." She firmed her voice. "And we will."

"Will you become Her Designate, in order to—what is the euphemism you daughters like to use?—ah, clean house?" Eyes on both chairs shot open, then narrowed with menace, for this was no idle question, but confrontation.

Kait rose to her feet, Maleonarial echoing the movement to stand by her shoulder, and which master was the greater threat? Neither, she decided, for both were afraid. "You listen to me, for I'll say this but once. The Eaters are the foe, not The Lady, not me. They don't belong in Tananen. As for what they plan? The longer these stay, chances are we'll be see'n it for ourselves."

Maleonarial stepped where she could see him. His face was set in stern lines, but he gave a small bow. "Agreed. The problem at hand is to be rid of our unwanted guests."

"Canna drown them." At their raised eyebrows, Kait felt her cheeks warm. "They come from the sea, don't they?"

"It's unclear." The historian's white shaggy brows collided in a frown. "The Brutes are theirs, but—these archives," the books hummed, "hold the writings of Tananen's greatest minds and thinkers, every known treatise on magic and mages—those that survived the school, though for some copies were made. I've found nothing to suggest the Eaters can cross The Hunger—an apt naming, Enyon notes—of their own accord. They must wait for a person—a host—to reach them."

"Hence the beheading of sailors," Maleonarial supplied.

"Yes. Though Nicti—no—" as another book prepared to move, "states 'evil can be called to evil.' I'd no context till now," Pageonarial apologized, as if they'd found fault. "We must assume Insom's Eater was able to call more to the hold."

"More reason to be done with these, then," Kait urged, envisioning tendrils of smoke crossing the land. To hide a shiver, she tugged at the quilt. The books refused to budge.

"But why come here in the first place? Why fourteen urns? Why just the masters, when we've students as talented. Is there any clue?" Pageonarial's voice rose as she gave the hardest pull yet and the books scampered in every direction. "Mal?"

Kait savored her small victory as she folded the quilt. No need to tell the owner what had been on it, or where it had been—

Her hands stopped moving as the answers slid into place.

"What is it, Daughter?" the mage asked her.

"I know why." As surely as if their dreadful muttering finally made sense. "Why here. Why you." She looked up, horror writ in her face.

"They're hungry."

Pageonarial hunched in his chair, which growled protectively, and Maleonarial didn't blame either, shaken himself. "You think they've come for the school's magic—Kait witnessed the Eater taking it from made-beasts in Tiler's hall," for the old master's benefit. The chairs whined. "Her Gift is a conduit, not magic itself. Why the—" but he knew, didn't he. "Only masters move throughout the grounds and buildings without question."

"Only masters can command students to write intention upon intention. They would and gladly, without the questions we would ask, without our—" Pageonarial passed a trembling hand over his eyes.

"—our appreciation of Her toll," Maleonarial finished, full of bitterness. Bad enough The Hag, now these Eaters?

"A snack," Kait said, clutching the quilt in both hands. "All the made-things here. All you could make. Your students." She thought of Leksand; he could see it in her eyes. "It won't be enough. I've felt their hunger. It's—bottomless."

"But what else—" Pageonarial fell silent and the mage didn't need to ask why. Since there'd been mages, every moment a school stood on these grounds, mistakes had been made. The result filled the border marsh and hills behind, hidden and sly, bold and full of frolic, each a glimpse of breathtaking wonder or gasp of the strange.

"Gossamers," Maleonarial said for him. "The Eaters are here for the school's gossamers."

Kait bit her lip, then nodded. "Aie. I believe they know it, too. Gossamers abandoned Tiler's. Yours have begun to flee, but I don't know if they can. Not from this."

"We've each made our share of gossamers. Would they know to run from possessed masters? Are we to betray them?" Pageonarial closed his eyes, then opened them. "Gossamers are Blessed by The Deathless Goddess. Will She not save them, Daughter?"

"I don't think She can," Kait replied. "Not alone."

Maleonarial heard the words like a call and wasn't the only one.

The historian struggled to his feet, helped at the last by an obliging boost from his chair. "Then we must aid The Goddess! To work!" He waved as he tottered to his desk, which bounced happily to be in use, then calmed to welcome its creator. Books stampeded to follow, racing one another up the desk's pedestals as if each were utterly convinced of its worth.

Maleonarial held in his doubt. "We'll leave you to it, Page. Call for us the moment you have something more."

White hair and bells, a head bent over books. The confident dismissive finger twirl.

Reassuringly familiar.

He and Kait walked down the corridor. With both holding lamps, the upper floor seemed smaller; with what they now believed, what slithered from their path vulnerable rather than dangerous, poison and teeth notwithstanding. "Do they outlive the mage who wrote them?" Kait asked suddenly, stepping over a made-cat that hissed and twisted and stared at them with hot angry eyes, then snapped up a pin-nipper in one gulp.

"They don't outlive the school's made-cats." He raised an eyebrow. "You didn't think we left those confined unprotected, did you? Once a week, mauls clear the empty rooms. Students make an abundance of them."

She lifted her lamp and looked ceilingward. "What about—"

He drew her arm and lamp down. "Best not."

"Aie," hasty agreement. A step later, "The hold daughter warned me Alden could destroy the school. That she would, if the Fell escaped. But what's up there—" her voice caught "—Maleonarial, that's to kill people. Mages and students."

"With whatever they might have created, yes. It's called Alden's bargain. A last resort if—when magic goes awry, as has happened." He glanced down at her. "Affar has a level head. She won't take lives if there's any other choice. Nor would I."

"Nor I," she said very quietly, and he felt it again, in the echo of Kait Alder's voice, in the way a made-cat backed away.

The edge of a question—gone.

Halfway down the stairs, Kait asked. "What of Harn?"

A daughter would sense the weakness of Her Gift in the boy, the way Her Words faltered in his mind.

It wasn't as a daughter she asked. Maleonarial stopped on the next landing. "In my time as scribemaster, we'd a student much the same. Tobin Piperson. He fell behind, tormented by what he couldn't do, mocked by the rest. I put him to work with the inkmaster, for Tobin had talent there. But it wasn't enough. It never is, Kait. Her Gift must be used. Resisting? We learn that to survive. But to be unable—it would be indescribable agony."

In the lamplight, she looked smaller, or had she hunched against a blow? "Tobin?"

The Hag had no mercy. Why should he? "We found him floating in a pond."

"Not Harn." Kait took hold of his jerkin, shook him with surprising strength. "You will not let that be Harn."

Maleonarial gripped her shoulder. Bent over her to say, his voice harsh, "The help he needs is the death of The Goddess. Help me do that. Help me save them all."

By lamplight, her eyes glistened, then an unexpected smile deepened the corners of her lips. Releasing his clothes, Kait patted his chest. "Well, ye kin start by check'n on the poor lad—make sure he's rest'n. Then get some yerself, mage. T'morrow we ha t'save Tananen."

Of its own volition, his hand left her shoulder and if a master of his years could recall the sensation? He'd just been comforted and sent to his bed.

"Where will you be?" the bewildered mage asked, the least of so many questions or was it the most important?

Her smile vanished. "Keeping watch."

Having made no promise to obey Kait Alder, after they parted ways Maleonarial found himself pulling up the hood of his cloak and heading for the back door from the kitchen. And if he cursed to himself as the cold night air hit his face, it was more because she'd made him do what he knew he should.

However damned inconvenient, with Eaters on the doorstep.

Harn wouldn't be in the room he shared with other students. Maleonarial had read the looks. Nor could the desperate would-be mage have followed the order he'd thoughtlessly given, to seek the supervision of a master, because he'd kept those masters in the hall.

Harn would try to write on his own.

Some things never changed. Students driven to write alone and in secret had the choice of risking the mauls who prowled the perimeter of the buildings by night, albeit the toothless variety who howled and slavered lovingly until the afflicted student fled inside.

Or they risked Slog's pond, where the mauls didn't patrol. Cruel, perhaps, to imply Tobin had ended his own life, but the result would have been the same whether the student jumped or had been pulled in while trying to write an intention: a floating corpse, drained of blood.

Rid had found Tobin, that next morning; the driver wouldn't speak to a master mage for months.

Maleonarial didn't need a light. The paths were populated with made-ants that gave off a faint glow at any approach. Besides, he knew the way.

He paused to look back. The upper floor was dark, its windows replaced with metal shutters. With the chill, windows on the staff floor should have been closed and snug, but one was open.

Kait, keeping watch.

She wouldn't see him unless she leaned out, but the mage found himself, again and unexpectedly, comforted.

The only other sign of life was the light limning the curtains of the kitchen. The cook, up to bake, and Maleonarial thought wistfully of bread pudding.

Before continuing on his way. There were three ponds here, impoundments of Helly Pelly Creek, deepening with each weir until the last was—

No one knew how deep. Toneonarial had made what slipped into the water twenty years ago, and at intervals it dug down, piling reeking muck like a canal dancer.

Perhaps that's what Toneonarial intended, but what he created was in no other way the same. The students named it Slog for no better reason than the name sounded less frightening; the masters had grates installed at once, because it was, in every way. In this one pond, the water never cleared. Around it, for a distance that kept expanding, implying an unusual pattern of growth for a made-beast, tentacles reached out, waiting. They resembled grass, or windblown leaves, or the stone of a path. Even snow.

Any living thing, made or real, that touched a tentacle would be snared and dragged into Slog's lair, to surface later, drained of whatever life-giving fluid had filled it. Rotting corpses being unpleasant to see floating around, there was a grapple and chain, a very long chain on a hand winch, to retrieve them.

Toneonarial had spent the rest of his life, the few months it took him to use up what life he'd left, on the upper floor. By the time Maleonarial was scribemaster, three attempts to remove Slog had failed, the latest costing Alden Hold a seasoned engineer and three of her crew. Alden Hold, understandably, declared the monster the school's problem, recommended stronger grates, and left.

Slog was a stationary risk; groundskeepers put markers a generous distance beyond the last known reach of tentacle, presuming common sense. Which inspired students of a certain risk-prone mindset to consider it a game, of sorts, to dash past markers and back again.

Or to sit by one, at night, to write magic alone.

Harn was where he'd expected, a hooded silhouette, a hand lamp by his feet. The light touched, but didn't penetrate, Slog's pond, and Maleonarial, seeing how far the markers had spread in twelve years, watched where he stepped and cursed The Hag under his breath.

Quiet, the night. He could hear his own pulse and Harn's anxious huffs of breath. Hear the scratch of pen to parchment. And before the mage could move faster, to stop the intention—

It flowed into life. Glowing bronze, aflame with sparks of laughter, what might have been a rabbit-sized butterfly but was more like an ache of the heart spread itself and lifted into the air and away.

Gossamer.

Harn bent over and wept.

Afraid to startle him closer to Slog, Maleonarial walked forward quietly, then crouched to grasp Harn's arm. "Easy," he soothed as the student did, indeed, start wildly. "It's me." He lowered himself to the ground. "I'm sorry, Harn."

"Because they're all I can write?" No longer tremulous and uncertain. This was a grown man's voice, deep-throated and bitter; in the lamplight, his shoulders were wider. Harn had left youth behind.

How many intentions had he made?

"No," Maleonarial said calmly, hiding his pity. "I apologize for not being here with you sooner. For whatever reason, Her Gift in you is different."

"Flawed. Weak."

"I'm not sure that's true. Kaitealyon reminded us of The Lady's love for Her Blessed Gossamers. Maybe this is the magic She wants from you."

"It's not magic anyone wants." A shoulder hunched further. "Did you hear what they call me? Rost and Callen and the rest? The Gossamer Mage. Because I can't hold Her Words in my head. Because they slide and slip out of order the harder I try, the faster I write. Because I'm useless and make useless things." Harn surged to his feet, throwing his handful of pens at the pond.

Maleonarial rose with him, bringing the lamp. By its light he saw a patch of ground move as though interested. He took hold of Harn's arm again, to pull him back.

Harn shook free. He'd gained height and weight, was able to look Maleonarial in the eye and as strong, but any fight left him. "Leave me, master," he said, too quietly.

"Kait would box my ears," the mage assured him. "Come, Harneonarial. Cook's in the kitchen, I for one am hungry, and you've done magic enough for the night." For several, by the age of him. "Tomorrow, we'll see the inkmaster. Time we both had master quality tools, don't you think? It could help—"

"Yes!"

Faint, the hope that pen, ink, or parchment would make any difference, but he'd guessed rightly Harn would take any offered.

Maleonarial looked up at a shuttered window.

As would he.

A word with Ansibel, the servant who came to call her to breakfast, produced a welcome change of simples and a bright yellow jerkin with colorful embroidery around collar and cuffs reminiscent of the sashes worn in Alden. Nothing to be done about her pants or cloak, and Kait felt like a flower out of season, but Ansibel promised her clothes would be washed and returned to her room.

Including those in the bag, Kait having removed the made-thrush and set it on the windowsill. Ansibel merely shrugged at the mess inside, as if nothing new.

Here, it likely wasn't.

The room, by the pleased look Ansibel cast the neatly made bed, was likely hers. She could take no credit, having not slept in it, but somehow the lack of sleep didn't matter.

Kait went down the stairs to find Leksand busy eating breakfast, box again on the windowsill.

"G'morn, laddie." She bent to kiss his cheek, taking the seat across from him. Places were set for more. "Where're the rest?"

He glanced up over a forkful of egg. "Dom said until there was a new scribemaster, he was staying abed." The corners of his eyes crinkled. "I think he's too sore to get up and won't admit it. I sent a tray with Hardly."

Kait nodded, helping herself to tea. "How's it work?"

"We help ourselves," he informed her, cheerful as any hungry youngster at the prospect. "Nelisti left eggs and sausages in the pan. There's a pot of porridge, bread, and such. She saved me bread pudding." He looked longingly at the bowl. "Would you like some?"

"Kind o'ye," she grinned. "But yer t'one grow'n." She liked rolling the words off her tongue as she would at home. Liked this unanticipated bit of privacy—but. "I'll get my plate, then." She lowered her voice though they were still alone. "There's ought you need to hear."

He sobered. "Aie."

Over breakfast, Kait told her son of Pageonarial, if not the upper floor. Of what the historian had to tell them, if not that he'd had himself confined in order to hide. She left out Alden's dreadful bargain in hopes to never think of it again, though she had, through the long night, but did speak of Maleonarial going to seek out Harn, though she couldn't speak to the result.

She finished what she was willing to say before Leksand tucked into the pudding, glad his appetite remained unspoiled while she forced food between her lips.

"I'm glad Harn has help," he told her between mouthfuls.

"Aie. If we don't take care o'those suffer'n, what good's the rest?"

"'The Lady loves best those who care for others.'" He smiled at whatever showed on her face. "You recited the *Tenets of a Daughter's Wisdom* in the kitchen for the entire week before leaving for Tiler's. Ferden and I couldn't help but memorize them too."

Kait laughed; there was nothing for it. "As if that lot gave a pig's snot." She pretended to frown. "Which is fine for me to say, student-prospect, and not you."

A spoonful of pudding lifted. Returned slowly to the bowl as Leksand gave her a somber look. "Momma, do you believe we can stop them? That Master Pageonarial will find an answer to the Fell in his books?"

"We—" Seeing Tercle approaching, Kait warned her son with a glance. "G'morning."

"Don't 'g'morning' me, Kait Alder," with a fearsome scowl. "We were up all hours watching for your damned owl. And saw nary a one for our trouble." Tercle stood at the end of their table, glaring at the place settings. "Where's the damesen?"

"I haven't seen her," Leksand replied. "I was first to breakfast, according to the cook."

"Nor have I." Kait pointed to a seat. "Join us? No owls," she promised.

"Humph." Tercle sat and poured herself tea. "The damesen's out for her dawn walk, then. A reprehensible habit," with better cheer. "I made sure to keep my head under the pillow."

Dawn was past. It looked, Kait thought, turning to glance outside, a fairer day than the last.

Maleonarial came through the door to the dining hall. Had he been upstairs? Not, she judged, by towel over one shoulder. "Good morning. Has anyone seen Harn?"

A scream answered.

Tercle had to see this, Pylor decided. She'd be seeing it now, but her friend, as usual, buried her head under a pillow rather than walk in the early morning air.

The object of the damesen's interest was the school's midden. With its daily load of fat trimmings and other wastes from the kitchen, it should reek like any other, but here made-roses formed a fragrant hedge around this necessity of life, even this late in the growing season. The plants were ugly and twisted, their flowers a multitude of smallish pink balls along thorny stems, and the roses didn't so much nullify the stench as crush it beneath their own.

Finally, a use for magic of which she could approve, of practical value. While hardly the glamorous magic she imagined students dreamt of creating, a newly graduated mage scribe could, with this and at the cost of a single bell, earn a favorable impression from hold lord to kitchen dreg—until those made-roses turned to ash, but by then, she supposed a prudent scribe would have found other ways to please.

Or left.

The made-roses improved the air; Pylor noted scavengers weren't deterred. Gulls and crows circled, bickering, intent on the prize below; rats and mice scurried within the hedge, safe from the made-cats who guarded the storerooms.

Movement, larger, caught her eye. Before she could worry, she realized it was the student, Harn, scurrying like a mouse himself as if to avoid notice.

Pylor hesitated, fingers light on the handle of her cane. She hadn't meant to send him away last night. Tercle had the right of it. She'd been too caught up in her own concerns. Thoughtless.

Where was he going at this hour?

She told herself walking the same way wasn't following him.

Maybe he sought privacy, a need she shared. Hadn't the chance to walk outside, alone, drawn her out despite the poor sleep of the night before? She was glad to let Tercle rest.

Poor Tercle. A damesen's rank meant nothing here. Their task—the one she believed they had—meant nothing. Tercle wouldn't linger abed for long, being eager to meet with the inkmaster, show their samples, and learn how much the school used and what, if any, stockpiles they possessed. Her apprentice had collected rumors along their route, while she'd been—preoccupied. Icot's mines were running out. Had run out. There had never been mines; the lapis ground in the school came via smugglers along the coast who expected magic in return. As if anywhere but Her Mouth offered a port, and magic could be bottled.

Pylor missed the coast. Missed the sea.

Missed mattering. She'd no role to play. Was that why her steps followed Harn's?

The mage and daughter had surely met last night, though Kait could only say she'd take over the watch, earning Tercle's sarcastic thanks. Was she herself so shallow that when left out of the councils of others, lacking magic or "gifts," she sought to make herself important? Be needed?

No. There were plentiful spots to sit alone. Pylor watched Harn pass them all, hunched over and now moving in haste.

His haste troubled her. His being alone out here, did. Most of all, her growing conviction she knew his destination. The hedge where Maleonarial had left the wagon with Insom's urns. It should be ahead, along the roadway past the first pond.

She looked around, seeking help, finding none.

Harn was almost out of sight.

Reluctantly, Pylor continued after him, walking by the low stone wall that impounded this and the other ponds. The mortar here was as patched and weathered as that of Tiler's Hold, unlike the school's main buildings, rebuilt, she'd been informed, fifty-five years ago. A student, it had been. Something to do with firemoths.

You think they'd learn not to create the things.

Fins and tails broke the surface. Mouths gaped, sucking down bits of debris. Stocked, no doubt, for the students' table.

And so of interest to gulls.

They wheeled overhead, skimmed over the pond. Looking for fish. Real birds, looking for fish, and that was all they were, but Pylor used her injured hand to pull her borrowed hood snug. Walked faster. Readied her cane.

The nearest gulls swerved aside with high-pitched rising squeals of indignation as one of their multitude dropped to the wall, wings outstretched as it waddled beside her on ungainly yellow feet.

Oh no. "Be gone!" She swiped at it with the cane's metal tip. It hopped out of the way, then came back down.

A beak longer than her hand, hooked and vicious. A beak that gaped open, as though begging a treat, and to her horror, but not surprise, Insom's voice issued from its throat, deep-toned and full of grief. "You're too late, cousin."

Her breath caught.

The voice became shrill. "Too late! Too weak. Too small. We can't be stopped. We won't be. We've starved too long." A laugh like the cry of a bird. "It's our time!"

Pylor swung the cane again, this time with both hands, missing as the damned bird hopped.

The beak gaped and the voice issuing forth was cold and strange. "Die now. Die now. Die now."

She stumbled back. "Get away!"

The beak snapped shut. White wings, that unnatural black roiling beneath, cut the air and the creature lifted away as if to convey her words.

Only to turn and dive.

It wasn't alone. She screamed as the first took an eye but the next ripped out her tongue, and as Pylor fell beneath the crush of beating wings and tearing beaks, a man stood watching.

Dolren?

Unable to say his name, she reached for him and he came close and she believed there was a chance she'd live—

Until he bent to smile at her, black lightning in his eyes.

He was out the door first, the rest hard behind, but they were too late. The heap of squabbling, feasting birds ignored their arrival and whatever lay beneath them?

No longer moved.

Leksand ran at the birds with a broom. They rose like bones tossed in the air, gore staining feathers and beaks, to hover overhead. Eyes intent. Waiting their chance to land again.

Maleonarial dropped to a knee, pulled out pen and vial and parchment, wrote with such quick clarity he had to step back or be buffeted by extraordinary wings as the made-eagle soared upward, shrieking its rage. Larger than a bird could or should be, it drove the panicked gulls and crows ahead of it and out of sight.

Far enough. As he stood erect, a twinge afflicted the knee he'd bent, another his lower back.

The Hag, never neglectful of Her toll.

He reached the body as Kait laid her cloak over the ruined face and chest, then took a sobbing Tercle in her arms.

Leksand stood, breathing in shattered gasps. Maleonarial took the broom from his unresisting hand. "Fetch help. There's staff in the dining hall. Go," when the boy stared at him.

Sense reentered those eyes, so like his mother's. "Aie." He took off at a run.

"I hate birds. I hate birds. HATE THEM." Tercle jerked free to kneel by the cloaked remains of her friend.

Gulls didn't attack and kill people, but they were opportunists, ready to scavenge, as were crows. Insom's made-gull would have struck first, but why? And why now?

"Mage." The daughter came up to him, whispering urgently. "Look. Her hand."

An arm outstretched. It might have been flung in the woman's final struggle, a desperate reach for the cane lying on the ground, but not the rigid finger, pointing toward—

"The urns."

Their eyes met. "I'll wait for help," Maleonarial told her. "You go."

"Aie."

The same grim acknowledgment as her son, but as Kait turned and left, stooping to grab the cane, the mage heard an echo like thunder.

"Hurry! There's been an accident!" Not that it had been, Leksand thought, holding the door open, waving to speed those inside out where they could be of use.

Not that they could help the damesen, who'd been kind to him and patient, but Tercle—

"The master's there," when they hesitated, not having Her Gift and unable to sense the blaze of Maleonarial's, fearing—as they should in this terrible place—what "accident" encompassed at a school that made monsters. "You'll be safe. Come quickly!"

Not that they'd be safe, any of them. The damesen had been slaughtered. What would the Eaters do next?

They ran through the door: Eaples with two women. One grabbed a stack of clean linens and jug of water on her way, as Momma would, so he gave her a nod as she passed.

Leksand came behind, pointing to where Maleonarial stood. "Over there." The women hurried onward.

Eaples halted, shading his eyes. "Hey!" he shouted. "You there! Stop!"

He broke into a run, going the wrong direction. "Come on. We have to stop the fool."

They'd one missing—Leksand caught up in two strides and the older man swung an arm to urge him on, panting. "Don't let him pass the markers or Slog'll have him!"

A figure walked toward the last pond before the stone fence. The area seemed innocuous, and what in Tananen was a "slog"? Surely the man should hear Eaple's continued warning shouts. Why didn't he stop?

He must have heard the damesen's scream. Why hadn't he gone to her?

Leksand ran faster, the fetid stench of crowded fish and stale water assaulting his nostrils. He could find his way home by smells at this rate—

Unlike the other ponds, this one was circled by narrow stones, waist-high and painted red. The figure walked between them. One step, two, while Leksand pushed harder, ran faster—

Huge snake-like things reared up from the ground—moved with horrifying speed toward the figure.

Who kept walking as though oblivious—

Or seeking their embrace—somehow, Leksand ran faster, for it mustn't be—

"Harn!!" he shouted.

She'd thought it a fair day, as if a clear sunny sky never looked down on death, as if the absence of storm implied peace.

Fool. Thrice fool and worse. The damesen had warned against doing what the Eaters wanted. Had confessed to fear and distrust and if Kait could have any moment back, it would be the one where she'd listened but hadn't heard, too full of her plans and Maleonarial's to appreciate who was in the greatest danger.

She reached the funeral wagon before realizing it.

Tidy lines of glittering ash marked where beautiful made-horses had stood, surrounded by empty harness and the memory of purpose. Atop the barren hedge, frosted tips caught the light but the sun had yet to do more than send skeletal shadows over the wagons and carriage.

Kait made her way through the harness and ash, stepped over the wooden tongue. She listened for what wasn't sound, as she had through the night, the deeper focus become almost second nature.

Nothing.

Which could be good news or the worst news and she wouldn't know till she caught up her courage and checked the bloody urns, would she? She tiptoed around to where the freight wagon had been left.

Maleonarial's tactic was obvious; he'd rammed the tail of the wagon into the shrubs and stone. A shame it had been for nought. Someone had taken a knife to the front canvas, cutting a slice from top to bottom of the panel behind the driver's seat.

Inwardly cursing her short legs and shorter body, Kait climbed into the well of the driver seat as quietly as she could. She steadied the cane as a club in one hand and put her hand on the nearest parted canvas, ready to step inside.

Harn's head appeared in the opening. "Good—morning?" The student eyed the club worriedly. "Is everything all right?"

Not with him, it wasn't, Kait saw plain as could be. He'd aged overnight, his jaw developing what would be jowls, the tousled ruddy ringlets subdued into brown wavy locks. His face, though, blushed as crimson as Leksand's when caught in misadventure.

"Don't you 'good morning' me, Harneonarial," she admonished, lowering the cane in relief. "What have you been up to?" Without waiting for an answer, Kait shooed him aside and climbed in after him.

"Nothing. The canvas was cut—I swear this was done before I got here," he babbled, stepping awkwardly between the urns.

Urns opened, their ornate seals tossed like so much litter to the floor below, the masters' accomplishments bent and broken.

"—I came looking for a better pen. Like Leksand's. A master's pen—" His voice fell away when she looked up at him.

It was quiet. Far too quiet in every sense. Kait clutched the cold rim of an urn, began to pull herself up to look inside, hoping to see black fumes, knowing she wouldn't.

"Don't bother. It's seawater. In all of them," Harn added, as if belatedly realizing more was wrong than his transgression.

Because it was. "We have to get back to the school," Kait told him.

If it wasn't already too late.

"Harn!!"

Others would care for the dead and grieving. Hearing Leksand's anguished shout, Maleonarial hastened to where Eaples and Leksand were trying to forestall another death. He took the shortest route, risking the slimy weir between the first and second ponds, jumping the gap, then running, sure-footed and quick, along the impounding wall. None of which his body could have done before Riverhill.

For once, he found himself grateful to The Hag.

He hadn't thought to warn Leksand about the dangers inhabiting the school, didn't know the latest himself for that matter, but someone should have—

Eaples was with the boy. Good. But Leksand was twice as fast, putting him first past the markers as he ran for Harn. Who kept walking into danger, not away, but there should be time. Slog didn't care for daylight as much. Like the made-toads on the walls, it grew sluggish with the cold, but the damned thing hadn't died of it.

Sluggish? All at once, what had appeared paving stones and bright moss rose overhead, tentacles whipping through the air as Slog abandoned stealth for speed, eager for the bounty in its grasp. One seized Harn, dragging him toward the pond. Leksand kept running after him. Eaples followed bravely. They managed to dodge the first but more tentacles rose, then more—

Pylor had been right. What good was magic? Maleonarial thought savagely, with no time to think of an intention of use, let alone write it if he did. What good was he, but as another meal for the monster?

He didn't slow. "I'm coming!"

As were others now, with rakes and shovels and who knew what. Courageous and foolish, but they refused to remain safe. Maleonarial feared all they'd accomplish was Slog would feast today—

Tentacles became ash, drifting sideways in the light breeze.

Momentum drove Leksand forward, when everything else seemed to have stopped moving. He ran through what had been a dangerous tentacle a heartbeat ago, throwing up an arm to shield his eyes from the ash. Which would be why he stumbled over the body.

It was a body, that much he could tell at once, having fallen on what was ice cold and squished and no longer remotely alive. He writhed free of the corpse with dismay, then as quickly leapt back to turn it, with fearful care, face up.

It wasn't Harn.

The Lady forgive him, he couldn't help but be glad it wasn't, when he should grieve for who it was, Dolren Keeperson.

Insom's servant. Here?

"It's not—" Maleonarial let out a long breath, making Leksand feel slightly better about his priorities in the newly dead. "Dolren was to stay in Alden Hold."

Great-uncle, who rarely made judgments of strangers, had called Dolren a slimy little worm, but not even a worm deserved such a death. Leksand looked up at the mage. "He could have hidden in the wagon. But why—" he shut his mouth over the words. The Lady save them. The urns.

"We called to him to stop, Master Maleonarial." Eaples was sweating, shaken. "Why didn't he listen?"

"That's why," Maleonarial said, pointing to the pond. "What rode poor Dolren knew what it wanted."

Leksand got to his feet, transfixed with everyone else as the water level plummeted, exposing the dark silt of the surrounding shore, dropping below the level of the grated weir at its outlet. Kept dropping, as if being sucked down, while the surface glittered with a growing layer of ash and he knew—

Slog had met a greater foe, one that sought out and consumed what was made with magic.

The Eaters were free.

With the moment come and doom most likely upon the world, Kait Alder found herself calm, almost cold. Oh, she ran as fast as she could, Harn with her, but when they took the turn in the road that revealed the doings behind the school, could see those around the damesen's bloody corpse, those gathered for doubtless as grim a reason by the distant pond, and her heart found Leksand before her eyes could—

None of that mattered. She knew where the Eaters would go.

Between the stones. Inside. To hunt.

Inside—

Kait stopped in her tracks, grabbing Harn to stop him too.

"What's happening?" he pleaded. "Where are the roses?" He stared over her head. "Is that—is that the damesen?"

"It is," she told him. "And more will die unless we get everyone outside, in the light, now. Can you do that, Harn?"

His eyes were round with shock, but he answered promptly, "Yes, Daughter. I'll tell Daisy—"

How didn't matter. If they could keep the Eaters in the stones, contained there—

"No one must do magic," Kait commanded. "Make sure. Go!" She gave Harn an encouraging push, using it to set herself in motion.

"Stay outside!" she shouted at Tercle and those attending to her as she rushed past. The still-open door to the kitchen saved time; dodging the cook's bulk didn't. "Get outside!"

Nelisti tried to hand her something. "Harrr—"

Leksand's box. Kait dodged that too. "Take it to him."

She'd no need to listen for the Eaters.

Inside, she could see them.

Smoke-like fingers stroked black through the hanging cages on either side as Kait ran past the counter to the larder to the stairs, extinguishing the firemoths within, ash dribbling to the floor.

Making it dark. They preferred the dark.

Fourteen. Would the Eaters stay together or disperse throughout the school? Would they seek out the masters or gorge on made-things first? Gorge, Kait decided, though the conviction came with its own horror.

The daughter took the stairs two at a time, relieved to find no one else inside. Hers was the fifth door, left side. With the light reduced to what came through a window at the other end of the hallway, she used touch to find it, fingertips running over the mortar and stone and whatever else paced with her.

There. Kait threw herself inside, bars of sunlight streaming through the window like Her Blessing. The bright-eyed made-bird waited on the sill, motionless and perfect, down to the little lump of shit growing beneath it.

Choking back what was more sob than laugh, Kait picked up the bird, letting it grip her finger with its tiny claws. She'd thought through her message on the stairs, what information Wendealyon needed, what not, and spoke, urgently and without pause. "The Fell are the Eaters, an ancient menace from The Brutes. One has possessed Insom, using him to send its kind to attack the mage school. The damesen is dead. We believe the Eaters have come for the school's gossamers. If they succeed, I fear The Lady is next. We must stop them here. We will. Her Blessing on us all." She stopped.

Its beak opened. Ursealyon's voice proclaimed, "I will deliver."

She hoped so, in case they failed.

Kait pushed open the window and tossed the bird into the air, holding her breath until it became a dot in the sky.

Now, to set a trap.

The expiry of Slog would have raised cheers from staff who'd risked their lives to place markers, only to fish out those who hadn't cared, but for the dead.

The dead, and the curious rain of ash down the stones of the building as cluster after cluster of hapless made-toads came to what Hardly Bakerson avowed a premature end, it not being cold enough.

Maleonarial's heart tightened in his chest. The made-toads turned to ash because the Eater from Dolren had finished one meal and now worked its otherwise invisible way up the wall for more. Where was Kait?

As if in answer, Daisy rose over the roof like a second sun, great white wings dazzling, to shriek a warning loud enough to shatter window glass. "Danger! Get outside. Stay in the light! Danger! Get outside! Do no magic! Do no magic!" The made-swan wheeled above, heading for the other building, continuing to sound the alarm.

"That's Harn's voice," Leksand said, staring up.

"Your mother's warning. The rest of the Eaters must be free." With Dolren's, fifteen of the things and they'd witnessed what one could do.

Leksand looked at him, face pale but determined. "Insom keeps lamps burning day and night. Momma said he did it to resist."

"They may not like it, but light's not stopped them," Maleonarial said grimly. Kait's warning had been accurate. She understood the first impulse of frightened mages, student or master, would be to create. Horses to flee. Mauls to defend. Goddess knew, some of the fools would make themselves living chairs to watch the end of the world in comfort.

And draw the Eaters straight to them.

"No magic outside," he told Leksand. "Kait wants the Eaters in the buildings as long as possible."

"Away from the masters."

Inside—

Maleonarial clapped the boy on a shoulder. "Maybe it's more than that." He jumped on a nearby bench. Before he could call for their attention, every head swiveled, every eye locked on him. The damned bells finally had their use.

Domozuk had a voice able to penetrate the corners of an audience hall. "Hark to the scribemaster," he bellowed, and no one denied the naming.

Good. He'd need that authority, their obedience, and more if they were to survive this day. "Gather everyone in the commons, quickly. Keep them outside and well away from any stone structure." If he was right and the daughter thought the same? There'd soon be none. "Dom, take charge."

"With me and quickly! Stay to the road." Dom, Rid beside him, marshaled the staff, sending someone to bring Tercle and those still by her side.

Those on the upper floor—including Pageonarial—couldn't flee on their own. Maleonarial didn't waste breath to explain. He bolted for the dining hall. Kait's son caught up with him at the door, wordlessly opening it.

"The Eaters are inside," the mage warned. "They wanted you here."

"I asked the woman of the woods to serve The Lady like my mother before me," Leksand replied, eyes clear and bright and brave. "Unless you doubt she'd go in, Scribemaster?"

Oh, he was quite sure Kait Alder would and had. "Come then."

The hall and tables should be well-lit for breakfast—exceptionally so, according to Dom, who'd said Saeleonarial had been at wit's end trying to stop the latest class of students making firemoths.

Cages hung or stood empty, glittering ash beneath. Nothing moved. Nothing made a sound. Tables were set and there were pretty dried flowers, but Maleonarial felt his skin crawl. This was no longer a place for the living.

"They know we're here," Leksand whispered as they walked across the open space.

"I don't think they care about us." He didn't add "yet."

A sober nod. Leksand wouldn't falter. Despite the boy's youth, he'd courage and uncommon good sense.

For his age, he was a fool. He knew better than grow fond of a student. Knew what lay ahead for the would-be mage and still, with every step they took together across that haunted room, Maleonarial swore to himself Kait's son would survive this.

Swore Leksand would live free of Her cursed Gift.

First, to live at all.

You did what work needed doing, without hunting up another to do it for you. Leksand grinned to himself, almost hearing his Momma's voice, because everyone in Woodshaven knew who'd find what needed doing and get it done. Usually before anyone else was awake.

Not that she and his great-uncle didn't expect him to do his share. Nim would find out. But at home, working together was the way, many hands and backs the custom. Otherwise, how could you enjoy the feast and rest to follow?

He hadn't seen it here, not until this terrible morning. Maybe the mage school was its own kind of village. Maybe he could make a home here.

If it survived. Leksand kept his eyes averted from the piles of ash, hurrying behind Maleonarial.

"Here." The scribemaster pressed his fingers in a pattern against what appeared a plain section of wood paneling. It slid aside, revealing a coiled metal staircase. "Take one."

Lamps hung from a hook, ready for use. Leksand ran his thumb across the flint knurl to ignite it, glad of the light. He looked up to see Maleonarial's face lit from below. It might have been carved from ancient marble, the utter black dread of what was above them held at bay by the flickering reflections from hundreds of bells, and his fear left him.

If anyone could save them, would save them, it was this mage.

Maleonarial made a peculiar noise, like a cough but not. When he raised his lamp to indicate the way up, his face was again mere flesh, jaw unshaven. A man worried but committed, who looked to him for help.

He would not fail.

They took the stairs at a quick pace, the mage leading. "This takes us to the upper floor," Maleonarial explained in a low voice. "There are five masters locked in their rooms. We have to get them out before any Eater finds them." A pause of two steps, then, "Don't waste time arguing with them. We'll carry them down if necessary. The stairs at the far end are wider."

Why were there locks? Leksand focused on the rest, cheered to know they were a rescue. "The masters are infirm?"

"They're dangerous."

Hence the locks. He swallowed what else he might have asked.

The light from their lamps chased bars of shadows around and around. He lost count of the steps before they reached the metal door at the top.

The scribemaster put his hand on the bolt. "Don't look to the ceiling, Leksand. Ignore what you see on the floor. If a door is open, stay out. Nothing will attack you unless disturbed."

"Like honeybees," he suggested.

An eyebrow lifted. "Like Slog. Smaller," as if that helped. "I'll do the doors to the right, you the left. Are you ready?"

Before Leksand could answer, Maleonarial drew aside the bolt and opened the door. He stepped through, so there was no choice but follow.

Things moved everywhere, fangs glinted, wet with poison, and if not for the mage walking steadily through the throng of, yes, they were small, but still nightmares, a sensible person would have turned to run back out the door.

Work needed doing, didn't it?

Leksand held his breath the first few steps, hardly able to believe the things edged out of his way, albeit grudgingly and at the last possible moment, with hissing and spit, but they moved, so he did.

Overhead he could hear more things slither and fought the impulse to look up, shuddering when something hot and black dripped onto his leather jerkin. He stiffened but joined the mage at the first door.

"I should have brought an axe," Maleonarial said abruptly.

"For the door?"

"No." With that disquieting word, the scribemaster slipped the bolt to one side and eased open the door. Before Leksand could see what was inside, he'd closed it again. "Goddess claimed." An inscrutable look. "It means Grafeonarial wrote an intention more than he should and She took the last of his life."

"The Lady's Bless—"

"The—" Maleonarial's voice broke. "This had nothing to do with paradise or blessing, boy," he snarled. "Use Her Gift and you will age and you will die. Most certainly before anyone you called friend at home."

Other things snarled in concert, and the lamp in his hand trembled so the light did until Leksand firmed his grip. "Aie, sir. The next master. Sir."

"'Aie, sir.'" The scribemaster shook his head, the tinkle of his bells now a dire, cold sound. "Take the left." Maleonarial went to the next door on the right.

A thing like a cat crouched, fangs dripping. Leksand stepped over it, promising to apologize to every real cat he met in future if it didn't attack.

The next two doors were open and he walked by without looking inside. Then, one closed and bolted. "Arcoeonarial," he whispered, reading the name. "Let's get you to safety, sir."

Leksand opened the door.

Through a window of delicate panes within a lattice of lead, Kait watched students and masters pour from the residences on the far side of the commons. Daisy flew low, causing hair to fly and cloaks—for those who'd grabbed them—to billow like wings themselves. Harn had done a superb job of evacuating the buildings, though credit to Maleonarial's creation.

Staff urged those newly outside away from the buildings and the central pond, collecting them like so many sheep in the small field near the entrance. Maleonarial's doing too, Kait guessed. He'd heard what she'd said about Eaters and stone.

Would know what to do.

Her role remained the same. To keep watch. She supposed this made the empty dining hall the Daughter's Portion, not that the mages would appreciate the whimsy.

To watch and listen.

There were no Eaters in view. No matter, they muttered. Above her. Everywhere in the school, for Kait had come to believe she heard those at a distance as well, as though they communicated with one another by shouting and she'd no choice but bear the cacophonous result.

Never words. Emotions. The Eaters were . . . pleased. Enthralled. Excited near to madness and she dug the nails of her fingers deep into the palms, using the pain to keep herself, herself, and not be drawn into their dark, ravenous hunger. She'd been right. Freed at last, the Eaters thought of nothing but to gorge themselves. They were chasing every wisp and scrap of magic. Consuming it only to hunt for more.

Not sated, not remotely close. If anything, what she heard and felt was a rising frenzy, as if the made-things of the school stoked the fires of their bottomless hunger.

She watched Daisy land on the highest of the connected roofs, crushing a chimney as the now ungainly creature attempted to perch on broad webbed feet.

Good. More bait to keep the Eaters where they were. Inside.

Kait silenced the mutters. Stood, feeling soiled. Staggered, and swallowed vomit so she risked a precious moment to calm herself as best she could, thinking of the wind through the pines and the feel of a baby's tiny hand around her finger.

She pushed her arms through the slits in her cloak, gave herself a settling shake, then walked briskly to the doors. Now to keep the mages milling outside in alarmed confusion from doing what they mustn't.

Maleonarial would go for the historian. Save his friend, save them. And if Pageonarial had no better answer?

They'd Alden's.

A floor and doors designed to keep in what the masters created might hinder the Eaters. It couldn't stop what moved between stones.

Maleonarial chose to be annoyed. Invisible evil magic-eating fume? The least it could do, he told himself, refusing to look down the corridor toward Leksand, was be tangible. Provide a target.

The Hag at least had the courtesy to inhabit a tower. According to legend, true, but those seemed real enough at the moment.

The bolt was drawn open on Pageonarial's door. If he'd bothered to check last night, most likely the bolt itself was magic and answered to the historian, who was too intelligent to be imprisoned by anyone but himself.

He hurried inside, the urgent, "They're here—" dying on his lips.

"Yes, I heard Daisy." Page sat on one of his leather chairs, surrounded by stacks of books and bubbles, the other chair and even the desk summoned to be part of what was a wall.

"You know this," Maleonarial gestured at the barricade of anxious things, "will only lure them. Come—"

"They're to keep you away."

Maleonarial took a step closer. Eyes of all manner of shapes and sizes narrowed in warning. The desk showed teeth like a bear's and he stopped where he was. "Have you lost all sense—"

"No, Mal." Page lifted that commanding finger. "You must listen."

"Be quick, or I'll write what can dispense with this and carry you out."

The old master gave his wise little smile. "I'm sure you could. Listen first. From Ingleton's annals. 'A host is selected. A host must be learned and the Eater prepared.' Do you see? Eaters must be shown—trained, if you will—a specific host. The lids you described to me, with each master's most memorable accomplishment—I believe they were to remind the Eaters which master to possess. That's why the Insom Eater wanted so badly to know about you, my potent friend. To prepare an Eater to possess you, if they could." His sunken eyes gleamed. "I believe they can't."

Scant comfort. "One arrived in Insom's servant," Maleonarial informed him. "Whether to be sure the damesen followed instructions, or to possess her, doesn't matter. They killed her instead. Now," with commendable patience, "will you come?" He took another step, met with a chorus of growls.

He drew out a pen and vial. "Page—"

"We don't know how they think, if they think. We don't know if there's one, with appendages, or hundreds. I need time!"

"We're out of it." Maleonarial knelt, setting down the vial, and brought forth a strip of parchment. Those, the pen in his hand, were Sael's, taken from the scribemaster's quarters, having followed his own advice to Harn. He'd be damned if he'd spill a second of his life using anything less.

"Scribemaster!" Leksand burst through the open door, registering what he saw without a blink—or perhaps he didn't see, for his voice was brittle and strained. "They're all dead, sir. Someone's—some thing cut off their heads."

Pageonarial's smile gentled. He twirled that finger and three of his blades rose from inside his wall of books and bubbles, one taking position on his shoulder, the others hovering too close. "Dinus disputed Ban's footnotes. 'Harm to the host is not harm to the Eater.' One should never take an anecdotal account for fact, but this suggests a preventative measure."

An axe to keep masters from being possessed? He should have remembered the one already here. "Page, we can get you out—"

"Look at you. Maleonarial returns." An unsteady chuckle. "Be grateful, boy. We should all be. For The Goddess needs Her scribemaster." The historian closed his eyes, as if falling asleep. "Snap!"

The made-flies were quick after all.

In a spray of blood and bone, Pageonarial's head fell from sight. Leksand cried out, but it wasn't from shock, or not shock alone.

The made-books were turning to ash from the bottom up. Those above broke loose and scampered for the ceiling, but any touching the wall became ash themselves. The rest were consumed even as they fled back to the chair and desk, and bubbles dissolved in midair—

Maleonarial thrust his pen, vial, and parchment in a pocket, taking Leksand by the shoulder to push him to the door.

"We've work to do."

There was only one reason The Hag needed a scribemaster at the school. Page had the answer after all.

Alden's bargain.

Fire.

At home, she'd cheerfully threaten the lot with a frying pan, the heavy black one.

At home, Kait thought with some impatience, she wouldn't need threats in the first place.

"I tried to tell them, Kaitealyon," Harn said miserably.

She nodded her thanks at him, then put fists to hips; the way a few backed up, they remembered the pose. "There'll be no writing magic till I say so."

"If you expect us to stay out here," a student near the front called, "let us make what'll keep us warm."

Another student shouted from back, "Master Xareonarial! Teach us how to write your made-cloak."

By the smug look on that master's face, a favored pupil had earned a reward.

Fools.

"You'll wait for the scribemaster." Domozuk had gone from determined to fierce, Kait grateful for his presence beside her. "And that isn't you," pointing a thick finger at he who'd looked ready to step forward.

A few other masters averted their faces, but she caught their grins. They were no better than their students for mockery and petty disputes. Were none here true friends? Then again, how could they be, Kait thought, for the very nature of mage scribes split them apart. The more talented among them aged out of sequence with the less. The most sought-after masters packed up and left, earning their living—and the school's—throughout Tananen.

Leaving those who found the school less demanding of their skills and life, if less lucrative.

Whatever their flaws, Kait intended to save everyone of the restive crowd before her. Unfortunately, while many had run outside at Daisy's alarm without coats, cloaks, or in some cases, shoes? All had a pen in hand. She didn't see ink, but presumably they'd pockets for such things.

After being on the upper floor, she'd no illusions about what a frightened mage might create to save himself. Or what would happen next. So far, she'd glimpsed Eaters flowing by windows, or flickering along the mortar of walls. No sign outside, near the masters. With luck, if any did emerge, they'd feed on the made-sheep and unseasonable plants and whatever lived at the sunken end of the chains first.

Frightening the mages as they did.

It was then Kait realized the uneasy murmur of complaints and protests had stopped, everyone staring up, at something behind her.

She turned.

In time to see Daisy become ash and drift away.

Leksand held himself still, though the press and draw of the pen felt like something alive, scoring through parchment and clothing into his skin. "There." A pat on his shoulder freed him.

Maleonarial set the parchment strip on the floor. Pink made-mice erupted from the dark blot of ink that had been words, Her Words, words Leksand had in his mind, but didn't know how to use. After the upper floor, he wasn't sure how he felt about such power.

The made-mice ran faster than any mouse he'd seen, naked tails erect, scattering in every direction. As they ran, they whistled in shrill harmony, a puzzle solved when the mage grabbed one to show him. The tail had holes like a flute. "I call them splits," Maleonarial said, dropping the wee thing as it tried to bite. When it landed, it bounced, split, and two began to run in opposite directions, whistling. The mage bent and caught both, tucking them in a pocket. "Handy when I wanted the library to myself. I was a student once too, you know," when Leksand continued to stare at him.

A troublesome one, no doubt. Leksand blinked, wondering how he could have missed the streaks of gray in Maleonarial's black hair. "Why make them now?"

"Snacks for our guests. And they've other use. Come on."

Moving quickly, he brought them to the main doors of the dining hall. Beyond were the rest of the mages, meaning his mother too, and Leksand reached for a handle.

But Maleonarial wasn't interested in going outside. He'd gone to the frame around the door, feeling along its outer edge. The wood—butternut, Leksand judged—was carved into fantastical shapes but other than the artistry involved, the piece looked no different from any other around the room.

"Ah." Fingers pressed, so, and a narrow opening appeared in the upright. Maleonarial hooked a finger inside, pulling forth a black twist of string. "This, Leksand, is the scribemaster's end of Alden's bargain. Can you make a spark?" His voice was calm, but he'd a strange, reckless air about him. "I trust a lad from the mountains travels prepared."

Wordlessly, Leksand produced flint and steel.

"Good. We need to do this together, so—" Maleonarial took an empty glass from the nearest table and turned it upside down over one of the splits from his pocket. He nodded outside. "I'll go to the gathering hall. When your split expires, light the wick and run."

He opened one of the doors, pausing to look around the empty dining hall, and it wasn't regret, Leksand thought.

But farewell.

Then Maleonarial was gone with a rush of chill fresh air, leaving him alone with the Eaters.

Who weren't a threat to him, not directly. Maleonarial had assured him, on the way down the twisting staircase, an Eater had to know its prospective host. Which wasn't the helpful thought he'd planned, since the mere possibility of being possessed, of being a puppet of ancient evil—

Leksand shifted the flint and steel to his other hand, rubbing sweat from his palm. He bent to take a closer look at their timekeeper.

The split put its front paws on the glass, tilting its head to look back. Other than the made-horses, and glimpses of oddities during the audience with Tiler's Hold Lord, he'd little experience with magical things. "Unless you count gossamers," he told it. "There's a goodly number in our forests." Nonetheless, he could see the perfection of this creation. The split was more than a whistle with feet. Dots of deeper pink decorated the skin beneath the fine hair. The whiskers curled upward, their delicate tips glittering—

Why make curled and glittering whiskers at all? Why think of pink dots?

Because Maleonarial could. Because he'd such fine and deliberate control of Her Words and magic he could make anything but chose to make everything—perfect. Craft. Skill. This called to Leksand as nothing about mages had—might he, one day—?

The split became glittering ash.

It wasn't an Eater come to feed. It mustn't be.

Leksand dashed to the door frame, came close to dropping the flint, but didn't, struck hard and true, sending a shower of sparks over the twist of black string.

It flared white hot in answer.

Those gathered in the commons would have spotted him on the bridge, had they not been transfixed as the Eaters consumed Daisy. His proudest accomplishment, the one that made him scribemaster and cost him a year. Maleonarial felt nothing but gratitude for the distraction.

And for Leksand Loggerson. No time to summon trusty Domozuk to help, or Kait, but he'd no doubt of the boy. Urgency beat through his bones; shortened his breaths. The Eaters had reached the upper floor—they'd taken Daisy from this roof. If they'd any chance, if it wasn't already too late, it had to be done now.

He entered the hall, forced to stop and let eyes blinded by sunlight adjust to the relative gloom. As in the dining hall, he heard ghosts, felt memories. Saeleonarial's laugh. The intricate splendor of Her Words and triumph of piecing them together—

The sickening moment he'd realized if mages were to stop dying for splendor and triumph, She had to end, and it was up to him.

His fingers found the catches quicker this time. Brought out the wick. He'd no trusty flint and steel, but no mage scribe used sparks to start fire.

Maleonarial formed the intention, checked it, then knelt with his pen filled with ink and ready, his eyes on the pink within his lightly closed fist.

And when the split became ash, he wrote what burned.

The concussion knocked her back, sent others to the ground. As Kait found her footing, she realized there must have been two blasts, for both main buildings of the mage school had collapsed in a mass of tumbling stone and roaring flame. The destruction spread in a wave, every building being linked to its neighbors, and none remained whole.

Good thing her son hadn't moved in.

Which was shock talking, she knew full well, because there was nothing good about this unless—

SCREAMS!

—not heard, but felt. Not from lungs, but from what writhed and burned, and Kait would have felt pity even for the Eaters if their death cries weren't threatening to boil the brain in her skull—

Silence.

She moved encased in it, oblivious to those around her, needing to be sure. Flinched when a billow of black smoke crossed her path, but that's all it was and she settled again.

Searing heat forced her to stop short of where the made-swan had greeted them, but that was close enough. Kait closed her eyes and listened.

Wind—

But it wasn't.

Breathing. Each breath steady as stone and slow as seasons. As if the world itself drew in, let out, what wasn't air at all.

Undisturbed. Untroubled.

Asleep.

Nothing more. She felt tears of relief spilling down her cheeks. Nothing more.

Hands grasped her. "Momma! Are you all right?"

A deeper voice, "Daughter, are the Eaters destroyed?"

Kait opened her eyes, smiled at faces blurred by tears, and nodded. "Aie."

Momma wasn't all right, not yet, Leksand told himself. She wouldn't leave the flames, for one thing, as if despite her assurance the Eaters had themselves been consumed, she kept watch nonetheless.

If she'd stop watching, he'd be able to tell her. How masters came to an end. How they succumbed to age while too young to die and how could it be kinder to write what could sever a head and leaving it staring up from a pool of—

"Leksand."

Leksand turned from his mother. "Pardon?"

"I said isn't it incredible?" Harn repeated patiently. "Maleonarial—and you—will be in history books across Tananen. This will." Grinning, the other waved an arm in case it was possible to miss the ruination to every side save one.

On that, the field and the gate and the road to Alden, people busied themselves. Made-horses sped messengers to the hold, though the twin pillars of smoke would take the news first. Three of nine masters, including Xareonarial, had also fled, to avoid being picked as scribemaster during the laborious period to come.

Of those remaining, one had made himself a shelter shaped like an amorous flower, another like a living furred hide, and more living constructions were popping into existence. Students huddled over parchments, pens working. Made-pigs, made-toads, made-firemoths.

"Why are they doing that?" Leksand demanded, listless. He didn't look at Harn, because Harn no longer was Harn, but someone much older who should be Harn's uncle or father. "Why aren't they helping one another?" The staff were. "Why make useless things?"

"They can't help it. I couldn't, if not for doing magic most of the night. And—they're afraid to be cold."

"It isn't cold." It was hot, so hot they risked eyelashes staying this close.

Harn made a sound; he didn't listen. Threw up his hands and left him.

Leksand didn't care. His name hung in Alden's hall. It didn't belong there or in histories. He'd struck a flint at the scribemaster's command. Managed to escape. Stood now as much a slave to the result's raging beauty as his mother, for there was nought else to do— nought else left—

As if she'd heard her name in his thoughts, Momma stirred, fluffing herself like a waking bird. "Tsk. Laddie, you've scorched your hand."

He made himself smile at her. "An ember caught me. It's nothing." But nothing would do save his mother produce a clean strip of cloth, like magic herself, to bind the angry red score. "Feels better," he said when she was done and regarding him a little too intently.

"The school will rebuild. It always does."

"It's n'that."

She looked to the crowd of useless, self-centered mages and snorted. When her gaze returned, her face was set and stern. "You didn't risk your life for them, Leksand. You served and defended The Lady. You've helped save Her."

Leksand opened his arms and gathered her up, resting his chin on her head. As long as he could remember, she'd known the words to lift his heart.

As long as he could remember, he'd told her what burdened it. "I don't want to be like them," he whispered. "Goddess forgive me, I don't want Her Gift any more."

He felt her stiffen, being a daughter, then sigh, for she was more. "Aie."

Maleonarial didn't watch his made-swift disappear into the clouds. It would find Affarealyon, most likely on the road and halfway here, and speak to her with his voice. He'd sent the hold daughter the blunt truth.

"I invoked Alden's bargain to destroy the evil we brought here. As my final duty as scribemaster, I charge you to care for those left homeless, knowing this is no light burden."

Then, more words had tumbled from his lips before he'd known he'd say them, or thought them, but they too were true. "Wait before you rebuild, Affar. There may not be another mage school."

Not if he could help it. With the end of the Eaters, the end of the school—with a body still hale and whole—was he not free to continue his quest? To end The Hag's rule over them. To save the Saels and Pages and Harns and the hapless fools wasting life to magic themselves warm when blankets were on carts heading up the road, because the feeling magic gave vanquished the fear and grief this day deserved.

End The Hag and magic, to keep poor battered Leksand where he now stood, in his mother's arms. Send him home. Both of them. He'd trust Kait could keep the boy from writing long enough for his mission to succeed.

Maleonarial strode faster toward the pair, ignoring the sparks and soot flying through the air like so many made-flies, the ground and pond painted red with flames' reflection. He'd make them a team for the carriage. If they left now, they could catch a barge—

Why was the cook heading for the pair too?

With something under her arm—

He broke into a run.

"Harrr." The cook held Insom's box out to Leksand, her sweat-drenched face beaming.

He didn't reach for it.

She thrust it at his chest with louder, less pleased "HAAARRR," as if to say she'd lugged it around long enough and he'd bloody well better be grateful.

"Thank you, Nelisti," Leksand said quickly, taking the thing after all. "Thank you very much."

"Narr."

Kait watched her walk away, a cook without a kitchen. "Hardly's family has a bakery. I wonder if she knows. What do you think, laddie? Leksand?"

He was no longer beside her. She looked around frantically.

There he was, walking toward the burning building, the box in his hands. She ran to catch up, half skipped to keep up. "What are you doing?"

He showed her the box. "I don't want any of this."

Fair enough. "N'need t'cook ourselves, laddie. Ye kin toss it from here," Kait suggested, heart aching at the despair in his dear face.

He stopped and she caught a reassuring glimmer of an earlier self in his abashed, "Oh, aie."

But as he lifted the red and black box, with its brass edges and catch, Kait remembered the feeling she'd had in the carriage, and the sealed inkwell belonging to Insom and Pylor's father before him. "Wait!"

Leksand raised an eyebrow at her, looking now about to laugh. "Why?"

She didn't hear or see anything.

They'd hidden before. "Take the inkwell and throw it first, into the hottest part of the fire."

His face went sickly pale. With exaggerated care, Leksand set on the ground the box that had accompanied them from Tiler's Hold to this moment, an object that, in hindsight, seemed determined to follow and find him. Kait watched him remove the lid and take out the gleaming metal inkwell. He stood and threw it with the same powerful arc that drove many an axe blade deep in the old pine at home.

Sparks shot up when it landed, in the towering flames of what had been a staircase, and Kait dared breathe again. "Let that be the last."

The lid flew next, then Leksand grabbed the box and aimed it at the fire. He hesitated to nod a greeting to the mage, who joined them and stood silently by. "I'll not need this. I'll not write Her Words."

By the fire's light, did she see a faint smile on Maleonarial's lips? "Do as you must, Leksand."

"I will." With that, Leksand flung the box, awkward in his timing and motion, so the parchment roll and pen came loose.

A spark caught the parchment midair, turning it to a torch.

The pen of Surano glass, made on an isle none from Tananen had ever seen, tumbled through the air, its amber and cream like frozen flame.

Struck stone.

Shattered into sparks of its own, sparks that did nothing to light the plume of black rising up, splitting into grasping fingers, and even as Kait shouted a warning that burned her throat and used Her Words— "ℒℬℽ"

The fingers found her dear boy—

And took him.

Flames blew out, then roared as if renewed. The stones of the bridge and circling the pond cracked and split, and whatever the daughter intended with her shout, the result was the breaking of the weir and the release of whatever lived in it. Maleonarial heard the cries from those now downstream and wading, heard Harn call out and Dom, but had no time for them nor care.

He faced what had been Leksand, seeing black lightning course through the whites of his eyes, eyes now cold and hard. Saw lips pull back in a pleased smirk those lips would never have made by nature, and it was only then he realized Kait had thrown herself at what had been her son and was beating it with her fists. "Outta him, damn ye! OUT!"

He pulled her back, held her tight against his chest so they could both stare helplessly. "After is too late," he said, to himself, not to her.

"No." Kait twisted free and spat at the feet of the Eater. "Give him back."

The eyes cleared, then filled with horror. Leksand put out a shaking hand. "Momma—"

Before their hands could touch, black flickered to stain the white and the smirk returned, became something darker. "Mine. Mine. Mine." This voice was foul. Was this what Kait heard in the stone? Too high. Too thin. Filled with echoes of itself.

A self delighting in pain of any kind.

But talking. Responding. "What do you want for him?" Maleonarial demanded. "Tell us."

"Nothing here. Here. Nothing." The eyes turned cunning, shifted to the crowd of mage scribes. "Feed us. Feed us. FEED US."

Her Words spoken by the daughter rattled the world. These were sly and dangerous. They tried to seize his heart, weaken his will, and Maleonarial didn't dare think of Leksand, trapped with that inside him. Most of all, he didn't dare think of the cleansing fire, so close, and how this body of his had the strength to pick up the boy and toss him in like an armload of wood.

There had to be another way.

"It's The Deathless Goddess you want. Her magic. I can take you to where She lives." A blow landed on his chest. Another and he caught Kait's fists in his hands but didn't dare look down at her. "We can use the carriage. She's not far."

In a dreadful parody of snake, or smoke, the body bent at hips and shoulders, twisting as the eyes, or something unseen, studied him. Then, high and thin, spittle forming at the edge of lips, "Liar! Liar! Liar!"

Distrustful creature. Maleonarial released Kait, who'd gone too still. "I want The Hag to end. I want my life and the boy's." Deliberately, he relaxed his stance, added a cutting mockery to his tone. "I've tried to end Her hold on us for years. Can you destroy Her or not?"

Eyes cleared, filling with tears. "No! You can't! We defend—" Kait whimpered as the black returned. "YES!! Where? WHERE?!"

"Not far," he repeated. "This is the bargain. You release Leksand, free and unharmed. I take you to Her Soul."

Dire muttering as if it argued with itself.

A hand, fingers like ice, took his. A broken whisper. "Not even for m'laddie, mage. Please."

Not looking down, he squeezed those fingers the slightest bit, before shaking his hand free. Aloud, "You'll be a mother again, not daughter and slave."

Trust me, he'd tried to say with that one touch. Could she?

"Ride host there. Free there. THERE!" The Eater's voice filled with anticipation. "FEAST. FEAST. DESTROY HER!"

Fear came like a tide with the words, with the stark hunger in that voice, the evil in it. Bile rising in his throat, Maleonarial fought to stand where he was and not run. Stayed where he was because Kait Alder stood, facing the Eater with him.

And when she spoke, he remembered courage.

"You go back to hiding and leave m'laddie be till then." She took a step closer, and did the ground tremble beneath her small foot? "I'll be watching. I'll know."

The black left Leksand's eyes. Bargain accepted.

Maleonarial made himself endure the boy's accusing glare.

Only the young could look so betrayed.

Her tongue probed her cheek, retreated from what felt a blister. Similarly, Kait's thoughts circled around a notion that felt—hazardous, to imagine. She'd used Her Words without hesitation or thought. What she'd said?

Made no sense at all. *To me.* Unless The Lady spoke through her lips to proclaim this the right and only choice, to sit and sway in a carriage she was coming to hate mightily, trusting the man driving what were surely the ugliest horses ever made.

To save her son, at unspeakable cost.

"You can't trust it, Momma," Leksand said, with the low tremor to his voice that spoke of fury and fear. Contained, barely. "You can't bargain with it."

"We'll see, won't we." She lifted her hand to signal no more. The Eater might be tucked away and quiet; it wasn't gone. Who knew what it could hear?

*To me.* On the other hand, those seemingly simple words had made sure no one would notice or care—not even Harn, busy aiding others— as the three of them hurried beneath the trees lining the brook become a flood, following the mage as he'd crossed by jumping from boulder to boulder.

A shortcut to where he'd left the wagons and carriage. The sole way to reach them that wasn't aflame, for the school kept burning. The audience hall and the residences connected to it. The more innocent dining hall and its kitchen and storerooms.

And not so innocent upper floor. Kait looked at her son. "Do you know what became of Master Pageonarial?"

"He killed the other masters then himself."

Her poor laddie. She resisted the impulse to pat him on the knee, for there was no comfort to offer.

Not even that his wish had come true, and Her Gift gone. Fled the Eater. Corrupted or withered by it. Whatever the cause, the person sitting across from her, disdaining the strap she held tightly, felt like the boy he'd been before Tiler's Hold.

And would be again, Kait vowed. She kept her watch, clinging to the hope offered by the press of fingers over hers.

The hope that the mage who'd spent years trying to end The Lady, was willing now to save Her.

What pulled the carriage bucking and rocking over the hill and down had legs and bodies to pull, mouths to take bit and rein, but otherwise? The six were fit for the upper floor, written to last no longer than it took them to run to Her Tears.

If the axles survived the punishment. Maleonarial, braced on the driver's seat, the wind of their passing blowing bell-laden hair behind him, judged it an even chance. After all, this was a hold lord's carriage. A wealthy hold lord at that. The road from Alden Hold to the far canal wasn't too far—

His teeth caught his tongue as wheels and seat dropped abruptly. He left the seat only to meet it on the way back up. The mage spat blood and grinned. For a man nigh death a handful of days ago?

He'd never felt so alive. "You found a way to stop Cil, Hag," he whispered. "Saved me. I'd thought it for spite. But that wasn't it, was it?"

The road at last. The team jumped the ditch with a disconcerting howl of joy. Maleonarial held on—

—they made it. The road was well maintained and they surged forward, faster and faster, until he had to pull his cloak over his mouth to catch a breath.

To talk, with no one near to listen. A habit.

"You did it for this, didn't you? To battle your enemy. All those years alone together. Did you come to know me so well, Hag, you'd known I would? I damn well didn't."

Despite the wind, something came to rest on his knee.

A gossamer, wings flattened, holding on with six hooked legs. Topaz eyes gazed up at him from what was an exquisite not-quite-a-rose nor fully-a-butterfly yet more beautiful than either. The head tilted, posing a question.

Maleonarial grunted. "I remember you. A nuisance. Tipped over my porridge."

The head rotated around.

His gossamer, this. "My fingers were clumsy with the cold," he assured it. Sprung from a moment's costly daydream, that too. He'd had those, as well as frustration.

He bounced his knee. "Scat. You don't want to be here any more than we do."

For a wonder, it obeyed, winking away rather than flying.

A tiny laugh in his ear.

"If you're trying to make me feel we've a chance, Hag," Maleonarial grumbled to the empty air, "it'll take more than that."

Though he did feel it, just a little.

He felt his mother's eyes on him and was grateful. Not for much right now, to be honest, but if she watched, the Eater would behave.

*. . . dark the well and deep and down you fall . . .*

Leksand shuddered.

"Laddie?"

"It's nothing." He could have told her, explained how the Eater snuck around and pulled him down, left trails of doubt and despair, but the effort daunted him.

And what more could she do?

She leaned forward, swaying with the carriage, to put her hands on his knees. "I can hear it. Muttering to itself. To you," with a perception he hadn't expected. "Try not to listen."

He stared at her hands, half as long as his, strong, though, with work. "Look at me."

Her tone raised his eyes, when he couldn't find the will. Her eyes— burned.

Which couldn't be, because this was his Momma and Leksand blinked furiously, finding her eyes familiar and brown. She sat back. "Better?"

"Yes, but—" All at once he could think for himself. "Set me on fire, before we get there," he said. "I've flint and steel."

*. . . no you don't . . . no you won't . . . down the well you fall . . .*

He fumbled them from his pocket only to lose his grip and drop them. In a victory over the yammering in his head, he picked them up before they slid across the floor and held them out. "Here."

"My brave laddie." His mother took the flint and steel, then tucked them away. "No."

"But—"

"The Eater lets you be, so long as it isn't threatened." Her eyes glistened. "I want to ride with you, not it."

*. . . weakness . . . weakness . . .*

It wasn't. It was strength, to insist on what they had, and not waste a moment. Leksand pulled open the curtains to either side, squinting in surprise to find the sun shining, relieved to feel the darkness in him retreat further. He pressed his nose to the window. "We've left farmland," he announced, willing, like her, this moment be normal. "It's a forest, but the trees are—Momma? What kind are they?"

She shifted sideways to see out without losing her view of him, then abruptly moved to her window.

"Those aren't trees."

Gossamers. Tall, seemingly still, and so many they appeared the edge of a forest, making Leksand's confusion understandable. But they weren't still. Rather than move with the carriage, the same gossamers reappeared in view over and over as though skipping through the solid world and Kait wanted to warn them to flee their company, the Eater, but it was too late.

Hadn't she summoned them?

*To me.* Words she'd spoken on impulse. Why? She sat back, staring across at Leksand, and tried not tremble. Was she, like Maleonarial, willing to conspire with the Eater, to pay an unimaginable cost, for her son's life?

Leksand pressed his lips together, the eyes meeting hers wide and round. Prudent, not to ask a question to inform what rode within him. Perhaps their survival, not to rouse it now to feed.

The carriage slowed without warning and he took another look outside. "We've come to another road. I'd hang on," he cautioned, hand seeking the strap. "It's not as—"

The rest of what he'd have said was lost in the protest of a well-built carriage hitting what had to be the worst road in Tananen. Kait hung onto her strap with both hands, counting it an accomplishment to stay near her seat, for there was no staying seated. She risked a look out herself, for anything had to be better than this, to see they raced between reed grass and brown-headed cattails, gossamers like a horizon of flickering bronze.

They'd entered the vast fen called Her Tears.

There were those who professed to know the mind and intent of The Deathless Goddess, which assumed there was a mind and intent to be known. Something Maleonarial often doubted.

What would those intimates say now? For instead of shielding Her Blessed Gossamers from the Eater, a plague of the things accompanied them, a number increasing the further along the rotten excuse for a road they traveled into Her Tears, and he knew them. Some were his—

Some were Cil's, watching him with topaz eyes that held the memory of his shape.

Maleonarial would have waved, but it took both hands to stay on the seat. At least he'd no need to guide the team; there was but one possible path.

Were the gossamers bait? The willful wisps of mischief hardly constituted reinforcements. Tippers of porridge. Tuggers of hair. Glimpses of glorious wonder—

The Hag stole socks.

And life, he reminded himself, his body no longer so young. She'd the unquestioned power to do that.

What else? The mage had a new and troubling sense whatever intervention he'd hoped to inspire—after all, what was one Eater against an undying omnipotent goddess, and The Hag owed them help for a change—the odds were excellent mere mortals might not recognize or survive it.

The carriage lurched and slipped, wheels close to mired in the steadily worsening surface. Kait and Leksand made no outcry, though being shaken and likely bruised.

Tough, the pair from Woodshaven. Close, that too. He'd met his share of villagers, hard-working and cheerful about it. Stayed with families, but this mother and son had a bond unlike anything he'd experienced. What that said about the paucity of his life, well, he'd had no choice in it, had he?

The boy's Gift had vanished. It must have happened when the Eater possessed him, but he hadn't noticed in the moment. Whether fled or consumed, the absence might be a mercy.

Though if whatever lay ahead included the best of all outcomes? The end of The Hag as well as the Eater? Freedom for every mage and daughter and acolyte?

He'd die a happy man. Would rather live as one, but he'd accepted the probable outcome when he'd walked from the school the first time.

They hadn't arrived yet. Maleonarial turned his thoughts to a practical problem. The team he'd made would expire soon and he'd prefer not to write another.

Hard to find bearings, between the ever-changing gossamers and featureless fen. It'd been summer when he'd ridden here to visit Her Soul. They should be close, but that could be as much wishful thinking as the end of magic.

If the team failed too soon, the Eater might keep Leksand's body in order to walk the rest of the road, if walking was what you'd call trying to pull boots from the cloying mud.

Unless the Eater, lured by the abundance of gossamers, left in pursuit.

Then what? What did an Eater gain by consuming magic, be it gossamer or Slog? He'd seen no sign it made the things more powerful. They remained as annoyingly mysterious as The Hag and he'd ask Pageonarial—

A death to lay squarely at whatever passed for the Eaters' feet. Add the months the historian had lived isolated and in fear.

Fear. Anger. Grief and regret. Even hope. Maleonarial stared straight ahead, jaw clenched. Emotion was the enemy of clarity. Of focus. He'd taught himself patience, those long years. Discipline. Concentration. He forced himself to relax, let Her Words float through his consciousness, stopping none of them. No need to examine this possibility or that. He was the most powerful mage scribe in Tananen, but intentions were of no use—

He sat straighter.

Ahead the sun failed to penetrate what wasn't a distant, indistinct rise in the ground, but a nearer bank of fog.

Her Soul.

⁓

*...close...close...closer...*

Leksand put his hands over his ears, but it didn't keep out the fell voice, with its *HUNGER*—

"Leave him BE!" Arms went around him, his mother abandoning her hold on the strap to join his struggle.

Whether it was her words or presence, or strength he gained from their contact, the voice retreated to a foul muttering. He lowered his hands in time to steady them both as the carriage leaned far to one side, then righted. "Better," he half gasped.

"Not if we turn t'jelly in this pisspot," she replied grimly, making him think of his bladder, for it had been a while.

And once thought? The jostling didn't help.

Such ordinary discomfort. He wasn't sure if he wanted to laugh or sob. Neither, given the state of things. "We're almost there," he began.

The carriage stopped, along with all sound. Even the Eater was quiet.

"Seems so," his mother commented, then gave him a fierce hug. "Ready to see The Lady's home, laddie?"

Leksand squirmed. She'd know, being a daughter, what would offend a goddess.

"Kin I take a piss first?"

There was nothing to see. Though the sun shone somewhere, perhaps everywhere else, here, at the end of the road, fog licked her boots and erased the fingertips of her outstretched hand. The made-team might stand in their traces, for all Kait could see from the now-essential anchor of a muddy carriage wheel.

Silence, save for companionable waterfalls by the other wheel. She'd taken care of her own comfort in that regard, quite sure The Lady had other concerns. Courteous of Leksand to inquire, given everything else, but he was that.

Moisture condensed on her skin, formed drops where it could. She ran her tongue over her lips, to find them dry.

Not fog, then. She waved a tentative hand back and forth. The gray stuff flowed with the motion, as if dancing—

A shadow loomed. Kait relaxed, hearing muted bells. The mage and her son, following the side of the carriage to rejoin her. "It wasn't this thick when I was here," Maleonarial said, frowning.

"It's not fog," she informed them. Something tickled her ear. Flew up her nose, making her sneeze. "These are gossamers."

As if they'd waited to be named, the gray bloomed every color and flowed in its dance this way and that, giggling like spring and flowers and all the joy in the world. They stood immersed in a shimmering rainbow of gossamers too small to be otherwise seen and Kait thrilled to the wonder of it.

"Here. HERE. HERE!" came the shrill and terrible shout.

Black fume moved like stabs of lightning, reaching everywhere. Taking—

He was free.

Why was it night? It hadn't been night—

And wasn't, Leksand realized. With awareness came searing agony, for he wasn't free. He stood rigid and unable to move, his mouth opened till the corners of his lips split and bled, while out poured what smothered color and stole light—

How could the Eater, which had hidden in a pen, continue to vomit forth from his mouth, so that he couldn't catch breath and felt darkness of another sort closing in—

And why did he taste the sea?

He couldn't see the Eater as could the daughter, but nothing else would roll back the gossamer fog in huge arching waves, letting through the sun, revealing their boots and the mud of the road, and the dead stalks of reeds.

Maleonarial turned to Leksand. Stopped in stunned horror. Blood flowed from either side of a mouth torn open, face convulsed in a rictus of soundless shout. He recovered and moved as the boy choked, unable to breathe. Supported him as he dropped to his knees and where was his mother, that she hadn't come to her son?

Intended words. Consequential phrases. Passages fraught and a syllabus too dreadful to endure. Her Words, all for this moment.

For the last, most perilous dictates to be uttered.

Kait turned her back on her suffering son and the mage.

*. . . black plumes grasp and take. As before.*

*She remembers.*

Took a step away.

*. . . gossamers break and are consumed. As before.*

*She remembers. Remembers, once, how hope failed and all was almost lost.*

Took one more step, ignored by the Eaters for their prize was in reach and they left all else to seize it. Her Soul. Not a tower. Towering. Not stone. Clear crystal spires, shot through with topaz sparks, rising to the sky.

*. . . exposed as what shielded them since the days of ice and fire, for there'd been both, She tried both, She remembers, fall to the enemy.*

Feeds the enemy. Not enough. *It hadn't been. She remembers.*

Wouldn't be. For what had been like Her, long ago and loved, had diminished to nothing more than appetite. Blind but cunning. An evil satisfied by nothing less than the end of things, and not even that.

Crystal spires filled with roiling shadows, black and thick and purposeful. Her ears, the ones that heard beyond this world, filled with their screams of triumph. United, again. All the magic of the world, all the life, theirs to plunder. *Again.*

*She remembers.*

But this time is different.

*This time She is not alone.*

Kait Alder, once a humble daughter from Woodshaven, opens Her mouth to speak. "ⵁ≈≈ꙅoꙅoⵖ⁀ꜿꜿꙅℓⴶℴ"

Her Soul. For a heartbeat, less, Maleonarial saw splendor beyond imagining or comprehension, as if he'd looked into the sun or the heart of the world.

So that he cried out in anguish to witness the spires befouled, darkness spreading out in seething waves—

Leksand heaved a breath, sobbed it out and coughed out blood. Maleonarial took hold of the boy and held him tight, having no idea what else to do. If this was the end, for what else could it be with gossamers disappearing and destruction spreading in all directions as if there'd been flames he hadn't seen—

Best this way.

"Look at me, mage." The command was rock against ice.

He held Leksand and looked up, for how could he not, and Kait looked down at him in her bright yellow jerkin and cloak, her eyes become hard glittering gems.

The answer to the question he hadn't dared think.

"No," he whispered. "No." But he'd known, hadn't he. He'd never met Kait Alder, for she'd never left her forests and village. Only her shape stood before him. "Her Designate."

"Yes," the roar of wildfire across grass. "As I became yours, for when you came and found what you called magic, what was left of me, you named me Lady and Goddess. And when you found those among you touched by magic, by me, you named them daughter and mage. You took from me like tiny Eaters, so I must take from you or dream myself into death."

Why weren't they dead now? He tore his gaze from Her face, or She allowed it, to see they and the carriage, the muddy road beneath, were all that remained. Around circled darkness and hunger. Above mocked a disc of cold blue sky.

Within was quiet as a tomb.

"Why aren't we dead?" he demanded, lifting his head. "Why save us, if we mean so little to you?"

"You mean everything. You create gossamers."

More than his share—but the mage hesitated, feeling on the cusp of understanding. "Why do gossamers matter to you?"

The murmur of raindrops through leaves. "Gossamers make magic." Kait's tender smile, those ancient, aloof eyes. "They were gone, once. I remember. The Eaters won and gossamers lived solely in my dreams of what was and would never again be, until you arrived and began to write them back into the world."

"Mistakes—"

The crack of lightning through wood. "All else you make is the mistake, mage. Twisting My Words to serve petty needs. Squandering what little magic has returned, so I must replenish it."

The drip of snow melt. The distant call of geese, returning. "You create gossamers when you forget greed and fear. When you dare listen to your dreams and mine. Hadn't you noticed, little mage? Gossamers like you."

This last in Kait's voice, so Leksand stirred in his arms and tried to speak.

"Easy, boy," Maleonarial said gently. The wounds to the corners of his mouth weren't life-threatening, but there was no telling the damage inside. "What now, Hag? We die together?"

Wind across frozen wastes. "Once, I'd the power to push the Eaters into the ocean. Since, My Veil and Fist kept them at bay." An avalanche ripping trees from a mountainside. "Now, they have found their way past my defenses. All are here. Soon, they will have this, too." Her hands indicated the tiny circle of road, then came to rest over her heart.

Death it was.

Leksand struggled to stand; Maleonarial steadied him. "W'came t'help." Blood cascaded down his cheeks with every word, but he didn't stop, or couldn't. "Wha'kin we do?"

"Laddie, ye did your share. You brought my enemy, our enemy, to-gether and here." Thunder rolled over a plain, freshening hope. "Only I can stop them. Not as this fragment. Most of me dreams, still. But you, Master Maleonarial, Hermit Mage and Scribemaster, you can awaken me." An unexpected laugh, as if between friends. "You almost have many times before."

He avoided Leksand's desperate pleading look. "I was trying to end you."

"No," and Her Voice was the first soft breath of spring, moving the bells in his hair. "You've tried to restore me, for there was nothing good or natural in the taking from one another. Nothing good about gossamers being thought mistakes and twisted made-things being judged right. Now, mage, awaken the rest of me."

Impossible. Ridiculous. What was he supposed to write? Maleonarial pulled out his pen, fumbled for ink. Heard Her laugh and dared frown. "What?"

"You've never needed to write magic. Only to believe in your intention."

It wasn't that easy. Had never been easy. He fumbled to understand. "I believe."

"In magic. Now believe in yourself, as I do. As Leksand does. As Kait." She went on tiptoe and he bowed so her lips met his forehead. Offering warmth and comfort, as a mother to a son. Belief, that too—

And when Kait who was The Lady and The Deathless Goddess and what he'd yet to meet and couldn't begin to comprehend smiled?

What could he do but smile back.

"Now, mage. The word you've always known, but not yet intended. My name.

"TANANEN."

Leksand watched comprehension light Maleonarial's face. Watched the mage lift his hand and write in the air with swift sure strokes.

Where he wrote, light followed, tracing Her Words so when Leksand closed his eyes, they shone still.

When he opened his eyes, the world had changed.

But what he saw first, all he saw, was the pile of glittering bronze ash where his mother had been.

And he wept.

What slept beneath the earth awoke to its name.

TANANEN.

The Eaters, ready to sup on all the magic in the world and bring destruction, did not see their doom coming, for it rose from the very earth to draw them down into a well both endless and dark.

Having nothing else to consume, they began to feast on themselves, muttering with delighted pain and thwarted plans and so did not see.

When flame followed, bringing an end.

It was given to Maleonarial alone the chance to see what he had done.

The crystal spires, cleansed, again rose brilliant and clear, with topaz glinting like sparks. Far above, flame writhed from jaws the size of mountains, wings owned the sky, and an eye like the sun, wild and bright, found him.

Winked.

Then vanished, leaving a laugh.

He'd made a gossamer.

And it wasn't the euphoria of magic spent he felt, but something better, something warmer. Joy, it was, and with that he realized nothing hurt, nothing of him had aged.

No taking. That's what She'd wanted. Only giving.

"I'm a Gossamer Mage." Was there a bell remotely big enough? Maleonarial half bent, hands on his knees, laughing. "A gossamer!"

"Sir?"

At the pained sound, he straightened. Poor Leksand. An intention occurred to him, and instead of thinking too much about it, the mage sent his finger scribbling through the air. Small twin gossamers popped into existence, flying at Leksand, who tried quite desperately to wave them away.

"It's all right," Maleonarial said, because it was, and the gossamers worked their tender magic on the boy's cheeks, so that an instant later, there were no wounds at all.

The gossamers pulled Leksand's hair and vanished.

Leksand felt his face in wonder, then his eyes dropped to the ground. "M'Mom. She died at home, didn't she."

The signs had been there. Only Kait could see the Eaters. Only she heard the singers. Not because of a special ability, but because She'd been Tananen all along.

"Yet was with us," the mage offered, believing that was true too. Kait Alder may have given her life to The Lady in Woodshaven, but what possessed her had let her be Kait until the very last. "The Lady let her stay with you."

The boy sniffed, but managed a brave, if wan smile. "Aie." He looked around. "What do we do now, sir?"

Maleonarial put his arm around Leksand's shoulders, feeling the inner strength of the Gift that came from Tananen.

"I believe we've gossamers to make."

# Fundamental Lexicon

*The world was once barren.*

Now it is not, for magic lives and breathes and loves again.

*We were once alone.*

Now we are not, for magic flows within those of us who dare to dream.

*Magic, once, was lost.*

Now it will never be, for magic is again part of the world and us.

And the stories we've yet to write, together.

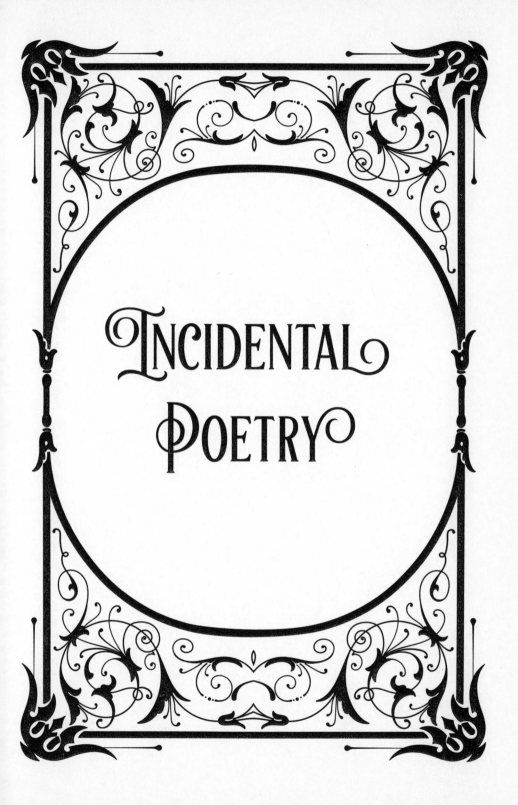

# Incidental Poetry

# ℐNCIDENTAL ℘OETRY

Wendealyon herself escorted Leksand Loggerson to the hold lord's closed door. "I feel the same," the hold daughter said abruptly. "How can that be?"

"We aren't what's changed." People will want answers, Maleonarial had said before their ways parted. Tell them what we witnessed and were told. Share the truth we know. So Leksand paused politely. "I've told you what happened. Tiler's was never abandoned to the Eaters. The Lady came as my mother to save you."

Her eyes filled with grief. "But . . . The Lady is gone."

No, his mother was. The Lady had never existed beyond a construct of smaller awestruck minds and that was a terrible truth.

Yet not the only one. "Listen for Her. Do you not feel Her Presence? Her Words?"

Grief faded. "I—do. I think I do. Yes," with sudden confidence. Then a flicker of confusion. "She's not the same."

No, She was again Herself, Tananen, the greatest gossamer of them all and the living fount of magic in the world, and the marvel? Wasn't any of those things, Maleonarial had said, and Leksand believed.

It was that She had a heart, one that valued and encompassed all that lived within Her realm.

As for Her Gift?

It might not comfort Wendealyon in this moment that some were born connected to magic, able to hear it speak, but from now on, Maleonarial believed, all would be.

Leksand put his hand on the door. "If I may, Hold Daughter?" He lowered his voice. "I have experience in such matters." And hadn't he tasted saltwater, as the Eater abandoned its host to join its kind? Hadn't he known its source?

The lungs of a man, almost drowned.

Wendealyon's grief returned. "You're as kind as your mother, Leksand, but there's nothing to be done for him. We've tried. We must choose the next hold lord. As you said, much has changed."

Her Veil being no longer a guarantee of death for those from outside, though the attention of newly bold gossamers was a filter of itself. The Snarlen Sea was no longer a barrier to those of Tananen who sought a wider world.

Or, just perhaps, to magic.

The change, Leksand thought, was just beginning. "Allow me to try, please," he told Wendealyon, and bowed.

To his embarrassment, she bowed back. "I'll leave you to it, then." And walked away.

Leksand opened the door, greeted by the smell of sickness. Missed the pot, his Momma'd say as she'd wipe up the mess or have him do it, for somehow they'd be the ones helping whoever had the croup or worse.

A fire burned in the grate. Lamps burned in every corner of what was a grand room, an explorer's room, full of globes and books. Maps hung on the walls and one had been worked into a bedcover, as though the form supine beneath needed to know where he was.

Or had forgotten.

Leksand walked to the bed and sat in the chair left beside it. Insom stared up, eyes seeing what wasn't there, his face writ in lines of anguish and despair.

Leksand found the hold lord's hand and held it tight. "I know, m'lord, that you can hear me," he said quietly. "I've been in the dark well and almost lost hope, but I didn't and you mustn't for we've won.

"The Eaters have been defeated. They're gone, perished in flame.

"Pylor knew you fought the Eater. More than anything, she wanted to save you."

A blink. A tear.

Leksand leaned closer. "I'm here to help you, m'lord. Follow my voice and climb out. It won't be easy.

"But I'll stay till you do."

Tambler's Inn in Alden Hold had a narrow raised stage for musicians, but few noticed, busy imbibing and embroiled in typically raucous conversation. Tonight, though, mugs remained midair and you'd have heard a pin drop, for on the stage, floating from side to side, was a singer the likes of which hadn't been heard since before the days of ice and fire.

When the last echo of song sank warm into hearts, the singer laughed and flew away through the ceiling.

Harn let out a blissful sigh. "See? That's singing." Then blushed, having written the gossamer, and looked helplessly around the table. "I can't go up now."

"You'd better," Dom told him with a mock scowl. "I put good coin down with Tambler to get you an audition. Go on."

Maleonarial joined the chorus urging Harn to the stage. When the former student broke into the first tentative line of a seaside ditty, the barge crew and dockworkers in the inn let out a roar of approval, mugs swinging in time. Relieved, Harn launched into the earthy refrain with vigor.

"Why?" Affarealyon pointed at the mage's head.

"It's lighter." Maleonarial combed his fingers through curly stubble, enjoying the sensation and its meaning. "I'm free. We all are." Mostly black his hair, with gray over the ears, as his body was mostly hale and strong, but mature. The knee complained of the approach of winter.

A season he'd live to see, and many more. Magic no longer had that ultimate, personal cost. No longer had that seductive pull stronger than food or love, though rewarding? Maleonarial smiled into his beer. Wait till the existing masters learned that magic had a mind of Her own and what they could now create?

Might serve a purpose, if interested. Or not.

More likely would giggle in their face.

Nedsom shook his head. "What I want to know is why you want us to rebuild the school. With magic itself awake and aware, and it's everywhere, by the way, even here. A gossamer swam in a bucket of mortar this morning. Mixed it well, but added—" He raised his hand, showing bronze glitter stuck to the palm. "With magic doing whatever it pleases, what's the point of more?"

A sensible question. The true answer, that She who was magic wished for the world to return to what it was before ice and fire and the Eaters, thus there must be more gossamers created to replace those lost, many more, was, Maleonarial decided, something for each person to discover on their own. The world would change. For people to have a place in it, they'd best hope gossamers continue to "like" them.

"The point of magic?" He formed an intention then wrote Her Words in the air. Small but intense the spark that followed.

Small but brilliant, the gossamer that appeared. It stretched like a little panther, rubbed around Nedsom's mug of beer, then disappeared with the flick of a tail, leaving behind the scent of baking.

And a generous heap of steaming battered fish.

"Help yourselves," he said, blithely taking a strip and plopping it in his mouth. Delicious, hot and spiced exactly as he remembered from a visit to Nor Hold's market, when he'd stopped for a meal at one of the vendors by the dock. "We need a school to teach a new kind of intention. How to give life to our fantasies without fear, and accept the result."

Affar sampled the fish. Her eyebrows rose in approval, then lowered to frown. "Not all fantasies are benign."

He'd made a promise to Nim, one no longer his alone to keep. "I believe nothing we create will cause harm to the land or its life. She won't allow it." He shrugged. "What we do to ourselves or each other— that may depend on the gossamers as much as us. They do have a sense of humor."

"We rebuild the mage school, then."

"A school for everyone who hears Her Words and wishes to create gossamers," he corrected. "Including daughters. Our ancestors, I'm told on the best authority, made one choice. We can make our own."

Their ancestors not having had the chance to see, as he had and would forever remember, the sky become wings and the sun an eye of dazzling topaz.

Maleonarial leaned forward. "What's your fantasy, Affar?"

And watched her face light with the astonished hope of a child.

Winter dressed the pines with white fluffy shawls and caps. Stilled the brooks and creeks, for a time. Nipped noses and rosied cheeks and Leksand Loggerson pulled his scarf close around his neck after he left Pincel's sled to walk the path home.

And there it was, snug in the clearing. Smoke curled from the chimney, tinged with the scent of curing sausage. Laundry hung, frozen stiff as boards. Someone didn't know to hang clothes indoors. Nim, helping his great-uncle.

Leksand slowed, then stopped. He was home.

But he wasn't, was he? He'd no home, now. Choices, yes. Insom the Second, recovered and understanding as no one else the wounds he carried, had urged him to stay, even offered the chance to sail the seas together and explore.

Maleonarial had sent word of a new school, for anyone who'd do magic. He was welcome, always.

He'd had enough magic for a lifetime. Didn't want, yet, to travel. As for what he did want?

Leksand shook his head wearily. Peace. Time—

"What's wrong, laddie?"

Because he'd always answered with the truth, as best he could, Leksand replied, "It's not home, Momma," before remembering he was alone and she was gone.

Then who'd spoken, in her voice?

A breeze, warm as spring, caressed his cheek. "Why not?"

"Because you're—m'Mom's dead. I don't blame you," for now he knew who spoke. The woman of the woods.

The world.

"She gave her life willingly," he told the air, told himself too. "I don't blame you. I'm just—it's not home, without her. Not anymore." He wiped a foolish tear from his cheek before it froze.

"I'd not be so sure, laddie." Snow lifted, became a shape, one his heart knew before his eyes. Color raced to cheeks and lips, swept over what was now a warm wool cloak, her favorite, and made a familiar pattern on sensible knitted mittens.

"Gossamer," he accused.

"Aie." A mittened hand gave his chest a familiar pat. "But also Kait Alder, who kept me safe inside her and saved us. All she asked in return was I care for you as she would."

He caught up the hand. Held it as he searched the face that couldn't be, but was, hers. Saw the gentle little smile bloom he knew best of all. "Momma?"

"For as long as you need me, laddie," she promised. "Now, let's get ye home."

*For it came to pass the goddess named deathless did die, praise to the great Maleonarial. Mage scribes from that day forward no longer gave life for Her magic—*

Sayshun, late of Lithua, looked up from the page. "Mage scribes? Really? I can't believe this is still required reading."

"Consider it informed metaphor." Her new friend and classmate didn't stop writing, tongue sticking out sideways in concentration, wings neatly folded.

"If magic agrees with your intent, you create with it. If it doesn't, you create in other ways. Everyone knows that."

With a laugh that smelled like roses, her friend put down her pen and gave her full attention. "You left one out. If you are magic," the gossamer said, "you share a name."

Sayshun shook her head. "That again? You can't all be Tananen."

Topaz eyes sparkled. "Don't be so sure."

# Key to Within

# Key to Within

*ealyon*, meaning: "promised to The Lady", pronounced: e-A-lee-on

*eonarial*, meaning: "debtor to The Lady", pronounced: e-on-AIR-ial

**acolyte**
woman who has received Her Gift and chooses to serve the hold daughter and The Lady; willing to give her life to The Lady as Her Designate

**Affarealyon**
Alden's Hold Daughter

**Alden Hold**
hold that stands between the mage school and rest of the world

**Ansibel**
servant at the mage school

**Aote**
heartland holding; one of the holds cleansed by The Lady

**Arcoeonarial (only as Arco)**
master mage scribe

**Arnsey ("Bitters")**
crew on russet barge, husband of Nanse, twin of Senert

**Atta Moss**
one of the three daughters of Woodshaven

**Ban**
student at mage school

**Bense Groomson**
driver of Insom's freight wagon

**Bettealyon**
acolyte of Tiler's Hold

**Boulderton**
village in Nor Holding

**Braneonarial**
Saeleonarial's younger brother; now a master mage

**Burgan d'Struth**
mapmaker from Whitehold Isles

**Callen**
student at mage school

**Caton**
author in mage school archives

**Cil**
Riverhill knacker's apprentice

**Corvinas**
author in mage school archives; wrote *Fundamental Lexicon of Tananen* Vol. 1

**Damesen**
title used in holds with elaborate courts to indicate a woman of the highest possible rank (not a Daughter)

**Dancers**
great beasts who dig silt from the canals, leaving it along the banks

**Darksmeri**
month corresponding to our December

**Daughter**
person with Her Gift able to speak Her Words; selected to rule the Daughter's Portion and reveal the dictates of The Lady to the holding

**Daughter's Portion**
area from which daughter and acolytes observe the court

**Daveonarial**
master mage scribe

**Derren**
northern holding

**Dinus**
author in mage school archives

**Dolren Keeperson**
Insom's manservant

**Domozuk (Dom)**
Saeleonarial's servant (scribemaster's)

**Eaples**
servant at the mage school

**Ella**
prospect for Tiler's Hold Daughter from Meadton

**Enyon**
author in mage school archives

**Esteonarial (Est)**
master mage scribe

**Ferden Haulerson**
Kait's mother's brother; Leksand's great-uncle; lives with them both

**firemoths**
made-moths able to start fires; popular student project

**Fisherson**
Sael and Bran's last name before becoming mage scribes

**Fujin**
author in mage school archives

**Garrod**
author in mage school archives

**Gillib**
northern holding

**Gudrun**
author in mage school archives

**Grafeonarial**
master mage scribe

**Hardly Bakerson**
servant at mage school; grandparents have bakery in Alden Hold

**Harn Guardson**
student mage scribe who accompanies Saeleonarial

**Harneonarial**
the name Harn would earn once a mage

**Helly Pelly Creek**
stream that runs through mage school to border marsh and canal near Alden

**Helthrom River**
largest river in Tananen, empties into Snarlen Sea at Tiler's Hold

**Her Fist**
mountain ranges protecting Tananen

**Her Gift**
a connection to The Lady that arrives in a dream at puberty; women with Her Gift serve The Lady and help govern; men with Her Gift become mage scribes

**Her Mouth**
sheltered harbor at Tiler's Hold; where the Helthrom River empties into the Snarlen Sea

**Her Soul**
tower reputed to be in the middle of Her Tears; home of The Lady

**Her Tears**
mist-shrouded fen hiding Her Soul

**hold, holding**
hold = capital city; holding = province

**Ichep**
country across the sea; trades at Tiler's; known for clever clockworks, etc.

**Icot**
holding in the mountains known for its lapis mines

**Ingleton**
author in mage school archives

**inkmaster**
devoted to the science of better inks

**Insom Fisherson**
Insom's name before becoming hold lord

**Insom the Second**
Tiler's Hold Lord. Pylor's cousin

**Jowen Hammerson**
inkmaster at Tankerton

**Kait Alder**
one of the three daughters of Woodshaven; mother of Leksand

**Kaitealyon**
Kait Alder's name in more formal courts

**Kaitie**
Kait's nickname

**Lekeonarial**
Leksand's name should he become a mage scribe

**Leksand Loggerson**
Kait's son; father Rogeonarial

**Leorealyon**
acolyte of Tiler's Hold; chosen as Her Witness and Designate

**Lightsmeri**
month corresponding to our May

**Lithua**
country on a distant continent; trades at Tiler's

**Locel**
northern holding

**loremaster**
anyone who studies the magic of Tananen

**mage scribe**
one with Her Gift able to write an intention using Her Words and create what didn't live before

**Mal Merchantson**
Maleonarial's name before becoming a mage scribe

**Maleonarial**
former scribemaster and loremaster; known as the hermit mage since leaving that post

**master mage scribe**
a mage scribe who has learned all he can from the mage school and goes forth to do magic-for-hire; masters retire to the school to teach

**Meadton**
village in Tiler's Holding

**Merr**
northern holding

**Mish**
prospect for Tiler's Hold Daughter

**Nabo**
author in mage school archives

**Nanse Heronsbill**
bargemaster of the russet barge

**Napen**
northern holding

**Nathrom River**
river in Tananen

**Nedsom**
Alden's Hold Lord

**Nelisti Barnswallow**
cook at the mage school

**Nicti**
author in mage school archives

**Nim Millerson**
farmer from Riverhill

**Nor Hold**
capital of Nor, a heartland holding

**Ottle**
author in mage school archives

**Ovon**
northern holding

**Pacthrom River**
river in Tananen

**Pageonarial**
master mage scribe and historian

**Pincel Hopper**
one of Woodshaven's daughters

**Pylor Ternfeather, Damesen**
Insom's cousin, chemist, very high rank in court at
Tiler's Hold

**Rid Smithyson**
scribemaster's driver

**Riverhill**
village in Tiler holding

**Rogeonarial**
mage scribe who fathered Kait's son in Woodshaven

**Rost**
student at mage school

**Sael Fisherson**
Saeleonarial's name before becoming a mage scribe

**Saeleonarial**
scribemaster

**Sayshun**
student at mage school

**scribemaster**
head of mage school; represents it to holdings

**Senert**
crew on the russet barge; twin brother of Arnsey

**Singers**
great beasts who grasp barges and pull them upstream along the canal using their wings

**Slog**
monster living in one of the mage school ponds

**Snarlen Sea**
ocean bordering Tananen

**Sult**
northern holding

**Surano**
island in the Whitehold Isles famed for glass work

**Tambler's Inn**
tavern in Alden Hold

**Tananen**
domain where The Lady rules

**Tankerton**
village in Icot holding

**Tarr**
northern holding

**Tercle Kelptassle**
Pylor's apprentice and friend; chemist; Tiler's Hold

**Terrhom River**
river in Tananen

**The Brutes**
rocky islands forming a barrier near Her Mouth

**The Hunger**
treacherous strait between The Brutes and Tananen

**Tiler's Hold, Tiler's Holding**
only place in Tananen touched by the outside world

**Tobin Piperson**
student at mage school

**Toneonarial**
mage scribe who wrote/created Slog

**Urray**
author of book in mage school archives

**Ursealyon**
senior acolyte at Tiler's Hold

**Wend Sharktooth**
Wendealyon's name before becoming Hold Daughter

**Wendealyon**
Hold Daughter of Tiler's Hold

**Whitehold Isles**
archipelago of islands that form a country; trade at Tiler's

**Woodshaven**
remote mountain village in Tiler's Holding

**Xareonarial**
master mage scribe teaching at the school

**Xcel**
heartland holding; one of the holds cleansed by The Lady

**Xol**
heartland holding

**Zor**
northern holding

# ᴀCKNOWLEDGMENTS

Unusual roots, this book has. *Mage* began as a novella for Eric Flint, eleven years earlier. Thinking it'd be science fiction, I set aside time for it, only to learn it had to be fantasy. Since I'd yet to write more than a short story, I—hesitated.

For one thing, I'd no ideas. (Other than my imaginings of what would become *A Turn of Light*.) Then I flipped through our Lee Valley Tools catalog and read about pens. I became consumed with the notion of written magic, of pens and inks, and of magic that lived. All of which would have stayed there, as the novella, except that I loved the concepts and world with such passion, I told my editor-dear, Sheila Gilbert (of two Hugos, yay!), I'd inadvertently discovered a book. She agreed with me.

Thus I published a novella, thanks to Eric, that was noticeably the start of a novel*, thanks to Sheila, and present you now with the rest.

Roger Czerneda, my other half, created the concept for the cover of this book. We went on a hunt for pens and inkwells for him, and me, to use. Yes, the glass pen featured in the story is real and came from The Kitchen Witch in Dundas, Ontario. The inkwell? Also real, and found at Rideau Antiques, possibly the oddest collection of stuff anywhere. Katie Anderson, of Penguin Random House, added her talents to finalize the cover design. The result is breathtaking and exactly right. Thank you both!

*Mage* kept adding unusual twists. In the midst of writing it, I broke my right wrist. Thanks to Dr. Anderson and Shawn, the amazing cast

---

* The late great Gardner Dozois gave "Intended Words" an honorable mention. When I'd the chance to thank him years later, he told me he'd have included it in his Year's Best had it not read like the start of a novel. I had to laugh.

maker, I was able to keep typing—encouraged to do so, in fact—finishing the book days before the cast came off. Whew!

Which meant Roger not only had his work to do, but me in his care for two full months. I couldn't have done the book (or my shoelaces or bottle tops or . . .) without his cheerful, unceasing comfort and help.

2018 was such a busy year for projects and family joys I curtailed my events. That said, I did some spiffy things with wonderful folks. I was a guest author for the Pixel Project's Read4Pixels Campaign to help end violence against women, ably helmed by the remarkable Regina Yau. Anushia Kandasivam helped me through the live video hangout, my first, and Steve Drew was there when I plunged into reddit/r/fantasy and did an AMA (ask me anything). Fundraisers need donors and I thank the following generous souls from the bottom of my heart for picking my items: Michelle Dubie Mitchell, Helen Merrick, and Wendy Shark. (And thanks for your patience with my cast, the postal strike, and all else.) Wendy? I hope you enjoy your Tuckerization as Wendealyon. Thanks for providing some intriguing quirks.

I was a featured writer at Smiths Falls Library's Open Door celebration, along with the splendid Marie Bilodeau. Thank you Karen Schecter, Sally Smith, Katie Hoffman, and others for your warm hospitality and assistance. Rhonda Parrish, thanks for inviting me to participate in your Giftmas food bank project. Bravo!

I'd no time to do publicity, but others stepped up for me. Edward Willett hosted me on his Worldshapers' podcast. Thanks, Ed! Special thanks to Lauren Horvath, Alexis Nixon, and Leah Spann for their hard work and enthusiastic promotion of my books. Lauren was instrumental in finding me terrific hosts online and reviewers. Thank you! Hugs to bloggers Rebecca Fischer (BookGirlsBookNook) for her love of Esen, Andrea Johnson of LittleRedReviewer for everything plus the *Mage* cover reveal, and the marvelous Paul Weimer for being there as well as here. Sara Megibow? You're incredible. Thank you for everything. And yes, I'll keep thinking up questions.

A special hug for Joshua Starr, who helped me through the final details of this book. You, sir, are a treasure.

Can*Con was again fabulous. Kudos to all involved! I'd like to thank the concom for graciously allowing Kevin Hearne, Kate Heartfield, Richard Larson, and me to take over the consuite for our "Shenanigans Book Launch." Such fun!

To all who came to my first-ever reading, at World Fantasy no less, from *Mage* and sat in stunned silence when I finished? Thank you!!!! That was epic.

Scott, I promised to put you in a fantasy novel. (Moms can do that.) Here you go! All the fine characteristics of Leksand's are true to life, so go ahead and blush. Oh, and thanks for your help with my dialects.

Last and never least, to our family. Proof the heart grows, the more you put in it.

—*Julie*